My Kind of Earl

"I don't normally allow strangers to . . ." She let her words trail off, but mouthed in a silent murmur, ". . . kiss me."

In response, Raven's gaze heated in a sudden flare, simmering to smoke as it rested on her mouth. Her lips tingled under his scrutiny.

As if he knew this and wanted to soothe her, the pad of his thumb skimmed that tender surface, too. "I bought a new book the other day."

The alteration in topic was unexpected. And yet, no other man could make such a statement sound so intriguing and so wicked at the same time. "What is the title?"

"Can't recall," he said mysteriously, stepping closer until his hip brushed her knee and the lamplight seemed to burn in his eyes. "Come upstairs with me and we'll read it together."

At once, she knew what he was doing and she covered his hand with her own, drawing it away from her blushing cheek.

"You are such a scoundrel," she said, but there wasn't even a hint of scolding in her breathless voice. Temptation, perhaps. But not scolding. "Why is it that whenever we're talking about your identity, you try to distract me with seduction?"

He flashed an unrepentant grin, and didn't even bother to deny it. "One is far more interesting than the other."

By Vivienne Lorret

The Mating Habits of Scoundrels Series
LORD HOLT TAKES A BRIDE
MY KIND OF EARL

The Misadventures in Matchmaking Series
HOW TO FORGET A DUKE
TEN KISSES TO SCANDAL
THE ROGUE TO RUIN

The Season's Original Series
"The Duke's Christmas Wish" (in ALL I WANT
FOR CHRISTMAS IS A DUKE and A CHRISTMAS TO
REMEMBER)
THE DEBUTANTE IS MINE
THIS EARL IS ON FIRE
WHEN A MARQUESS LOVES A WOMAN
JUST ANOTHER VISCOUNT IN LOVE (novella)

The Rakes of Fallow Hall Series
THE ELUSIVE LORD EVERHART
THE DEVILISH MR. DANVERS
THE MADDENING LORD MONTWOOD

The Wallflower Wedding Series
TEMPTING MR. WEATHERSTONE (novella)
DARING MISS DANVERS
WINNING MISS WAKEFIELD
FINDING MISS MCFARLAND

My Kind of Earl

The Mating Habits of Scoundrels

VIVIENNE LORRET

AVONBOOKS

An Imprint of HarperCollinsPublishers

First Avon Books mass market printing: October 2020

Print Edition ISBN: 978-0-06-297660-4
Digital Edition ISBN: 978-0-06-297661-1

Cover illustrations by Jon Paul Ferrara

FIRST EDITION

20 21 22 23 24 QGM 10 9 8 7 6 5 4 3 2 1

For my readers,
thank you for welcoming my stories
into your homes and hearts.

Acknowledgments

I'd like to thank my editor, Nicole Fischer, and the entire Avon Romance team. This book would never have found a reader without your dedication and efforts. Thank you, all, so much! In my thoughts, I'm always sending hugs to you. And many thanks to my agent, the lovely Stefanie Lieberman, for your support in keeping this dream alive.

A huge thank you goes to my sisters. To Cyndi, for being my cheerleader, champion, and first-draft reader. To Deanna, for your generous insight, encouragement, and conversations. And to Katie, for your wry humor and our shared laughter.

And finally, I want to thank all the readers at Avon's Kiss-Con Chicago 2018, who rallied on my behalf for a chance to write this *Tarzan in London* story. This one is for you.

My Kind
of Earl

Chapter 1

October

Not many men would dare walk the London streets at three o'clock in the morning, all fancied up in a tailored coat of black superfine, brushed top hat and polished boots. Raven knew he looked like easy prey, flush in the fob. Just the kind of gent he'd have pickpocketed as a lad. Or the kind he'd seen gutted and left by the Thames far too often.

But he wasn't worried. Nearly every day of his twenty-eight years had taught him about back alleys, crooked dealings, ruffians and cheats. And despite his unsavory beginnings, he'd made a good life.

It was going to stay that way, too. All a man had to do was follow a certain philosophy. He'd come up with four rules—or *keeps*, as he liked to call them—years ago and they served him well.

One: keep a watchful eye.

Two: keep your nose on your own face (and out of some other bloke's business).

Three: keep what's yours safe and sound.

And *four:* keep anonymous.

For an orphan raised in a foundling home, the last *keep* should've been simple. But he'd run into more scrapes than he could count just by being noticed. So, he'd learned the hard way to blend in.

It was a good skill to have, especially now.

This was the hour of cutpurses and wastrels. An earlier rain had sent the latter to the shelter of the mews to warm themselves by sputtering dustbin fires. But the former tended to lurk in the shadows, waiting for the telltale sounds of the rich—the plink and clatter of coins, the rasp of folded notes, or the distinctive *clap* of hard-soled Hessians on the damp pavement.

To avoid announcing his presence, Raven kept his footfalls in time with the night watchman on the other side of the street. The sharp measured strike echoed within the gathering snakeskins of fog that curled along the cobblestones and would disorient any thug listening in an alleyway.

Up ahead, an old beggar woman sat huddled beneath a streetlamp with a basket of yesterday's wilted violets on her lap. She squinted through the chilly mist, then gave a familiar toothless grin as he approached. "Why, if it ain't the randy gent back fer the second time this week."

"I had to drop by to visit your flower shop, didn't I?" he teased, touching the brim of his hat in greeting.

"Bah," she sniggered, shooing her hand in the air. "The only visitin' yer doin' is to the bawdy house up a pace. Well, 'ere's yer posy, then."

Pretending great offense, he asked, "Now, when have I ever bought only one posy from you, Bess? That'll be three posies. I've made promises, after all, and a man must uphold his word."

She clucked her tongue at him and fished through the basket. "Three girls in one night. A cryin' shame. Why, if I were me younger self, I'd have left you too weak to visit another bed. Buried two husbands, I did. A' course neither were fine gents. Not like you."

Raven smiled to himself. She didn't realize that they'd crossed paths dozens of times when he wasn't in his gentleman disguise.

He was usually dressed in a regular coarse wool suit and

shirtsleeves on his way to Sterling's gaming hell, where he worked as a general factotum. His straight black hair wasn't often parted and styled with pomade beneath a black Regent as it was now. And he didn't parade about in a stiff pointed collar and cravat.

But he'd learned long ago that people saw what they wanted to see and he used it to his advantage.

"Your promises are impossible to resist." Bending down to lift her vellum-skinned hand to his lips, he stared soulfully into her eyes. "Run away with me, Bess."

She snatched her hand back and cackled, spots of color tingeing her wrinkled cheeks, her breath misting in the air beneath the flickering glow of the lantern. "Get on with ye now, randy gent. I've said before, I'm too much of a woman for ye. Now, take yer posies before there's nothin' left of 'em. A' course"—she hesitated, holding tightly to the limp, string-tied bunches, her thin brows inching higher with meaning—"should ye ever need a new cook for yer fancy pile of bricks, ye know where to find me."

Believing this was her way of negotiating for more coin, he fished a bob out of his pocket and dropped it into her waiting palm. She bit down on the tarnished silver token before sliding it into her frayed gray bodice.

"Aye. You'll be the first on my list." Then he tipped his hat and went on his way.

Once he was out of sight, he stowed the flowers in his pocket. The women working at the bawdy house wouldn't appreciate the disrespect of wilted flowers, but buying them helped Bess gain a meal or two while still keeping her dignity.

Raven knew from experience that, sometimes, pride was all a person possessed.

Keeping a watchful eye, he walked on, not letting the stillness of these early hours fool him into complacency.

Even so, London almost seemed like a cathedral at this time of morning, hushed and reverent. On the street, a dingy yellow hackney lumbered by in a solitary procession, disappearing into the congregating fog toward some unseen altar. It chanted in a disembodied *clip-clop-clip* of horse hooves and rang bells of rigging. The sounds reverberated off the shingle and brick facades of boardinghouses and shopfronts that stood tall like pew boxes filled with sinners. And the incense that burned to purify the worshippers was little more than the charred, heavy soot that sifted down from chimney tops and mingled with the damp, fetid odors rising from the gutter.

He drew it deeply into his soul—the sounds, the scents, and the sights of his world.

Raven's steps took him beneath a trio of painted wooden signs that hung from curlicues of wrought iron in front of darkened shop windows while their proprietors slept abovestairs. Here, houses, rented flats, and shops intermingled. All of a man's necessities were within a short stretch of the legs—a barber, a tailor, a mercer, and a pleasure house.

Yet, Moll Dawson didn't hang a sign out front. Not even a placard. She didn't have to.

Moll ran the most exclusive brothel in London, catering *solely* to haute society nobs. Strictly invitation only. She even spun a tale that her girls had never been touched by common hands and were trained by courtesans from all over the world.

Raven was as common as soot. But, three years ago, when he'd started working at Sterling's gaming hell, Moll had approached him with a secret bargain.

She'd grant him admittance to her infamous gilded parlor, with girls draped in silks and bathed in perfumes . . . as long as he directed the high-stakes winners at Sterling's to her establishment instead of her rival's.

After being spat upon by foppish aristocrats all his life,

the offer was too tempting for Raven to refuse. So, whenever he came to Moll's *entertainment emporium*—as she liked to call it—he dressed the part. He even mimicked the gestures and the air of supremacy that he witnessed at the gaming hell.

But she never let him forget his place. He was allowed inside solely by the favor of her graces.

It shouldn't have made any difference to him. After all, a man with such humble beginnings shouldn't expect anything better. And yet, something inside him had always wanted more.

Raven tucked that thought away, as he usually did, and paused in the shadows near the narrow ginnel between buildings, taking careful measure of his surroundings.

Outside the bawdy house, a pair of fine black carriages waited, the bobbing orange glow of a cheroot signaling a driver's position high on a perch. The main floor windows were dark behind the drawn curtains, but lamplight flickered beyond the first- and second-floor shades. Faint stirrings of music drifted down, along with the frenzied creaks of straining bed-ropes and occasional guttural groans.

All was as it should be . . . or so he thought.

In the next instant, however, he heard a scuffling sound from the dark gully beside him.

His ears perked, homing in on the sly shuffle. A lumbering footfall followed.

He hesitated, scenting the air for the ripe stench of desperation. Footpads and cutthroats often lurked outside of brothels for their chance to take a lust-addled man unawares and rob him blind.

But what he heard next wasn't the sound of any ruffian he'd ever encountered.

"Hurry, cousin," a feminine voice whispered just before a quick, pattering step rasped against the pavement like a rush of hailstones.

Peering around the corner, Raven saw only the faintest of movements in the gloom, accompanied by the unmistakable rustle of petticoat and skirts. He'd know that sound anywhere.

"I don't get why you've got to go in through a window," a gruff male voice said.

Raven suppressed a chuckle. He'd heard tales of women sneaking *out* of bawdy houses through a window to escape in the night, but never one stealing *in*.

Even so, he didn't concern himself with the matter. Moll Dawson employed a big, blond Viking-like bully to guard the door. Sure enough, they'd sort this all out on their own.

"This is part of my research for the book I'm writing. It is of the utmost importance that I observe the . . . um . . . objects of my study without drawing attention to myself, ergo the window. You might even say that this is a scientific endeavor upon which I am about to embark," that softly feminine voice answered.

The unexpectedly highbrow words caused Raven to pause once more. The cultured tone was as different from Moll's distinctive husky growl—or any of the women here—as the crown jewels from paste gems.

Curiosity bade him closer. Blending in with the darkness, he edged along the constricted path until his eyes adjusted enough to spot two figures—a large hulking male and a small female in a dark cloak.

"If you say so, Jane."

"Now, if you would be so kind as to boost me to the ledge. It is a bit taller than I calculated on my sketch of the establishment."

The flesh of his brow furrowed as he listened to the odd exchange. There was something familiar about the bloke's voice, too, but it was the woman who'd ensnared Raven's attention.

In the sliver of lamplight that penetrated the darkness, he

could see the outline of her form. He became acutely aware of every breath, every shift. The tilt of her head. The roll of her shoulder. The unfolding stretch of her arms to the sill. And if hearing her voice hadn't already told him that she was a blue blood, then her movements would have done.

They were fluent and graceful, as if she'd spent years learning dance steps and the proper way to pour tea. A high-society chit.

Now, why would someone like her be shimmying in through a brothel window?

Even though it went against his own rules, he knew there was only one way to find out.

THERE WERE far too many mysteries in life and Jane Pickerington intended to unveil as many as possible.

Even if her quest required stealing into a brothel in the wee hours of the morning.

But this wasn't a mere whim. No, indeed, she was fully prepared for any situation that might arise. Hers was, quite possibly, the most exquisitely formulated plan of the nineteenth century. Complete with exterior and interior architectural sketches. And, of course, she made certain that the room was empty before she'd climbed inside.

But it turned out that she wasn't alone, after all.

Stepping away from the window seat, Jane instantly found herself nose to nose with a hard, unblinking face. On a gasp, her gloved hand flew to her throat.

Her mind rapidly calculated seven means of escape and three methods of incapacitation . . . until she realized who or *what* her would-be assailant was.

"A statue. Only a statue," she murmured on a breath of relief.

Her pulse quieted as she surveyed the snug, darkened

study of the proprietress, illuminated by the faint orange glow of dying embers. Three more statues stood along the wall behind her, but no other sentient inhabitants.

Thank the stars. This errand was far too vital to deal with any unforeseen complications. Her research depended on discovering the differences between gentlemen and scoundrels.

And what better way to learn about the male species than to study them while their objective was purely primal?

In Jane's opinion, this quick sojourn through a brothel was akin to touring the wilderness to visit creatures in their natural habitat.

She and her friends were writing a book on their findings. After all, too many young women were ill prepared for the potential perils that awaited them in society. And Jane refused to allow another one of her friends to face ruination or be eschewed from London in disgrace, like poor Prue.

With a new Season beginning in a few short months, there was no time to delay.

Swiftly, she turned away from the statue. Then she jerked to a sudden halt, caught on something. Her eyes drifted down the marble form—correction, the *nude* marble form—and there, she found the culprit.

Her eyes widened in astonishment. The statue wasn't adorned with any sort of fig leaf at all. Then again, it would likely take a banana leaf to conceal this artist's rendering of male genitalia.

Unfortunately for her, the gold-threaded cord from her red paisley reticule had wrapped around a rather gargantuan priapic member.

She tried to tug herself free. When that failed, she considered breaking off the phallus entirely. It would likely be the quickest method of extrication.

Taking him in hand, she glanced up at his patient expression apologetically, then leveraged her weight on the turgid slope with a faint grunt. But she quickly discovered that his was a surprisingly solid and immovable appendage.

Using both hands this time, she tried again, adding a little hop to her movements.

It didn't work.

Jane frowned down at the tangled disaster. Now, the tip of her left glove and middle finger were caught in the cord.

A problem-solver by nature, she sank to her knees for a better vantage point. But, not too far in the distance, she heard a door close, a heavy footfall, and an exchange of a curt greeting. *Drat!*

She worked faster, using her teeth to cut through woven silken strands. Silently, she prayed that this phallus wouldn't lead to her ruination.

While she doubted anyone entering the brothel through the front door would walk directly to the proprietress's study, she couldn't rule out anything. She'd tried to account for every possible scenario or mishap—a lesson she'd learned after her first experiment with gunpowder.

She was immensely grateful that both of her eyebrows were currently intact. Yet, for the majority of her second season, she'd possessed only one. The other had been a poorly sketched impersonation, giving her the appearance of an unfinished portrait of an exceedingly plain girl.

But she would not permit this erection to blow up in her face. No, indeed!

A few seconds later, her hand slipped free of the glove, along with her reticule. *At last!* But some of the unraveled cording remained firmly wrapped around the shaft *and* her glove.

She would simply have to leave it behind. Time was of the essence and her cousin wouldn't wait forever. Duncan was more apt to forget the reason he was waiting in the alley. Though she loved him dearly, he tended to be more than slightly beef-witted.

Jane adeptly maneuvered a path through the copse of nude statues, past the tufted rose hassock in the center of the carpet, and stopped behind a large fern on a pedestal near the camouflaged servant's entrance.

And she was just in time, too.

At the precise instant that she stepped into the narrow servant's corridor, she heard the unmistakable turn of a lock across the room. Someone was coming into the study!

Closing the door carefully, she hoped that no one would discover her *or* the scandalously affixed glove she'd left behind.

Chapter 2

Using the dim phosphorescent light from a small jar of glowworms—*lampyris noctilua*—in her reticule, Jane stealthily navigated the concealed passageway. She was immensely grateful for the architectural drawings she'd committed to memory beforehand. Otherwise, she might have taken a wrong turn and found herself in the kitchens.

Instead, she stepped through another hidden door in the corner of the main parlor. Tucking her makeshift lamp away, she went inside to learn all she could about a man's primal nature.

A potted palm concealed her entrance from the small gathering of gentlemen and their paramours. An entrancing melody of flute, lyre and spinet drifted down from an ovoid minstrel's gallery perched high in the far wall, effectively muting the click of the latch as she closed the door behind her.

The room was precisely as it had been described. Honestly, it was positively astounding what gentlemen spoke of at soirees when they forgot a member of the female sex was among them. Then again, she supposed that being practically invisible to men ought to have *some* advantages.

And now here she was, inside a veritable womb of wickedness.

Red-tinted globes diffused the sconce light, giving the room a crepuscular glow. Walls papered in oxblood silk were trimmed in ebony wood and adorned with long gilt-framed mirrors. Overhead, the vaulted ceiling was painted with a fresco of nude heavenly bodies in unabashed poses that, in many cases, appeared anatomically impossible. And, in a nearby corner, stood a mysterious curtained alcove swathed in black brocade.

The interior was completely immersed in darkness. It would be perfect!

Hidden behind her cloak and a convenient copse of palm trees, she crept to the shadowy nook like a zoologist on a London jungle expedition. The air was thick with jumentous body odors, poorly cloaked in perfumes. And peculiar porcine swoughs and squeals drifted down a recessed staircase tucked into the far wall beneath the gallery.

Utterly fascinating!

Peering through palm fronds, she spotted a pack of wild gentlemen—*genus intoxicatus*—playing cards at one of eight linen-draped tables. They tossed back their amber libations and communicated in grunts, snorts and nods to the cyprians draped in silken petticoats and colorful corsets.

In turn, these rouge-cheeked and kohl-eyed women fawned and fussed over them, enswathing their patrons' necks in bare-armed embraces, displaying their voluptuous adornments in a proximity very near to smothering.

Strangely, the men appeared to enjoy the oxygen deprivation.

Jane pursed her lips in scholarly contemplation as she skirted, unnoticed, into the dark alcove. Absently, she speculated if a simple test to discover the difference between gentlemen and scoundrels might be the duration in which one could hold his breath. Perhaps, the longer the interval, the greater likelihood that he was, indeed, a scoundrel. *Hmm . . .*

To ensure she recalled this hypothesis later, she reached

inside her reticule and withdrew a small ledger to scrawl a hasty note.

Lifting her gaze to the inhabitants of the room once more, she caught sight of a man standing beneath the arched doorway. He was lean and broad-shouldered. A fine figure of a man. But there was something guarded in the alert glance he swept over the room beneath the shadow of his brim. He was so intent in his scrutiny that even she scanned the room in speculation once more. Then her study returned to him as he doffed his hat, revealing hair as black as jet and eyes so pale and bright that she could see the glow of them from a distance. Her entire attention was ensnared by them.

A strange current of static electricity skittered up her spine and burrowed into the wispy brown curls at her nape, lifting them. If she were given to flights of fancy, she might even make note of the occurrence and think about it later. However, her pragmatic self reasoned that his arrival had brought a waft of air from the opening of the outer door. Said *waft* merely swept into the alcove with enough force to disturb her coiffure, albeit without moving the drapes. An architectural oddity was all it was.

Even so, she couldn't look away.

And she wasn't the only one either. Every female eye veered in his direction. Even the musicians in the gallery abruptly stopped playing.

In the quiet that followed, Jane heard a slow sigh from one of the women, the susurration dissipating in the air like the slow evaporation of steam from a Watt condensing engine.

He was unlike other men she'd observed before. There was nothing stiff-shouldered or aristocratic about the way he prowled along the perimeter of the room. His body moved in a lithe pantherlike stride, arms slightly forward as if prepared to defend himself from unseen assailants at any given moment. The hard set of his angular features and razor-cut mandible looked positively feral, especially with his inky black brows lowered.

He appeared unduly focused on the task that brought him here. Though, if his primary objective was to find companionship, his intensity was surely unwarranted. He *was* in a brothel, after all, she thought with amusement.

Her gaze wandered appreciatively over his form. Jane told herself it was no different than a scientist studying a prime example of any species. But she must have become too distracted. Because, before she realized how close his steps had brought him, he suddenly halted.

Directly in front of *her* hiding place.

Jane held her breath and remained perfectly still. Even though the mirror across from her proved that she was fully concealed in the shadows, her pulse did not care. It hopped like a kernel of popping corn prepared to burst from its pericarp.

She watched the slight tilt of his head. Heard the deep inhalation through his nostrils. And saw the satisfied smirk curl the corner of his mouth.

Newton's apple! Surely, he wasn't intending to enter into this alcove?

He issued a murmur deep in his throat. The sound was little more than a low growl, but the deep timbre vibrated inside her and caused the rush of her blood to purr feline-like in her ears. It made her peculiarly dizzy, befuddling her senses.

"Ah ha," he said quietly. "Here you are."

She startled. It took every ounce of control over her central nervous system not to gasp, or shift, or move in any way to alert him to her presence.

He couldn't be addressing her. Could he?

No, of course not. He must have a habit of speaking to

himself. Perhaps his introspection was directed at one of the cyprians he'd hoped to encounter this evening, which would explain his concentrated perusal of the room.

But Jane, no matter how curious, did not turn her gaze to see which woman had earned his attention. She dared not even blink for fear of discovery.

Then, after what felt like an eon of continental shifting and tectonic plates rumbling beneath her feet, eroding her balance, he moved on.

Finally! Her relieved lungs staggered out a breath and then in, her pulse gradually slowing. Even so, Jane kept an eye on his progress, watching as he dropped his gloves inside his hat, exposing one long-fingered hand after the other.

He took inordinate care in choosing a table, pausing to cast a sweeping glance about the room from each position.

By the time he sat down, not one but *two* of the women from the minstrel's gallery had rushed down to join him, leaving the spinet player on her own. The lyrist and flautist wore expressions of patent delight, crowns of golden laurel leaves in their upswept ringlets, and . . . nothing else beneath their Grecian-fashioned robes of transparent white gauze.

She watched them both choose a well-muscled thigh to perch upon. They peppered his face with adoring kisses, their hands snaking inside his coat. And Jane felt a disturbance in the epidermal layer of her cheeks, a telltale prickling as the temperature rose by at least two degrees.

She was blushing, of all things. Though, frankly, she did not understand why she should blush now when she hadn't while observing the smothering embraces of the other women to their men. Quite perplexing, indeed.

He turned his head to whisper something in their ears, and Jane found herself leaning forward on the balls of her feet, as if she might hear that low timbre again. From this distance, it was an absurd notion to have. Nevertheless, whatever wickedness he spoke was enough to make his companions giggle with glee before they kissed him, then raced back up the stairs.

They appeared again at the oval gallery that overlooked the parlor. Only this time, instead of picking up their lyre and flute, they drew a diaphanous curtain as one would across a stage. The lamps illuminated behind them caused a shadow-puppet effect against the silken wall, the outline of their forms on perfect display.

Jane had only a moment to wonder what sort of entertainment the cyprians were planning. Then, with the spinet playing on, a wordless enactment began. It was a dance of sorts, a graceful movement of limbs twining, necks arching on soft sighs, bodies brushing and embracing.

Curious about the intended goal, Jane studied the audience, noting that the cardplay and conversation at the table halted. With rapt attention, every gaze lifted to watch the performance.

Well, all except for one.

The very man who'd sent the women upstairs, and seemingly for this purpose, looked away.

He did not sweep the room at a glance.

He did not fish in his pocket for a watch to check the time.

Instead, his piercing gaze settled directly on the alcove, as if those unfathomably pale eyes could somehow peer through the darkness . . . and directly to her.

⚶⚶⚶

WHEN RAVEN had entered the bawdy house shortly after the little trespasser, he'd been surprised to find the study empty. She'd simply disappeared like an apparition. And yet . . . a scent lingered in the air.

The subtle, powdery essence was far different from the

profuse odor of musk and the cloying perfumes of the bawdy house girls. No, this smelled clean and soft like the late autumn cuttings of lavender he'd once seen hanging from a frilly swag over an open window of a fancy corner bookshop.

Instinctively, he knew the fragrance was hers. Much like the dainty glove he'd found dangling limply from one of Moll Dawson's prized statues.

With a smirk and a swift tug, he'd tucked the black silk into his pocket and continued his search, knowing the trespasser couldn't have gotten far.

And he'd been right.

The instant he'd stepped into the parlor, he caught the barest trace of lavender and followed it to a curtained alcove in the far corner. Standing there, he could feel the warmth emanating from her body in sweetly scented waves. He'd even been tempted to reach inside and pull her out into the open.

But he hadn't. He understood the need to keep secrets, better than most.

Even so, he was curious about her. The curtained grotto was used by both voyeurs and exhibitionists alike and it made him wonder if she was waiting for a lover.

Had she slipped inside this brothel for an illicit tryst? Or was it something else altogether, like that peculiar *research* she'd mentioned outside?

He did not have an answer and, if her silence was any indication, she hadn't been prepared to reveal herself. At least, not to him.

So he'd done what came naturally—he'd walked on but kept a watchful eye.

At first, he'd wondered why the other men hadn't taken notice of her. Then again, most blokes weren't used to searching every dark corner as a matter of life or death. Yet, as he moved through the room, studying the nook from each angle, he discovered that she was almost completely concealed in the shadows. *Almost.*

He'd smiled to himself as he lowered onto a straight-backed chair at the far table. This vantage point provided just enough sconcelight to reveal her. And after sending Hester and Venetia upstairs, he eased back to proceed with his own *research.*

The debutante was a mere wisp in a fine black cloak and wore the hood pulled low. Much of her face was still hidden, except for a wide mouth and a narrow chin. A pair of deep red lips moved faintly as though she were murmuring to herself. Then she paused, her head cocked toward the gallery as the music and *entertainment* were reaching a crescendo.

Sighs and moans drifted down like a siren's call. There were few greater visions in life than watching a pair of comely women pleasure each other. It was no wonder that the audience's attention was ensnared.

All except for his.

Raven was more intrigued by the trespasser's response and how her mouth fell still, relaxing to a plump pout. Strangely, the sight of it stirred him more than the kisses and caresses from Hester and Venetia had done. So much so that he was aware of his breath exhaling in a rush across the surface of his own lips and how they tingled in response.

Nearby, the gents from the other table and their evening's paramours stood, heading for the stairs to sate their appetites. In the alcove, the trespasser's subtle spellbinding incantations resumed.

His gaze drifted lower, edging along the satin trim that lined her cloak to a pale hand and a dark glove. But it was the objects those hands held that perplexed him—a palm-sized booklet and the stub of a pencil.

Was she taking notes . . . in a brothel?

Blast me, he thought with a wry smirk curling one corner of his mouth. Were all debutantes as peculiar as this one?

Regrettably, he was so engrossed in watching her reaction to the orgy unfolding overhead that he missed the instant another man staggered into the hall.

Raven stiffened when he saw it was Ruthersby. The baron was a dissipated drunkard known for leaving welted red handprints on the girls. Just one more reason to hate self-entitled blue bloods.

Whatever the little trespasser was doing here, she needed to steer clear of a man like that.

Fully alert, Raven sat forward, poised to intervene. The baron tottered sideways as he neared the alcove, his attention on the sights and sounds of the minstrel's gallery. He righted himself, wavered one-footed, then set off again.

But gravity seemed against him. He staggered backward, swinging a silver hawk-handled cane in a wide arc to right his balance. The pointed tip struck somewhere in the middle of the shadows and earned a soft gasp from the trespasser, her lips parting.

The baron didn't seem to notice her. He simply wobbled on. And Raven, adhering to his second rule, resumed his seat.

Until the baron stopped, and turned.

With the tip of his cane, he probed the alcove with purpose. Then he reached inside.

Raven was already across the room when the drunkard hauled the young woman out by the wrist. The hood slipped to her shoulders, baring a lopsided twist of honey-brown hair and a slender mask of black lace. A pair of almond-shaped slits revealed wide eyes that shot past the baron and centered directly on Raven.

At once he was struck by irises so pure and blue it felt as if she'd stolen the tint from his clear icy gray. A shock spurred his pulse, filling him with the uncanny desire to steal it back.

"What have we here?" Ruthersby slurred in singsong. "A fresh new piece for me to—"

Before the baron could finish, Raven gripped the man's arm, forcing his fist open on a wince.

With the deb free, he took hold of her gloveless hand and tucked her behind him for safekeeping. "She's mine for the hour."

But she misunderstood his better intentions and jerked out of his grasp. He thought she would make a dash to the door, and he was ready for it. But she merely stood apart from them and lifted her hood in place.

"For your information," she said, "I belong to none other than myself, in this hour and in any other."

Raven frowned. That highbrow tone was too self-assured under these circumstances.

But the baron grinned and adjusted his hold over the head of his cane, his gloves creaking with the effort to stretch over those fat fingers. "Mmm . . . You speak like the governess I once had. Quite strict and quick to temper. Tell me, my dear, do you have a fondness for a firm hairbrush?"

Her head tilted and those lips pursed in confusion. "I hadn't really thought about it. However, I suppose a firmer bristle is more efficient than—"

"Don't say anything more," Raven warned and tried, again, to shield her. Of the three of them, he seemed to be the only one with enough sense to see that she didn't belong here. To the baron, he growled, "Lay a single finger on her and you'll regret it."

The baron's liquor-flushed cheeks turned florid, his gaze gleaming with fast fury. "Listen here, usurper! I saw her first."

"Actually, that isn't correct," she informed him, peering out from behind Raven. "This man was watching me from the table before you arrived. Though, I hadn't had the opportunity to discern the reason before you stumbled drunkenly past me on your way to the stairs. A man your age really shouldn't imbibe so heavily."

The more she spoke, the more the baron's eyes gleamed with debased hunger. No doubt, he was already imagining all the cruel things he would do to her. "Name your price, my dear. I'll double it—whatever the amount. I refuse to let this gentleman stake his claim."

She huffed in exasperation. "Apparently, you were not listening a moment ago when I said that I belong to no one. And, besides, he isn't a gentleman. You can tell this simply enough by his button."

The hair on the back of Raven's neck rose. Moll Dawson's arrangement with him depended on his convincing charade. For the past three years he'd never incurred the slightest suspicion.

The baron squinted at him but shook his head in dismissal, and Raven knew there was no possible way this debutante had seen through his guise.

Even so, his own gaze skimmed over his togs. Pretending snobbish effrontery, he crisply intoned, "There is nothing amiss with my button."

"I beg to differ." A dainty bare finger pointed as she spoke in a confident but dizzying rush. "The third one down on your waistcoat has been reattached with brown thread instead of black. The stitches are slightly twisted, as well, which suggests an untutored hand. From these observations, I can surmise that you mended the button yourself, using whatever thread you had available. Undoubtedly, you mistakenly believed that one dark color was like any other. A wife, housekeeper, or a valet would never have made that error. This leads to the natural presumption that you are neither married nor wealthy enough to employ servants. Therefore, it is my conclusion that you cannot be of the same ilk as the gentlemen who call upon the headmistress of this exclusive establishment."

Raven studied her with deceptive calm. As if blood weren't rushing in his ears. As if she hadn't just laid his secret bare and obliterated his bargain with Moll in the process.

Damn it all! That's what happened when a man ignored his own rules. And yet, if Ruthersby didn't believe her, Raven still had a chance to recover.

Unfortunately, one look at the baron and that last hope fled.

Ruthersby had his own agenda, after all. Flicking a glance from Raven to the debutante, his eyes suddenly gleamed with cunning and triumph. He drew in a barreled breath and bellowed, "Imposter!"

Then all hell broke loose.

Chapter 3

A footman in pink satin livery rushed in from one of the unseen corridors, holding fast to his powdered wig like a stage actor late for a curtain call.

Baron Ruthersby brandished his cane at Raven and shouted, "This man is a commoner in a patently poor disguise. How could you have allowed him admittance?"

"My lord, I—I assure you th-that I had n-no idea," the footman stammered.

"Never mind your excuses, man," the baron blustered. "Summon that brute at the door and call the guard at once!"

Raven, keeping to his disguise, coolly intoned, "This gentleman is clearly deep in his cups and raving like a lunatic. Fetch his driver before he embarrasses himself further."

The footman's expression contorted in confusion as he looked from one to the other. Then he set his hand on the baron's shoulder as if to escort *him* out.

"How dare you lay a finger on my person!" Ruthersby's ruddy face turned aubergine as his grip on the cane's hilt tightened. Without warning, he whacked the beak to the footman's forehead before swinging back to Raven. "And *you*! How dare you speak to me in such an insolent manner!"

"In point of fact, this man was speaking to the footman *about* you, not directly *to* you," the debutante interjected absently as she sidled up to the servant. Handing him a handkerchief, she advised him to attend the wound in the kitchen *post haste*. Oddly enough, he obeyed without a backward glance, as if she were somehow directing this disastrous play.

"And, frankly," she continued with authority, slyly stealing past the baron and toward the doorway, "I believe the point of embarrassment was breached the instant you stumbled into the alcove. Now, if we could simply put this unfortunate episode behind us . . ."

As she spoke, the giant Viking bully who guarded the door marched into the parlor, apparently having heard a disturbance. Blond, barrel-chested and burly-framed, Ivor took in the room at a glance, paying no attention to the uninterrupted hedonism in the minstrel's gallery.

Instead, his gaze settled on the cloaked feminine figure. "Yer not one've our girls. 'ow'd ye get in 'ere?"

"I do not believe my answer is of any relevance since I'll be leaving directly."

"'ow's about we just let Moll decide?" The brute blocked the path and looked down at her in a way that suggested he ate debutantes for afternoon tea and used their pinky fingers to pick his teeth afterward.

Raven was already at her side, steering her out of immediate danger. From beneath her hood, he heard her mutter, "Well, this is an unforeseen scenario. It's like the gunpowder incident all over again."

Gunpowder? He shook his head, having no idea what she was talking about. Not that it mattered. At the moment, they had other concerns.

He bent his head to speak low in her ear. "Just stay close to me. I'll take care of this."

"You needn't *take care* of anyone but yourself. I can manage on my own."

She stiffened beneath the hand he splayed against the curve of her lower back and lifted her gaze to his in a show of stubborn resolve. The movement caused the satin trim of her hood and a few errant, wispy curls to slide in a fragrant caress against his cheek, momentarily distracting him.

It was long enough for Ruthersby to step past the two of them and stand in their way. If it weren't for the cane he brandished in one hand, he'd have looked like a caricature of a boxing man—shoulders straight, knees bent, one fist raised high.

Behind Raven, Ivor took two hard steps forward, shaking the ground beneath his feet.

"Bloody hell," Raven cursed under his breath. He knew he could handle himself, but he didn't want to think of what would happen to the deb in the meantime. Not only that, but he would have to go easy on the baron. He didn't want to hang for murder when this was all over.

Keeping the bespoiler of his night's pleasure behind him, Raven gauged his opponents' positions as they closed in from opposite sides. "Fear not. I won't let anything happen to—"

"Look out!"

She yanked his sleeve, tugging him aside, just as a big ham-sized fist swung out with enough force to stir a breeze against his jaw.

He mumbled a grunt of gratitude and answered the attack with a solid facer. Ivor blinked, stunned. Wasting no time, Raven gave another and another. Pummeled and muzzy, the bully rocked back on his heels and stumbled into a nearby table. Tripping over a pair of chairs, he went crashing down onto a pile of tangled furniture.

The deb harrumphed while blindly reaching inside the seam of her cloak. "*I* do not require *your* assistance. However, you may wish to duck."

Just then, the baron's cane came scything down in a hard arc toward his head. Raven dodged to the side, but not soon enough. The edge of a fat ruby in the hawk's eye sliced a burning path into the flesh of his jaw.

Ignoring the sting, Raven buried a right jab into the baron's gut. But his knuckles encountered hard ribs of steel corseting over a dense balloon of blubber. Smarting, he drew back on a curse. *Bloody vain fop!*

Still, the blow sent the baron tottering back and he flailed blindly to stay upright. The silver beak of his cane came down again. This time it slashed through the shoulder seam of Raven's coat, carving sharply through the superfine wool that had cost him a half a week's wages.

Damn it all! That was enough. Stripping the cane from the baron's grasp, he slammed it down on the hardwood floor with a resounding *thwack*. The hawk head broke off and went flying across the room.

"Why you lousy ratbag—"

Before the baron could finish, the little deb stepped forth and blew a cloud of dusting powder into Ruthersby's face. He sneezed, then began to cough, doubling over and wiping at his eyes.

"Good job, you," Raven said to her with an appreciative nod.

"Thank you. I always come prepared with measures to extricate myself from any unfortunate situation."

He didn't like the sound of that. The high-society chit was out of her element. Proof of that was her presence here. He doubted she knew anything about the darker side of a man like Ruthersby's nature.

But there wasn't time to explain or to argue.

Ivor regained his feet. He was now on a chair-smashing rampage and headed straight for them.

Raven kept her near him as he darted around the maze of tables toward the door. But the Viking shoved a table aside and lunged forward, catching Raven off guard with an uppercut.

A universe of stars flashed behind his eyes. He staggered back, trying to shake it off. Then Ivor came at him again, full charge. Lifting him off his feet, he drove Raven hard against the wall beneath the minstrel's gallery.

"Oof!" The last of his air came out as a groan as the big man struck him over and over again, keeping him pinioned to the wall. And all the while, the lively sounds of a spinet tune played on overhead.

Through a dim haze, Raven saw the baron recover. Ruthersby seized the opportunity and chased the debutante around the upended tables.

It was like watching the plot of a penny dreadful come to life. She was always one step ahead of him . . .

Until suddenly, he snatched the hood of her cloak and dragged her back. Her hands flew to her throat, pulling at the enclosure. But it was too late. The baron had her now.

Something snapped inside Raven.

For years, he'd learned to subdue his baser nature—the feral *survive or die* part of him that had lived through nightmares in London's underworld. He didn't even allow himself to think about those things. But seeing her struggle and flinch to get away from Ruthersby's groping hands unleashed his inner beast.

An animalistic roar rose from his throat.

Still smashed against the wall by the bully, Raven lashed out with fury, delivering blow after blow, wherever he could reach. An elbow to the shoulder. A knee to the ribs. A dig to the throat and a bunt to the head. But Ivor shook it off, his skull apparently made of solid rock.

So Raven shifted to cinch his arms tightly around the Viking's neck, and held fast, listening to the strained wheeze of each breath.

"Unhand me!" the little deb shouted as she turned to face her assailant. "If you do not release me this instant, I should be forced to employ measures that will most likely end with an injury to your person."

"Be a good girl now and—"

The baron never had the chance to finish.

Quicker than a Covent Garden pickpocket, she thrust her arm forward and hooked her foot behind Ruthersby's knee, taking him off-balance. Down he went with a grunt, the back of his head striking the edge of a chair before he fell boneless to the floor.

"I did warn you," she admonished coolly as she pressed two fingertips to the pulse at his throat. "You'll likely have an immense headache for at least a week."

Then, stepping over the supine form, she looked toward Raven just as Ivor passed out and toppled like a felled tree.

And there they stood, with two bodies on the floor at their feet, as a chorus of moans and music drifted down from overhead.

Catching his breath, Raven stared at her. He felt strangely mystified and exhilarated as if he were a lad seeing fireworks light up the night sky over Vauxhall for the first time.

"And to think," he said, "all this happened because of a button."

"Oh, it was far more than a mere button that gave you away." There was a curious gleam in those midnight-blue eyes, but she didn't elaborate further. She only held his gaze for that single instant, then darted through the door, disappearing from sight.

"Wait," he called, giving chase. But the pain in his bludgeoned ribs made him slow and he didn't catch up with her until they reached the study.

There, the muted glow from dying embers lit the trespasser's silhouette against the open window on the far wall. Just as he closed the door with a quiet *click* behind him, she boosted herself up and straddled the sill, looking over her shoulder at him.

"Come any closer and I shall be forced to use this," she

said, holding an indistinguishable object in her hand that looked something like a fat candle. "And I must warn you, it has the potential to be quite dangerous."

Pretending to appease her, he stayed where he was beside a fern on a marble pedestal. It would only take him four strides to reach her. Three if he leapt over the tufted hassock.

He watched her with rapt fascination as she placed the object on the sill with extreme care. But then he caught the flash of uncertainty in her fine-boned features.

A slow grin tugged at his mouth. "You're only trying to hoodwink me."

"And what purpose would a baseless warning serve in such a place? Surely, you cannot suspect that I would come to a brothel defenseless."

She reached inside her cloak once more, withdrawing flint and steel.

He shrugged. "You're a stranger. I've no idea what you're capable of doing."

"I suppose that makes two of us," she said with a light laugh, flashing a grin that revealed the smallest, most intriguing little gap between her two front teeth in an otherwise perfect arrangement of pearly whites. "Nevertheless, please remember that I did warn you. And, whatever you do, *do not* come near this window."

With a quick strike, she lit the strange candle on the sill. Then she ducked her head and slipped out the window, holding onto the edge.

He rushed forward to keep her from falling. But she dropped lithely to the ground before he could reach her. Emitting a shrill whistle, she then loped gracefully toward the back alley.

Hoisting his leg over the sill, he prepared to follow.

Yet, hearing the creak of the floor behind him, he turned to see Moll, her tall voluptuous form draped in a gown of burgundy velvet and trimmed in ostrich feathers.

"Who was the girl, Raven?" she asked, her voice curling and raspy like the smoke rising from the cigar pinched between her thumb and forefingers.

He cursed, hoping that tonight's cockup hadn't put a nail in the coffin of him ever being allowed back in her good graces. "I can explain—"

But before he could utter another syllable, the candle flared suddenly, crackling in sparks. Then, all at once, it quieted on an ominous *poof* as a dense cloud of thick pink smoke began to flood the room.

✂✂✂

JANE'S BREATH caught as she closed the carriage door and saw billowing curls of pale smoke rolling from the brothel window. Grinning, she clapped her bare hand against the gloved one in muffled glee.

Her *urgent escape smoke* experiment had worked marvelously!

Withdrawing the ledger, she angled it toward the lamplight to jot a quick note of the ratios she'd used. She would require more of these in the future, she was sure.

But, before she could lick the tip of her pencil, all the events of this evening flooded her at once. She sank back against the squabs as her cousin spurred the horses and they set off toward home.

A brothel! Only now were the dangers of her escapade beginning to seep into her sentient mind, her heart racing beneath the shallow rise and fall of her breast. She'd barely survived the encounter unscathed!

But the things she'd learned made it all worthwhile. Why, with another visit, the primer on the marriage habits of the native aristocrat would be so full of useful information that every finishing school in England would teach from it.

Jane beamed from ear to ear. She could already imagine

the future accolades. Scores of young women would line up at bookshops for the only tome that would change the course of their lives.

Her lashes drifted closed as she tried to commit the night to memory. But all she could see were a pair of gray eyes, so pale they nearly lacked color altogether. And that voice . . . so deep and rough-edged, it still seemed to be inside her, belaboring every pulsebeat.

She's mine for the hour.

How positively primal! His tone had been so authoritative and commanding that even she was tempted to believe him.

Then, and now, it caused tingles to race over her skin in anticipation, tightening every hair follicle and gathering in her lungs. A breath stuttered past her parted lips. What might it have been like to be *his* for an hour?

But there, her mind went as blank as a freshly mopped slate. She had absolutely no experience in being the object of a man's desire. Had this episode been removed from the allure of a brothel and placed in a sedate ballroom, he would have looked straight through her.

Even so, his actions toward the lecherous gentleman who'd pulled her from the alcove were nothing short of predatory. She'd never witnessed such an aggressive display of dominance. Quite thrilling!

If only she could study him for the primer. It would surely be the most fascinating chapter in the entire book. The subtitle would be: *The Primitive Man in All His Glory.*

It was a pity she'd never see him again.

Feeling the carriage slow to a crawl, she opened her eyes and tapped on the hood. "Cousin, we mustn't dally near Haymarket at this time of night."

"But I've got to stop," Duncan called down through the small square flap, thick titian eyebrows knitting perplexedly above his thrice-broken nose. "It's Raven and I couldn't run him over."

Jane smiled up at him patiently, knowing that beneath his battered Wellington and the burly exterior of an ox, Duncan Pickerington had a heart of toffee pudding and a brain the size of a walnut. "I'm certain the bird will instinctively fly away before the horses can trample it."

"Oh, but he isn't a bird. I work with him at Sterling's. Although . . . I don't know why he's pink."

Now it was her turn to be perplexed. Sometimes Duncan said the strangest things.

But curiosity had always had a way of taking over her better sense. So she opened the door, intending to lean out and have a look for herself.

"A raven would be black, certainly not pi . . ."

Her words dissolved away as a form emerged from the shadows and stepped into the light of the carriage lanterns.

Suddenly, she was face-to-face with those frost-gray eyes again.

"Raven," her cousin called down with a merry chuckle. "How did you come to be so pink?"

The man seethed at her, nostrils flaring. "I ran into a meddlesome little debutante who had no business being where I found her."

Jane swallowed down a rise of nerves. "Goodness! Your skin is quite caryophyllaceous, isn't it? Must have been the dried beet powder I used for fuel. I'll have to make a note of that."

However, when lifting the ledger earned her a low growl, she thought better of it. Perhaps she would jot down her findings later when it was more appropriate.

"Don't worry, Raven. Jane can set you back to rights. She's brilliant. Comes up with all sorts of things."

Dark brows arched sardonically over those icy eyes, and

every deep syllable he spoke spilled acidly from his lips. "Is that so? How lucky for me."

"I sense a trace of unnecessary sarcasm in your tone. I assure you that—"

"Pickerington," he interrupted, calling up to the perch but without taking his gaze from her. "Mind delivering me to my flat? I think I'd like to have a chat with the *brilliant* Jane."

She studied the long-fingered hand that fell on the door and recalled his ferocity when battling those men, especially the largest one. And she was never more aware of her petite stature as she was in this moment. "Regrettably, we have no time for a detour."

"Oh, but this is *Raven*," Duncan said with an awed elongation of syllables as if he were describing a mythological god. "He's never asked me for anything before. I'd love to see his flat and I'm sure it won't take but a minute. Please, Jane? Just this once? I won't pester you for anything ever, ever again. I promise."

She bit down on her bottom lip, worrying the soft tissue between her teeth. Her gaze strayed to the cut on the man's cheek, then to the tear in his sleeve. And was that . . . *blood* saturating the fabric?

"Very well," she said on a tight breath of guilt.

Perhaps the least she could do was to set him back to rights.

But when he gave her cousin the address in Covent Garden then climbed inside the abruptly close confines of the carriage, she felt it necessary to add, "Duncan will come to my defense if I emit the barest squeak of distress. I won't be held responsible for what he does to you."

The man she knew only as Raven eased back against the squabs across from her and folded his arms over his chest. "But who will protect *me* from *you*?"

Chapter 4

———

Jane sat stiffly on the cushioned bench as the carriage trundled along the street toward Raven's dwelling. In all the hours she'd spent formulating a plan to enter the brothel and study the inhabitants, she'd never once fathomed the possibility of leaving *with* a scoundrel in tow. And certainly not one so grumpy.

It wasn't her fault that he was pink. Well, not entirely. "Just so we're clear, I never asked for your assistance."

"And I never asked you to ruin my life," he hissed back and she hated that his voice was still so dratted appealing.

"If the sum of your existence revolves around admittance to a brothel, then you have far more to worry about than the color of your skin. In fact, I recently read a medical journal on a certain . . . *ailment*, shall we say . . . which some men have contracted when visiting houses of ill repute."

Within the slitted confines of her lace mask, she slid a purposeful glance down his form to the shadowed juncture she'd read about in the journal.

"I don't have the pox," he growled, shifting beneath her scrutiny. "I use French letters."

Taking up her ledger once more, Jane sat forward with interest. She wished the carriage lanterns were brighter. If nothing else, she would use this unexpected opportunity to compile more research.

"I've never seen one before, but I've read about them.

How do they operate, precisely? Is it a difficult contraption to manage?" She licked the tip of her pencil then gestured to the general area. "And do you have one on your person this instant?"

"No, I'm not wearing one *now*. That isn't how it works."

The scientist within her was inordinately disappointed. She slumped back and tucked the ledger away. "I suppose that ought to be a relief. After all, I shouldn't want to share a carriage with a man who was merely waiting for the next opportunity."

"*You* don't have to worry about that. I prefer my women more worldly. *Not* little debutantes who go places they don't belong."

Jane knew she was plain. And yet . . . she'd never had it confirmed so blatantly by a stranger before. In the very least, he might have had the decency to imagine her a prostitute the way the other man had done.

"You must be exceedingly familiar with *all* the women who work in that establishment to know instantly that I wasn't one of them," she said, trying to keep the slightly bruised portion of her ego from sounding too waspish.

The amused rumble in his throat told her that she'd failed. The blackguard didn't even bother to confirm or deny her suspicion, which left her without a further understanding of his species.

"So tell me," he began with a sharp nod and a growling edge to his voice, "what was the other thing that gave me away, aside from my damnable button?"

It likely shouldn't please her so much to know that her comment had irritated him.

But it did.

She felt a grin tug at the corner of her mouth. "Frankly, I'm surprised that a man your age isn't more self-aware. I do not know how long you've kept to your disguise, but I saw through it the minute I clapped eyes on you."

Ha. Let him stew on that, she thought, crossing her arms.

Without a word, he stared at her with steady intensity as if fully prepared to either wait for her to divulge the rest, or to bore through her skull, sift through the contents and glean the information for himself.

And, drat it all, she couldn't leave it alone. It wasn't in her nature to leave a question unanswered.

"Very well," she said, resigned. "You possess a certain . . . feral quality that is never seen in a ballroom or at a dinner party. You prowl rather than walk as if you've just emerged from a den and are in search of your next meal."

"And I'd be feasting now if it weren't for you."

A weary sigh faded from her lungs. "Are we to return to this topic again and again? I shudder to think what the world would be like if all men were as singularly focused on sexual congress as you are. All my research this evening on the differences between gentlemen and scoundrels would be for naught."

"So that's what you were up to with all your note taking."

She gave a nod that may or may not have been rather smug. "My friends and I are writing a book to aid future generations of our sex."

"Smart as all that, are you?" His brows flicked upward and his mouth slanted in unmistakable derision.

She didn't answer.

"Well, *professor*, I hate to be the one to shatter your illusions but, stripped of all society's trappings, men *are* all the same."

Of course, he made his speech without a modicum of remorse for his attempt to *shatter her illusions.* Yet it was his cool smirk in the lantern light that tweaked her ire.

"All alike? No, indeed," she said. "The majority of men aren't quite so pink, I'm sure."

He skewered her with a steely glower. Then, in one smooth

motion, he moved to the edge of his seat, reached out and lifted her hood in place before she could even gasp at his sudden nearness.

Her lips parted all the same. The scent of him—some enthralling combination of leather and raw earth—invaded her olfactory sense. And those pale irises were impossibly close. So close, it seemed as if she were peering into the depths of a fathomless lake that had frozen into one solid block of ice.

"Word of warning, Jane. It isn't wise to anger a hungry animal when you're about to step into his cave."

In that moment, she realized the carriage had stopped. She peered out the window toward the redbrick facade of a ramshackle terrace in Covent Garden.

Newton's apple, a scoundrel's flat! She most definitely hadn't planned for this.

❧❧❧

RAVEN CROSSED the threshold and closed the door, effectively shutting out the light from the streetlamps and immersing them in blackness. He noticed that the soles of Jane's shoes shifted nervously on the hardwood floor.

Good. She deserved to feel uneasy and uncertain after all the trouble she'd caused him.

"And I thought you were merely goading me when you mentioned a cave," she said under her breath, her sardonic tone extracting a reluctant rise of amusement within him.

He didn't mind the darkness. At least, not anymore. He'd grown accustomed to using all of his senses to take measure of his surroundings.

Already his eyes adjusted to the pale rectangle of light bleeding in through the transom above the door. He tasted the closed-in staleness of the air that told him no one had been here to disturb the dust since he'd left.

But there was a new fragrance here now, teasing his nostrils with the allure of something warm, powdery and feminine—a scent that belonged here about as much as a debutante belonged in a brothel. And, in that instant, he knew this was a mistake.

He never should have invited Pickerington and his meddling cousin to his home. Surely, he could have figured out some way to leach the pink from his skin, even if he had to scrub himself raw with lye to do it.

So then why had he brought them here?

He wasn't used to having visitors. Wasn't even used to having a home of his own. In fact, other than Reed Sterling, this peculiar debutante and her cousin were his only guests in the six months he'd lived here.

So it came as a complete surprise to realize that, in some small way, he wanted them to like it. Or, more to the point, that he wanted her to see that he was more than just a brown thread.

What a clodpole he was.

"I'll just light a taper or something," he muttered, trying to put the ignorant thought out of his mind as he moved past them to the console table.

It wobbled when he slid open the drawer for the tinderbox. The short third leg was on a long list of things he'd yet to fix. But he'd get to them all in time, he thought as he lit a tallow candle and a thick curl of smoke rose from the wick.

"So, this is where Raven lives," Duncan Pickerington said as the golden light flickered to life, gilding dust motes in the air of the narrow foyer. His block-shaped head fell back to look up at the flat ceiling, his mouth falling slack on an awed exclamation as if gazing up at the heavens instead of huge yellowed scales of torn plaster. "Where's your landlady?"

"On holiday," Raven lied, never one to share more information than he had to.

After lighting all six tapers in a bronze brace, he turned his head and saw the inquisitive Jane lower her hood to scrutinize her surroundings. Framed by the mask, her midnight-blue eyes reflected a circlet of flames. Her lips began moving in that soundless murmur again and he waited for her to say something—an observation, a cutting remark, anything— aloud. But she kept her thoughts frustratingly hidden from him.

"You're lucky," Pickerington added glumly. "When me dad and me lived in our last flat, we was always being hounded by the landlady. It was likely her who'd done put him in debtor's prison."

Jane lifted a hand to her cousin's shoulder. "Your father will not always be there. Just as soon as his debts are paid, he will be free once more and reunited with the entire family."

Mollified, Pickerington nodded and commandeered the candelabra with a careless swipe of his meaty grip, guttering two of the candles. Holding the brace aloft, he began to tromp up the stairs ahead of them, leaving his cousin behind. So it was up to Raven to ensure her steps didn't falter in the more rickety places. He was planning to fix those, too.

In the meantime, he took Jane's slender wrist in his grasp and tethered her to his side. Touching her bare skin, he instantly recalled the glove he'd stowed in his pocket. But he wasn't in a hurry to return it. If she could keep her secret thoughts to herself, then he could keep his.

But when she lifted a round-eyed glance to him and he felt the tender spurring of the pulse nestled against his palm, he reflexively stroked his fingertips over the downy skin to soothe her. "The railing isn't secure."

"Even so, you cannot simply seize a woman whenever you wish. You offer her your arm and wait for her to accept," she chided softly. Slipping free, she maneuvered his arm as one would a puppet in a *fantoccini* then curled her slender limb around him to rest her hand on his sleeve. "This is the proper way to escort a woman up a questionable set of stairs."

Dubious, he looked down at the disheveled topknot of golden-brown hair, her head coming only to his shoulder. It seemed that his was the more proper way because, like this, he could feel the warm, small curve of her breast press against his arm through the tailored wool.

"If you say so," he offered. "But take care on the next tread. It might be loose."

When she pressed even closer, a grin tugged at his mouth. Who was he to argue against *propriety*?

Reaching the first-floor landing, he led them down an L-shaped hallway, the walls stripped to the lath and creaking floors underfoot. These repairs to this old boardinghouse were also on his mile-long list.

His carpentry and pargeting skills were learned primarily by trial and error. *Plenty of error*. But he found he enjoyed the labor, the process of demolishing and clearing out the old in order to make way for the new. And beyond this door at the end of the hall, everything was new.

The agitation that had been with him downstairs dissipated on a slow exhale of expectancy as he turned the key in the lock.

The door swung open on oiled hinges that no longer screeched like a cat. Candlelight gleamed against cream-colored walls.

Stepping inside, Raven breathed in the scent of fresh paint and admired the gloss of his waxed floor. It had taken a good deal of sweat to make this space shine and there was plenty more work ahead of him as well. But all he could see when he looked around him was a life of his own making.

Puffed with pride, he glanced down at Jane's upturned heart-shaped face.

Her feathery brows knit together above the slender strip of her mask and her lips formed a frown. "*Where* is your furniture?"

Clearly, they weren't seeing the same room.

She slipped her arm from his and he was struck by an uncanny impulse to draw her back, to feel her slight form at his side while he explained the hours he'd spent toiling and cursing and despising crown molding. But instead, he shrugged against the taut bands of tension gathering along his shoulders.

"Most of it was broken and moldering. Sold the lot for a few crowns," he said and felt the fool for expecting her to marvel at the bare floor and walls when the true show-stopper was in the next room. "Besides, everything I need is just through there."

Taking the brace from Pickerington, he moved toward the varnished door on the far wall and knew that curiosity would oblige Jane to follow. Then, standing just beyond the threshold, he kept his grin tucked away and waited.

This room was sure to impress even the likes of a pampered debutante. It hosted two tall windows, draped in deep blue brocade. They flanked a wide canopied bed with thick walnut posts that dominated the space. On the far wall stood a round-bellied wardrobe at least twice the size of the rat-infested cupboard that he'd been stuffed into whenever he'd been caught running away from the Devil's workhouse.

An involuntary shudder slithered through him at the errant memory. He swallowed and shook it off, reminding himself that those days were as far gone as the rubbish he'd cleared out of this room.

He followed Jane's inquisitive gaze as it skimmed quickly past the bed and to the glossy Chippendale side table with a gold tasseled key resting in the drawer lock. She only gave a cursory glance to his spindled corner washstand, paying no attention to the pristine porcelain basin that didn't have a single crack or chip along the rim. And he'd wager she didn't know that the tall, leather wing-backed chair by the hearth was more comfortable than any other chair in the world, he was sure.

Every luxury a man could ever want.

In this light, he could see the thick fan of sable lashes around Jane's wide eyes as they ventured back to the bed. He was especially proud that the mattress ticking and pillows were stuffed to bursting with downy feathers instead of straw or horsehair. It was like sleeping on a cloud.

There was a bit of smugness in him when he asked, "What do you think now?"

In the seconds that followed, Raven waited for those eyes to light up with wonder. Waited for her to exclaim that she'd never imagined such opulence. And waited for her to offer a shy apology for assuming she knew everything about him at a glance.

Brown thread, indeed.

Before she could respond, however, her cousin tromped in behind them and exclaimed, "Damn, that's a right giant of a bed. I bet the whole house was built around it. I bet"—he nudged Raven and lowered his voice to a dull roar—"you could fit four girls in there at once."

Jane cleared her throat. She crossed crisply to the far corner and retrieved the chamberstick from the nightstand, her movements brisk and agitated. "Cousin, there's no point in dawdling. Light a fire in the hearth, if you please. I'll need as much light as possible in this iniquitous cavern."

Raven's ego took a facer. *Cavern?* This debutante obviously took for granted such lavishness. Likely didn't have a clue about how hard a man had to work for everything he wanted, especially when he'd started out with nothing.

But he wasn't about to enlighten this overeducated bluestocking. Rule number four—keep anonymous.

Besides, her opinion didn't matter in the least. All he needed was for her to take the pink from his skin and then good riddance.

And the sooner the better.

Chapter 5

It was Jane's nature to see the merit in ominous beginnings. There was always something to be learned, after all. And what could be better for the book than studying the intricacies of a scoundrel's mind whilst standing inside the den where his secret ponderings and aspirations sprouted to life from dreams?

The problem was, this scoundrel only appeared to be interested in sexual congress.

What a dismal end to her evening! Was she to learn nothing new about his species—like, perhaps, how women fell for their seductions in the first place?

She unfastened her cloak and dropped it on the counterpane. Her unmated glove came off next, the black garments mere slivers against a veritable sea of dark blue linens. Without her permission, her mind conjured that very scenario—which Duncan had mentioned an instant ago—of four women sprawled on every corner of this continent.

Until this evening, she would have thought such a carnal overindulgence an impossibility. But after seeing Raven so easily manage the two *minstrels* earlier, what were two more? Certainly nothing to a man like him.

She expelled an irritated breath.

"I don't see what has you in such a lather," he said crossly, his attention on one of the dark bedposts as he turned his thumbnail along the carved, decorative swirl. "You can drive the good humor out of a man like a hammer to nail."

Watching his slow, careful movement into the slender groove—as if he were intent on ferreting out a secret from the recesses of the woodgrain—she felt a strange tingling sensation along her spine. It started at the sacral curve and traipsed lazily up to her nape, distracting her . . .

At least, until Duncan snickered behind her and she remembered why she was so piqued. Ah yes, the four women.

Jane chose to ignore both men and untied the reticule from her waist. Reaching into the ruched opening, she withdrew an assortment of little green jars, small brown flacons and phials, and a miniature wooden spoon. Then she lined them up on the ledge where he kept his shaving cup and razor. With renewed agitation, she flicked open lids and pulled stoppers, and began combining powders and liquids into a composite at the bottom of the washbasin.

She wasn't entirely certain it would work to remove the profuse pink staining from his skin. But she didn't particularly care either. She just wanted to end this unsatisfactory night once and for all.

"What else do you have in that bag of yours?" Raven asked, peering across the distance with speculation.

She speared him with a glare, then reached for the pitcher. *Empty*, of course. She gave him another hard look for the inconvenience.

Turning to her cousin, she said, "Duncan, would you be so kind as to find the kitchen belowstairs and fill this with clean water, *tout suite*? Oh, and take this *rat de cave* with you and be mindful of the stairs."

"A' course," he said with eagerness, dusting his hands together after he added a log to the crackling kindling and tinder bundle in the grate.

Taking the ewer and spiral chamberstick, Duncan set off immediately with loud, lumbering footsteps and headed out the door.

Left alone with the instigator of her foul mood, she set her hands on her slender hips and faced Raven. "Come here, if you please, and make haste. I've wasted enough time dealing with the likes of you."

"You look like an angry pixie with your arms flared and your foot tapping away like that," he said, arching a supercilious dark brow as he pushed away from the post and ambled toward her, taking his time. "Now, why do I get the sense that the little professor is mad at me? It should be the other way around, don't you think?"

"Do I think? Why, yes, I do. All the time, in fact. Would you like to know what I'm thinking right now?"

"Something tells me I don't."

"I'm thinking about how disappointing it is to realize that there are men in the world like you," she said, her eyes narrowing into slits. "Ones who will sell their meager possessions just to visit an exclusive brothel. Ones with no higher aspirations than a night's fornication."

"That isn't exactly—"

"I'm thinking that the book my friends and I are writing will be less of a primer and more of a tragedy, warning all women away from your sex. And I'm thinking"—she paused to swipe a loose hank of hair from her forehead—"that I should let you remain pink."

"You're awfully full of spite for someone so small," he said, smirking down at her. "And don't forget, it's your fault that I can't return to Moll's."

"I'm certain you won't have trouble finding a woman to bring here. Although you may lose sight of her on this vulgar expansive land you refer to as a bed. I shouldn't be surprised if you'd purchased it by the acre."

"I plan to add tenant farms in the south quadrant."

On a tiny growl, she seized his wrist in a strong grip and hauled him over to the washstand. Before he could utter another word, she scooped up some of her gray concoction and slapped it against his hand.

Scrubbing the grit over his skin, she heard him issue a gruff grunt, deep in his throat. She took it as a sign of his displeasure. Imagining his utter torment only encouraged her efforts. So, she continued to unleash her anger in a rough massage over his palms, down the lengths of his fingers, and in between.

"Is this supposed to be a reprimand for my roguish ways?" he asked in a teasingly low timbre. "I hate to disappoint, but it feels like heaven. Your little hands are as soft and warm as a kitten's underbelly."

"And your provocative comments are falling on deaf ears," she claimed, working him into a pink lather.

But she lied.

Her entire body was now tingling from his words and she was suddenly quite aware of the feel of her skin on his. Every nerve ending was heat-stung with pleasure. The dichotomy of grit and smooth flesh was a decadent treat for her gluttonous senses. He was warm, too, his hands so much larger than hers, with broad palms and long fingers that likely knew all sorts of wicked ways to touch a woman.

"Are they, *really*?" he asked with a dubious curl to his voice, his hot breath stirring a wayward tendril by her temple and sending a delightful shiver tumbling through her.

It seemed to go on and on, swirling inside her, especially around her middle, coiling tightly. And she would like to explore this at length . . . if she didn't know precisely what he was doing.

He was feigning a flirtation in order to unsettle her because she'd prevented his evening's licentious festivities.

Her vigorous scrubbing continued. His declaration was nothing more than a pretense of seduction. She'd been laughed at before for being odd. Normally, she politely pretended she didn't understand or didn't hear the insult.

Tonight, however, she wore a mask. Anonymity made her feel a bit braver and freer to speak her mind. He knew her name, but not her face. And should she ever see him in the light of day—highly doubtful considering his nocturnal escapades—she would be spared any residual embarrassment.

Although, at the moment, all she felt was annoyance.

"I can see right through you, I hope you know," she said with a sniff. "Then again, you're not terribly opaque. After all, your only furnished room is a bedchamber. Clearly, bedsport is your sole priority. And I am ashamed to recall my fleeting thought of dedicating a full chapter to you. From your mildly chivalrous actions at the brothel, I thought you lived by your own philosophy of scruples. Instead, I've discovered cunningly disguised moral turpitude."

A disapproving growl rumbled somewhere in the vicinity of his chest. "I've had about enough of your boundless accusations. For your information, I have money *and* aspirations."

She scoffed. "I doubt you even own a single book, unless it contains nude etchings."

❦❦❦

RAVEN WENT still, his entire body rigid. The last accusation stung like lemon on an open gash.

Having only been educated to a rudimentary level in the foundling home, he'd taken great pains throughout his life to become a self-taught man. In fact, whenever he'd earned enough money to spend, he'd always bought a book.

Always wanted to better himself.

Always wanted to thumb his nose at everyone who thought he was rubbish.

"I don't see that it should matter to you"—he jerked his chin toward his bedside table—"but take a look in there. Go on."

"Fine. I will, but only to further my understanding of the debauched life of a scoundrel. I'm certain nothing can surprise me now."

Clenching her jaw mulishly, she wiped smears of mauve-colored grit on a scrap of flannel then turned the tasseled key. And when she slid open the drawer to reveal his collection of books, she gasped.

He grinned self-righteously and turned his attention back to his ablutions. "There. Now you can stop grousing at me."

Glancing down, he noted the pink stain on the cuffs of his shirt and the powdery film on his waistcoat. Likely his entire suit was ruined and would need to be replaced. He didn't relish the idea of being fitted and measured by a tailor again. The last one had treated him like a flea-infested mongrel, saying directly to him that such a suit for a plebian man was nothing more than a waste of fine wool.

"Why are these not displayed properly on a shelf?" she asked with sharp disdain.

Raven rolled his eyes and muttered under his breath, "And still the harping continues."

"And look at this!" She tsked. "You've dripped candle wax on two, and doubtless because you couldn't read the titles within the dark recesses of the drawer."

Jane ran the pad of her index finger over the worn spines, her lips murmuring the titles soundlessly. He watched her, transfixed by her mouth and the fond caress of her fingertips over the books. Her nails were manicured into softly rounded crescents that carefully scraped away the wax. At the quiet rasping sound, his skin prickled warmly beneath the fine lawn of his shirtsleeves, along the broad muscles of his back and down the length of his spine. The errant sensations pooled low in his gut, distracting him.

"I keep what's mine locked up," he said, his voice taking on a husky edge that drew her inquisitive attention.

Her head tilted to the side, wispy brows lifting ever so slightly, like a brown-and-gold butterfly testing the air before flight. "Even in your own bedchamber?"

"Aye. When you wake up in the foundling home to find that the other boys have stolen the stockings off your feet, you learn to keep—"

He broke off abruptly. *Bollocks!* He hadn't meant to let that slip.

Turning back to the basin, he made a swift attempt at diverting her attention by adding, "Have you read any of them?"

"Yes," she answered simply, softly now.

He could feel her probing stare on his profile, hear every hesitant breath she took. But he refused to turn to see pity in her expression.

"I didn't realize you were an orphan. That must have been dreadfully lonely."

"*Crowded*, is what it was. Never a moment alone, or a moment's peace. Much like now."

Carefully, she closed the drawer and turned the key. When she reached inside the basin once more, his first impulse was to pull away and tell her that he could manage on his own. But he had a greater desire to let her know that he wasn't bothered by his admission. So he pretended indifference.

He had nothing to be ashamed of, after all. He *was* an orphan. There was no changing that fact.

The instant her hands settled over his, Raven sensed an alteration in her demeanor. Her scrubbing was gentler, the smooth edges of her nails tracing along the curve of his cuticles. Her thumb worked circles into his palm, soothing places he never knew were tense in the first place. And it had the dangerous effect of relaxing his guard.

His lids grew heavier. Dimly, he watched her retrieve another flacon from the night table.

Wariness would usually have him withdrawing, but a glut of languor and pleasure had overtaken him. He simply let her drip that unknown, clear liquid into the cup of his palm without question.

At once, his nostrils were assailed by the same fragrance that scented her skin. Was this . . . lavender water? He drew in a deeper breath, his lungs filling with the heady elixir, his flesh tingling with every press and rub.

Jane Pickerington wasn't what he expected. The society debs he'd encountered on the pavement or in the park had their noses up in the air. He'd heard tales of fainting spells when they met with a shock or anything that disturbed their prudish sensibilities.

So, naturally, he'd thought they were *all* uptight and high-strung.

This one had her moments, but she was more apt to surprise him. Like she was doing now.

Looking down at their warm, entangled hands, he noticed his own skin color gradually emerging. Mystified, he asked, "What's in this paste you made?"

"Oh . . . crushed eggshells, salt, potash—which may sting, by the way—and your own shaving soap," she said absently as she added a few more drops from the flacon, filling his bedchamber with her powdery, pure scent.

Raven wanted to lie down and let the round pads of her kitten hands work their magic all over him. Perhaps even pull her down with him. Start off by giving that opinionated, full mouth a good-night kiss . . .

"How old were you when your parents died?" she asked, shattering the cozy image he'd conjured.

Tiny knots of agitation returned to the tendons stretched like baggage straps across his shoulders. He straightened and dragged in another deep lungful of air, only to find that the scent's relaxing properties had faded.

"For all I know, they could still be alive," he said, keeping his tone impassive as he slipped out of her clasp and reached for the flannel to wipe off the gritty residue. There was still a pinkish hue to his flesh, but it was far better than what it had been before. With another scrubbing, he'd be back to rights. "I was found on the doorstep of the foundling home and there's nothing more to tell."

"But surely there must have been a note of some kind . . ."

He arched a brow. "A heart-torn scrap of paper pinned to my swaddling with a fervent plea from my mother to take care of her poor helpless child?"

Jane nodded. Those wide, inquisitive eyes looked up at him, filled with reflections of firelight and so much naive hope that a humorless laugh escaped him.

"So, you're a bluestocking *and* a romantic? Well, little professor, it may surprise you to learn that some children are simply left to make it on their own."

Her gaze slid from him in a downward arc like a falling star brought to earth as nothing more than a rock.

A pang of irritation abraded him like a pebble in a boot. "Don't give me any of your pity."

"I'm not offering any. It's just . . ." She trailed off as she made a slow procession over to the bottle of whisky he'd left on the far side of the mantel. "I'm startled to learn that we have something in common."

He doubted it. From where he stood, there were no similarities between his life and hers.

"But more than that," she continued, facing him as she returned with the bottle, "I haven't been very fair in my judgments of you this evening. My apologies, Mr. Raven."

"It's just Raven. There's nothing else."

She inclined her head in a nod of understanding, then struggled to work the cork free.

He reached out and twisted the stopper loose. "Care for a glass? Or do you prefer to swig directly from the bottle?"

She slid him a sardonic glance as she reached into her sleeve and withdrew a frilly handkerchief. Remembering that she'd already given one to the wounded footman earlier, he wondered if she kept one up each sleeve. For all he knew they were tucked into her corset, too. But he didn't bother to ask. He didn't want to be curious about her.

Upending the bottle, she dampened a corner of lace, then lifted it up to the cut on his cheek. Pausing halfway, she said, "Bend down a little. You're too tall for me to clean it properly."

"I don't need to be coddled," he said, but found himself moving around her to sit on the edge of the bed, regardless.

"You're being ridiculous. I'm only making certain that your jaw doesn't develop some horrible festering pustules like the ones I've seen sketched in medical journals. I find that it's always best to be prepared for the worst."

"How reassuring." His droll reply ended in a sharp hiss the instant the liquor-soaked cloth touched his open wound. "And where did this philosophy of yours come from?"

"The correct wording would be *from where did your philosophy come*? Tilt your head a bit, if you would. Thank you." She paused to make a gentle pass, biting down into the cushion of her bottom lip. "I do not suspect you have cause to worry. This laceration on your jaw should heal quite nicely. At least, as long as you refrain from picking at the scab that will form. Before I go, I'll leave you a salve to aid in your recovery and keep you from scarring."

He noticed that she sidestepped his question, but let it pass. "I won't need it. I've always been a quick healer."

"As you will." She shrugged and continued her ministrations. "My little sister, Theodora, is terrible about scratching open her wounds and I fear her four-year-old knees will bear the scars for years to come. I will be grateful when our brothers return from university for their winter holiday. She will be less likely to fall since she practically lives on Theodore's back. She pretends that he's her pet rhinoceros."

"Wait a minute." He felt his brows inch higher. "You have both a brother *and* a sister with nearly identical names? Is that after an ancestor or something?"

Jane quickly averted her face to fuss and fold the handkerchief. "Not exactly. Theodora was born in autumn, and with the three older boys away at school, Mother and Father had simply forgotten about them. I've heard that happens in larger families, on occasion."

Raven knew what it was like to be considered just one face among dozens of orphans in the foundling home. They'd been treated as shells of children, like those Russian nesting dolls. No single individual mattered or earned attention, unless they'd misbehaved. Otherwise, he and the others had simply been stacked up and shipped off to the workhouses, leaving the orphanage ready to take on another set.

But he never expected it would be the same in a family.

Her account made her life seem somewhat lonely. He knew all about that. A sudden sense of recognition prickled over his scalp, as if one hollowed-out spirit had inexplicably found another.

An instant later, he balked inwardly. What a crackbrained notion! He brushed it off like lint on a sleeve. The two of them were as different as two people could be.

"How many siblings do you have?" he asked for the sake of conversation, not because he was interested in the answer. As a matter of fact, he wasn't interested in anything regarding Jane Pickerington.

Well, except for that mask.

He stared fixedly at that scrap of fabric and realized that

he'd grown tired of seeing it. The appeal of mystery was long past and he was itching to take it off.

"There are eleven of us in all," she answered simply, leaning in to study his wound.

Eleven, he thought with amazement, imagining a world with nearly a dozen Jane Pickeringtons in it. No brothel would ever be safe again.

His fingertips idly brushed the soft violet skirts bunched between his parted thighs. He was getting agitated, his blood stirring. Her nearness was getting under his skin, the heat of the fire intensifying the fragrance of lavender.

Didn't she realize her vulnerable position? No, because she felt safe behind that blasted mask. Too safe in the company of a scoundrel, even one who had no interest in her. Not really.

"How did you come to be named Raven?" she asked, drawing him out of his vexed musings.

"From a birthmark on my arm that looks like a bird."

His dismissive comment earned her full, abrupt attention. And her eyes were so fixed on his that he could see the individual striations of dark indigo and sparkling sapphire.

An ominous shiver stole down his spine, but he shook it off. After all, how could he know that such a simple statement was about to take the life he'd built from nothing and turn it on its ear?

Chapter 6

"Might I see it?" Jane asked, feeling a thrill sprint through her. "Birthmarks have always fascinated me. Neither myself nor my siblings have any extraordinary markings. In fact, we're all quite plain."

He gave a snort of wry amusement, a smirk playing on his lips as he asked, "So, you want to have a look at all the places that aren't pink, do you?"

She rolled her eyes. "Has it occurred to you that I'm merely inquisitive about everything?"

"Oh, it's occurred to me. And there's nothing *mere* about your curiosity. You've got the lion's share, to be sure."

Indignant, she sniffed and dabbed harder against the laceration along his jaw, earning a gratifying hiss. "Certain people prefer the advancement of knowledge. While *others* sell off their furniture in order to pay for illicit pleasures at a bordello."

He growled. "For the last time, I didn't sell my furniture for a swive. I have money, damn it all. In fact, I own this bloody house." His exclamation echoed inside the plaster walls. But then he stiffened, his eyes widening slightly for reasons beyond her understanding. "Just don't tell Pickerington, if you can help it."

"Why shouldn't you wish my cousin to know?"

"Not just him. I don't want anyone to know. Word gets

out and before you know it, people start to plot, wanting to take what's yours."

She cocked her head in inquiry. "You haven't told anyone?"

"No one but Reed Sterling. I had a room at his gaming hell for a while. Didn't seem right to keep it after he married."

Oh, *now* she understood. Her mouth curved in a smile as the softer side of the scoundrel was beginning to unfold. "You must hold Mr. Sterling and his wife in high esteem if you wanted to shield them from your constant parade of prostitutes."

"There was never a parade of—" He broke off. "Look. If I'd wanted a woman in my private rooms, I'd never have gone to Moll's in the first place."

She nodded sagely. "Perfectly understandable, especially when your life had taught you not to trust anyone. Which is the reason you haven't hired anyone to look after your loose buttons."

"I can look after my own damnable buttons," he grumbled under his breath.

"Perhaps," she said, humoring him. "Though, I must say, I'm honored to be privy to your secrets and to have earned your trust after such a brief and turbulent acquaintance. I cannot imagine that trust is something you give easily."

She could see a hard pulse beating in a rapid rhythm beneath the taut flesh of his throat. Then he raked a hand through his hair. But he must have forgotten about the cut on his shoulder, for he winced.

Roughly, he jerked out of his coat and tossed it aside.

"I don't trust you," he barked. "I don't even know you. You're just some reckless, peculiar debutante I rescued from a brothel."

"Correction—I rescued myself. Then I rescued you," she

said, already leaning in to examine the wound with the blot of the handkerchief and a sharp hiss from him. "Is this the arm of your birthmark?"

Without waiting for his answer, she began to carefully peel apart the torn seams at the shoulder. He inched back, twisting at the waist, and the fabric slipped from her fingertips. "Has anyone ever told you that you're too bloody curious for your own good?"

"All the time, I'm afraid."

His jaw hardened and he stared intently at her face, roving over every inch. "It would have turned out far different for you in that bawdy house if I hadn't been there. Or if you hadn't been wearing this . . ."

Before she could react, his hand deftly stole around to the back of her head and untied the mask with a small tug.

Her breath hitched on a gasp as the scrap of lace fell, unheeded, between them.

Shocked, she stared at the triumphant gleam in his gaze, unblinking. Without the mask, the aura of mystery—which had likely been the sole reason men had fought over her in a brothel—was gone. Stripped bare, she was her ordinary self again.

"Whyever did you do that?" she scolded, her tone accusatory and cross.

"To see who you really are."

"That makes little sense. You already know my name. You even work with my cousin who has verified my identity."

"Are you always this logical?"

She swallowed, trying not to reveal how exposed she felt. "I strive to be, which is more than I can say for you. One minute I'm inquiring about your birthmark, and the next—" She stopped as a thought suddenly occurred to her. "You took off the mask to distract me from asking about your birthmark. Surely, you're not afraid of what I might think of it."

"Afraid," he scoffed.

Then, as if she'd issued a challenge to prove his manhood, he reached across his chest to the diagonal tear on his shoulder. Her hand splayed out to stop him, but it was too late. He tore the sleeve clean off with a *rip* that cut through the air.

"I could have mended that for you."

He arched a brow. "Mended the pink dappled shirt of a stranger you'll never see again?"

"Point taken," she offered with a slight shrug.

Now they were both exposed and, in her opinion, on equal footing.

Her attention shifted to his arm. Or, more precisely, his bare, undeniably masculine arm. His skin bore a slightly olive tint, and beneath the swarthy surface, he appeared to be comprised of a knight's armor, with the clear delineation of the thick deltoid shoulder cap over the hard, woven bands of biceps and triceps.

Seeing him this way caused a peculiar reaction to her physiology. Her head felt giddy. Her skin prickled with heat. Her fingertips tingled with the desire to touch the dusting of dark hair that grew in a downward arc along his forearm. Stranger still, saliva pooled beneath her tongue. Her sense of smell seemed heightened, his scent invading her nostrils in an absolute olfactory domination.

"What's this?" He clucked his tongue, smirking at her. "Jane, you've proven yourself a modern, scientific woman. Surely the sight of a man's arm shouldn't make you blush, considering where you were tonight."

"I'm not blushing, I assure you," she said, even while suffused with evidence to the contrary.

A low laugh escaped him. "Must be the heat of the fire."

She nodded in tentative agreement, her teeth biting down on the cushion of her bottom lip. What made her reaction more embarrassing was the fact that she hadn't even given his birthmark a passing glance yet.

Not wanting to appear the lecher, she pursed her lips studiously. "Would it be too much of an imposition if I were to . . . possibly . . . touch you there? Merely to further my own understanding of the nevus, of course."

A slow rakish grin curled his lips and his deep voice curled her toes. "You can touch me anywhere you like, professor."

Jane immediately thought of a new chapter for the book. A rather scandalous chapter. And, for a long while after that, she completely forgot she wasn't wearing a mask.

❧❧❧

RAVEN KEPT a watchful eye on Jane as she leaned in, still not knowing what to make of this debutante.

He thought he was prepared for the first tentative brush of her fingertips, that soft silken press of her flesh against his. But he wasn't. Gooseflesh rippled down his arm in a prickling wave, raising each hair in a way that begged to be smoothed by the stroke of her delicate hand.

And he certainly wasn't ready for her unreserved *"Oh"* of wonderment. The soft exclamation drifted across his skin and sent a surge of blood gushing through every vein in a molten flood.

Then her lips began to move in that soundless murmur once more. Seeing it from such a close proximity tempted him far more than he'd thought possible, considering how much trouble she'd caused him in such a short amount of time.

"Why do you do that?" he asked, his voice hoarse and gravelly from this unfathomable desire.

The spell caster's concentration was still diverted and she issued an absent, "Hmm?"

"It's like you're talking to yourself right now, but you're not speaking aloud."

"I'm simply jotting down a few notes in my mind," she whispered.

"And what are you saying?"

Her hand splayed over him, curving around his bicep, her examination growing bolder. "That it's quite remarkable. I never imagined your arm would feel so different from my own. It's as if your musculature is formed of those thickly braided ropes that keep massive ships moored. The surface is as taut and smooth as an overfilled wineskin, and an enticing heat emanates from your flesh. Do you feel feverish?"

"No," he lied. "Well, not unless you're about to order me to lie down. But, be warned, I plan to take you with me."

"And this birthmark of yours," she continued as if she hadn't heard a word he'd spoken, "is inexplicably detailed. I've seen other birthmarks and normally one has to employ imagination to see shape and form. But not with this. Would you like to hear something quite odd, Raven?"

"You don't realize it, but you almost always say something odd."

"Prepare yourself then, for I recognize that mark."

He grinned at the absurdity. "Is this how you flirt with all the men you examine?"

"You misunderstand," she said, turning her head to meet his gaze. "I have an uncommonly detailed memory. A mnemonic sketchbook, of sorts. Once an image is inside my mind, it's nearly impossible to remove. And I've seen that bird before, exactly as it appears on your arm."

There was enough gravity in her expression to cause a shiver to roll down his spine once again. Every muscle on his skeleton contracted and tightened. And he decided at once that he didn't want to be under anyone's quizzing glass. Not even hers.

She went back to tracing the outline, and at the sensation of her warm breath coasting over his skin, he felt a restless need to stop this conversation by any means necessary.

So he settled his hands on her hips.

Jane issued a faint squeak of surprise, but didn't bolt. She merely watched him with those deep blue eyes, as if deciphering and calculating his movements like a player counting cards in a deck.

"It's only fair. You're examining me, after all," he explained baldly, ready for her to back away.

He wondered how many thoughts were turning in her mind as she looked from his face to his hands. Was she gauging his intent? Absorbing the feel of his fingers as they flexed in appreciation over the unexpected roundness of her hips, and skimmed upward to span the narrow channel of her waist?

"You're a surprisingly curvy little creature," he murmured as his splayed hands inched higher to the base of her rib cage. "And you're not wearing a corset."

"They needlessly . . . restrict respiration," she said on a shallow breath.

"Wouldn't want that," he agreed absently, enjoying that spears of whalebone weren't hindering his discovery of the supple warmth just a layer or two away.

He imagined peeling the garments slowly down her body, exposing patches of creamy ivory and blushing pink and dark sable. And he imagined how easy it would be for him to lift her out of her pooled skirts, and for her to straddle him . . .

Those visions pulsed thickly in his blood, making him forget the reason he'd touched her in the first place. Making him forget that he wasn't interested in debutantes.

Now, every heartbeat was like a heavy thump of a drum, the rhythm rousing the more primitive side of his nature.

The part that was driven by the baser desires of *want* and *need* and *claim*.

Usually he kept this inner beast locked tightly away, but there was something about Jane that made it reach through the bars and rattle the cage.

Distracted, his thumb began tracing the shallow rim of her navel through the violet muslin. The innocent touch caused a tremor to roll through her and into him. The faintest puff of air left her and the sound told him she was just as surprised as he.

"I wonder where Pickerington has gotten to," he said as his gaze took a meandering climb over the rise and fall of the firm hillocks of her breasts, to a pair of full, parted lips that had tempted him from the very first moment.

The dark pink tip of her tongue darted out to wet them and he could easily imagine plundering the warm recesses of her mouth. Tasting the sweet release of her inhibitions.

"Considering Duncan's appetite, he's likely found the larder," she answered with her usual logic, thinking nothing of how honesty might work against her in this circumstance.

"Then he could be gone for some time yet."

Certainly long enough for Raven to seduce her, if he chose to. And the idea of tutoring her to the ways of pleasure was surprisingly appealing.

As if she'd read his mind, she gave him an alert glance. He held it and smiled in invitation.

Oh, the things I could show you, Jane Pickerington.

But she wasn't like the women he bedded. Prostitutes understood passion and primal appetites. They knew that swiving was nothing more than a transaction from beginning to end—a give and take to satisfy both parties.

Jane was only a naive debutante on a foolish errand to study scoundrels for her book.

Even so, he knew he could tempt her. There was enough

to encourage him in the way her hands rested on his shoulders, her fingers curling over his muscles in artless exploration. And there was curiosity in her eyes, too, her pupils expanding like spills of ink on midnight-blue silk bedlinens.

She studied his features intently, her gaze roving from his brow to his mouth to his eyes, and to his mouth again, lingering.

A few kisses and caresses in the right places and he could have her underneath him, gasping his name, before she even considered the insurmountable regret that would follow from losing her virginity to a man she would never see again.

Raven had the sense of mind to know that he should be shocked by his thoughts. And by the simmering temptation to put action in the place of idea.

"I believe you're either teasing or underestimating me again," she said with a calm that belied the fast pulse bumping the underside of her bare throat.

He wanted to put his mouth to that flawless skin and soothe that tender throbbing place with his tongue. "Am I?"

"If you like, I could demonstrate how a young woman with seven younger brothers has learned precisely where a man is most vulnerable."

Taking him off guard, she suddenly shifted her stance to press her knee against his groin. Hard.

On a sharp inhale, he inched back on the bed and out of the direct path of danger, releasing her. The inner beast shrank away from the bars of the cage.

Raven shook his head to clear it. He should have seen that coming. "If it makes you feel any better, I wasn't planning to seduce you."

She glared at him on a huff. Then she moved to the washstand and began returning her jars and flacons into the confines of her red reticule with tiny, agitated *pings* and *clinks*.

"Worry not, I won't call out for my cousin. I am fully aware that a man who prefers the favors of *worldly* women would never find me desirable."

I'm just as stunned as you are . . . he thought but kept silent.

Scrubbing a hand over his face, he found it thoroughly perfumed with lavender. This would surely haunt his thoughts for hours.

Feeling the need to put this behind him, he bent to swipe his coat up from the floor.

"Here is the salve I mentioned," she said, leaving a small gallipot on the ledge. "And I will likely recall where I have seen that mark on your arm by the end of the day. I'll send word."

He expelled an exhausted breath and slipped the left sleeve over his shoulder, clenching his jaw against the discomfort. "Don't bother. There's nothing I need to know."

Those wispy brows furrowed again. "There's always something to learn."

Taking hold of the reticule, he dropped in the remaining phials with a clatter, cinched it closed, and handed it to her. "Not everyone is like you, Jane. Some of us are satisfied with our lives just as they are. In fact, some of us don't want anything to change. And you've already cost me enough this night."

He punctuated his statement by draping the cloak over her shoulders, then prodded her toward the door with a little shove at the small of her back.

"But when I remember, and I *will* remember—"

"Jane has a brilliant memory," Pickerington interrupted, lumbering into the room with the chamberstick in one hand, the water pitcher in the other, and crumbs littering the front of his coat.

"Perfect timing. You were just leaving," Raven said, striding forward to take the jug in a grip so tense he thought he'd crush the curved glazed handle. "Found the buns in the larder, I see."

Pickerington spoke over the hefty bite he was masticating. "Well, Jane did say *two sweets*—"

"*Tout suite*, Duncan," she clarified, then shook her head as her cousin began licking his fingers one by one. "Oh, never mind."

"I only ate the stale ones to get them out of your way, Raven. Left all the fresh ones." Pickerington's hearty chuckle sent a gust of pungent, liquored breath into the room.

Raven's eyes stung from the fumes as he set the pitcher down.

"I'd say you're more than half-sprung, as well. I hope you left some brandy for me. In the meantime, best keep you away from candles or else we all risk going up in flames. So, off you go." Without delay, he began steering the big ox into the other room.

Then he went back to prod Jane along. "If you don't mind, I'd like to get back to my old skin. Thank you for the paste. I'll manage the rest on my own."

He was surprised, albeit relieved, that his guests went down the stairs and out to the pavement without any further comment. And, more importantly, no probing questions from Jane.

The mark he bore was so thoroughly enmeshed with the nightmares of his youth that he could scarcely look at it without brutal recollection.

At the carriage, he had one hand on the open door and the other trying to usher the little debutante inside. But Jane refused to budge.

He should have known it wasn't going to be that easy to get rid of her.

"I cannot blame you for your eagerness to see the last of me, considering how pink you still are. However, if it wouldn't be too much trouble"—she paused to gesture to her cousin who was currently grappling tipsily for the nearest lamppost—"could you put Duncan inside the carriage? He cannot possibly drive in his condition."

"Surely, you don't expect *me* to drive you."

"Of course not," she said, a quizzical smile flickering on her lips in the lamplight. And, damn it all, he was intrigued by it. What was she thinking?

He found out in the next instant as she skirted to the side and deftly scampered into the driver's perch like a cat in a tree.

He was relieved that he wouldn't be called upon to spend any more time with her, he told himself, and refused to look a gift horse in the mouth.

It took effort, but he managed to stuff Pickerington's drunk arse inside the carriage. The bloke was already snoring against the squabs before the door closed.

Walking toward the front, he lifted his eyes to the small form on the bench. She looked almost like a child holding the reins.

An unforeseen shock of worry overcame him and his next words came out before he could stop them. "Say, do you know what you're doing?"

"Who do you think taught Duncan?" she asked, handling the ribbons like a seasoned hack.

Always full of surprises, this one.

She lowered the brake and he waited for her to go.

Yet, she hesitated.

In the dim light that barely illuminated the heart-shaped face and pixie-like features beneath her hood, he spotted that inquisitive gleam in her eyes again. He felt a responding jolt, a kick to his pulse. And something in his gut told him that she was about to mention the mark again. She was too curious and tenacious by half.

"No," he said before a single utterance could pass those tempting lips. "Leave it alone, Jane."

"You don't even know what I was—" She broke off when he arched a brow. Then she offered a half shrug of reluctance. "I cannot help it, you know. To me, questions must have answers or else there's no peace."

"So, even though you and I will never see each other again, you are still determined?"

She nodded on a resigned sigh. "I'm afraid it is an unbending part of my nature."

"It's your own time you'll be wasting."

"Perhaps," she said. "But who knows? That very mark could be the one thing that leads you to discovering who you really are. Haven't you ever been plagued by a puzzle that must be solved?"

She didn't wait for a response, but broke their connected gaze and gathered the reins. Then, with a sharp whistle that pierced the damp early morning, she drove off.

Hell's breath. He really wished she hadn't left him with that question hovering in the air like a specter, demanding an answer.

He narrowed his eyes at the carriage as it trundled down the street and out of view, believing she'd done it on purpose. She was smart enough to know that every orphan was haunted by the same questions—*who am I* and *why in the bloody hell didn't they want me*?

He'd buried that yearning to find his parents long ago. Moving on from childish hopes had been his only way to survive. His only way to hold onto the man he'd become. To keep the life he created.

But because of one luckless meeting with a debutante, he felt that awful stirring again.

It was like having the ground shift beneath his feet, unsettling the earth just enough to reveal the corner of Pandora's box hidden below the surface.

Any man who liked his life just the way it was wouldn't dare open it. He'd turn around and walk away.

So that's just what he did.

Determined to forget all about this night, Raven pivoted on his heel, stuffed his hands in his pockets and . . . found Jane's glove.

His fingers clenched around it, cushioning the soft silk against his palm. *Damn.*

But only a fool would think about returning it.

Chapter 7

$\overline{}$

Jane wasn't about to drive directly home with her intoxicated cousin in the carriage. It was far too probable that he'd accidentally let it slip that she hadn't attended a perfectly respectable soiree at Upper Wimpole Street like she'd told her parents.

Of course, it was equally probable that the Viscount and Viscountess of Hollybrook would dismiss his drunken rambling. Their nephew rarely fell under their notice. In fact, they hardly knew their own children existed. For most of their lives, Jane and her seven younger brothers and three younger sisters—*the horde*, as she affectionately called them—had been very much on their own.

Nevertheless, there was one thing that Lord and Lady Hollybrook could never abide, and that was an unfavorable light shining on the family name.

As such, Jane had learned to embrace her invisibility since entering society. And until tonight, she'd never come close to ruination.

Newton's apple! Who'd have thought that plain Jane Pickerington would ever be alone in a scoundrel's bedchamber? A breath of astonishment escaped her lips in a puff of lamplight-gilded mist.

She drove by rote through the streets, distracted by her thoughts. With her hands gripping the reins, her fingertips tingled at the recollection of touching his warm, bare skin.

And he had touched her too, in ways that no man—pink or otherwise—had ever done.

She should have stopped him, she knew. But the sensations had been so startlingly unfamiliar that she'd been unable to resist the opportunity to explore them further. Her pulse had reacted with a foreign and pleasantly labored arrhythmia. Her nerve endings had seemed to multiply beneath her skin, welcoming the heated press of his hands over her hips and midriff with exhilarated enthusiasm. Even her inner organs quivered in heady delight.

In fact, if not for the somewhat alarming giddiness—which surely had resulted from a series of shallow breaths—she may have decided to see what would happen next. For research purposes, of course.

In hindsight, however, she doubted Raven had any intention to do more. His flirtations had coincided too conveniently with her probing questions. It was clear he'd only meant to distract her. And, therefore, the guarded scoundrel's caresses had been little more than a blockade.

She closed her eyes briefly, acknowledging this truth.

Then, all at once, the excitement of the night began to take its toll and weariness crashed over her on a great yawn.

It was no wonder, for she hadn't slept in twenty-two hours. So she decided to drive to Upper Wimpole Street, toward the modest brick town house where she was supposed to have dined.

Seeing the pale golden glow of a lamp beyond the white framing of a narrow second-story window, she smiled with gratitude. Her friend was already awake. Then again, it was nearing five o'clock in the morning and Elodie Parrish was a notoriously early riser.

If there was anyone who would be eager to learn all about her findings on the habits of the primal male, it was one of her co-authors. Not only that, but a short visit would allow Jane to rest her eyes while her oblivious, slumbering cousin found sobriety.

Leaving Duncan to the land of Nod, Jane stole inside the town house through the servant's entrance by way of the small back garden. She crept up the stairs to Ellie's room, making certain not to disturb either of the spinster aunts whose chamber doors flanked the wainscoted hall just beyond the shadowed portraits of their niece's late parents.

Scratching quietly on Ellie's door, Jane turned the knob. She saw her friend at the vanity table, tucking a tortoise-shell comb into her twisted mane of glossy black hair, and already dressed in a morning gown of apricot taffeta even before the servants were about.

Catching a movement in the looking glass, Ellie turned with a start, amber eyes wide.

"Jane!" Then her breathless exclamation turned accusatory in a blink. "Whatever have you done this time? If I'm not mistaken, you're wearing evening attire. Please don't tell me you've stayed out all night . . . and without me."

Jane held a finger to her lips and closed the door with a quiet *click*. "I had to this time."

"Had to," Ellie tutted. "You know very well that I had no engagement last evening."

Crossing the room with familiarity, Jane ensconced herself in the window seat. As she spoke, she issued an inconsequential shrug to lessen the alarm she knew would follow. "Well, I knew you would not approve of this particular errand."

"Surely, it cannot be worse than when you . . ." Ellie's voice faded and her next words came out in the barest whisper. "You went through with it, didn't you? That preposterous idea you blurted out last week about visiting a . . . a . . ."

"Take a breath, Ellie. It was only a brothel."

In the steady blue flame of the oil lamp, Ellie's porcelain

skin appeared ghostly beneath her dark fringe, and a whimper of distress escaped her.

Jane sighed. "This reaction is precisely the reason I didn't tell you that I'd already made up my mind about going. You do have a tendency toward fatalism, after all."

"I should think it understandable in this particular instance. You just casually told me that you've broken into a house of ill repute—*this very evening*—as if it was nothing more than a shopping excursion for ribbons and gloves." Ellie scoffed, her concern rapidly altering to irritation as twin spots of pink rose to her cheeks.

Accustomed to these diatribes, Jane eased back against the recessed shutters and tucked her feet beneath her. She was far too tired to argue. "Every subject requires a firmly established foundation of knowledge. Especially this one."

"Perhaps *that* is the problem. You have convinced yourself that all knowledge is good."

"And it is."

"No, it isn't. After years of listening to sermons about Eve, I'm sure of it," Ellie said, lamenting. "Oh, couldn't we return to a time when all I had to worry about was you setting yourself on fire? Or kidnapping Lord Holt off the street?"

Then Ellie stood and began pacing the floor while wringing her hands. Once she was in a dither, it was nearly impossible to get her out of it.

"That kidnapping was an accident and *you* were part of it," Jane reminded on a yawn.

"*Hmph.* Well, it was your idea to tie him up and put a sack over his head. I wanted to release him straightaway."

Jane flitted her fingers offhandedly and rested her heavy lashes against her cheeks for a moment. "It all worked out well enough in the end. After all, he married our Winn and they are still basking in the glow of nuptial bliss on their honeymoon."

"But it could have been much worse. Oh, and I should hate to think about what might have happened to you tonight!" Ellie exclaimed, each breathy syllable enmeshed with fresh, well-rested dread. "A brothel, Jane? How could you! You might have been ruined just like our dear Prue then eschewed from London like a criminal. And all she had done was fall for the charms of a disreputable rake, certainly nothing compared to this. The loneliness in her latest letter should have served as warning enough for you to reconsider your foolish errand."

Jane recalled the last lines of the letter, as if she were staring at the page right then.

I know you would not have been swayed by moonlight and soft words. No, you would have kept your head firmly on your shoulders and saved yourself. And, therefore, you would never need to live your days from one letter to the next.

Until the next . . .
Your Friend,
Prudence Thorogood

Jane expelled a slow breath, thinking carefully about her decisions this evening. Yes, her errand had been dangerous. But she wasn't filled with doubt and repentance. Quite the opposite, in fact. The words in the letter only reinvigorated her determination.

"Prue's situation reaffirms that the risks I took tonight will only serve a greater purpose in the future, once we finish our book."

"You and I know very well that no one will print it if there's a single mention of"—Ellie cast a fretful glance over her shoulder to the closed bedchamber door before whispering—"*prostitution*. As women, we are taught to pretend we've never heard of the practice."

"I wonder if there are a pair of prostitutes having a conversation right this instant, pretending they've never heard of debutantes."

"Do be serious, Jane."

Still in hysterics, Ellie continued pacing back and forth between the rosewood vanity and a mossy green canopied bed. Her skirts *shushed* loud enough to rival a squirrel crunching through a walnut shell.

Blocking out the noise, Jane closed her eyes again and lifted her shoulders in a soundless shrug. "We'll simply use veiled references in the book."

"*Veiled?* They would need to be stitched in a shroud if we expect anyone like the persnickety Miss Churchouse to teach a lesson in her class. She nearly had an apoplexy when you inquired about the acceptable moment for a gentleman to press a lady's hand. And the answer was *never.*"

"Which is likely the reason she is still *Miss* Churchouse," Jane said with a smirk. But when her attempt at humor was met with silence, she cracked one eye open to see her friend glaring at her. In her own defense, she said, "I'll have you know, I gained valuable research. Sometimes calculated risks must be taken. After all, we're doing this for our own friends as well as for ourselves."

"If you ask me, *you* are doing this more to satisfy your own rapacious curiosity," Ellie sniffed. "And you know what happened to the cat."

It was not the first—or even the fiftieth—time Jane had heard this argument. "Yes, yes. The poor fabled creature was killed by inquisitiveness. But instead of always thinking about that one singular feline, try to concentrate on the millions of others with nine lives, hmm?"

"Then you are likely down to your last one."

"Nonsense. I'm certain I have at least . . ." She paused, mentally recalling the number of experiments that had gone awry and ticking them off one by one. But when she ran out of fingers, she cleared her throat. "Well, the number doesn't really matter. Every misstep has offered new insights."

"Perfect. That's precisely how I would have comforted your brothers and sisters if you'd been caught tonight. *Never fear, children, your sister likely gained some 'new insights' before her untimely demise.*"

"I'm certain that Death isn't looming nearby with a scythe in a skeletal grip the way you are forever thinking he is," Jane said with nonchalance as if the chastisement hadn't struck a chord within her. But it had.

She loved her siblings dearly and couldn't imagine ever being separated from them. Before she'd even entered society, she'd vowed never to wed a man who didn't love her family. And after Prue's unfortunate expulsion, Jane had also decided never to allow herself to be seduced outside of marriage and sent to live apart from them.

Not that it had ever been a viable consideration. Of the three admirers who'd demonstrated a passing interest in being invited to tea, each were quickly frightened away as soon as they'd met *the horde*. And since she hardly inspired men with the desire to dance with her at assemblies, let alone conjure illicit fantasies, she'd been certain imminent seduction was an impossibility.

Of course, she'd never once imagined herself venturing into a scoundrel's bedchamber. And, had he been genuinely interested in seducing her, she might have need to worry. But in the end, as always, her plainness had been her virtue's savior.

"I should hate to think of what might have happened if

you'd encountered a man who was more determined than you," Ellie said, as if reading her mind.

"Actually, I did," she said, matter-of-fact. But seeing her friend's eyes alter from almond-shaped, to round and stark like amber gems dropped in snow, Jane realized how her statement must have sounded. "Not *more* determined. Perhaps, *similarly* would be a better adverb. I left unscathed. Well, minus a glove but missing nothing irreparable. In fact, I'd even go so far as to say the gray-eyed scoundrel was quite chivalrous at times and . . . *Oh, bother.*"

Ellie had gone still and white as paste, her breaths shallow like froth on a pot of boiling potatoes. Her fingertips were fanned out over her lips as if to stop a sudden torrent of unwarranted, retrospective panic.

Jane began hastily fishing through her reticule until her hand closed around a brown flacon. Standing, she lifted it and removed the stopper. "Breathe, Ellie, or you'll force me to deploy this vinaigrette."

Her hyperventilating friend's porcelain features grimaced in swift distaste. "Put that away, if you please. The last time you waved it under my nose, I couldn't smell anything for a week."

Jane took no offense. Even though it was her own concoction, she wasn't yet satisfied with the results.

Dropping it into her bag again, she watched absently as Ellie walked over to her bed, pulled back the coverlet, and slid in—*fully dressed*—and closed her eyes tightly.

The melodramatic scene caused a spark of mirth to erupt in Jane. "What are you doing?"

"I've determined that this has all been a terrible dream and I am preparing myself to awaken at any moment."

Jane shook her head in fond exasperation and glanced out the window to see her cousin had emerged. The lantern light cast slanted shadows over his squared jaw and confused expression as he scratched his chin and gazed from one town house to the next.

"I'd better go before Duncan decides to drive off without me. I'll have to share the details from my errand with you on the morrow. And trust me, they aren't as dire as you might imagine." Especially since she'd just decided to keep the more salacious aspects of what happened at his bedside to herself.

What Ellie didn't know couldn't hurt her, she thought as she went to the door.

"Jane," her friend sleepily called, halting her for the moment. Ellie turned her head on the pillow, her gaze curious despite her fatalistic fears. "What did it feel like when you met the gray-eyed scoundrel? Was it different than meeting an average gentleman?"

Jane considered her answer carefully, making a mental note of the sudden escalation of her pulse as she pictured Raven's face. How peculiar.

After forty-seven rapid beats, she said, "Do you remember when it was our last day at the academy and Prue and Winnie and you and I were being terribly silly and dancing the waltz until we were all so dizzy we had to lie on the grass for our heads to stop spinning?"

"I was certain we were all going to die of some strange spinning brain fever."

"Well, I felt like that again tonight," she admitted and her cheeks grew hot. "What do you think it could mean? Part of me fears that it is a warning from my mind to steer clear of him. But the other part wants to spin around in circles and laugh."

Ellie closed her eyes on a fretful sigh. "I think you should avoid anything that makes your head spin. It almost always means something dire is about to happen."

Chapter 8

Jane was sure nothing calamitous or scandalous would happen with a little more research. Certainly not when she was at home. Therefore, the instant she stepped inside her parents' Palladian mansion in Westbourne Green, she went straight to work.

The library at Holly House was a towering, rectangular room, surrounded by an inaccessible upper gallery with walls merely painted to look like an upper library arcade. Mother was fond of *trompe l'oeil* and had hired artists to paint false representations of reality all throughout the house.

In Jane's opinion, anything that looked like a bookshelf ought to be an actual bookshelf. She'd thought so even as a child, when she'd built a rickety ladder—her first contraption—to take her five-year-old self all the way to the wrought iron catwalk.

To this day, there remained a broken arched pediment above the far window and a crescent-shaped scar on her shin from her first failed attempt.

With her third attempt that same year, she'd succeeded. She'd gained the platform but then came to the disconcerting realization that her construction skills were sorely lacking when her ladder collapsed, leaving her stranded.

Thankfully, her uncle had dropped by for a visit and found her. He'd suggested that, perhaps, her time was better served by expanding her mind in *reading* the books instead of building shelves for them. And, over the years that followed, she'd read every tome in this space cover to cover, finding the answers to many of life's mysteries.

Just not all of them.

Now, amidst the rows and stacks, she tried to find another. Her memory flashed with a picture of the mark on Raven's arm. Then it flashed again with the sketch in a book, of a bird surrounded by a wavy-edged circle.

But in which book had she seen this particular raven?

Unsure, she simply took every title remotely ornithological.

Piling them on the trolley that she'd built when she was eight, she made her way to the opposite end of the house. But the old cart heaved and squealed under the immense mound of research. It was like walking with a stubborn pig on a leash who kept digging his back hooves into the floor. She simply pulled harder, tugging the beast along the variegated marble floor. She passed several oddly placed murals in the main hall, each marking her mother's brief interests.

First came the Parthenon flanked by pilasters, when having a folly in the south garden simply wasn't enough. Then came a landscape meadow of sheep, from Mother's brief knitting period. The third was a sea of silver-capped waves with gulls flying overhead, before holidays in Brighton had lost their appeal. And the most recent was a desert pyramid, commissioned after Lord and Lady Hollybrook returned from their tour this summer.

They'd left Jane and *the horde* behind, of course. Traveling with one's children simply wasn't *de rigueur* and they always abided by popular opinion.

Unfortunately for them, their plain, bookish, and odd daughter was decidedly *out* of fashion. While she was accomplished in many areas, they weren't the *right* areas.

A debutante needed to demonstrate to society—and her future husband—that she would be a graceful ornament for any man's arm, an asset in his home. She should be whole-some, modest, and delight others with scintillating conversation, as long as it was about art, music, or the weather.

A debutante never spoke of scientific matters, ideas for inventions, or writing a book. Therefore, Jane would never be truly accomplished. At least, not according to the *ton's* standards and not her parents' either.

Tucking that thought away as she always did, Jane took a right turn at *Egypt* and steered the cart down the arched vestibule between the main house and the conservatory rotunda.

Inside, the air was cool and fresh and humid. She drew in a deep, invigorating breath and felt every ounce of exhaustion lift from her shoulders, floating up to the misty glass of the domed ceiling.

Beyond the eastern wall of mullioned windows and past the winding canal, she saw the dawn slumbering on the horizon beneath downy bands of coverlet-clouds in shades of apricot and lavender. Pastel light crept in through thousands of diamond-shaped panes to brush the eager leaves that overlapped the narrow stone path within the conservatory. And as she tugged the cart along, a plethora of potted flowers, plants, climbing vines and trees—which she'd cultivated herself—now greeted her, brushing against her shoulders and cheeks.

This jungle was her real home, the place where she had spent many a happy hour, deep in her studies.

The foliage opened up to a glade, where her desk waited. Leaving the cart, she deposited her reticule on a grayed and stained trestle table that was cluttered with vials, jars, galli-pots and even a Leyden jar. Then she flitted around the semi-circular clearing, lighting lamps and adding kindling to the embers beneath the curfew in a small cast iron closed-stove.

But when she turned back to the cart to begin her hunt for the raven, she stopped short.

The pile was puzzlingly small. It had been much larger when she'd left the library, she was sure.

In that same instant, the aged butler appeared in the doorway, his arms overladen with the books that must have fallen during her lengthy trek through the house.

"Good morning, Miss Jane. Up early with your research again?" he asked without any inflection in his tone or alteration in his ever-grave expression. And yet, for most of her life, Jane had a sense that there was a wealth of untapped mirth hidden deep in his jowls.

Mr. Miggins was a somber man of established years with gently rounded shoulders under his black livery. He wore his hair styled in a comb-over of dull gray hair streaked with white that, regretfully, reminded her of bird droppings on a statue. Of course, she'd never told him that. He'd always been kind and patient with her and *the horde*.

"Actually, I haven't been to sleep yet," she confessed, knowing that he would keep her secret. "The evening filled me with a dizzying array of new questions and I'm not certain I'll ever be able to close my eyes again unless I find the answers."

"I've no doubt you will," he said with his usual unblinking certainty that she'd always found comforting. He shuffled down the slope and proceeded to stack the books on the cart again.

Already skimming through the pages of the first one, she paused briefly as a new curiosity formed in her mind. "Mr. Miggins, suppose you were an orphaned boy. Wouldn't the foundling home have assigned you a Christian name and a surname?"

Familiar with her random odd observations, he answered without question. "I should think so, miss."

"Then, what might be a reason not to accept the surname?"

He continued his task, carefully arranging the books in an orderly pile. After a moment, he said, "Perhaps I'd be waiting to know who I truly am. Every man deserves to know his own origins in order to make a name for himself."

Thrumming her fingers against the cloth cover, she thought about Raven and wondered if that was the reason he only went by a solitary moniker. Perhaps there was a part of him—whether by conscious choice or by some internal guidepost—that wanted to know who he truly was.

"I believe I agree with you," she said.

He inclined his head as if he never doubted she would. "If that's all, miss, shall I have the kitchen send your usual tray?"

"That will be lovely. Thank you."

Jane didn't wait until he left to dive headlong into the stack of books. She carefully surveyed page after page, feeling shivers of anticipation gathering beneath her skin. The answer was near, she sensed it.

She didn't know how much time had elapsed before she was disturbed by a peculiar tapping on the glass. But it was probably just a bird pecking at its own reflection. Ignoring it, she ambled over to the cart for another book.

Unfortunately, the first seven had not contained the sketch she remembered.

Beside the stove, she noticed that the mahogany and brass serving trolley from the kitchen had been left, and so she poured herself a cup of tea to take back to her desk. However, by the time she set it down, the window tapping had grown more insistent.

"For heaven's sake. That bird must be in love with his own reflection," she said, stalking toward the foggy mullioned door that led to the garden, fully prepared to shoo the creature away.

But when she reached the door, she saw that it wasn't a bird tapping on the glass. At least, not the avian type.

Beneath a shock of feathery black hair, a pair of frost-colored eyes peered through the glass.

Chapter 9

For a moment, Jane just stood there, staring at Raven.

He looked wild and windblown, eyes bright, hair tousled in black layers that fell carelessly over his forehead. He'd changed clothes, too. Now he wore a blue shirt with a short, buttoned collar beneath a brown coat.

In her mind, she could still see him shrugging out of torn black wool and rending the seams of white linen to bare his tightly loomed arm. She could still feel the smooth texture of his skin, the hardness beneath. Still sense the sure grip of his hands encircling her waist, his thumb coasting circles around her navel.

Her pulse raced as if it were happening all over again, her heart pounding in rapid spurts beneath her breast.

"How on earth did you find me?"

His mouth curved in a slow, mysterious grin. "You're not the only one who knows things, Jane."

The sound of her name, spoken in that low, growling drawl sent a warm flutter to her midriff. Within her cranium, her gray matter tilted ever so slightly on its axis as if preparing for a series of revolutions. She feared that the peculiar dizzying rush would take her unawares again.

"Are you going to loose the hounds on me?" he asked with a smirk playing at the corner of his mouth, his breath fogging up the glass.

"Our dog died this last summer," she said inanely. "Besides, I'm not afraid of you. It's just taking my brain a moment to orient itself to this unforeseen outcome."

"While you're busy puzzling it over, let me in."

"I really shouldn't."

He was a scoundrel who didn't follow the rules of society. He lived in a world of gaming hells and bawdy houses. He did whatever he liked, whenever he liked. His only furnished room was a bedchamber, for heaven's sake! And he had an uncanny and stealthy ability to appear before her eyes when least expected.

"Likely not," he agreed, seeming to read her thoughts like the pages of a journal. "But it's hardly fair that I allowed you into my home when you won't do the same."

Well . . . Put that way, it seemed rather hypocritical of her. He had trusted her, after all.

Drawing in a deep breath, she slid the bolt free.

A shock of frostbitten morning air rushed over her, the cold blast lifting fine tendrils from her nape as if in warning. As if she'd just unlocked a panther's cage.

Raven crossed the threshold, instantly shielding her in a cocoon of warmth and the fragrance of leather, raw earth, and the clove from his shaving soap. Then he laid his hand over hers and slowly eased her fingers away from the latch before closing them both inside.

The conservatory had never felt so small.

She blinked up at him. "I'm glad the paste worked."

"As am I. Though I'm surprised I'm not blue at the moment. It took an age for you to let me in." He cupped his hands and blew a steady *huuuh* of air into them as he looked her over. "Mind if I share your warmth?"

Share her warmth? She'd never been asked so bold a question. Frankly, she was surprised a man so primal would bother asking permission instead of merely hauling her into his arms.

She blushed, recalling every moment in his chamber, the way he'd sat on his bed with his legs spread, the heat emanating from him, the grip of his hands . . .

It had been the most intimate experience of her life.

"Well . . ." She hesitated, not knowing quite how to respond. "I don't think that would be entirely proper under the circumstances."

"I meant your fire, Jane." And there was that smirk again, slowly bracketing one side of his mouth. "It may not have occurred to you yet, but we're still standing on the mud rug while the little stove is all the way over there. Then again, *if* you prefer a more carnal method, I'm fully at your disposal." He winked. "Think of it as research for your book."

Her cheeks flooded to scarlet, she was sure, as she realized that she'd been blocking the path, a pair of urn-potted yews on either side of her.

"Yes, help yourself," she said as she took a step back beneath the branches. Then, seeing his eyebrows arch, she quickly added, "To the fire."

He offered a reluctant nod. "I suppose it'll have to do . . . for now."

As he brushed past, she tilted her head quizzically. Was that a flirtation? If it was, then it made little sense, considering his preference for worldly women. Not only that, but she'd already surmised that he'd only flirted with her before as a means of distraction.

Puzzled, she followed a few steps behind. "I thought you were fairly determined to put an end to our acquaintance."

Warming his hands at the stove, he said over his shoulder, "I was. Then I found myself standing alone in my bedchamber, dripping wet from head to hoof with pink water in a basin, and staring down at a scrap of black lace on the floor . . ."

With rapid strokes, her mind sketched the illicit image

and her breath caught, her throat suddenly dry. Gentlemen *never* spoke of bathing rituals openly. And she had a strange, almost desperate, desire to know if this man had used the bit of toweling to dry the water from his skin, or if he'd stood nude in front of the fire instead.

She swallowed, imagining the latter.

". . . so I came by to return it," he continued, unaware of the scandalous spinning of her thoughts.

Though, in her own defense, this mental voyeurism was not wholly without scientific merit. In fact, she was certain his anatomy would make an enthralling study.

Dimly realizing that she hadn't responded, Jane shook her head to rouse from her daydream and found Raven staring at her. She blushed as if caught peeking at nude etchings . . . of him.

"What were you thinking about just now with your eyes all dark and drowsy, hmm?" He clucked his tongue as if he already knew the answer. "Naughty, Jane."

She cleared her throat. "I've no idea to what you are referring. And I cannot fathom why you've come all this way for a mere *scrap of lace*, as you put it."

He averted his attention to the stack of books on the cart, lifting one after the other. "Seems someone's developed a sudden interest in birds."

"It should come as no surprise. I declared as much when I left you. And you made it perfectly clear it didn't matter. So, whatever I discover, is for my sake alone," she said, wondering what had actually compelled him to seek her out. It certainly wasn't to return her mask.

She had her answer when he spoke again.

"There's no reason for you to think that my birthmark has any real significance. And it is lunacy to imagine, for a single bloody second, that it could tell you where I came from."

Ah, there it is, she thought and smiled to herself in triumph.

Would a man who was determined to let the matter rest truly come all this way simply to repeat himself? Or was he reluctant to acknowledge his own curiosity had been roused after a lifetime of never finding the answers on his own?

She scrutinized his profile as she approached.

He wasn't as aloof as he pretended to be. She knew the signs of curiosity well—the quick eye movements over every title, the splayed hand denoting the desire to absorb the contents of the book through his fingertips, the faint *hmm* of interest that he tried to cover by clearing his throat.

"You could be correct," she said in stealthy agreement. "However, I try to look at everything through a broader lens. To see potential and possibility that, perhaps, others cannot." She picked up a penny that rested on the corner of her desk. "A coin, for example, is not only a matter of currency but a scraping tool, a prop for an uneven table leg, a piece of jewelry, a hoe for digging a trench through a small patch of dirt for planting seeds, and so much more. Therefore, in my way of thinking, that extraordinarily detailed mark on your shoulder could be more than it seems."

"It isn't. It's just a mark and nothing more. An accident of birth. It couldn't be anything else. Even if it were, why should I care? That's all in the past."

"'The' man 'doth protest too much, methinks,'" she said, borrowing a line from *Hamlet* after seeing the slender volume in his bedside drawer earlier.

"'. . . and the lady shall say her mind freely,'" he retorted, adding, "even though she's wrong."

"The fact that you are standing here in my conservatory proves otherwise."

He growled at her smug expression. "Listen to me carefully, Jane. I have no desire to become a new project to research, like your primer. It may start off with a bird in a book. But I know where it will lead. You'll get it in your head to discover what it must have been like to grow up an orphan in the Dials, and put yourself in another precarious predicament."

At first, she took umbrage to this presumption, imagining that he thought she was an idiot. But then she saw a shadow flicker beneath his heavy brow and high cheekbones, his features set with firm resolve. An uncanny light seemed to shine from within his gaze, burning white-hot in the icy depths with warning, and yet, something about it warmed her.

"Are you actually . . . concerned for my welfare?"

He issued a low, gruff grunt through his nostrils and turned back to the books, thumbing through them absently. "I'd be more worried about the rogues of St. Giles coming to my doorstep and blaming me for unleashing a bluestocking plague upon them."

She nodded, easily accepting his truth. After all, she'd already theorized the true reason he'd come here and it wasn't because of her. He was interested in information about the mark, even if he refused to admit it.

Seeing him pause on a page she'd marked with a slender red ribbon, she moved beside him and pointed to the illustration. "I thought, perhaps, the bird might have resembled a cormorant instead. The wings are similar, you see."

"Mmm . . ." he murmured in agreement. "But the bill is wrong."

"Precisely. Yours is rather like"—she drew an invisible arc over the book's depiction—"that."

"No, it's more like this," he said, covering her hand with his, guiding her fingertip.

"I beg to differ, but it's like . . . this . . ."

It was only when the roughened pad of his index finger glided with tingling friction along the length of hers that she realized they were essentially holding hands. Miss Churchouse would be scandalized. And they were standing quite close, too. Close enough that, if she were to tip back on her heels, her head would rest against his shoulder, and the superfluous cushion of her buttocks would brush his thigh.

Her skin contracted at the realization, drawing tight beneath her clothes. But she made no move to stand apart from him. She lingered instead and listened to his steady, even respiration and felt the instant that her own lungs assimilated to his rhythm without conscious effort.

A strange development in her own physiology, indeed. A current seemed to flow between them as if they were both holding the coil of a Volta battery.

Infinitesimal seconds passed. She studied their fasted hands—his nails trimmed nearly to the quick, the skeletal rise of scarred knuckles beneath tanned flesh, and a dusting of dark hair peeking out from beneath his cuff. His manus was a fascinating combination of elegance and strength and savagery, much like the man himself.

"How does that memory of yours work, exactly? What did you call it . . . *nee*—"

"Mnemonic sketchbook," she said distractedly, rambling on as his finger continued an analysis of her digits. "And I'm not entirely certain. When I was much younger, I used to imagine a tiny artist standing at a paint-spattered easel on the front portico of my brain. Then an army of bespectacled clerks would take each page and file them away in an endlessly cluttered cabinet that has never been sorted to this day. Regrettably, the process frequently keeps me from recalling information precisely when I need it."

"Mmm," he murmured low and deep, as if it made perfect sense to him.

Strangely, she wasn't sure what she'd just said. It was all a blur. And it only became worse when he turned her to face him with a tug of her fingertips. Lifting her hand, he examined the lines of her palm, the pad of his finger tracing tingling paths along each shallow trench.

"Such soft little hands," he said. "I should think you'd want to wear gloves to protect them. And yet, I noticed that you were only wearing one earlier. I have to wonder where the other might have gotten to."

A ragged breath stumbled out of her as her mind conjured the image of her lost glove dangling scandalously from the statue's appendage. And when she looked up at Raven to see a glint in his eyes, she felt a flush of embarrassment rise to her cheeks.

There was no way he could know . . . Could he?

Before she responded with a declaration of innocence, a familiar crash and cheer rumbled through the house from the direction of the north wing.

Raven glanced toward the door. "What was that?"

"The twins trying out the toboggans on the stairs," she said, furtively slipping free. She stepped over to the little stove, busying herself as she waited for her blush to ebb. "For the past fortnight, they've scrambled out of bed at dawn to see who can fly faster. We have a tradition to race down the hill toward the canal every Christmas, and the winner always earns the right to keep the family trophy at their bedside. The boys like to practice when they feel the first nip in the air. But don't worry, it will be over the instant that Mrs. Rice heralds her trumpet and orders them back to the nursery to breakfast on porridge."

Just then a rather pathetic bleat of a trumpet sounded, followed by a more robust call to arms.

Jane nodded toward the hall. "See?"

He came to her side, his brow furrowed as he looked to the arched corridor. "Is it always like this?"

"Of course not. It's usually much worse. When Theodore,

Graham and Henry are home from school, those devil-may-care lads actually rattle the windows. Admittedly, Henry has become more sedate in recent years. Though, my nine-year-old sister Phillipa, has taken up the reins he left behind. Fair warning, if you happen to hear someone shout 'take your marks, get set, go' be fully prepared to glue yourself to the wall and wait until the blur dashes by. She is forever challenging our brothers to races and besting them every time."

"And what do your parents have to say about all this?"

She shrugged. "They pass through the halls and, if they happen to notice something amiss, summon the servants."

"And what do the servants do?"

"Come to me. Then I see to the children and sort things out. Oh, you needn't look so surprised. It is a method that has proven successful for years, ever since I was Phillipa's age."

He was quiet for a moment, considering. "What will happen when you marry?"

It was kind of him to say *when* and not *if*, she thought as she busied herself by adding a splash of tea to her waiting cup.

"My husband and I will live here and look after my siblings," she said. "Of course, that is easier said than done. Thus far, I haven't met anyone who wants to return to my house after the first visit, let alone one who is eager to bestow his heart and soul to me."

"Heart *and* soul, hmm? Is that all you want?"

"It is all I demand," she clarified after a sip and primly dabbed a bead of moisture from the corner of her mouth. "There has to be something more to marriage than procreation and the exchange of capital. The future readers of my book will want to know how to find love."

He issued a grunt of disappointment. "I thought you were more levelheaded, Jane. How about I save you loads of wasted time by telling you that a heart is just a blood-pumper? That's all it does. As for a soul . . . well, I wouldn't know. If I ever had one, I'm sure it has shriveled to dust by now. Trust me, you'd be better off keeping to your scientific theories and leave the romantic delusions to the poets."

"I find it hard to believe that a man who has read *Romeo and Juliet* does not believe in love."

"I've never seen actual evidence of it. Have you?"

His accusatory tone put her on the defensive. "Perhaps if you spent more time away from a brothel you might have done."

He jerked his chin up and a smirk bracketed his mouth. "But I'm not the one writing a book on it. Aren't *you* supposed to prove it?"

"I plan to," she said crisply. "In fact, I've already created a hypothesis regarding the emotion. I compare it to a skill one possesses, much like a head for mathematics. You either have the ability, or you do not. After all, there are those who go their entire lives with never having fallen in love or"— she paused to swallow down a slight catch in her voice— "having been loved in return."

It was her greatest fear that she would be one of those people.

He stared at her, his gaze far too probing for her liking.

She shifted from one foot to the other, holding her teacup in front of her like a shield and feeling as though he could see directly through her. She might as well have proclaimed herself unlovable right then and there.

Mortified, she turned back to the books and continued in haste. "In order to prove any scientific theory, one builds up from the bottom. Knowing what love is not, aids in defining what it is. Much like your birthmark."

"Also another pointless quest," Raven said, but his tone was gentler now.

She didn't want his pity. Needing to resume a less embarrassing topic, she set the teacup down and tapped her index finger against a stack. "In this pile, we've already established what it doesn't look like. It's simply too detailed and upraised to resemble one of these drawings. In fact, it's like a scar that has healed over time."

"Don't be ridiculous," he scoffed, the return of his mocking tone driving away her momentary discomfiture. "Do you actually think that someone carved into my infant flesh to brand me?"

"Well, not when you say it like that. It would be cruel to consider. All I know is that it is no ordinary birthmark. In fact, it's quite out of . . . the *ordinary*." She gasped as a fresh new thought sparked to life. "Yes, of course!"

She turned away from the table and went to the library cart, shuffling through the contents in a haphazard fashion.

"And what has brought on your sudden excitement?" he asked, peering over her shoulder.

"I'll tell you in a minute as soon as I've—*ah ha*! Here it is." She held up the hefty book with triumph. "This is a book of ordinaries, a heraldry of family crests."

Her finger skimmed quickly through the index. Finding the page number, she riffled over the cut edges until she found her place. Then she went back to the trestle table and spread open the book.

There were a dozen crests on either side, but only one that stood out from the rest. *His mark.* Her breath caught the instant she spotted it and, behind her, a strained hush settled over Raven like a breaking wave suddenly withdrawing from the shore.

The image was nearly identical to the supposed birthmark on his shoulder. The only alteration was the arrow and laurel branch in the raven's talons.

She knew they both saw it, but she laid her finger beneath the drawing and the surname of *Northcott*, regardless. While she wasn't familiar with the family, she also knew that it was only a matter of looking through the right book. *Debrett's* would have it, to be sure.

"That doesn't prove anything," he said after a minute, every syllable drawn tight as if gathering momentum for an argument.

"*Prove?* Perhaps not," she said logically. "However, it is clearly something worth investigating further. Something that possibly links you to this Northcott family."

He turned his hard glare from the page to her and growled in warning. "Why are you bent on disrupting my life, turning everything upside down? For your own amusement?"

Stung, she straightened every vertebra in her spine. "Because everyone deserves a chance at a family!"

"Even if I don't want one?"

"You may have a sister out there who is alone, or a little brother who needs guidance. Would you really turn your back on them? Leave them feeling as if they didn't matter?"

She was breathing hard now, her question reverberating in pings that bounced against the glass overhead. It was only then that she realized she'd raised her voice. Her throat was somewhat raw. Her heart and lungs felt raw, too.

He didn't respond, but a pair of inscrutable eyes assessed her in the tense silence. She might as well have been standing before him, garbed in the gauzy Grecian robes of those cyprians.

Embarrassed by how much she'd just revealed, *again*, she said, "I fear it's been a rather long night, and my passions have gotten the better of me. I'm not usually so sentimental."

His brow quirked in doubt, and the grim line of his mouth softened. But whatever Raven's thoughts were, they would remain a mystery.

Mr. Miggins cleared his throat from the doorway. "The

children are ready to begin their lessons, miss. Will the gentleman be joining you?"

"I don't believe so, Mr. Miggins. This gentleman was an unfortunate casualty in one of my experiments and he only dropped by to—"

"She turned me pink," Raven interrupted with a dubious grin. "But she set me back to rights."

"Miss Pickerington always manages to find a way," the butler said, his monotone never revealing his unfortunate high degree of firsthand knowledge.

"As I was saying," Jane added. "Raven will be leaving us shortly. However, *if* he should choose to stay, he is welcome to look over our copy of *Debrett's Peerage*. I believe it can be found in the library."

"Very good, miss," Mr. Miggins said with a bow before he withdrew.

Turning her attention back to Raven, she said, "I mean it. You *are* welcome. However, I have a feeling that this really is the last we'll be seeing of each other. You've made it perfectly clear that you like your life just the way it is. So, I shall desist making a nuisance of myself and keep whatever findings I discover far from your doorstep."

"You're not still going to—" He broke off on a curse, raking a hand through the inky layers of his hair. Then he expelled a lengthy sigh as if he finally realized the futility of asking her to stop her quest. "It doesn't matter what I say. You're too stubborn to listen."

"I prefer *tenacious*," she said with a grin and held out her hand. It wasn't her practice to bid farewell in such a manner. A nod of the head usually sufficed. But some inner mechanism had lifted her arm beyond conscious understanding.

The answer came to her the instant he enfolded her hand in his grasp, securing her palm to his. Her skin reacted to the touch, tingling as the caress of his fingers teased warmth into her blood. Then her brain and heart and stomach all spun together in a single revolution. The force of it caused her body to sway ever so slightly, listing forward on the balls of her feet.

Raven stepped closer, steadying her with his other hand over the small, rounded curve of her shoulder. "At least promise me you'll get some rest."

"I will," she said, feeling strangely tipsy all of a sudden. "I have a particularly cozy chaise longue in the corner behind those palms. It has proven to be the perfect spot for a nap while the children are in the garden. Many brilliant ideas have come to me there. It is also an excellent place for mulling things over and . . . reading books on the peerage."

Slowly, he released her and withdrew a step. "I'm years ahead of you at mulling."

"I understand," she said, prepared to walk him to the door.

But just then a small bouncing giggle interrupted from the corridor and she turned to see a naked, curly-headed two-year-old toddling toward her with his arms outstretched. "Janejanejanejanejane . . ."

Leaving Raven, she scooped up her brother, his plump, fuzzy bottom resting on the underside of her arm. "Peter, whatever are you doing out of the nursery, and where are your clothes?"

"Blocks," he said with simple gravity.

"As you can see," she said to Raven, "Peter is our philosopher. He just imparted the meaning of life in a single word."

"A lesson I shall remember always. Play blocks with Jane and never wear clothes."

She pressed her lips together to hold back a laugh. The man was such a scoundrel, even now. "Peter, this is Raven. Can you bid him a good morning?"

In response, her brother timidly buried his face in her shoulder. "Bird."

"And a good morning to you, as well, Peter," Raven said with a bow.

Peter giggled and lifted his head. "Bird. Book."

"Hmm . . ." Jane said with an arched look down to the cart. "My brother is very wise. Not only is he expressing his mastery of all words beginning with the letter *b*, but he's telling you to look through that book before you leave."

"Well, Peter, I'm afraid I have to go."

"Blocks," Peter said with an understanding nod.

"Yes, you're quite right. I must go to my own house to play with my own blocks and sadly," he said, shifting his gaze to her, "without Jane."

She drew in a breath, tasting the staleness of finality in the air on the back of her tongue. It was bittersweet. There was nothing more she could do to persuade him. It was his life, after all. And yet, part of her wished she could change his mind.

Keeping that thought close to her breast, she inclined her head and committed this moment to memory. Then she turned and left the conservatory.

Chapter 10

The blast of a gunshot jolted Raven awake.

He bolted upright, a rush of blood roaring in his ears, pounding hard in his chest. His lungs heaved like an overworked bellows. Looking around, he half expected to see the crimson-stained stones of the wharf. To taste copper on his tongue. To hear the slap of water against ship hulls and the gulls screaming overhead.

But he wasn't by the docks at all. That had been three years ago. He had the puckered scar on his side to prove it.

Instead, he was in some sort of wilderness, surrounded by trees and climbing vines and the rapid shuffle of footsteps nearby.

"Set that one there, thank you," he heard someone say and the familiar feminine voice brought him to full awareness.

He scrubbed a hand over his face to clear away the drowsy haze, realizing where he was—in a jungle conservatory in Westbourne Green. With Jane.

To be fair, he'd never intended to linger. He'd been on his way out the door and ready to put this futility and madness behind him. Then curiosity had got the better of him.

All he'd wanted was just one look at Jane's favorite napping spot. But when he'd entered this foliage-thick corner, secluded like a long-forgotten hermitage for the first explorers of the world, he'd felt a waterfall of peace and calmness wash over him. The air was so heavy and damp that it felt like breathing in purified waters. And the overstuffed age-softened chaise longue was so inviting that he'd given in to temptation and sat down. Then her soft powdery scent had enveloped him like a downy coverlet.

He'd felt so at ease that he'd closed his eyes . . . for just a minute, he'd promised.

Now, lifting his gaze to the domed glass ceiling, he saw the flame-bright circle of the sun shining down from a pale blue sky and heard the distant laughter of children in the garden. He must have slept for hours. *Bollocks.*

Not wanting to be discovered, he stood, ready to quit this place without Jane any the wiser.

But when he peered around the corner to where the door was nestled between palm trees, Mr. Miggins made a sudden, unexpected appearance.

The heavily bejowled butler bowed calmly as if he hadn't just taken a year off Raven's life. "Pardon me, sir, but would you care for anything from the kitchens?"

"How did you—" Raven felt the flesh of his brow pucker. "How long have you known I was here?"

"Ever since Miss Jane went to teach her lessons and I came to clear away the tray, sir," the butler said blandly.

"Does she know?"

"Of course, sir. When I informed her, she begged that I not disturb you. As for the matter of the kitchen . . . we have an excellent selection of cold meats, cheeses and pies."

Embarrassed, he raked a hand through his hair, combing through the uneven layers. He wasn't used to being caught unawares. *Keep a watchful eye,* he reminded himself mockingly.

But ever since meeting Jane, he'd noticed that his own rules were falling by the wayside, and fast. Well, not anymore.

"Much appreciated, Miggins," he said. "But I'll just have a cup of tea and be gone."

"Very good, sir." He bowed as if to leave, but hesitated. "Also, I regret to say that the family's copy of *Debrett's* is not currently in residence. It has been at the bookbinder's since Master Charles and Master Tristram launched it from their trebuchet last week."

Raven was struck by a rise of reluctant amusement. This house was a regular Bedlam. "How far did it go?"

"All the way from the pyramid to the Parthenon. As you might imagine, there was much celebration in the hall."

Miggins walked away after that, seeming pleased even though his impassive expression never betrayed him.

Left alone, Raven straightened and stuffed in the tails of his wrinkled shirt. When he walked around the maze of plants into the open area, he expected to find Jane waiting to gloat.

Instead, he found her kneeling before an open trunk, sifting through the contents in a frenzy. She lifted books and various objects from the depths for cursory examination before hastily casting each one aside in scattered piles on the stone floor.

Sliding a glance his way, she grinned and spoke as if they were already in the middle of a conversation. "I had an epiphany."

"And I had an accidental nap," he said, walking past the labyrinth behind her to the tea trolley.

As he poured a cup, his hungry gaze swept over the crystal dish of deep red jam and the slices of toast, cut on the bias and lined up like gabled rooftops inside the silver claw-footed rack. But no. He refused to linger long enough to break his fast. Already he sensed that one more delay would only lead to another.

So, he would drink this and then go, he told himself. And he most definitely wasn't going to ask about her epiphany.

Gulping down the tea in two scalding swallows, he moved nearer to the trunk. "I'll be leaving now."

Still immersed in her exploration and bent over the side in a fine display of her curvy bottom, she gave an absent wave. "Be sure to steer clear of the open garden beyond the wall. Phillipa has talked Charles and the twins into racing backwards down the hill. There are sure to be casualties."

He took a step, then hesitated. "Why didn't you simply tell them not to?"

She lifted her head just enough to brush a wisp of hair from her temple and stared at him dubiously. "They're children. How are they expected to learn about gravity, or cause and effect for that matter, if they're locked in their bedchambers? Every moment is an opportunity for learning. Not *all* of us choose to turn our backs on enlightenment."

The scolding edge of her tone did not escape his notice. "I see what you're doing."

"I have no idea what you could mean."

She blinked, innocent and owl-eyed, but then gave herself away by biting her lower lip. She did that, he noticed, whenever she was keeping herself from saying what she really wanted to.

"You're pretending that it doesn't matter a whit to you if I walk out that door."

She went back to rummaging, but he caught sight of her cheek lifting in a grin. "It worked before, didn't it?"

"That was an accident. An accidental nap."

"There's no such thing. You chose to stay. Aristotle said 'choice, not chance, determines your destiny' and that 'the ideal man bears the accidents of life with dignity and grace, making the best of circumstances.'"

"Well, what did he know, anyway?"

She burst into laughter, the sound bubbling over the sides

of the trunk like an overfilled pot of jam on a cookstove. It was so sweet and rich that he wanted to taste it.

Sitting back on her heels, she gazed up at him, her tempting lips parting in a smile. "Ask me about my epiphany."

"No," he said, feeling in serious danger of liking Jane Pickerington. "I'm leaving now before I do something I regret."

Without another word between them, he turned and walked toward the glass door.

Then, just as he set his hand on the bolt, she called out, "I think my uncle knows the Northcotts."

Raven went still. His feet were suddenly leaden and weighted to the mud rug.

He tried the bolt. But his hand wouldn't obey, the tendons seemingly enervated by interest.

The problem was, he'd been thinking about her comment earlier, regarding his birthmark being a scar instead. The only reason he gave it a passing thought was because he remembered something from long ago.

When he was near the age of seven, an old caretaker had confessed that he'd been the one who'd found Raven on the doorstep of the orphanage.

"Never seen such an angry babe a'fore. There ye were, half-frozen, howlin' loud enough to shake down the walls, and waving that arm marked with a bird as black as pitch. Determined to survive, ye were. Must be in yer blood. Never forget that, lad."

And Raven hadn't forgotten.

. . . a bird as black as pitch . . .

Could that have been a scab on his skin from a cut? A scab that had healed and left him with the pale red scar that the beadle of the orphanage had told him was a birthmark?

He didn't have an answer. But what he had in abundance was something he'd been trying like hell to deny—overwhelming curiosity.

A heavy breath evacuated his lungs. Damn her and her epiphanies!

❧❧❧❧

RAVEN SLOWLY turned on his heel to face her and Jane knew she'd piqued his interest beyond a mere passing curiosity. At last!

Now, to keep hold of it, she mused.

The problem was, she didn't have any proof to validate her claim. At least, not yet. She was sure it was here, somewhere. All she knew was, if she could discover a bit more about his origins, it would not only benefit him but the primer as well.

To her way of thinking, the more time she spent in his company, the more she would understand the mindset of scoundrels and how they came into being.

"As you may recall, my uncle—Duncan's father—is in prison," Jane began. After years of telling bedtime stories, she'd learned that the more salacious the opening scene, the more eager her siblings were to listen.

"And?" Raven said with gruff impatience.

Oh dear, she would have to speed this up to hold his attention long enough to make her point.

"Uncle Pickerington is the black sheep of the family. And, much to my father's dismay, his youngest brother chose the vocation of tutor instead of something more respectable like a cleric. But that is neither here nor there . . ." she said, realizing she'd started to ramble. "The point I'm making is that he was a tutor for many notable members of society—politicians, military leaders, dukes, earls, and viscounts—and he was highly regarded. Until, of course, his debts got the better of him and he was sent to Fleet. But we have his things here in the garret. There are trunks

brimming with ledgers and books. And this very morning, during the children's lessons, I suddenly remembered
that I'd seen your mark—without the arrow and laurel
branch—in one of my uncle's ledgers."

"So you've found it, then?"

"Well . . . no. But he had the habit of sketching things
from his surroundings along the margins. So, I know it's
here, somewhere in his vast collection. The footmen are
carrying down two more trunks."

In the same moment, a pair of older men trudged into the
room, arms stiff and straining with the cumbersome straps.
All at once, the heavy portmanteau dropped, hard on the
stone tiles.

Jane startled. The sharp *crack* even caused Raven to
flinch ever so slightly. Which surprised her. Even during his
battle in the brothel, he'd maintained a cool facade. And
since he didn't seem like the type of man to become alarmed
by a sound, she made a mental note of it to ponder later.

"Let's say you do find the sketch," he said after the footmen had withdrawn, his features inscrutable once again.
"That still won't prove anything."

She tiptoed over the clutter toward the tea trolley. Famished after a long night, she munched on a corner of toast
and poured a cup of tea. "Correct. At least, not without more
evidence to support my hypothesis."

"Dare I ask what it might be?" He came to her then, his
fingers white-tipped and pressed tightly to his temple.

Jane almost felt sorry for him. He wasn't the first one to
whom she'd given a headache in the course of her life. But
it couldn't be helped. She was determined to entice him to
stay until they unraveled this mystery together.

Handing him the cup, she held up a finger and said, "I
need a bit of sustenance first, so that I am forearmed against
your inevitable counterarguments."

If the way he greedily drained the last drop was any indication, it seemed he was willing to wait. So she took another bite of toast, then sank a large spoon into the dark jam. Lifting it to her lips, she savored the sweet, tart flavors that spread over her tongue on a sigh of pleasure. There was nothing better to break one's fast than toast and jam. Barely pausing to swallow let alone draw a breath, she dug in for another heaping spoonful.

Raven came closer. She felt the enthralling heat of his body at her back as he peered over her shoulder. His warm breath sent a tingling caress along the column of her neck, stirring the fine hairs at her nape.

"You're barbaric when it comes to food," he said. "You do realize that you're supposed to put the jam on the bread first and eat them together, don't you?"

The low vibration of his amusement teased a flutter into her midriff. Reflexively, she settled a hand over the tilting, lifting sensation, and wished she had a jar of his voice—a deep, rich conserve—that she could put on her tongue and languorously lick the bowl of the spoon after she'd finished.

Nibbling away the residual stickiness on her bottom lip, she turned. Somehow, she knew that he wouldn't stand apart from her like a gentleman. She was already learning a bit about scoundrels.

Toe to toe, Jane and Raven shared an enticing bubble of static heat that made her skin exceptionally sensitive, the way it was after a steaming hot bath. Even the soft cambric of her chemise abraded her in taut, pleasure-stung places. It made her breath quicken. And standing this close in the daylight, she could see that his pale gray irises contained filaments of sparkling silver that surrounded the dark expanse of his pupils. Those bright slivers were like a source of heat within a vapor of smoke, white-hot and smoldering.

"That's what everyone else thinks," she said, trying

to sound informative even as her voice turned peculiarly hoarse. "However, if you take something that is dry and porous—the toasted bread—and combine it with something wet and sticky—the jam—then the dry will invariably begin to absorb the wet, thereby becoming soggy. Why, it completely negates the entire purpose of toasting the bread in the first place."

"Do you think this much about everything?"

A grin from anyone else, and she might have thought they were laughing at her. It was something she'd grown used to over the years. But with Raven, the slow curl of his lips was accompanied by a simmering hunger in his gaze, and she sensed that his thoughts were on a different trajectory.

"Well, not *everything*. There are many things I have yet . . . to encounter." She faltered as those filaments flared with more heat. So much so that they scorched the apples of her cheeks.

"If you have a list that's particularly wicked, then I'm at your full disposal."

Jane was breathless for a moment, imagining what it might be like to have him at her *full disposal*. Just think of all the anatomical research she could conduct!

"What are you thinking of?" he asked, his eyes narrowed in rakish speculation.

She cleared her throat, her teeth sinking into her bottom lip as she straightened her shoulders to present a more scholarly air. As if she hadn't just imagined his body laying bare on the trestle table for her to examine.

"The correct phrasing would be, *Of what are you thinking?* Here," she said, handing him her toast. "You look hungry."

As if seeing her grammatical lesson for what it was—a sly evasion—the scoundrel chuckled and took a bite, holding her gaze all the while.

She ignored the unspoken accusation. Relieving him of

the teacup, she averted her scalding face to drink the last remaining drops, then set the cup on the trolley beside her spoon.

Dusting her hands together, she said, "All I want from you is your time and patience."

"Pity," he said, taking another greedy bite and not appearing a bit sated. "But I have a life to get back to."

She darted a calculating glance to the trunks. "Give me three hours. Working together, we're bound to find it. You'd finally have answers. And I know you're curious, too. You needn't be ashamed of it."

"Bloody hell, Jane. You could badger an escaped prisoner back into gaol." He looked from her to the door, lingering with longing on the latter. Then he heaved out a sigh. "I'll give you an hour. No more."

"Agreed," she chirped, bouncing up onto the balls of her feet. She felt like clapping, but it wasn't time to celebrate. At least, not yet.

He grumbled under his breath, "I don't know why I'm doing this. It isn't going to change anything."

"That's not quite true," she offered. "If my hypothesis is correct on these two points"—she lifted one finger, then another—"one, that the mark on your arm is actually a scar; and two, that it's related to the Northcott lineage, then that could very well mean you were born into the aristocracy. In fact, I'm almost certain of it already."

Raven stared at her for a moment without blinking.

Then, all at once, he laughed. Shaking his head, he laughed some more and so hard he nearly choked on the toast.

"The theory wasn't meant to be amusing," she huffed and handed him a freshly poured cup, which he drank down after a few fading chuckles. "Startling, perhaps. But you're acting as though I've suggested you're a descendant of flamingoes."

"After last night, I would believe that more readily."

She sniffed, marginally offended, and marched over to her desk to withdraw the hourglass perched on the corner. "You weren't *that* pink, and it was only temporary." Coming back to him, she held the timepiece between them. "All I'm asking, is for you to look through a few trunks. And you gave me an hour. Well, I want the *full* hour."

His brow arched with intrigue. "You shouldn't say that to a man. It gives him all sorts of wicked ideas."

She knew he was only flirting with her out of habit, wanting to distract her. There could be no other reason. And yet, that low gravelly drawl made her wonder what, precisely, those *wicked ideas* were.

Her mild irritation over his laughter was completely forgotten. Now, inside her mind, a tiny eager scribe sat at a desk—hair in complete disarray, spectacles perched on her nose, heart pounding—and waited with fresh ink and paper.

"If it wouldn't be too much trouble," she heard herself ask, "could you . . . um . . . list them? For research purposes, of course."

Raven's gaze strayed to her mouth and lingered.

Was this a mere flirtation? Truth be told, in this moment, she wasn't entirely certain. And it was the first time in Jane's life that a trace of doubt left her feeling giddy and warm from head to heel.

Perhaps he was thinking of demonstrating? A firsthand account *would* be far more thorough than a list, to be sure.

"Tell you what. I'll tackle those trunks with you first." He took a step toward her to breach the distance. Lifting his hand, his index finger skated a tingling path along her jaw to the crest of her chin, and he tilted up her face as her pulse hopped beneath the thin, susceptible skin of her throat. "Then we'll see if there are any grains of sand left in the glass, hmm?"

The dark promise in his smoky gaze sent a frisson of heat spiraling inside her. Jane offered a wordless nod in agreement.

Inside, however, her inner scribe gasped, bosom heaving in anticipation, poised pen all aquiver.

Raven released her and took the glass to start their time, propping it on the trestle table. All the while, Jane was dividing the hour into minutes and those into seconds. If they found what they were looking for within the first few then, by her calculations, that should leave plenty of time for quite a thorough and scandalous list.

Chapter 11

Raven knew they weren't going to find anything. The only reason he'd stayed was to exhaust Jane's determination on the subject of his mark and the absurd idea that it was related to the Northcott family crest.

It was just a coincidence. An aberration, like seeing faces or shapes in woodgrain or wallpaper flowers. Stare at anything long enough and you might even believe it was actually real. But not him. He wasn't fool enough to be taken in.

He honored his word, however, and examined the contents of the trunks with diligence and a critical eye. A *very* critical eye. He didn't want to give Jane the opportunity to accuse him of being less than thorough and try to cajole him into staying longer.

When they finished here, the search would be over for good. He'd make sure of it.

Even so, it surprised him to find that he and Jane worked well together. They each took one side of the first trunk until there was nothing left, then moved on to the second, sifting through books and ledgers with the same meticulousness.

Occasionally, Raven caught himself reading and absorbing the pages instead of thumbing through them with hurried purpose. Whenever that happened, he schooled his features and cast a surreptitious glance her way. Thankfully, she was always too immersed in her own perusal. It was becoming an onerous task to hide his utter fascination and awe at all this knowledge and literature so close at hand.

A few minutes later, he found himself accidentally and deeply ensconced in *A Sentimental Journey* by Laurence Sterne when Jane suddenly said, "You may borrow that book, if you like."

Guilty and embarrassed, he slapped the cover closed and swiftly stacked the slim volume off to the side. "Why would I want to do that?"

After years of earning ridicule, censure and even beatings from being found with a book in his hands, it was ingrained in him to deny any interest at all.

Jane lifted her shoulders in an inconsequential shrug, still perusing her side of the trunk. "You have a certain way of grunting when you find something that interests you."

"Grunting?"

She nodded while fanning through a book and absently remarked, "A deep, truncated sound at the back of your throat that pushes a short puff of air through your nostrils, like this . . ."

She mimicked it and Raven was caught somewhere in between amusement and insult.

The latter won out. "I don't grunt."

"Imagine what you will," she said dismissively. "You also growl in a certain manner when you're frustrated and then paw through the pages. This usually happens when you've come across one of the ledgers written in French. However, when you stumble across a book you like, you issue that little grunt and hold the cover protectively as you slowly turn the pages."

Staring at her profile, he felt a rush of unfamiliar discomfiture wash over him. It was as if she could see through him, and she wasn't even looking his way. Surely, he wasn't that transparent. He'd never been before.

"And there's that disbelieving grumble I first heard when I mentioned your brown thread," she said with a *tsk* and a sly glance. "Fear not, your secret is safe with me. I won't tell any of the other scoundrels that you're not what you seem."

Damn it all! He glared back at her, but she merely grinned and kept to her examination of the trunk.

Standing, he went to the tea cart and downed the dark brew, the leaves having turned bitter. He picked up a slice of toast and chewed it crossly, wishing she wasn't so bloody perceptive.

He caught himself grumbling again but stopped short. Then he realized there wasn't a reason for his foul temper. He'd already revealed his collection to her. So, there was no need to hide his fascination for books. Not with her. Gradually, his irritation faded.

With the ever-present need to be on his guard soothed for the moment, he returned to her side. Wordlessly, he nudged the cup against her shoulder. In response, she issued a pleased hum as she took the tea, sipped and then handed it back to him.

"I just had the most amusing notion," she began with a quizzical smile. "Surrounded by all these trees and vines, it's as though we're in the jungles of Africa with only a single teacup between us. While other explorers might require more pomp and circumstance when breaking their fast, we'd survive quite well like this, I should think."

She finished her statement by taking his toast. And he had to admit that he agreed with her. It was strange to imagine that sitting on the floor with a high-society deb could feel like the most natural thing in the world.

Though it wasn't as if he had a lot of experience to compare this with. The society women he knew liked to gamble and flirt and whisper daring invitations in his ear while their husbands were at other tables. But Raven wasn't interested in being anyone's pet again. He preferred to live his life on his own terms.

At the thought, he glanced over to the hourglass and saw the pile of silver sand was higher on the bottom than on the top. Soon he would be back to his life. They were halfway through the third trunk now.

Jane held a ledger out for his inspection. Clamping a wedge of dry toast between her teeth, she pointed to the frayed edge along the center. *"Mrf ink bersa bay mrfing."*

"Didn't quite catch that," Raven said with a smirk. "Perhaps you should try grunting as a form of communication." Apparently, it worked for him.

Pulling the toast from her mouth with a tug, he finished the slice.

"I think there's a page missing," she clarified without the impediment. "Perhaps more than one."

"I've found that in a few, as well, and stacked them in a separate pile, here." He gestured to the growing stack of twelve—now thirteen—age-softened leather ledgers.

"Hmm. My uncle must have used the paper to send a missive. Father would often receive correspondences from him on torn scraps of paper." She flipped the pages back and forth, reading them. "It appears that this ledger was from when he tutored the Wellesley children near the turn of the century. I imagine it could not have been easy for a child in a military family during the French Terror. There's quite a number of pages missing. Oh, but look here. This is one of those sketches I was telling you about." She turned it toward him. "It's a knight's armet. From my brief perusal of the book of ordinaries, I recall that this sits at the center of the Wellesley family's crest. Which further cements my belief that we are bound to stumble onto something from the Northcotts as well."

"Not if we don't hurry it along," he said with a glance back to the hourglass.

"Drat," she muttered and resumed a more frantic search.

An unexpected sense of urgency filled Raven with every grain of sand that fell. There were only a handful of minutes left.

Together they displaced items of no relevance with the detachment of archeologists discarding dirt from a dig site. They skimmed pages, found nothing, then cast each ledger aside. Over and over again.

Raven knew the exact instant that the top of the hourglass was empty. It felt like the jarring jolt of a carriage wheel hitting a rut and stopping dead in its tracks.

With his hands curled over the lip of the trunk, he stared down at the bottom. All that remained atop the cracked leather was a smattering of yellowed letters and torn pages, along with a folded cravat in the corner, tea-stained with age.

But there was no sketch of a raven. Hadn't been one in any of the trunks.

Pushing away, he stood and left Jane at the edge. His footfalls snapped against the stone tiles as he walked around the conservatory, a gnawing tension gathering in his limbs. To relieve it, he cracked his neck on one side and then the other. He'd known all along that there'd been nothing to find, so it shouldn't bother him to come up empty handed. And it *didn't* bother him, he told himself. Not in the least.

Pausing at the door, he peered beyond the windows to a leaf-scattered view of the garden. A deep exhale emptied his lungs and fogged the glass.

"It isn't possible," Jane said, drawing his attention. She reached into the trunk's abyss to pick up every tiny sliver of paper, her short, rounded nails dragging over the bottom in ever-increasing desperation. "It has to be here."

"Nothing to fret over. An additional hour of my day is hardly a matter of life or death, and I'd snagged a good nap earlier."

"But I never forget things that I've seen. They're always in my head. What's the point of it if I can't figure out where and when I saw them? And I was so certain." Her voice was roughened with exhaustion and emotion and she flung a piece of cloth to the floor. "It was all for naught."

"You're just tired, that's all," he said. "Besides, it doesn't really matter."

"Stop saying that. It *does* matter. I wanted so very much to find something for you."

The afternoon sun streamed down through the domed ceiling, illuminating the angry tears in her sapphire eyes. And in that instant, Raven believed that it truly did matter to her. Perhaps even more than it did to him.

So when she bowed her head and her kneeling body folded like deflated bagpipes, he knew he couldn't leave her. Not yet.

"Poor little professor," he said, not unkindly, and returned to her in a few long strides. "Come now. Don't let this trouble you. I am eons ahead of you in understanding futility. After a time, you'll get used to it, like a splinter that's gone too deep beneath the skin to remove."

Sinking down beside her, he ran the flat of his hand over her back and peered into the empty trunk. Correction . . . the *nearly* empty trunk.

Only now did he notice the folded edge of yellowed paper, sticking up from some hidden place near the corner. "Jane."

"No one deserves to suffer, Raven. No one deserves to feel alone and abandoned. Just thinking about you as a little gray-eyed boy, staring out the window of the orphanage and wondering—"

"Jane," Raven repeated, taking her by the shoulders.

He fought the urge to roll his eyes as he started to brush the wet rivulets from her cheeks with his thumbs. "Listen to me. You're overtired and letting your emotions get the better of you. Frankly, I'm disappointed. I never took you for a missish chit. Now, we aren't going to go any further unless you promise me there'll be no more tears, hmm?"

She sniffed again and swiped the back of her hand beneath her nose. "But it's over, regardless."

He shook his head. "Not quite. The trunk has a false bottom. But I don't want you to get your—"

Her gaze swerved to the corner. Her lips parted on a gasp. Then she scrambled to retrieve it, diving headlong over the side before he could even finish his sentence.

"—hopes up," he concluded.

For a long moment, she didn't say anything. Just simply stared down at the letter.

Bollocks. He shouldn't have mentioned it. Continuing this wild-goose chase would only leave her feeling more defeated in the end.

"I was wrong," she said.

Guilt ate at him in gobbling bites like a worm in a cherry. He should have stopped this nonsense before it began. "Like I said, it's neither here nor there for me. In fact, I don't even know why I stayed after the sand ran out."

"No, Raven." She shook her head, her eyes glittering with unshed tears. "I mean, it wasn't a drawing I remembered. It must have been a seal."

Then she turned her wrist to show him the broken red wax, split in a horizontal line. And there, as if it had been taken directly from his flesh, was the bird.

The *raven*.

Numb with disbelief, he didn't move at first.

Surely his eyes were playing tricks on him. He truly never expected to find anything and a noticeable tremor shook his hands as he reached for it.

"This is the seal from the Northcott family," she said. "Though, how the identical design came to be on your arm, I do not know."

Dazedly, he unfolded the letter. He studied the looped scrawl with fascination, the right-sided slant, the spots of ink here and there. Skimming over the page, he tried to piece together the contents but only cursed in frustration. "This is in French. I thought the Northcotts were English."

"Correct," Jane said, leaning in to read it with him, her lips moving soundlessly. "Water has made many of the sentences run together, so I cannot read it all. However, the handwriting appears feminine. And from what I gather, this letter is a request to hire a tutor to speak her husband's native tongue. And here it says"—she gasped and her hand fell atop his sleeve with a squeeze—"it says that she is newly married and would like to speak like a proper English lady before her child is born. And do you see the date?"

Speech failed him at the moment, so he nodded and issued a grunt of affirmation.

1799.

Mr. Mayhew, the beadle in charge of the orphanage, had told him he was abandoned in January of 1800.

Raven had never come this close to finding anything before. But there it was in his grasp—the wax seal that matched the mark on his arm, the letter written just months before he was left on the doorstep, and the surname . . . *Northcott*.

Was that *his* name?

Raven's heart stopped beating. Instead, it rushed in his ears, roaring like a caged animal and he hated it. Bloody hell! He shouldn't still be wondering about his name. What did he care? He was a grown man, not a child.

Lowering the page, he drew in one breath—*two, three.* He needed a moment to shut out all the distractions and to gather his reliable cynicism.

So, he stood and focused on his external senses, ignoring the erratic clamor of his heart rising up the constricted path of his throat. Breathing in, he smelled the cool earthiness of freshly watered soil in the pots, the misted leaves on the branches, and the clean, powdery scent of lavender. But those things weren't helping him. They were far too sweet.

Swallowing, he tasted tea on his tongue and the residual char from the toast. And there was the bitterness he needed. He let it fill him.

Jane's cool, soft fingers curled over his wrist. A slender furrow had worked its way into the creamy flesh of her brow as she gazed up at him with concern.

The jaded part of him wanted to laugh at the absurdity of her reaction. They were mere strangers, after all. Why should she care what the letter may or may not have revealed? This had no effect on her life whatsoever. And yet . . .

Another, unnamed, part of him wanted to soothe her. To shield her from the inevitable disillusionment that would follow when this turned into nothing. And it would turn into nothing, he was sure.

He shook his head. "There's no reason to make any ridiculous leaps. It's merely a letter."

To prove it, he dropped it down into the trunk again and watched as the weight of the seal carried the page in a downward plunge, like the sail on a sinking ship.

"Raven, this is *not* a coincidence. You have to realize what this means." Hands on hips, she stood in front of him like a miniature blockade.

Caught somewhere between amusement and exasperation, he took her by the shoulders. He drew her closer and felt the stiffness in her muscles, the tight coils that had been tormenting her for the past hour. Beneath the heat of his hands, he began massaging them away. "You're getting ahead of yourself."

"And you're trying to dismiss everything we've learned."

"Seems to me that I'm the only one thinking clearly at the moment, instead of rushing to judgment. Just relax,

Jane. Let those pixie wings fall to the side. Yes, that's right. It's been a long day for both of us," he crooned, watching her eyes blink drowsily as the tendons and tissues yielded to his tender kneading. Moving along the slender slope, he cupped her nape, his fingertips probing in circular motions. The softest of moans escaped her. The unexpected sound sent a surge of arousal through him and he tried not to wonder what other noises she might make under his hands. "Soon I'll walk out that door and you'll only ever think of me in your naughtiest fantasies, like the one I'm having of you right now. Would you like to hear it?"

"You're just trying to distract me," she said crossly. "This woman—"

"No. You're getting all tight-shouldered again. Let it go. I mean it, now."

He didn't want to hear any more about the letter or the mark. All he wanted was time to think. He couldn't take any more of this upheaval.

Cupping her jaw, he gently tilted her head back to give her the hard, unquestioning stare that had warned many a man to keep their distance.

But Raven made the mistake of setting his thumb against the cushion of her lips. His gaze was instantly drawn to the supple pouting flesh that had tempted him from the start.

This spell-casting mouth had gotten him into all sorts of trouble with her silent incantations, brown thread declarations, probing questions, and earth-shattering epiphanies. Not to mention, the tantalizing mouthfuls of lush red jam.

Just the thought of it made his pulse start to riot, his blood running hot. Was it any wonder that he'd reached his limit?

"You may not want to hear it," she continued, undeterred, "but this woman might very well be your—"

He silenced her with a kiss. Capturing the tender sweetness of her gasp, he finally found the respite he needed.

Chapter 12

Clearly, Jane had pushed Raven too far.

Otherwise, he never would have overlooked the fact that the recipient of this sudden smoldering kiss was a plain bookish debutante and not a worldly woman. She attempted to draw back to alert him to his error. But when his warm mouth settled over hers with firm possession, she forgot what she wanted to say.

Clever scoundrel that he was, he seemed to read her thoughts and then assured her in the tender way his strong hands cradled her skull that he knew what he was doing.

Oh, he most certainly did.

Deftly, his fingertips worked a tantalizing massage into her nape, keeping her right where he wanted her. Which, coincidentally, was precisely where she wanted to be. Only she hadn't known it until just then.

She yielded to his mastery of the subject as he nibbled softly into her flesh. The heat of his breath slipped inside the narrow seam, bathing her tongue with the flavors of their shared breakfast and the taste of something else—an unknown delicacy—that made her inexplicably hungry. She wanted more of it.

A budding pressure grew beneath her lips. The tender-swollen skin felt like grapes coming to full succulent ripeness in the hands of an expert wine maker. She needed to be plucked off the vine, harvested by his mouth, crushed into pulp and juice, and readied for fermentation. *Oh, sweet fermentation!*

Without thought or any true skill of her own, she kissed him with firm compressions to soothe the pulsing pressure. Her hands splayed over the coarse wool of his coat, grazing up and over the heavy stitching of his lapels to his shoulders, and earned his gruff grunt of approval.

Her body reacted to the primal utterance. Her small breasts grew taut and aching with a peculiar heaviness. A bewildering, unexplored gravity pulled her closer to him and she listed forward on tiptoe until only a sliver of space remained. But the force was too great to resist, the air crackling like static between them.

Succumbing to momentum, she swayed against him. Somehow her arms found their way under his coat where he was warmest, and wrapped themselves around his narrow waist. His soft linen shirt was thin from wear and washing, and it molded enticingly over the musculature of his back beneath her seeking hands.

This time, he growled in a way she had not heard before. The husky, savage sound made her knees tremble, her legs as insubstantial as ivy vines. But he shored her against him, his broad palm skating down the curve of her spine to the small of her back.

"Open for me," he whispered against the damp seam of her lips, nuzzling into the corner of her mouth. "Don't be stingy with your tongue."

Tongue? she wondered dazedly, never thinking that the wet, budded surface would be something another person would wish to investigate. "Whyever would you want that?"

"Trust me. It's part of the process."

The trace of amusement in his tone made her question his authority on this portion of the lesson. "Do you have reference material to which you might direct me?"

She felt his grin against her lips and then a playful tug of his teeth into the flesh of her bottom lip. A zing of pleasure spiraled through her, swirling tightly, deep inside her middle. Who knew that a bite under the right circumstances could feel so pleasant?

"You can't learn everything from a book," he coaxed, nipping her again. "There are some things you just have to try for yourself."

Curious, the willing grapes parted for him, waiting for him to surge forth and explore her taste receptors.

But he did not. Instead, he continued his small sipping kisses, sampling her nectar, weighing her readiness for the bottle. *Good gracious, the bottle!*

Jane blushed at the thought, purple inside her skin as she bore the sweet agony of his kiss, one drop at a time.

Then, at last, he nudged her mouth open and delved inside the dewy cavern. The unexpected pleasure, the slow glide of flesh against flesh, the thrilling rasp of his tongue against hers, sent tingles cascading through her in a hot deluge, quivering deep down inside her stomach.

She felt like purring.

Her arms lifted, slipping out of his coat, and her hands glided around his neck to delve into the mink-soft hair that was just long enough to brush his collar. It all felt perfectly natural to her now. A successful experiment—one she would like to repeat as often as possible.

Sliding closer, she rose up on the toes of her slippers to satisfy all the new sensations pulsing into full wakefulness. Raven assisted her. He settled her body into some faultless orientation against his own, where the hardness of him met the softness of her.

The sublime configuration definitely deserved further study.

No one had ever kissed her or held her like this. And

even without having compiled any research on the subject, she suspected that this was the way it was supposed to be done.

His hands fisted in the back of her gown, pulling her tighter against him. She could feel the buttons of his shirt and, further down, the hard, unmistakable and imposing ridge of his erection.

He was aroused, she thought, awed by this entire sequence of events. Her body reacted to this knowledge with a low liquid throb that urged her hips to tilt of their own accord against him, and a strained whimper escaped her throat.

Chasing the sound she'd made, his lips drifted hotly along the underside of her jaw and down her throat to the V-shaped niche in the center of her clavicle. And when his tongue touched that susceptible place, laving it tenderly, she whimpered again, clinging to him.

He growled that new growl again. "Do you taste this sweet everywhere, Jane?"

"It's only the jam," she assured him, even though she wasn't feeling sure of anything at the moment. In fact, she was barely holding onto her wits as he nibbled a path to her earlobe and raked the flesh softly between his teeth.

"Currant?"

"Damson plum," she breathed, her neck arching against the delightful scrape of his whiskers along her throat. An excited pulse sped on a current through her body, settling where their hips aligned. "I cannot fathom how you kiss worldly women. The pleasure must cause them to burst from their skin like overripe fruits."

Raven went still, clutching her tightly. The hard pounding of his heart inside his chest matched the same harried rhythm inside her own. Then a slow breath staggered out of him.

She shook her head when he gradually eased his mouth away. "No. I don't want to stop."

In response, he pressed lingering kisses against her cheek, her temple, and her brow as he held her excitable, breathless body against him. He stroked a hand down her back, calming her in slow passes. "You need to get some rest."

"But the letter. We have more to—"

"I don't want to talk about the letter anymore today. And if you continue to push me, then you'll soon find yourself carried to that napping spot and thoroughly kissed in places you've likely never even read about," he warned darkly.

Taking her chin in his grasp, he let his gaze fall to her lips as if preparing another assault to her senses.

A wanton thrill raced through her and her lips pursed in inquisitive contemplation. The scientist within her was reminded of the importance of being thorough. Her inner scribe was disheveled and eagerly reaching for a fresh pen.

But even she understood that this was less of an offer and more of a threat, like the snarl of a cornered animal.

She'd pushed him too far already. In the past twelve hours, she'd done quite a lot to upset the course of his life.

"Very well," she said. "I'll send word to you as soon as I translate the letter, as well as whatever I discover from our copy of *Debrett's*. After it is mended, of course."

"Of course," he said with a small grin and she could almost taste it against her tingling lips. She wished she could taste it.

But no. That was a dangerous thought. Her head was beginning to clear enough for her to realize that more kisses would only lead to ruination and being eschewed from her family. She wasn't willing to take that risk just for research.

Decided, she straightened her shoulders. "Once it is all in your possession, that will be the end of my interference in your life. I trust that will be amenable to you?"

He offered a nod. But before he released her, he took her lips once more, stealing the last of her senses.

Then, several breathless and intoxicating minutes later, he set her apart, pivoted on his heel and left, cursing under his breath about *bloody irresistible damson jam.*

Chapter 13

For the following week, Raven was glad to get back to his own life. He put his focus where it belonged—on refurbishing his house, keeping his employment—and *not* on any unreliable debutantes.

He enjoyed his position at Sterling's. After three years, the red silk wallpaper was as familiar as the color of his own blood.

When Reed Sterling had first offered him a position, Raven had started out as a mere usher, but quickly worked his way up to a croupier. Now, as he prowled through the rooms, he oversaw the tables and the bank, kept the books in order, and took care of patrons' requests. He also supervised the list runners and made sure the ushers filled the whisky glasses.

It all kept him busy. Far too busy to think about Jane Pickerington. Or to wonder why, after pushing and pushing to find a link between the mark on his arm and the Northcott family, she'd suddenly lost interest.

Not that he cared. In fact, he was glad she hadn't pestered him once in the past week. She hadn't sent the translation of the letter like she'd said she would either. That didn't bother him at all. And, apparently, her copy of *Debrett's* was still at the bookbinder's because she'd sent no word regarding the family name.

More than likely, the absentminded bluestocking had forgotten all about it and had moved on to something new.

It wouldn't be the first time that had happened to him. Wouldn't be the last, he was sure.

Of course, if he were truly interested in knowing, he could always purchase his own copy of the book. It could be good for a laugh, if nothing else.

But, since none of it mattered, regardless, there wasn't any point in wasting hard-earned money. He put the whole ordeal out of his mind and cracked his neck from one side to the other.

Stopping near the door of the hazard room, he cast an absent glance over the crowd at the green felt table. As usual, gents were shouting and raising fists stuffed with pound notes while sconcelight glanced off their sweaty pates.

He was familiar with most of the men who walked through Sterling's doors. Knew their names, their secrets and indiscretions. Knew who'd lost their shirts at the tables and who'd begged for a loan from Reed Sterling. London, however, was a big city and he couldn't know everyone. So, when a stranger walked in, Raven always noticed.

Though, lately, he'd become even more shrewd in his studies. He'd found himself taking careful note of the men in their middle years with gray or grizzled hair, and whether or not they were of a similar height and build to his own. He'd searched faces for resemblances—the shape of the eye, the cut of the chin, anything. And on more than one occasion, he'd caught himself wondering if any of the men had married a French woman who'd once needed an English tutor.

It was madness! And it was all Jane Pickerington's fault.

So before he acted the fool and started sizing up this crowd, too, he stalked toward the faro tables. He wasn't going to let one luckless encounter with a little debutante distract him any longer.

"You there, boy," a man called out as he passed.

Raven felt the hair at his nape stand on end. He knew he was being hailed, but it had been years since anyone had dared call him *boy*.

Even as a lad it bristled him to hear the condescending sneer that forever accompanied it. But he'd never been cowed by it. He'd always been too proud.

At the orphanage, Mr. Mayhew had beaten him time and again and told him that his arrogance would be his downfall. Devil Devons at the workhouse had told him the same, right before he'd lock the door to the rat cupboard. But Raven, no matter how bloodied afterward, had continued to stand before them, straight-shouldered and staring them directly in the eye.

His competence and assuredness had gained the admiration of his fellow workers. And the majority of the patrons treated him with respect, or kept a wide berth.

Normally, he would turn and stare down any man who thought he was nothing more than muck on a pair of boots. Usually, that was all he needed to do.

But tonight, his temper was rough-edged, like a blade that begged to be sharpened. Deep in his gut roiled the upheaval and uncertainty of the past week, and he knew he wasn't as self-possessed as he needed to be. So, he decided to ignore the pompous gent's insult and walk on.

"I say, there . . . boy."

Raven gritted his teeth but did not turn around. At least, not until the prig clamped a hand on his shoulder. Then he whipped around on a low growl.

The gent's blue eyes widened with a start. A glare instantly followed, his heavy tawny brow furrowing above a hawklike nose. The man—older by about thirty years—regarded him with the chilly disdain that aristocrats must teach their young from the cradle. "Fetch me a whisky."

Raven stiffened. Even worse than being called *boy*, he

despised being treated like a dog and asked to fetch the master's slippers.

Even so, he knew how to be diplomatic. He wouldn't have gained this position if he hadn't proved his ability to keep a cool head when dealing with pompous aristocrats. And since he'd never seen this gent in Sterling's before, he granted him a little leeway. A very little.

Maintaining an inscrutable expression, Raven cleared his throat, preparing to politely inform the gent that all he had to do was give a nod to Tom. After all, the usher was standing only six feet away with a complimentary whisky tray in hand. Any beef-headed buzzard could have discerned as much.

But then the man spoke again.

"Be quick about it and there'll be a shilling in it for you."

Raven tried to shrug off the provocation. But, damn it all, this had been a shite week and he'd had enough. The rough edge of his temper sliced through his composure just enough to break the surface. "A whole shilling?"

The man squinted, jaw ticking. "Are you mocking me?"

Raven signaled Tom, offering the gent a mere passing glance. "Of course not. I would have to be of superior birth to condescend to the likes of you. And wouldn't you know it, seems I've forgotten my crown at home." When Tom approached, Raven reached out and took the whole tray. Then he pushed it toward the gent, all the while knowing that reflex would force any man to take hold. And when he did, Raven flashed a cold grin. "Your whisky, sir."

He sketched a proper bow and stalked into the faro room.

Of course, that wasn't the end of it.

A quarter hour later, as he was taking a stack of profits to the safe, he saw that self-entitled arse standing in front of Reed Sterling in the main card room, his beak sniffing with effrontery.

Spotting Raven, the gent pointed with a hard sweep of his arm, the silver buttons on his cuffs winking as they caught the light.

Sterling followed the gesture, his unreadable gaze raking over him. And even though no discernable reaction flickered over the former prizefighter's famously calm exterior, Raven knew they'd soon be having a chat.

So, at the end of the night and with the accounting ledgers in hand, Raven went to Sterling's office as usual.

Inside the paneled room, Reed Sterling was standing at the window behind his desk, staring across the street at the white stone town house where he lived with his wife and her uncle.

Raven laid down the ledger on the desk and eyed his employer, taking note of the set of his square jaw. The dark-headed man was an imposing figure, especially when he had his arms crossed over his chest, with the sconcelight silhouetting his form. Years of pugilism had given him broad shoulders, a burly build, and a right hook that could fell a tree.

Without turning around, Sterling said, "I trust that whatever issue you've been having with the clientele this week, you'll remedy by tomorrow."

Hmm . . . Apparently, this wasn't the only night he'd unleashed a small portion of irritability on the high-society nobs. But he was tired of looking at gents of a certain age and wondering if any of them had left a child to nearly freeze to death on a cold January night, discarding him like refuse in the gutter.

"Done and over," he said, but made the mistake of shrugging. The action caused his shirt to catch that blasted scab left over from Ruthersby's cane—right above the mark—and his words came out sharper than he'd intended.

Sterling turned, a dubious smirk lifting the nick on his

upper lip. "This wouldn't have anything to do with a rumor I heard about a certain man—and one who strangely matches your description—having been involved in a brawl at Moll Dawson's, would it?"

Sterling had eyes and ears all over the city and nothing ever got past him, so Raven expected this. But that didn't mean he was willing to talk about it. As far as he was concerned, the less he mentioned about that night, the better. "Perhaps I have a twin in London."

Sterling's mouth twitched as he scanned the columns of the ledgers with a deceptively absent air. "I also heard another tale about Duncan Pickerington visiting your flat—as he calls it. Yet his account was so completely absurd that I dismissed it."

Raven cursed under his breath, his back teeth grinding together.

"I also believe," Sterling continued conversationally, turning the page, "there was mention of a girl involved."

Raven stiffened, shoulders ramrod straight. "Pickerington never should have mentioned any of it, especially nothing about her."

"Why is that?"

Knots of tension rose like hackles down his spine, and Raven didn't quite understand the sudden anger he felt toward Pickerington. But it was there, nonetheless. "Isn't it your rule that well-bred women aren't discussed beneath this roof? At least that's how it was when you were courting your matchmaker."

In response, a pair of mismatched irises—one, a solid indigo and the other golden at the corner—lifted from the ledger. A dark brow arched in a clear warning to tread lightly in matters that concerned his wife. "We both know Pickerington, and I'm sure he meant no slight. From what I understand, the girl is his own cousin."

"Then he should do a fare sight better at protecting his own family, not let them fall into danger. A man keeps what's his safe and sound." Raven growled before he thought better of it and saw the keen flash of interest in that gilded eye.

"Made an impression, did she?"

"Nothing of the sort," he answered tightly, wanting an end to this conversation.

But that didn't stop his skin from tingling from the unwanted and ever-recurring memory of her taut, fragrant body pressed against him. Bloody hell! He wished he could just forget already.

Fisting his hands, he swallowed and inwardly rued the day he'd ever met the little jam-eating bluestocking.

Sterling closed the book and offered a nod as if that was the end of it.

Raven turned on his heel to leave. But just as he got to the door, Sterling had one more question for him.

"So tell me," he said with a trace of amusement, "were you actually turned . . . pink?"

Raven was going to kill Pickerington for having such a big mouth.

Looking over his shoulder, and mustering as much pride as he could, he stared pointedly at the budvase on the windowsill. "As pink as that posy you're taking to Mrs. Sterling."

◦◦◦◦◦◦

JANE COULDN'T let another day pass without sharing her findings with Raven. She just hoped it would be enough to convince the hard-won skeptic. However, if the wax seal hadn't persuaded him to believe, then she likely had a battle ahead of her.

Peering through the slit between the carriage window drapes, her gaze skimmed over the ramshackle terrace in Covent Garden. She'd expected Raven home by now. According to her watch fob, it was a quarter past three o'clock in the morning.

The news she had for him needed to be delivered in person.

Unfortunately, finding the time had been challenging in between lessons for the children, daily disasters, and social obligations that Ellie refused to let her cancel.

In fact, Ellie was with her now, asleep on the blue velvet bench beside her. Ellie's aunts, of course, believed they were both still at the Willinghams' ball with Jane's parents. And her parents believed that their daughter was spending the evening at Upper Wimpole Street with Ellie and her aunts.

It was the perfect stratagem. Or, at least, it would be if Raven ever showed up.

Jane was ashamed to admit that she'd caught herself wondering—and not for the first time this week—if he'd found a new brothel and was holding and kissing cyprians the way he'd held and kissed her. But of course he was. It was logical to conclude that a man she'd met in a brothel would continue to seek his pleasure in such establishments.

But her stomach refused to agree with her mind. Every time she thought of it, that organ churned with peculiar ferocity. The frequency of this occurrence in the past seven days had compelled her to carry a placket of mint leaves. Their soothing digestive properties had become necessary after the artist on her mental portico started painting a series of scandalous portraits involving Raven and scores of beautiful women.

Reaching for her reticule, she began fishing through it. But the flickering glow from the lamppost dimmed as a form emerged beside the carriage.

She did not jolt in startlement. Even before she turned her head, she knew who it was. Only Raven made her skin contract in an all-over body tingle of gooseflesh. Only he caused her heart to stumble awkwardly out of rhythm as if it just tripped over an artery and collided with the wall of her rib cage.

The queer sensation irritated her all the more as she thought about the lateness of the hour. She wondered if he would reek of women's perfume. Grumpily, she reached out to unlatch the carriage door, but he instantly took control of it.

Swinging the door open on a growl, he issued a gray-eyed glower. "Isn't it a bit late for you, Jane? I believe your driver has fallen asleep and this is hardly the place to leave yourself unprotected."

She sent him a glare of her own. "You only have yourself to blame. I wouldn't have needed to linger if you'd bothered to come home at an appropriate hour. Where *have* you been, or dare I even ask?"

"You harp like a fishwife," Raven muttered under his breath, his voice sharp as an ice pick. "It may surprise you, but there are people who have to earn a wage if they want to eat. They don't have the luxury of flitting about out of a need to escape boredom, passing time between dinner parties and foolish, reckless escapades."

At the rumbles of their gathering argument, Ellie stirred with a small mewl of protest, but did not awaken. She merely rolled closer into the corner and pressed her cheek more securely to the bunched-up shawl she was using as a makeshift pillow.

Jane sniffed the perfumeless air surrounding him, marginally mollified. "I was under the impression you did not want me to contact you unless I found something definitive."

He crossed his arms over his chest, his dark coat pulled taut over the tightly loomed muscles. "I didn't care if you found anything at all. Like I told you, nothing's going to change for me. I just find it amusing that your determination to upend a man's life runs on a schedule."

"*A schedu—*" She stopped on a growl. This was not how their encounter was supposed to commence. She wanted to convince him to believe in the possibility, not completely disregard it. "I'll not allow you to goad me. This is too important."

He shrugged, then nodded indifferently toward Ellie. "This one of your book-writing friends?"

"Yes," she said stiffly. "I would introduce you to Elodie Parrish; however, once she decides to fall asleep, the end of the world could not rouse her. Even so, I knew I had to stay until I saw you."

"Miss me, did you?"

She ignored his mocking tone and turned her attention to her reticule again. Reaching inside, she curled her hand around a scroll, then held it out for him. "I took the letter, applied a restoration technique with the juice of a lemon and uncovered the name written at the bottom. I've translated much of the contents as well."

He slowly unfolded his arms, eyeing the paper as if it were a miniature cannon ready to fire. Taking it in hand, he unrolled the letter, skimming over the contents.

"Arabelle," he murmured, his gaze fixing on the looped scrawl.

If it were anyone else, Jane would imagine that the bland expression indicated disinterest in the subject, or even boredom. Raven was quite skilled at pretending indifference.

But she knew it meant more to him than he cared to let on. When they'd been in the conservatory, there had been moments when she'd looked into his eyes and had seen something familiar buried deep down in their depths.

It was longing.

She'd seen the same look in the mirror her whole life— that need to belong somewhere, to have her existence matter to someone, and to know that she wasn't merely an easily discarded byproduct of procreation and nothing more.

"Arabelle Foreaux Northcott, to be exact," Jane supplied.

She was careful to affect an offhanded tone for the purpose of easing him into the rest of what she would soon reveal. From their brief encounters, she already understood that he tended to retreat when pushed too far and it took a devil of a time to bring him back. Either that, or he attempted to distract her by any means necessary. Even with a kiss.

After many thoughtful hours of mulling over their startlingly passionate osculation, she'd come to the conclusion that he hadn't actually desired her. No, indeed. His response had been more of a means of self-preservation against a sudden glut of life-altering information.

"As you know," she continued, "I had intended to research that family name in our copy of *Debrett's*. Regrettably, on the very day that it arrived from the bookbinder, another disaster befell it." Jane shuddered as she recalled the event. "I had just opened it when Theodora came to me, complaining of a *sleepy* stomach. I soon learned that, when her stomach falls asleep, it decides to regurgitate its entire contents in a rather terrifying spectacle. I'll spare you the more gruesome details but only say that, by the time I returned to my desk, I discovered that much of the book had been ruined beyond repair. Including the pages regarding the Northcotts. Nevertheless, that did not halt my efforts, for I found—"

"How is your sister?" Raven interrupted.

She blinked at him, surprised by the thoughtful concern softening his tone and features. A kernel of warmth glowed beneath her breast. "Theodora is well now, thank you. Her fever broke by midweek and her stomach is happily awake and enjoying the biscuits that the cook and every maid have been leaving in the nursery for her."

"I'm glad to hear it," he said with a nod.

For reasons beyond her understanding, the tension he'd seemed to have carried with him from Sterling's dissipated in that same instant. He shifted closer to the carriage, his movements no longer stiff or agitated. It was as though some inner tumult had come to a peaceful conclusion.

Whatever it was, Jane was grateful. His mellower mood eased the worry she felt over what she would reveal next.

"As I was saying," she continued carefully, "I still managed to discover information on the Northcotts. It happened quite by accident. I was using a map for the children's lessons when I noticed a tiny hamlet in Hertfordshire of the same name. And from there, my research led me to this." Reaching across to the opposite bench, she drew the shawl-wrapped book onto her lap. Unwrapping the hefty tome, she handed it to him.

He looked at it, skeptical. "And what is this?"

"The baptismal record from the small chapel."

"You *stole* this from a church?"

"Merely borrowed it from an unwitting vestry clerk. I'll return it before anyone realizes it's missing," she said in self-defense. "I've marked the page of December 1799 births with a violet ribbon. But take care of the binding. It's quite brittle."

"But how did you know the month . . ." He shook his head without bothering to finish the question and drew in a deep breath. "Let's just see what you've found, then."

His index finger slid along the rough-cut edge to slip in between the pages where the ribbon lay. Then he opened the book with the caution of a man expecting a venomous snake to spring from the margins.

Skimming the handwriting, his eyes settled on a narrow, slanted script about halfway down.

Even though he didn't read it aloud, she knew what he was seeing. Merrick Northcott, born 1st of December, to

Edgar Clay Avendale Northcott, Viscount Northcott, and Arabelle Foreaux Northcott, Viscountess Northcott.

His gaze lingered for a moment, then he simply closed the book and gave it back. Jane waited for his reaction. A skeptical arch of a brow. A blink of amazement. Anything.

But he offered nothing, his gaze as unreadable as ash in an abandoned hearth.

Disappointed and heartsick, Jane looked down at the book and sighed. Had he truly gone so long without hope of finding his family that there wasn't a single shred of it left?

She didn't have an answer.

Feeling the throb of a sudden headache, she pressed her fingertips to her temples. Then, without warning, she felt his hand gently cup her cheek, the warmth of it startling on this chilly night. His touch was so comforting that she nestled into the curve of his palm reflexively.

She realized she'd missed him these past seven days. How peculiar. She could number the length of their acquaintance by the hour and yet his touch and his scent were already part of her, like an indelible mark upon her skin.

His thumb trailed the insomnia-bruised flesh beneath her weary eyes. "Have you slept at all this week?"

"Some," she admitted. "After Theodora felt better, the twins decided to invite an entire family of squirrels into the nursery. It has been a bit chaotic."

"In addition to the research," he added with a knowing look, chiding her with a slow shake of his head. "You shouldn't have been so determined. Especially not on a stranger's behalf."

"Well, I'd say that you and I are more like acquaintances. After all, I don't normally allow strangers to . . ." She let her words trail off, but mouthed in a silent murmur, ". . . kiss me."

In response, his gaze heated in a sudden flare, simmering

to smoke as it rested on her mouth. Her lips tingled under his scrutiny.

As if he knew this and wanted to soothe her, the pad of his thumb skimmed that tender surface, too. "I bought a new book the other day."

The alteration in topic was unexpected. And yet, no other man could make such a statement sound so intriguing and so wicked at the same time. "What is the title?"

"Can't recall," he said mysteriously, stepping closer until his hip brushed her knee and the lamplight seemed to burn in his eyes. "Come upstairs with me and we'll read it together."

At once, she knew what he was doing and she covered his hand with her own, drawing it away from her blushing cheek.

"You are such a scoundrel," she said, but there wasn't even a hint of scolding in her breathless voice. Temptation, perhaps. But not scolding. "Why is it that whenever we're talking about your identity, you try to distract me with seduction?"

He flashed an unrepentant grin, and didn't even bother to deny it. "One is far more interesting than the other."

She took that as another evasion. After all, she knew his preference for worldly women. Her own thoughts cooled and she focused again on the reason she'd come here.

She thrummed her fingers against the book on her lap. "I wish I had more proof to offer. Unfortunately, I have no other information on Merrick Northcott, yet the lack thereof leads me to speculate over the high probability that you and he are linked in some way."

The more time she spent thinking about Raven and his peculiar "birthmark," the firmer her conviction became that he was connected to the Northcott family. And as cruel as it was to consider, he would not have that intricately detailed mark on his shoulder unless someone had put it there in order to claim him as their own.

But was he the child mentioned in the letter? Plausible.

However, without evidence at her disposal, she couldn't be certain. He might have been a ward, or even an illegitimate child.

"You're making leaps in logic again," Raven said, his eyes slowly frosting over.

Drat! Had she gone too far? Perhaps her proclivity to find solutions to puzzles was working against her better intentions.

Scrambling to keep him from retreating altogether, she hastily said, "Then prove me wrong. Help me find Merrick Northcott and this will all be over."

He shook his head. "You're too tenacious. You would only find another name, and then another."

"I won't," she said. "I give you my word."

"No," he said firmly and took a step back. Then his hand fell on the door, ready to shut out every possibility.

Hope left her on an extinguished sigh.

Carefully, she wrapped the shawl around the book. His gaze followed as she placed it on the bench across from her, a frown knitting his brow. Was he still thinking about the contents of the baptismal record? Considering the possibility?

She couldn't be certain. But his questioning expression was enough to breathe the last dwindling ember of hope to life again.

Jane quickly thought up a new plan. Perhaps if he saw the little chapel himself and imagined Lord and Lady Northcott standing there with their child, it might sway him toward believing.

"I'll just return that later this morning after I drop Ellie at home, and then change clothes," she said plainly, as if she intended to put the matter behind her as well. "The parish in Hertfordshire isn't too far of a journey, fewer than two hours when the weather is dry. And the roads are quite safe, I'm sure. Well . . . mostly."

Raven gave her an alert glance, a low growl of warning rumbling deep in his throat. "What do you mean *mostly*?"

"One can never know if there will be bloodthirsty highwaymen lurking about at dawn, lying in wait for the next unsuspecting carriage driver. From what I understand, criminals tend to use the bleary light of dusk and dawn to their advantage," she said with a shrug and a nonchalant flip of her fingertips in the air.

His brows arched over his narrowed eyes. "I see what you're doing, but it won't work. I'm done with all this. I'm going to go into my house, close the door, and get back to my own life. And you're going to get back to yours, too."

As if the matter were settled, he stormed away from her to gruffly wake the driver, then came back, fairly steaming with agitation.

Jane, however, wasn't agitated at all. She'd heard him speak in this same manner in the brothel when he was determined not to follow her, and again in his bedchamber when he professed to having no curiosity about the mark. A scientist of the human condition would likely interpret this as predictable behavior.

Suddenly, her small ember of hope flared brightly, igniting. "Has anyone ever told you that you have an authoritative tone? In fact, it's quite . . . aristocratic."

Apparently, he wasn't in the mood for her teasing.

He closed the door firmly and glared at her through the glass. "Additionally, I want you to send a messenger to return that book. You're not to go alone. Don't you dare smile at me, and stop biting your lip. I mean it, Jane. Send a messenger."

The carriage shifted as the driver released the brake and called out to the horses. Then she was off with a merry wave to Raven, leaving him to curse epithets into the cold night air.

Chapter 14

Raven grumbled all the way to Hertfordshire later that morning. He hadn't slept a wink. And the last thing he wanted was to ride across the countryside on the back of a borrowed horse.

Reed Sterling had warned him that the big stallion was as insolent and short-tempered as his namesake. Savage had been given to him by his friend, Lord Savage. The only way to deal with the brindled beast, in Sterling's opinion, was to put him out to stud at his country estate.

Raven agreed. It wasn't just because he hadn't ridden in years—not since he'd been plucked from the workhouse by Devons' widow and groomed to be her young lover—but also that the animal was unruly.

He wouldn't be surprised if the snarling steed was possessed by a demon.

But he'd needed a horse today, regardless, to stealthily follow Jane's carriage. He'd refused to give her the satisfaction of seeing his face at her conservatory door this morning, revealing that her manipulation had worked.

So he put up with the stallion. Whenever Savage tried to assert his dominance by baring his teeth, straining against the lead, or rearing back, Raven growled down at him. Strangely enough, the gruff sound seemed to work. And, by the time they cantered past Watford, they'd reached something of an understanding.

Even so, after an hour and a half, Raven was sorely glad when they reached their destination.

Up ahead, the carriage stopped around a curve in the narrow lane in front of a slender fieldstone chapel with a steepled, moss-grown roof and pointed spire.

He dismounted near a stream tucked away on the outer edge of the forest glade. Both he and Savage needed a drink. Though Raven would have preferred his to be something stronger, he drank down the cold, clear water in grateful gulps.

Wiping the back of his hand over his mouth, he watched Jane step lithely down from the carriage. She was dressed in a deep red, fur-lined pelisse with the shawl-wrapped book in her arms and, doubtless, her infamous reticule tucked beneath it.

He expected her to traipse into the chapel and return forthwith.

Instead, she took time to speak to the driver. She pointed him in the direction of a dozen black-thatched cottages that stood in a winding cluster beneath the base of a hill, as if asking him to drive elsewhere and without her. But why?

Frowning, Raven stroked the flat of his hand down the tiger-striped hide along the horse's brawny neck. The carriage drove away, leaving Jane alone in front of the chapel.

She cast a furtive glance around, then went to the heavy oaken door, opening it—just a crack—to peer inside. Apparently not seeing what she wanted, she closed it and slyly crept around the corner, disappearing behind a hedgerow.

His plan to keep her from knowing that he'd followed quickly fell by the wayside. So he left Savage tied to a bare elm branch that hung above tufts of sweet grass growing up from between the rocks.

Just as Raven entered the small side garden, he saw Jane bending over to position a wooden pail beneath a window ledge. A cool breeze buffeted the crimson wool against her bottom, outlining the lush curves that made his fingertips and palms tingle from want. Made his blood pulse thickly through his veins.

He was shocked by his increasing desire for a woman who wasn't remotely his type. And even more so by the fantasies that had beleaguered him at all hours of the day and night. In fact, ever since he'd kissed her and tasted the innocent, unschooled glide of her tongue in his mouth, his mind had conjured all sorts of improper things to teach the little professor.

The errant thoughts meant nothing, of course. He was merely randy and out of sorts because he hadn't yet found a new brothel. A few hours of female companionship and he'd be back *in* sorts, with the likes of her never to enter his mind again.

Assured of it, he moved silently over the grass. "Why is it that I always find you sneaking into windows?"

She turned with a start, her bluer-than-blue eyes widening against a sea of white, which was exactly the reaction he wanted. But then she smiled, which was not at all what he wanted.

"I knew you would come," she said with a small, but exuberant, bounce up on her toes. "Admit it, you're just as curious as I am."

He glared at her. "I'm only here to see for myself if you were actually going to jaunt across the countryside, alone, and with a complete disregard for your own safety."

It was the truth. Any interest he might have had about the contents of the book was eclipsed by the anger that burned in his veins at the thought of this reckless fool putting herself in harm's way.

She bristled at the sharp edge in his voice and adjusted her cargo tighter against the high, firm hillocks of her breasts.

"I have arrived safe and sound. Regardless, I don't need anyone to look after me. I've been doing finc on my own for years. Therefore, you may leave me in peace and go back to your own life."

If only he could. Knowing that there was no one else to stop her from these escapades compelled him to take up the role of her guardian, whether he liked it or not.

"That cart went dashing off with the horse the moment I met you," he said bitterly, striding toward her and ready to end this episode. "I'm not about to let you go in there alone. So, stand aside."

A look of triumph and excitement flared in her eyes. He chose to ignore it, slipping past her to open the window. Seeing that the small vestry chamber was vacant, he navigated the sill.

Inside, the air was pungent with the sweetness of aging books. Turpentine and beeswax polish had worked its way into every grain of umber-dark wood, from the old warped floor to the table in the center and the shelves that lined three of the walls.

Raven turned to Jane. "Just give me the book and I'll leave it on the table."

"Not on your life," she declared crossly, already tying the shawl around her shoulder and waist in a makeshift sling to hold the large book against her torso. She hiked her stubborn chin and climbed up on the wooden pail. "It's either both the book and I, or neither of us."

Arguing with Jane was not something a man without sleep or patience would ever undertake. So, he only bothered to issue an annoyed growl as he leaned out and slipped his hands under her arms. She issued a slight gasp as he lifted her smoothly inside, careful to keep her head from hitting the window casing.

His irritation vanished the instant her scent filled his

nostrils and her slender form yielded against him in a soft, supple press, her hands gripping his shoulders. In the seconds that followed, her wide eyes searched his. And the color tingeing her cheeks and lips matched the fur-lined pelisse, making her look like a delectable little fruit, just ripe for the tasting.

She paused to wet her lips and the dark drops of her pupils seemed to mirror his thoughts. But instead of giving in to the hunger that had plagued him all week, he set her apart and issued a firm warning.

"This is the last time, Jane. No more of these foolish errands. Now, put the book—" He glanced down and saw that her shawl was empty. "Where is it?"

Jane blinked and looked down, equally mystified. Then they both went to the window and saw it resting against the rocks.

Raven retrieved it, realizing belatedly that he should have felt it between them a moment ago if he'd been paying attention.

Coming back, he brushed off the bits of dust and leaves and gave it to her. "Put this back where it belongs and then we're leaving."

"Leaving? But surely you didn't come all this way just to stop."

"Stop? I never planned to start in the first place."

All he knew was that, the instant her carriage had disappeared from sight in the dark wee hours this morning, he'd stalked into his house and cursed a blue streak into his empty bedchamber. Then, before he knew it, he'd found himself banging on Reed Sterling's door and asking to borrow his newly acquired horse.

Thankfully, Sterling hadn't asked the reason. Because Raven was damned if he knew it himself.

Dressed only in trousers and open shirtsleeves, Sterling

had· simply sent a hasty missive to the stable yard before darkly commanding never to be disturbed when he was alone with his wife . . . unless the gaming hell was on fire. Then he amended that with, "And it had better be a damned conflagration."

Raven only hoped that Sterling would be as indifferent about the sudden requirement for a horse in the dead of night when they saw each other later. He didn't want to answer any questions regarding Jane or his reasons for following her. Especially when he wasn't entirely sure himself.

Standing in front of her now, he raked a hand through his hair and exhaled frustration through his nostrils. "Just put it back."

Finally, she did. Then she faced him, hands on hips and arms flared. "There's no sense in leaving until we explore furth—"

Her words halted as they heard the creak of a footstep on the hardwood floor.

They both turned as a slight, elderly man dressed in a dark cassock shuffled into the room, distracted by an open prayer book in his gnarled hand.

Lifting his rawboned face, he saw Jane across the room and a smile creased his cheeks. "Ah, Miss Pickerington, back again so soon? Strange, but I didn't see you come in through the chapel."

"My apologies, Reverend. I always find myself drawn to different books in different places. A failing of my own, I'm afraid."

"If that is a failing then we should all be similarly stricken. I'd have thought I'd exhausted you and your charming friend with talk of this parish's history yesterday. I do tend to drone on and on, or so my wife says . . ." He glanced toward the window and caught sight of Raven. "Oh, I see you've brought someone new today."

"Indeed. This gentleman is my . . . um . . . cousin who insisted on serving as my chaperone. He can be quite stubborn."

"A pleasure, sir," the vicar said with a nod and a serene smile. "To my mind, stubbornness is a forgivable transgression when one is putting another's welfare first."

Raven stood taller and flicked an arched glance in Jane's direction. "Then I shall continue, knowing all the while that I'll be pardoned."

"And you are most welcome here," the vicar said affably. "We have so few travelers nowadays. Ours has become such a small parish since the terrible fire."

"My apologies. I did not realize you'd had a fire," Jane offered, her expression guilt-stricken as she furtively glanced toward the bookshelf.

He shook his head. "I beg your pardon, for I've done it again. I always speak of the tragedy as if it were a recent occurrence. To my doddering mind it still is, I suppose. That January of 1800 will forever linger with me as the night of devastation."

An icy shiver snaked down Raven's spine.

"Eighteen"—Jane swallowed, her complexion unnaturally pale—"hundred?"

"Simply heartbreaking," the vicar said with sadness haunting the depths of his cloudy gaze. "Not a soul in the manor house on the hill survived. Not the fourteen servants. Not even Lord and Lady Northcott."

Raven's throat went dry. Only this morning he'd read those names. Only this morning he'd imagined the pen in a capable, manicured hand, dipping into a pot of ink before scrawling the names in the register, a head bending to blow a stream of breath to dry the page.

This morning, just hours ago, those strangers had been alive to him. Now they were gone. The vision in his mind evaporated like a curl of smoke from the last ember in a grate.

In the moment that followed, the soft rasp of Jane's slippers on the floor was the only sound to disturb the solemn quiet. She came to his side and curled her hand over his sleeve, either in comfort or regret, or perhaps both.

"Was there a child?" Raven heard himself ask the vicar.

The old man nodded, looking heavenward. "Such a great and woeful loss. He was so small that there were no remains found to place in the family crypt. I like to believe that he was so precious to the angels that they chose to take him in body and spirit."

Jane went unnaturally still and Raven knew they were both focusing on the same three words—*no remains found*.

Raven shifted from one foot to the other. An uncomfortable, itchy awareness covered his skin, the primary discomfort residing at the mark on his shoulder. It seemed to contract and pulse like a fresh wound trying to heal. He wanted to scratch it until it bled. Until the skin was scraped raw.

He didn't like those three words. There was no real finality in them. It left too much room for the most dreaded of all things . . . hope.

Jane's fingertips brushed over his sleeve in a small, comforting caress. "Wouldn't it be possible that the baby might have survived by some miracle?"

"Hope is one of humanity's greatest gifts, Miss Pickerington. Though, in this particular circumstance, I've also discovered that it is a tool used by charlatans and opportunists to bring further pain to the remaining family. It would have been better if they'd been allowed to grieve their loss in peace and be healed."

"And just what are these charlatans trying to gain?" Raven asked, confused.

But the answer that came was nothing he ever could have expected.

"Why, the earldom, of course."

∞∞∞∞∞

THE PIECES fit together for Jane in a sudden breath of enlightenment. "The Earl of Warrister. I'd completely forgotten the rumors."

Looking up at Raven, she saw a brief flash of shock in his expression an instant before his handsome features rearranged themselves into inscrutable lines and angles. She felt guilty for luring him here for such terrible news. And yet, even as she was dismayed to hear about the tragedy, she was also filled with a sense of certainty.

The mark was not a coincidence. It couldn't be.

"The Earl of Warrister is quite reclusive, though 'tis no wonder, what with the accusations," the vicar added with a sigh.

"From what I now recall, his lordship still holds fast to the idea that his grandchild survived the fire, does he not?"

"Sadly, yes, even after all this time. There are some who believe that the earl's mental faculties are somewhat . . . diminished. His nephew, Lord Herrington, has been the most vocal about his own suspicions."

"Then Lord Herrington must expect to inherit," she mused absently.

"The law of primogeniture will make it so, I'm certain. The baron is, after all, the eldest of the earl's nephews. And better he than a usurper." The old man's age-rounded shoulders lifted in an inconsequential shrug as he began to cross the room with his prayer book in hand.

Jane's gaze strayed to the baptismal record. *Drat.* In her haste, she'd put the book on the wrong shelf and it wasn't pushed in all the way either. She only hoped the vicar wouldn't notice or else he might imagine they were a pair of those *charlatans* he mentioned.

"Regrettably," the vicar continued, "many are ensnared by the promise of money and power. Why, even in the wake of such a catastrophe, there were those who swarmed the rubble left behind in order to see what treasures they might take for themselves. A pity. Especially because Lord and Lady Northcott were always so kind and generous. There wasn't a single parishioner who was ever infirm or hungry that her ladyship did not try to lend aid to in some way or another. His lordship beamed whenever she was on his arm, as any man would have done, I'm sure."

"She was pretty, then?" Raven asked, his voice more tender than Jane had heard before. And in the muscled forearm beneath her hand, she felt the faintest tremor.

"Aye. None lovelier."

She witnessed a soft smile touch Raven's lips. A wealth of emotion welled in her throat as she thought of that fire and the child who'd lost his parents—the child who'd grown into a man who was starting to believe.

"What else do you know about the Northcotts?" she asked, completely missing the fact that the vicar had gone still, his uplifted arm half-suspended in the air.

With his prayer book in hand, he hesitated at the sight of the misplaced baptismal record. When he turned around to address his guests, his genial manner was gone.

He looked carefully from Jane to Raven, his wizened gaze narrowing. "And just what is your name, sir?"

"That," he answered with a mystified shake of his head, "is a very good question."

Chapter 15

After their unceremonious departure from the chapel, Raven walked with Jane to the hill where the Northcott house once stood, his thoughts distracted and distant.

The last day of October seemed to be exiting in proper gloomy fashion. As they approached the top, a chill breeze sent crisp leaves skittering along the path ahead of them, rushing from the dark clouds gathering overhead. They settled, shivering against the remains of the manor house foundation.

Even after all this time, the memory of that night showed itself in the scorched fieldstones, laid out in long rectangles like an ancient skeleton that the earth was slowly devouring. The fire had destroyed everything else.

Or nearly everything, Raven mused.

Was it possible that the child had survived? Perhaps, like the other items looted from the ashes, the child had been taken away as well.

But for what purpose? Surely not to be left on the doorstep of a foundling home. After all, why go through all the trouble of saving an infant only to abandon it?

Raven didn't know the answer. In fact, he was no longer sure of anything.

He felt altered, rearranged. It was as if someone had taken an egg whisk to his insides and was waiting to see what kind of pudding would come out after he steamed.

Jane stood by him, quiet aside from the silent murmur of her lips as she made her *mental notes*. He was oddly comforted by the familiarity of her habit. With so many uncertainties surrounding him, he found himself gravitating to the only things he knew.

Absently, he brushed his thumb over the delicate softness of her hand, not knowing exactly when he'd reached out and taken hold of it. Or even when he'd removed her glove. But he discovered it was gripped in his other hand, nonetheless.

Refusing to ponder over it too much, he merely focused on the tender cushion of her palm nestled into his, the clasp of her fingers, the feel of being tethered to something—to someone—real.

Without her beside him, he might later convince himself that it was all a strange dream.

"The vicar became quite reluctant to share any more information, even eager for us to leave," he said. "I think he suspected us of usurpering."

"Of *usurpation*," she corrected quietly. "Is that what we're doing, Raven? Are we . . . claiming your birthright?"

"No." That much he knew for certain. "There isn't anything to claim because neither of us has proof."

"True. We cannot say definitively that you are Merrick Northcott. At least not yet. However, I've already begun to compile a list of places to visit once we return to London, as well as individuals who may have answers."

He looked down at her and shook his head. "Jane, don't push this any further, hmm? Not right now."

"You just found out who your parents were. Surely, you aren't going to stop there."

"I *might have* just found my parents," he clarified tightly, feeling the egg whisk spinning inside him again, faster and faster. "I *might have* learned that they didn't abandon me after all. From what the vicar says, they were good people. So they likely didn't deserve all the hatred I unleashed on them in my thoughts over the years. And I'm learning all this now, only to lose them all over again. I dunno how you'd manage all this but, for me, it's a great deal to take in all at once."

"Oh, Raven, I . . ."

Her words trailed off as her blue eyes started to brim with an ocean of tears, her trembling fingertips covering her mouth.

Bloody hell. This was why he kept his thoughts private.

Pulling her close, he wrapped his arms around her and tucked her cheek against his chest. "Don't cry, little professor. If you do, then I'll have to kiss you and we both know where that will lead." Pressing his lips against the top of her head, he inhaled the soft fragrance of her hair on a deep comforting breath. "In a fit of passion, I'd carry you to that tree line over there for a bit of privacy in order to ravish you thoroughly on a bed of pine needles. You'd get sap in your hair. I'd stain my trousers . . ."

He affected a sigh of inconvenience and gained the quiet laugh he was hoping for. But as he held her, his body began to warm to the idea. He even glanced to the edge of the surrounding forest, where sunlight speared through evergreen boughs and gilded the tips of the stubborn oak and maple leaves that had yet to fall. A bed of pine needles wouldn't be all that bad . . .

"Then I shall not cry," she said, surreptitiously swiping a hand against her cheek on a sniff. Then she smiled wanly up at him and pressed her hands against his chest to ease out of his embrace. "Besides, a gentleman would not unleash his feral appetite in public. And we should not stand thusly either. One always has to presume there are unseen eyes watching."

She took her empty glove from him and proceeded to slip her fingers into it, but Raven confiscated it again, enfolding her delicate hand once more. Then he set off down the hill, along the winding, overgrown lane.

"You cannot do this either," she chided with a gentle squeeze before she withdrew.

He frowned. "Why not?"

"Pressing hands is something men and women only do when they have an understanding."

"I understand you well enough," he said with a shrug and snatched her hand again, tugging her closer to lift it to his lips. And it was clear that she understood him, too.

"No," she said with a small laugh. "I meant that they have pledged themselves to each other. That they will marry."

He eyed her dubiously then curled her arm over his sleeve, because he knew she couldn't argue against propriety.

"Surely, you don't have an understanding with all the men you dance with, or those who assist you out of a carriage?" He gave her a look of mock gravity. "There are laws against marrying so many men, Jane."

"Tease if you like, but you will have to adhere to these rules if you wish to go further in society."

"I don't care about claiming some clodpole title. What would I do with an earldom?"

"I shudder to think," she quipped, grinning up at him. Then, her expression sobered. "I don't believe you're the scheming sort, but rather a man who wants to claim the family he never had."

"Little good it does me now . . . *if* any of this is even true." He made an absent gesture over his shoulder and they both turned their heads to glance up the hill toward the emptiness where a grand house once stood.

To believe that a child had survived such complete devastation seemed too unrealistic. A mere fable.

"But if it is true, there is a brighter side. Your grandfather is alive. You could meet him, perhaps."

"I'd like that," he said, surprising himself with the reflexive and unguarded reply. Uncomfortable, he cleared his throat and added, "Just to have a look at him, that's all. To a bloke like me, seeing an earl would be like touring the curiosity shop."

She gave him a knowing sideways glance. "You don't have to be nervous. Remember what the vicar said—the Earl of Warrister is still holding onto hope. I'm sure he would be glad to meet you as well."

"Apparently, you forgot about the charlatans. He's probably grown leery over the years. I know I would have done."

"Hmm . . . true. And there's Lord Herrington to consider. He would be your biggest adversary. Not to mention, you would have the entire *ton* to win over." She speculated over this in the silent movement of her lips and he knew she was thinking of a plan. "If you are to meet your grandfather, you should be fully prepared with the ways of society before entering a hostile environment."

"What do you have in mind, then? Going to tutor me, Jane? Teach me your ways?" His voice dipped lower and he winked. "I'll teach you some of mine, if you like."

She laughed. "I think I've already gained an understanding of *your* ways."

It was on the tip of his tongue to tell her that it wasn't all about kissing for him. He liked her. In fact, he'd never been with a woman in this way before, conversing and sharing ideas and such. And it wasn't half bad.

Yet, in the end, Raven didn't say it.

"I'm not going to change the man I am," he said firmly. "I don't need any lessons on how to behave in society because I don't live in your world. *If* I ever decide to meet the earl, it will be on my own terms."

"Very well," she said with a resigned sigh. "Then I suppose, the only thing left to find out is where his lordship currently resides. Though, I have a faint recollection of someone mentioning that he kept a town house in St. James's Square, once upon a time. But it would have been closed up for years now. I could ask Ellie's aunts, of course. They are the only ones I could trust to keep this quiet and, better yet, they know the names and whereabouts of absolutely every unmarried or widowed gentleman in society."

"Quite an interesting skill to have."

"Oh, they're not alone by any means. The *ton* is filled with aunts, mothers and debutantes with that very same preoccupation. You'd be surprised by how aggressive and intimidating an aristocratic female can be when given the right incentive. Which, I'm certain, you'll discover for yourself when you change your mind and decide to pursue your birthright."

"That isn't going to happen," he said, but with a trace of wry amusement at her doggedness. "And your sheer determination will not make it so. My own will is as solid as granite."

He kicked a stone on the path with the toe of his weathered boot to punctuate his statement. It skittered to a stop a dozen paces in front of her.

Taking her turn at it, Jane gripped his forearm to keep her balance and sent the rock sailing up ahead, off the path and down the slope of the ditch. Smirking up at him, she added, "Then, perhaps, it is equally as moveable."

Unable to help himself, he laughed. He'd never met anyone like Jane Pickerington.

Together, they walked the rest of the way in companionable conversation, with her speaking about the hazards of having tea with the dragons of society who were sticklers on propriety. The tales of napkin and fan debacles kept him in a state of curious amusement. She truly lived in a world apart from him.

Too soon, they rounded the bend where Jane's carriage waited. The driver offered a friendly wave and lifted a paper-wrapped parcel.

Jane waved her bare fingers in a cascade, her flesh tinged pink from cold, and Raven recalled that he was still holding her glove. Distractedly, he returned it to her.

"And what's all that about?" he asked with a nod toward the driver.

"Nothing really," she said, nonchalantly slipping into the kid leather that had been dyed to match her pelisse. "When I hired his carriage this morning, he was somewhat reluctant to drive out of London with only a single occupant's fare. I explained that I was writing a book and that my errand was vital. This gained his interest. He then shared his own desire to write a book but that he'd never taken the time to begin. This was when I informed him that Hertfordshire made the finest paper, and perhaps, all he needed to inspire him were the proper supplies. Fortunately for me, Ellie and I had stopped by the little shop when we were here yesterday so I knew they had a lovely selection of stationery."

"And what would you have said if you'd met a driver who hadn't wanted to write a book?"

"The odds of that were quite slim. I haven't encountered a driver yet who didn't have a few stories to tell."

Raven felt the flesh of his brow furrow, his mouth drawing taut, his mood darkening. "Crafty one, aren't you?"

"Merely informative."

"But you got what you wanted anyway."

"It's lovely when the two coincide," she said, her lips curling in a pleased as punch grin.

But Raven wasn't smiling as they reached the carriage. For someone as brilliant as Jane, she seemed wholly unaware of the things that could have gone wrong.

He growled down at her. "You need to stop putting yourself in danger. No more of this flitting off on your own for research nonsense."

"But I wasn't alone, was I?" she challenged smugly. "You were riding behind my carriage the entire way."

Firm in his resolve, he held her gaze as his hand lifted to cup the delicate line of her jaw. He was surprised by the gentleness of his touch when he felt such a powerful, unexplainable vehemence coursing through him. "No more acting on whatever impulse comes to mind. I know you think you're always prepared. But if you truly care for your siblings, as you say you do, then stay out of any situation that requires whatever it is you carry in your reticule."

She stared back at him in perplexed silence, her lips unmoving. A crimson blush stole to her cheeks.

He anticipated her diatribe. She would come up with at least seven retorts on why she could do as she pleased and how it shouldn't matter to him, regardless.

Raven tensed, welcoming the argument. She could say whatever she wished. He had a counterargument and deflection for all of it at the ready.

But what he didn't expect was her quiet, acquiescent, "Very well."

Her eyes turned petal soft as she gazed up at him as if suspecting some tender emotion was behind his command. But she kept the accusation to herself.

This exchange left him unsettled. The muscles along his shoulders and neck were as tight as a yoke. He would have felt better arguing with her.

Handing her into the carriage, he eyed her shrewdly, thinking that this was another easy victory. Too easy.

He studied her every gesture for a sign of deception. But he found nothing amiss in the graceful way she lowered her hood then carefully arranged her skirts, or in the subtle shift of her feet that brought the small toes of her leather half boots peeking out from beneath her hem.

What he did find was a scattering of burs gripping the red wool. He began to pluck them away, and his tension gradually receded with each pointy barb he tossed to the ground.

In turn, she sat forward to groom him, brushing a lace-bitten leaf from his sleeve as if these intimacies were perfectly natural. They may well be for her, given her caring nature. But they weren't for him.

He'd never taken hold of a woman's hem without intending to lift it.

The temptation to explore the inner pleats and ruffles to trace the slender, stockinged ankle and trim calf was there, of course, but he didn't give in to it. When the burs were gone, he slipped away and put his hand on the door instead.

Strangely, he felt better now, more himself. Whoever that was.

"Oh, I nearly forgot," she said, reaching into her reticule. Withdrawing a small object wrapped in brown paper and a string, she handed it to him. "This is for you."

He took it, weighing it in his grasp, eyeing it carefully. "And what is it?"

"Damson jam," she said with a smile on her lips and in the new-bellflower blue of her eyes.

Reflexively, his fingers tightened over the parcel and he wordlessly nodded his thanks.

"By tomorrow," she continued, "I should have more information from Ellie's aunts about the Earl of Warrister, including where he resides. Will you come to the house for tea?"

The question took Raven off guard on a rise of reluctant amusement. First a gift of damson jam and then an invitation to tea? When had his life turned into this?

It was all because of her, he thought ruefully.

A smirk tugged at his mouth. "Yes, Jane. I'll come to tea."

✤✤✤✤

BUT RAVEN didn't wait for Jane to tell him where the Earl of Warrister had once resided. He'd found out on his own.

The following morning, dressed in a working man's suit and reeking of patron-sloshed whisky, he walked steadily on the pavement through St. James's. These early hours were lit only by lamplight shimmering through a silver-gray veil of fog.

His measured footfalls echoed off the towering white stone facades. There was no hurry in his pace. This was only a stroll. A mere stretch of the legs, he told himself.

After a long night of calling out cheats and breaking up drunken brawls, he needed to walk. Needed to quiet the restlessness that had been accumulating in his limbs since the chapel vestry in Hertfordshire.

And while he didn't want to admit that he'd left Sterling's gaming hell with a destination in mind, his stride slowed and gradually halted altogether not too far from a pair of ivory columns flanking a broad black door. Which happened to lead inside the grand town house of the Earl of Warrister.

He didn't plan to linger overlong, or to speculate what rooms lay behind the windowpanes and tightly closed curtains. He tried not to wonder about the portraits hanging above mantels, in halls, or climbing the staircases that might contain a face distantly similar to his own.

He failed in his attempts, so much so that he didn't hear the quick step clipping along the pavement until a willowy form collided with him. The startled face of an older woman looked up from beneath the brim of the black bonnet she was clutching to the top of her head.

"Dear me!" she said, her eyes growing wider and wider the more she looked at him. And once again, she called out in a fretful tremble, "Dear me!"

Enswathed in guilt for having lingered in this place for too long, Raven lifted his hands slowly so as not to startle her more. "I mean you no harm, ma'am. Merely on my way home after a long night of work. Beg your pardon."

And with that, he left abruptly in a swirl of fog, hearing faintly in the distance behind him another "Dear me!"

Chapter 16

Jane was determined to convince Raven to pursue his birthright.

He could deny his interest all he wanted to, but she knew better. As he'd gazed at the scorched remainders of the Northcott manor, his desire to have answers for his life and to know his own family had been written all over his face. And the pain of his loss had been just as apparent in the fervent clasp of his hand.

For such a hard-edged scoundrel, however, he was terribly skittish about moving forward.

Therefore, she planned to make Raven's transition into society as smooth and gradual as a fish reanimating after a winter thaw. Then, before he even realized it, he would be swimming effortlessly into the life that had always been meant for him.

He'd come much closer to believing yesterday. She only hoped he didn't return to second-guessing as he tended to do.

To keep progress moving in the right direction, she decided that tea should be without any fuss or ostentation. She'd serve it in the morning room—or the Gull Parlor, as she called it, given the seaside mural outside the door. The cerulean blue walls and the butter-colored damask upholstered chairs, surrounding a simple table, provided an easy and relaxed environment. Aside from the conservatory, it was the most modestly decorated of all the rooms in Holly

House. And it was imperative that this tea was particularly unassuming.

So, with that thought in mind, she went to the kitchens.

"A brown Betty pot and the plain porcelain teacups and saucers that the children use will do nicely," she said to the dimpled Mrs. Dunkley who'd been with the family since before Jane was born.

The cook wiped the back of a flour-dredged hand against the frown corrugating her forehead to brush aside a hank of short, silver-blond curls beneath a ruffled cap. "Surely, Miss Parrish would take offense to using such meager wares. You two girls having a spat?"

"No, indeed. Ellie and I are still the best of friends," Jane said absently, busy examining the hole-punch perforations on a tin box grater. Angling away from the trestle work table, she held it up to the window in speculation. She then picked up a nutmeg grater and gave it the same attention.

"Well, if that's true, I'm not sure I understand the point of it."

Still distracted, Jane only listened with half an ear as she then studied a round, low-walled sieve. She ran her fingertip over the fine screen that was used for making caster sugar, after it had been cut from the large conical loaf and thoroughly pounded to separate the granules.

"The truth of the matter is," she said after realizing her response was required, "I've also invited a gentleman and this tea is more for him than anyone else. I want it to be perfect and plain."

Holding the sieve aloft, a dusting of residual downy sugar fell on her face. She summarily fell into sputtering and sneezing and missed the instant when Mrs. Dunkley's eyes brightened with sudden clarity.

"Splendid. Then it'll be just as you asked for, miss. *Perfect* for your gentleman."

The sound of a peculiar lilt drew Jane's attention to the—now beaming—cook. She knew at once there'd been a misunderstanding.

"And plain," Jane reiterated, brushing away the sugar from her cheeks and lips. "It's imperative that we don't scare him off."

"I'll make it plain as the nose on his face," Mrs. Dunkley assured with an even bigger grin.

Glad that was settled, Jane left the kitchens with a quick, light step.

In the main hall, she passed Mr. Miggins, who informed her that Miss Parrish had arrived and was waiting in the conservatory. Wasting no time, she went directly to Ellie and summarily learned all the pertinent information on the Earl of Warrister and where he resided.

Yet, when it was all laid before her, a shadow of gloom seemed to hover coldly nearby.

"In Bath all these years," Jane said on a sigh, chafing her hands over the long gigot sleeves of her lilac dress. "Is his health truly so dire?"

Ellie shook her dark head. "No one knows. The earl does not go to the Pump Room but has the water brought to him. Though, since he has been out of society for a number of years, it is likely that he's infirm. Or worse."

"Let us hope that his lordship is not flirting with the specter of Death quite yet, for Raven's sake." Standing at her desk, she absently traced the sketch she'd drawn of the Northcott family seal. "I don't want Raven to face any more disappointments than he already has done."

"Are you certain it is ideal for you to spend so much time with a man you met in a brothel? Your parents would surely not approve if they found out their daughter had a frequent male visitor who was neither a gentleman nor courting her in the open. Are you not concerned for the safety of your virtue, if not your reputation?" Ellie asked from behind her.

Jane scoffed. "Raven is hardly courting me and has likely never given the notion an inkling. But he is a gentleman, at least by birth. We just have to prove it. That is why I feel compelled to aid him in his quest." Turning around, she saw a pair of amber eyes drawn tight with concern, sooty lashes bunching together. Placating her friend, she added, "As for my reputation, I will take better care than I have done thus far. And I won't even think about visiting another brothel for the time being."

"Thank the saints for small favors," Ellie muttered wryly. "But you neglected to say whether or not you are concerned that he might try to seduce you."

Jane had given this matter some thought. After analyzing the moments that preceded the kiss and then the stripping of her glove before holding her hand, she'd come to the conclusion that this was merely part of Raven's lexicon.

Whenever he met with information that was new and perhaps overwhelming, he processed the feelings in a more primitively physical manner rather than a verbal one. It really had nothing to do with *her* appeal or lack thereof.

But on the other side of that coin was the fact that she'd learned a heady amount of useful information about her own physiology and the delicious sensations a debutante might experience when confronted by a skilled seducer. And any scientist who set out to study the differences between gentlemen and scoundrels wouldn't think of stopping quite yet.

After all, it was vital to note these things for the primer.

Therefore, if she managed to convince him to continue onward and he happened to kiss her again . . . well . . . she decided to persevere. For the sake of research.

"Never fear," she said to Ellie. "I have everything under control. There is absolutely no need to fret about my virtue."

Unfortunately, any possibility of convincing Ellie of that fact was obliterated a moment later when Raven came to the conservatory door.

A rush of eagerness made Jane's pulse skip with light effervescence as she traipsed down the leaf-crowded path to let him in.

Instead of coming directly inside, Raven stared at her with a quizzical arch of his brow. "Little professor, why are you covered in prisms? You're practically glowing in the sunlight."

Dimly, she looked down. Her trim bodice and the modest inches of exposed flesh above it were speckled.

"Hmm . . . and so I am," she said, absently brushing at them. "I was in the kitchen a moment ago and started to wonder if the grating devices would be sturdy enough for ice, in order to make a false snow on Christmas morning for the children, if need be. Though, it appears I've covered myself in sugar, nutmeg and"—she paused to inspect an opaque white morsel with a sniff—"cheese."

"Had I known you were serving yourself for tea, I'd have arrived much earlier." A simmering pair of gray eyes roved over her in a slow but thorough sweep. He reached out to brush her cheek with the pad of his thumb, then put it to his lips. "Mmm . . . you are positively scrumptious."

His low growl of appreciation sent floods of scalding heat to every exposed inch of her epidermis. And every un-exposed inch as well.

From behind her, she heard a delicate cough. *Ellie!* She'd nearly forgotten. And now her friend had likely heard an earful that would cast doubt on Jane's previous statement.

Trying to compose herself, Jane willed her cheeks to cool. It would be much more effective if she had a fan to wave or a sudden blizzard to walk through. "I've invited Ellie to our tea. I'd like to introduce you, if I may."

"All three of us? This high-society tea is getting more interesting by the moment." He clucked his tongue in mock scolding, his gaze warm and playful as he leaned in to whisper, "I s'pose I should've known about your wicked tendencies, considering where I found your glove the night we met."

"My *glo*—" Jane stopped, and she knew her eyes must be as round as magnification lenses. *The statue. The phallus. Newton's apple!* "It was all perfectly innocent, I assure you."

A slow grin curled his lips. "Strange, but I'd always thought the word *innocent* meant something else entirely."

Turning away from him before her cheeks actually combusted, she walked back to where Ellie was waiting.

Her friend's expression possessed a wealth of speculation. But Jane merely shrugged her shoulders and shook her head as if to say that none of what she'd overheard had been a real flirtation.

Behind her, Raven prowled into the open glade to join them. He'd taken his hat and gloves off on the way, tossing them both on top of the desk with a careless air. This left him in a gray coat that fit the breadth of his shoulders to perfection, the brushed wool only a shade or two darker than his eyes. His simply knotted white neckcloth made his dark features and rakish grin all the more disarming.

Ellie's eyes widened. Her cheeks slowly saturated with the pink flush of appreciation—a telltale sign that her heart was beating faster.

Jane couldn't blame her. In fact, her own heart had been suffering frequent bouts of arrhythmia ever since she'd met him. She'd tried several herbal amalgamations, steeped into teas but, thus far, none of them provided suitable cures.

"Raven," Jane said, hoping he would begin to behave with

a semblance of propriety, "I should like to introduce you to my dear friend, Miss Elodie Parrish. Ellie, this is Raven."

The scoundrel stepped forward and took Ellie's gloved hand, bringing it to his lips. "You're even lovelier when awake, Miss Parrish."

Ellie's porcelain complexion turned scarlet and she was unable to form a coherent response. "I . . . hmm . . . that is . . . I believe . . . you're quite . . . yes, indeed."

He was certainly not on his best behavior. In fact, he seemed to have come here with the clear intent to scandalize.

"Raven, kindly release my friend from the thrall of your potent masculinity," Jane said dryly. Then, under her breath, she added, "We are not a pair of cyprians you can balance on your knees."

But the scoundrel heard and slid her a knowing look as if he thought her jealous. *Absurd!* He chuckled and dropped the hand—paying no attention to the way Ellie staggered back a step, gripping the table for support—as he moved closer to Jane.

"Your pixie wings are flared," he murmured in her ear with amusement.

The low vibrations of his deep voice tunneled through her in tornado swirls of tingles and flutters, distracting her. Otherwise, she never would have allowed him to take her own hand and curl it around his arm. By the time she realized it, her fingertips were pressed firmly, almost possessively, to the coarse wool of his sleeve.

Her own response confused her. After all, Ellie was her co-author. An understanding of scoundrels would benefit them both.

And yet, Jane realized with a degree of befuddled dismay, she did not want to share him.

"So, where's this tea, hmm?" he asked with an uncharacteristic eagerness that drew her thoughts away from the surprising conclusion. He even flashed a practiced smile. "Been saving my appetite all day for these high-society victuals."

The tense emphasis he continued to put on the words *high society* offered Jane a sudden insight into his overtly flirtatious behavior. He was acting as though he were being cornered again, and his manner of lashing out in defense was by saying shocking things.

She brushed her fingertips soothingly over his sleeve before she led him out of the conservatory, and hoped that Ellie had recovered enough to follow.

"I'm afraid this will greatly disappoint you, then," Jane said with a glance over her shoulder to see that Ellie had come out of her daze and was joining them in the hall. "Tea, after all, is nothing more than leaves sitting in hot water."

He issued a grunt of disbelief as his gaze toured the polished marble floors and intricately molded arched ceiling. Then he gave a sideways glance to a baroque tapestry hanging above a pair of gilt bronze maiden lamps and a gold snuffbox, resting on a glossy bombe chest.

She didn't want him to focus on the disaster of opulence that had been born from her mother's desire to impress her guests, but to think of this as just another house.

"I'm in earnest," Jane said, drawing his attention back to her as they approached the seaside mural. "There will be scones and possibly a small sandwich or two. It will be much like our sharing tea and toast," she added quietly. "Nothing at all elaborate. This is merely a simple . . ."

She stopped just inside the parlor, stunned into silence.

Much to her dismay, the modest room had been completely transformed by a buffet fit for the king. Atop the humble round table—now draped in crisp white linen—was a centerpiece of a swan ice sculpture with ornately carved fruits piled between its wings. A bouquet of celeries in a crystal vase stood beneath its graceful neck. And on silver platters and pedestals sat an assortment of cakes, tarts, and scones, along with a hilltop of small meat pies surrounded by a valley of sandwiches and hardboiled eggs.

"Nothing at all elaborate," Raven mocked with a laugh. "Jane, I think I should read your dictionary. Mine clearly doesn't have the right definitions for some of the words you use."

⁂

BY THE time tea was over, Raven felt more relaxed. Part of it was because he'd gorged himself on plates upon plates of delicious food until his appetite was subdued. And part of it—perhaps even most of it—was because of Jane.

She quieted the restless sense of separation he'd felt all his life. Her peculiar observations and unaffected airs were a welcome reprieve from the world he knew. And now that it was just the two of them, standing alone at the conservatory door, he almost hated to leave.

"I can see why you became friends with Miss Parrish. Much like you, she isn't at all stuffy or condescending, but charming in her own way," he said truthfully.

She was also pretty, polite and quick to blush. Raven could tell that he made her nervous. She'd cast surreptitious glances toward him throughout the hour, like a visitor to a zoo checking to see whether the lock on a lion's cage was secure or not. And he'd rattled the bars a bit, flirting outrageously for his own amusement *and* to make Jane jealous again.

For reasons unbeknownst to him, he felt a perverse amount of satisfaction every time he saw the flash of a thunderstorm darken her eyes. Just like now.

"Yes, Ellie is quite charming," Jane said tersely. "Though I regret to inform you that she has been in love with her next-door neighbor for most of her life and has little interest in any other men, not even for a mere flirtation. So, perhaps, you should focus on the information she brought with her rather than her *charm*."

"Jane," he crooned, "you know I only want to flirt with you. Come now, don't be so cross."

"I'm not cross. I'm just—" She bit down on the rest of her reply, pressing that delectable mouth in a stubborn line. Then she straightened, chin high. "Today we learned that the earl resides in Bath. Do you intend to visit him and introduce yourself?"

"No and no," he answered. "By all accounts, he sounds frail and, as much as I might have liked to meet him, I would not jeopardize his health by causing him undue stress."

Raven had made the swift decision when he'd first learned the news from Miss Parrish. It was difficult to think of getting this close to potentially knowing his family only to stop, but he knew it was the right thing to do.

"But what if you had proof before you introduced yourself? Surely that would only bring the earl joy."

"And just when did this proof suddenly come into being? I'm afraid I missed that part of our tea conversation," he said wryly.

"I was thinking that my uncle might know something. After all, we did find the letter in his possessions. It's possible he was still working for them after you were born, or even knew of people who tended to come and go from the manor house . . . like someone who may have rescued a child from the fire?"

"The odds of that are unlikely," he said. "Besides, I don't believe the person who left a child on the doorstep of the foundling home wants to be found."

"True, but my uncle is our only link to your family. It would make sense to explore all avenues," she said with a slight shrug.

The sunlight streaming in through the diamond window-panes caught the movement, gilding her skin with myriad sugar-sweet sparkles. Imagining how they would melt on his tongue, his mouth abruptly watered. His sated appetite roused again with vigor, pulling him a step closer.

"Of course," she continued, oblivious to the new directions of his thoughts, "it would make sense for me to go with you. But my parents do not approve of me visiting the debtor's prison. They prefer to distance the entire family from the black sheep for the sake of our collective reputation, such as it is. And, sadly, my uncle abides by their wishes by telling the turnkey to keep me out whenever I've made an attempt to see him."

Raven heard the hint of dejection in her voice and set his hand on her shoulder to soothe her. But his thumb strayed beyond the ribbon trim to the softness of her exposed skin. The slight contact caused her breath to hitch, lips parting, her skin reacting in an instant rise of gooseflesh.

Their gazes met—his hungry, hers shocked at first, then openly curious. Whatever conversation they were in the midst of was now gone from his mind.

He was fascinated by her in ways he couldn't explain. He wanted to see the world through her eyes. Wanted to explore it and taste it and touch it through her senses.

With the pad of his thumb and then the tips of each finger, one after the other, he slowly traced the delicate decline of her clavicle, from the silken crest of her shoulder to the base of her throat. And by the time he reached the V-shaped niche, a sheen of perspiration bloomed on her newly flushed skin, dissolving the wayward sugar particles into an irresistible glaze.

"You shouldn't look at me that way," she said on a panted breath, "as if you intend to kiss me . . . in the full light of day . . . when anyone could happen upon us."

"If it's any consolation, I wasn't planning to," he said. "But this is your own fault, you know. You failed to calculate a scoundrel's restraint when faced with a sugarcoated bluestocking." Crowding closer, he drew her scent deeply into his nostrils. "Now hold still, Jane. I'm going to need a minute to examine my findings."

He lowered his head and felt her tremble beneath the brush of his lips in that delicate hollow. Heard the soft broken sigh she expelled at the first warm lick. Tasted the sweet vibration of her passion-laced mewl as she unabashedly arched her neck for him.

"Oh," she breathed and her hands found purchase on his shoulders.

He slid his arms around her waist, pulling her into the bow of his body. "You like this, hmm?"

"Mmmhmm," she hummed, her fingertips skimming through his hair. "I've quickly concluded that the heated, salebrous texture of your tongue is quite . . . beyond exceptional. And that flicking, swirling motion you're doing is causing the most wondrous arrhythmia."

He smiled against her delicious skin. No one else could make scientific deduction sound so erotic.

His lips grazed over the column of her throat to the fluttering pulse. There, he tenderly laved each harried beat before he blew a hot breath over that vulnerable place.

But she was right. This small sampling of her flesh was too dangerous. He could easily lose himself in her taste and soft sounds of pleasure and forget that there was a houseful of people nearby.

So, while he was still able, he straightened.

She whimpered softly in protest as he held her trembling body close. Her hand drifted down from his nape to his chest, beside her resting cheek.

"You did it again," she said after a moment. "We were in

the middle of discussing ways to discover more about your family and then you tried to distract me with seduction."

He pressed his lips to the top of her head. "Not so. It was you who did the distracting *and* the seducing by dressing yourself as a confection. I am an innocent pawn in your scheme, madam. But I am magnanimous enough to forgive you."

"How kind," she said with a laugh and eased out of his embrace to stand apart. "Then what do you say to meeting my uncle?"

She was shamelessly tenacious. Briefly, Raven wondered what it would be like to have all of her driving focus centered on him *and* on pleasure instead.

Dangerous was the answer and he decided to leave that thought alone.

"I say that it is fortunate for you that I know the turnkey."

"You do?" She smiled at him, her eyes so bright and clear, they were almost violet in their brilliance. "Does this mean you're willing to pursue your birthright, even without my incessant prodding?"

He knew what she wanted to hear—that he knew he was Merrick Northcott, the infant that had somehow survived the fire. But he couldn't allow himself to believe it. He knew the bitter disappointments that awaited him too well.

Raven denied it with a shake of his head. "I'm doing this because, if I didn't, you'd likely try something dangerous to manage it on your own. I already know you too well. I'm likely the only one of your acquaintances that can smuggle you inside the prison safely. And"—he paused to tuck a wayward chestnut wisp behind her ear—"it's clear from the wistful sound of your voice whenever you speak of your uncle that you miss him."

"Greatly," she said. "I am indebted to him for shaping my

life into what it has become. He's the one who first taught me to read, and that I could find answers in books."

His fingertips trailed along her jaw to the tip of her chin as he gazed down at her, feeling none of the chill that seeped in through the crack in the door, but only the warmth of that November sunlight inside him.

"I have a sense that you would have found all the answers regardless," he said. "It's that lion's share of determination in your blood."

Her lips curved in a smile so soft and welcoming that he wanted to feel it against his own. But before she could tempt him any further, Raven left her standing there, wishing he didn't still have the taste of her on his tongue.

Chapter 17

A week later, a dingy yellow hackney drove Jane to Fleet, bumping along the streets on a dreary overcast morning. Peering through the small window, she saw Raven waiting for her outside the iron gate of the debtor's prison.

Beneath the brim of his hat, his storm-cloud eyes watched the carriage come to a stop. Without a word of greeting, he swiftly opened the door and slipped a parcel inside. "Put this over your head before anyone sees you. I had to pull some strings to make sure no one would be asking too many questions. From what I gather, everyone knows everyone else's business around here. So, today, you're the widowed sister of Bill-Jack Rollins."

"And who is Mr. Rollins?" she asked, unfolding a length of black lace from the unwrapped paper and slipped the mourning veil in place.

Raven disappeared for an instant to toss a coin up to pay the driver and bid him to wait. Then he returned with his grumbled answer. "Just someone I knew from my other life."

Reaching inside with impatience, he set his hands around her waist, assisting her to the ground. He secured her arm in the crook of his, then cast a furtive glance around as they approached the gate.

The turnkey eyed them with a brown-eyed glare and an intimidating set to his square unshaven jaw. The man was stocky-framed and sure of himself. He wore the brim of his hat pulled low, which cast eerie shadows over his features. And he had the look of a hardened prisoner, not of a man who kept them locked up.

Jane crowded closer to Raven, a fierce shiver stumbling through her. Perhaps this wasn't such a grand idea.

The man set the key inside the lock and the mechanism tumbled with an ominous *clank*. Then the heavy door groaned open.

With an impatient gestured, he bid them inside the fortified gatehouse before closing the door behind them. After a quick glance around, the man reached out and punched Raven on the shoulder, hard. "Why, you old dog."

"Hullo, Bill-Jack," Raven answered with a reluctant grin.

"Just look at us scrawny saplings now. All those days of trying to outrun Devil Devons 'as made the pair of us into 'andsome blokes. Yes, indeed. A' course I see a few o' the others from the workhouse, a time or two, strollin' in to visit the tenants. But most of 'em are up to no good, if ye ken my meanin'. Not like us respectable types." Bill-Jack puffed out his chest and guffawed, slapping Raven on the shoulder again. Then he turned to Jane and waggled his thick eyebrows. "And whot 'ave we got 'ere, a fine lady on your arm, eh? Must be someone special for you to bring 'ere. From what I recall, you ain't too fond of boxes or places wif locks on the outside."

Raven stiffened beside her and beneath her hand, she felt the muscles tense. "Some things are better off forgotten."

"Yeh," Bill-Jack uttered on a heavy exhale, his eyes appearing unfocused and distant. "But I still think about those two days you spent shackled in the cupboard while that devil got 'iself killed in the alleyway. Blimey! Must've been awful with the rats and such."

Jane's breath caught and her gaze shot to Raven. His profile revealed nothing, but she felt the confirmation of the story in the shudder that coursed through him. But all he said was, "I'd rather not talk about that, if it's all the same to you."

Her stomach turned, roiling at the frightful visions trampling through her mind. She'd been naive to imagine that being an orphan and having no family to comfort him had been the worst he'd suffered. What other horrors had he experienced?

As if knowing her every thought, he flicked a disapproving glance down at her and issued a short, low growl.

He didn't want her pity. But that wasn't what she was feeling. She hated what he'd suffered. If it was in her power, she would ensure that the rest of his life was wholly different than the beginning. And if she could just prove his identity and help to prepare him for society, then perhaps it would be.

"A' course. A' course," Bill-Jack said with a nod. "That's all behind us now."

Raven reached out to shake his hand. "Much appreciated for all you've done today and"—he paused, and cleared the gruffness from his throat—"for all you did back then."

Bill-Jack pumped his fist and clapped him on the shoulder with a wink. "Who'd've thought the two of us would end up being the ones who survived it all? But I just followed your lead. Wily as ever, I always knew you'd come out of it. Born under a lucky star, you were." Then he turned his attention to Jane and flashed a yellowed grin. "Take good care a' this bloke, eh? If it wasn't for 'im, I'd a starved to death nine times over."

"I will. I promise." Jane extended her hand as well, and Bill-Jack grinned shyly as he wiped his own against his trouser leg before accepting. "Thank you for this favor. If there is anything you need, please don't hesitate to ask."

"Aw, it ain't nothing. It's like I said, if not for this bloke, I wouldn't be 'ere. Now, I got myself a right good job 'ere and a family at 'ome. One little 'un and one more on the way."

He gestured with a jerk of his head. "That's the door over there. Just follow me."

They walked through a courtyard, passing bedraggled children at their games, chatting women at their needlework, and harried men at their pacing. Entering the prison, they climbed the stairs to the gallery like mourners in a slow procession. All the while, she was still haunted by the images in her mind of Raven as a boy, locked in a cabinet filled with rats. Tears collected in the back of her throat, stinging the corners of her eyes.

He expelled a resigned breath and bent his head to whisper, "Put it out of your mind. Don't let it become part of you, too."

She wobbled her head in a nod and swallowed, glad he couldn't see her eyes.

Once they reached the upper gallery, she was able to focus on her surroundings. They moved through the narrow corridor, passing rooms on either side. Many doors were open, revealing lavishly furnished interiors with every luxury a man could want—canopied beds, brimming bookshelves, desks, tables and chairs.

Bill-Jack muttered that those were special acquaintances of the warden, indicating with a sly slide of his thumb over his fingers that monetary compensation was involved.

Reaching the last room at the end of the hall, Mr. Rollins gave a curt knock on an oaken door with substantial black iron hinges. He slid a metal plate to the side, allowing the faint gray light from the room within to slip through the exposed grille. "Yev got visitors, Mr. P."

Without waiting for a response, he turned the key in the lock. Jane stood in the doorway, waiting for the familiar sight of her uncle to appear.

Instead, an old man with a haggard face and sloped shoulders slowly stepped forward. He was pale and thin, aside from a paunch that pushed at the buttons of his camel waist-coat. His hair was a disheveled combination of brown and gray, and his green cutaway had a frayed hem.

His blue eyes raked over her and Raven with marked distrust.

Too unprepared for this alteration in him, Jane belatedly realized that she'd forgotten to remove her veil. She did so in that instant and tentatively stepped forward. "Good morning, uncle."

"Jane," he said flatly, his disapproving tone startling her even more.

An uncomfortable laugh tittered out of her and she felt Raven's arm at her elbow. "Are you not glad to see me?"

Her uncle began to mill anxiously around the room, straightening an upended cup that sat on a desk of cluttered papers. This was not as elaborately furnished as those others, but sparse and void of warmth. While he possessed a bucket of coal for the fireplace, there were only two pieces in the grate. His bed was little more than a straw pallet elevated no more than six inches from the floor. He had a rug, but it sat beneath a trunk, which lay open to reveal the disorder of clothes and books within. And yet, she knew her father paid handsomely for his upkeep, as well as a steady allowance to assist in paying off his debts. So, where was all the money being spent?

Surely a man who'd been in prison for a number of years would have wanted to make his room a home of sorts. Wouldn't he?

"You shouldn't have come. Think of your parents. If my brother were to find out . . ." He cast a cursory glance to Raven. "And who is this?"

"This is Raven. We are hoping you may have some information regarding his family. Do you recall tutoring a French woman to learn English?"

He waved his hand in a dismissive gesture before walking toward the window set high in the stone wall. "I've tutored many. It would be impossible to recall one without having my ledgers to consult."

"I hope you will forgive me, uncle, but I've looked through your ledgers. At least, the ones that are in the trunks you keep at our house. However, the dates we're interested in are from the latter part of the year 1799, and I noticed that there aren't any ledgers from that time."

The instant the words were out, Jane felt Raven's intense scrutiny on her profile. She realized that she hadn't pointed out this fact to Raven on the day they'd found the letter, but hoped he didn't suspect her of withholding anything vital. After they'd discovered the image on the wax seal, all else had faded into unimportance.

Until now, when every detail seemed crucial to proving his identity.

Looking up at him, she saw that his brow was furrowed in contemplation, yet he offered her a quick nod of understanding.

She turned her attention back to her uncle. "I was hoping that you might have those ledgers here with—"

"No, I most certainly don't," he said before she could finish, his voice increasing in volume and agitation. "And why would I? It has been so many years since I've been part of that world. Most of it is lost to me. It will be many more years to come before I've paid all the . . . debts I owe."

"What about the name Northcott?" Raven asked, surprising her. "Ring any bells?"

"It does not," Uncle John responded hastily, without even pausing long enough to draw in a single breath or bat an eyelash. His left hand started to twitch, tooth-bitten fingernails snagging against the side of his trousers. "You never should have brought her here. My niece is the firstborn daughter

184 VIVIENNE LORRET

of a viscount. She has responsibilities to her family and a reputation to uphold in society. She cannot gallivant around in a debtor's prison. I don't know who you think you are but it is clear that you must cease your involvement with my niece at once."

Raven bowed stiffly without another word, then took a discreet step back. But Jane stayed by his side, curling her arm around his. "Uncle, he does not deserve your scorn. It was all my doing."

"Jane, you know you are expected to marry well, to increase the wealth of the family, to set an example for those who follow. Whatever I have done to sully the family, you and your siblings must undo. It is imperative. Therefore, you cannot waste time dallying with derelicts," he said, flicking a contemptuous glance to Raven.

She stiffened, taking umbrage. "You have no cause to speak to him so harshly. You know nothing about—"

"Go!" her uncle yelled, his color rising. Then suddenly, he came forward, advancing with threatening shooing motions, flinging his arms. "Go now."

She stumbled back, but Raven held her securely, guiding her safely past the threshold the instant before the door slammed shut, the echo reverberating through the corridor.

Jane was stunned. For the life of her, she couldn't understand his extreme agitation, as well as his instant dislike of Raven. It made no sense. And whyever would he call him a *derelict*, of all things?

Making one more attempt to gain something worthwhile from this hapless visit, she lifted her face toward the iron grille. "Uncle, if you remember anything about the Northcott family and your time with them, will you please write to me?"

"I will not recall the name," he shouted, adamant. "Now begone with you and do as I say. Take care that you abandon this newfound acquaintance of yours. It will come to no good."

That was the last glimpse she had of her beloved uncle. And with it, the last hope she had of discovering any information that might lead to proving Raven's identity seemed to fade, as well. What could they do now?

"I don't understand," she murmured, dejected. "He was never like this before."

Raven replaced the veil over her head. "Try not to hold on to this visit, little professor. Time in confinement will change any man. Some are hardened, while others break."

She nodded, taking comfort in his presence here with her, but not without a degree of guilt. After all, according to Bill-Jack's account, Raven had firsthand knowledge about time in confinement.

She swallowed down the tightness collecting in her throat as he drew her down the hall and toward the stairs. "I apologize for my part of this wasted morning. I truly thought he would know something, otherwise I never would have subjected you to coming here. I understand how you must abhor places like this. No wonder you were so gruff when I first arrived. Though, I wish you'd told me beforehand. I never would have put you through this."

"I wanted to do this for you," he said quietly as they approached the gatehouse, curling his hand over hers. "But my mood, such as it was, had nothing to do with being here and everything to do with a rumor I heard before I left Sterling's earlier this morning."

She lifted her face to his with inquiry and alertness, only to see him shake his head.

"Not yet," he said with a discreet nod toward Bill-Jack up ahead.

He waited until they bid farewell and the gate closed behind them. Then, once they were next to the hackney, he continued. "Late last night, there were some gents in the card room talking about the Earl of Warrister's return to London."

Jane gasped. "Do you think it's true?"

"They seemed convinced of it."

"Then he must not be as ill as we feared," she said in a rush, her spirits leavened by the news. "And you know what this means, don't you? There will be a caretaker or a housekeeper we could apply to for a tour of the house."

Raven made no comment, but she distinctly heard a grunt of interest escape his throat as he tried to appear aloof.

She smiled at this and slipped her hand in his with a tender squeeze. "There's no need to be nervous."

"I'm not," he said too quickly. Then he looked down at her through the veil and expelled a sigh as if he knew he wasn't fooling her. "Not much."

When he handed her inside the carriage, she worried that he might simply send her home without even considering it. So she tried harder to persuade him.

"No one would ever have to know. And"—she paused, hoping to incite his interest—"from what Ellie's aunts have said, his lordship has quite the extensive library."

Raven's expression remained unchanged.

In that instant, she began to fear that his stubborn resolve would mark the conclusion of their quest. After this failed visit with her uncle, their final avenue had reached a dead end. There was no reason to further their acquaintance.

Without his willingness to proceed—begrudging or otherwise—this truly would be the last time she would ever see him.

In the silence that stretched on between them, she knew that they both realized it.

He disappeared from the doorway, taking with him the only thing that brightened this dreadful morning. A bereft breath caught in her throat. She hadn't prepared herself for goodbye. There was nothing in her reticule for this.

Jane sank back in the seat, the veil hiding the tears collecting along the bottom rim of her eyes.

But then something unexpected happened. Raven returned and, as he climbed inside, called up to the driver, "St. James's Square."

Chapter 18

Raven didn't know how long he'd been sitting inside the carriage, peering past the window shade at the town house. But it was long enough that the driver banged his fist on the hood.

"In circumstances such as this," Jane said with a teasing tone from the other bench, "one usually walks up to the door and knocks. After all, if there is a housekeeper or caretaker inside, it is highly doubtful that he or she is privy to our thoughts and hopes of entering the house."

He slid her an unamused look. "I'm taking note of the surroundings. It's important to keep a watchful eye no matter where you are."

She nodded thoughtfully and pursed her lips. "I see what you mean. That scullery maid who just passed by, carrying the market basket, is clearly about to make turnips today, and that *is* a dreadful crime. No one likes turnips."

At the sight of her disarming grin, he instantly felt more at ease. He also felt like a fool for admitting to her earlier that he was nervous, but he could tell that she had known it anyway. Jane had an uncanny ability to see right through him. And for some reason that thought helped him breathe easier. The roiling sea inside his stomach faded to a gentle lapping wave.

Exiting the carriage, he handed her down and paid the driver, bidding the man once more to wait. But as he reflexively reached for Jane's hand, she withdrew and shook her head, moving further away.

He frowned and advanced to her side.

"It wouldn't be proper in this circumstance. Additionally," she added, "you cannot call me *Jane*. When in the presence of others, you must refer to me as Miss Pickerington. Using my given name suggests an intimacy of close acquaintances, an understanding between us, or—in your vernacular—that you have claimed me."

"I think I would have remembered that," he said, flashing a devilish grin.

When he faced forward, he saw that they were already at the steps. She'd done it again, distracting him just long enough to keep him from second-guessing, or wondering what he was going to say if someone opened the door.

Climbing the short rise of stone stairs, he felt her warm gaze on his profile and heard the tender smile on his lips when she whispered, "You'll do splendidly."

Straightening his shoulders, he drew in a deep breath and rapped his knuckles on the door.

It opened almost instantly. Unexpectedly. And by the very same woman who'd crashed into him on the street the other day.

"Dear me! I'm supposin' you're real after all," she said, though her doubtful expression and shake of her head seemed to contradict her statement. "Well then, you'd best come inside before there's a spectacle. Rumors'll be flyin' across chimney tops by day's end."

Confused, Raven looked over his shoulder toward the street but saw nothing amiss. Then again, this woman seemed to have a few dice missing from her cup.

"Are you the housekeeper?" he asked as they entered.

She bustled around them in a flurry to close the door. "Mrs. Bramly, at your service."

"We'd like a tour of the house," he said, getting straight to the point. But when Jane cleared her throat beside him, he added, "If that would be acceptable, ma'am."

He knew this wasn't going to work. After all, if some strangers had asked to take a look at his house, he'd be the first to show them the pavement instead. Then he'd leave his boot print on their arses.

But this skittish woman surprised him by saying, "Right this way, sir, miss."

Taking Jane's hand, he settled it over his sleeve. Before she could balk, he said to her, "There's no telling what condition these floors and those stairs are in. I could be saving your life."

She pretended to be exasperated, but he saw the smile tucked into the corner of her mouth.

They followed Mrs. Bramly out of the foyer and up a gleaming staircase. Raven absorbed every detail of wainscoting and gilded plaster molding as he moved from one archway to the next, their steps muffled on the runner. The scent of orange and clove pomanders tried to drive the mustiness away, but it hung on, clinging like damp shirtsleeves to the skin, impossible to ignore.

He looked around at all the polished candlesticks and gold-inlaid tables and pulled at his cravat. These long, narrow rooms were choking on fine furnishings, with little clocks and porcelain figurines on all the mantels. Each time his thigh bumped a marble table and nearly sent an oil lamp or a bit of bric-a-brac crashing to the floor he felt clumsy and closed in.

If it were up to him, he'd have opened these walls to make breathable spaces. A place where a man could think or read a book without suffocating to death.

In the back of his mind, he already knew this would be the only time he'd ever come.

The gents talking about Warrister's return at Sterling's

had speculated that the earl was coming here to name Lord Herrington his heir, and to give his blessing at last. The more Raven thought about that, the more he knew he didn't belong here.

He wasn't educated or reared like an aristocrat. He wasn't proper. And he never would be either, not with a past like his.

It was foolish to think that someone like him could just walk up to an earl and say, "Oh by the by, I think I'm your grandson."

So what in the hell was he doing here touring the house in the first place?

"Jane, this was a mistake," he said in her ear when they entered another long, narrow room. "Let's go back to the carriage, hmm?"

He was fine with his life just the way it was.

Beside him, Jane stopped but didn't respond. He squared his shoulders, preparing for her attempt to cajole him into finishing the tour.

But when he searched her face, he didn't find stubbornness. Instead, he found tears gathering in her eyes as she stared fixedly toward the wall ahead.

Instinctively, he gathered her close, while a few steps away he heard Mrs. Bramly's voice. "And this is the portrait gallery. Seven generations of the Northcott clan hang upon these walls . . ."

Slowly, Raven turned his head.

Then he stopped breathing. The pulse at his neck beat so fast that it caused a high-pitched ringing in his ears, like a wine-slicked finger sliding around the rim of a crystal goblet, over and over again.

All he could do was stare at the two figures in the portrait on the wall.

There was no need to read the engraved placard at the bottom of the frame. He knew who they were.

Edgar Northcott had been a tall, lean man with broad shoulders and a wealth of sandy brown hair that curled over his temples and brow. He had a hawklike nose and a hard-set jaw. His eyes were a periwinkle blue that seemed to glint with some unspoken secret, and an almost indiscernible smirk lifted one corner of his mouth.

And then there was Arabelle Northcott.

She wore a shimmering silver gown, with her hair piled high in an elaborate coiffure. Inky black ringlets cascaded down to frame the delicate features of her face—the fine arch of her brow, the slim line of her nose, and the angles of her cheeks, jaw and chin. She was beautiful.

But it was her eyes that arrested Raven. They were a soft, downy gray that seemed to reach out beyond the canvas and blanket him with their warmth.

He felt it in the center of his chest—a tender, burning ache. And suddenly he knew.

The breath fell out of him. The ringing in his ears turned into a deafening rush as his heart pounded in panicked beats inside his rib cage. Years of pain and longing and hope stormed through him all at once.

He looked to Jane but his vision was blurred, everything gray around the edges.

He needed to leave. Now.

Without a word, he left the gallery. He would apologize to Jane in a few moments when he could think. When he wasn't so overwhelmed.

Yet in his haste to retrace the steps they had taken, he ended up in an unfamiliar corridor, facing a stained door, partially ajar. He growled in self-irritation. Stripping off his hat, he raked a hand through his hair. Why did there have to be so many bloody rooms?

Trying to orient himself, he pushed open the door to see

if this was the one that led to the upper gallery and the stairs. But then he caught a scent that halted him in his tracks.

Before he could even blink to focus on where he stood, he knew he'd found the library—a room they hadn't had a chance to tour.

The air was permeated with the familiar sweet fragrance of old books that calmed his straining lungs and even quieted the roaring in his head. And he simply stood there in the partially open doorway to collect his thoughts.

His gaze roamed from floor to ceiling, each inch filled with books. A light flickered over a multitude of leather-bound spines and he heard the faint crackle of a fire in an unseen hearth.

He nudged the door wider, the hinges screeching in protest. And Raven stopped abruptly on the threshold the instant he realized he wasn't alone in this part of the house.

An elderly man sat in a wing-backed chair by the fire, wearing a burgundy velvet morning coat and a gray shawl draped over his lap. He seemed to be staring sightlessly into the flames, as if considering some great mystery of the ages.

Then he turned slowly toward the figure in the doorway. Without a start or a gasp, he merely said, "I thought you would come again."

"I beg your pardon, sir," Raven said in self-defense, feeling like a child caught shimmying into the baker's window. "But I've never been here before."

The man eyed him shrewdly. "Not inside perhaps. But you startled my housekeeper on the pavement a sennight ago. She wrote to tell me she'd seen a ghost."

Numbly, Raven absorbed this. He swallowed and could have sworn that the sound was loud enough to fill a theatre. "So then you are . . ."

"The one who owns this house."

His mind whispered *grandfather* in a hushed awe as if anything louder would disturb this hallucination and Raven would find himself out on the pavement, none of it real.

"Come closer. The firelight is dim and my eyes are far too old to discern one apparition from another."

Raven obliged and moved into the room.

"Uncanny," the man murmured under his breath. "You even walk like him. He always had something of a swagger. 'Proud and prowling,' his mother used to say when he would come home from school, eager to fit the world in the palm of his hand."

"Where did he go to school?" Raven heard himself ask, accepting this dream as reality. And that was only one of a thousand questions crowding on his tongue. *What was he like? What were his interests? Did he read all these books? Can I read them, too?*

"You don't know?" The old man scoffed. "Surely, you've done your research. You've been to Hertfordshire, after all. Aye, the vicar wrote to me as well."

"I didn't want to know too much. And yet," he said on a breath, feeling a need for complete honesty, "I wanted to know everything. That is the reason I startled your house-keeper on the pavement last week. I meant no harm, then or now. So, if you'd like me to go, you have but to say the word."

"Stay," he said without hesitation. "Sit by the fire if it's not too warm for you. My bones are like ashes that can no longer support an ember. Tell me, what brings you here at this particular time in the winter of this old man's life? Trickery? Deception?"

Raven smiled at this familiar cynical frankness. He understood it well.

Taking the invitation, he eased back into the opposite

chair and answered. "It all began last month, when a debutante turned me pink and robbed me of the life I knew . . ."

He told the story of the mark on his shoulder and how it led to a letter, which took them to Hertfordshire and the registry of parish births and deaths, and eventually to here.

The earl stared into the firelight, his bony hands steepled contemplatively. He never asked to see the mark, or for proof of the letter. He just listened, as if he'd been waiting in his chair for someone to step into this room and start telling him a grand, and even unbelievable, tale of an orphan found on a doorstep, once upon a time.

When Raven had finished, he was relieved to have it all out of him. It felt as though he'd overcome an illness and sweated a fever through his pores.

Remembering that Jane was likely waiting for him at the carriage, he rose. "I should go now. Jane is likely formulating a plan to find me, and one that involves at least three of the mysterious objects she keeps in her reticule."

No sooner had he spoken than he heard quick steps on the runner. Then he saw a blur of violet rush past the door and caught the faint scent of lavender swirling in the air. Striding to the door, he called her name.

She stopped at the end of the corridor, pivoted on her heel, and hastened back to him.

"There you are," she scolded, but her features were fraught with concern as she clasped his extended hand between both of hers. "I'd feared you'd gone, that this was all too much."

"Bring the worrywart in here. Let me meet her."

The instant Jane heard the old man's raspy voice, she paled and her wide eyes looked to the open doorway.

Raven grinned and tugged her into the room at his side. "This is Jane. And, Jane, this is the Earl of—"

"You may call me Ableforth," the old man said. "Formalities are often tiresome, especially later in life when there isn't anyone left to use your given name."

She curtsied low. "It is an honor to make your acquaintance . . . my lord . . . Ableforth."

The earl nodded, pleased. "So, you're the creator of pink smoking candles, hmm?"

Standing, she cast a startled—and accusatory—glance up to Raven as her cheeks turned the color of beet powder. He could tell by the faint tapping of her foot on the rug that he was going to get an earful for revealing her part in his story once they were back inside the carriage.

Smoothing her hands down her skirts, she cleared her throat and opened the cording of her reticule. Reaching inside, she withdrew a fat, bright green object and presented it in the palm of her hand. "As you see, they are not always pink. I've just made this one using dried mint leaves. I have not set a flame to it yet, but I hope the smoke will emit a pleasant aroma, rather than turning everyone and everything within its surroundings green."

The earl chuckled and steepled his fingers once more, keeping his thoughts hidden behind wizened periwinkle blue eyes. "Perhaps you'll discover the answer and inform me of the results on our next visit."

"It would be my honor," she said, curtsying again.

Raven sensed the man's requirement for solitude and peace. In fact, he needed his own to put his thoughts in order.

Bowing, he said, "Until a later day, then."

"Not *too* late." The earl smiled, then turned back to his study of the logs piled on the grate, as if this had all been a dream and nothing more.

Perhaps it was.

OUTSIDE AND standing in the cool drizzle falling on St. James's, Raven's head was spinning. He could hardly believe what had just happened.

The only thing that was real and tangible was the feel of Jane's hand in his as they entered the carriage. The lowered shades slapped against the window as the driver set off toward Westbourne Green.

Across from him, Jane blinked as if stunned. "Well, this was certainly a startling develop—*Oh!*"

He didn't give her a chance to finish.

Needing to settle his thoughts and find peace, he pulled her onto his lap and eased his mouth over hers.

He tasted her soft gasp and then the warmth of her sigh as it filled his lungs like Lazarus's first breath in the stone tomb. Without hesitation, her arms encircled his neck. A deep grunt of contentment vibrated in his throat.

He'd never been one to think too much about kissing. His first experience was with Mrs. Devons, the Devil's widow. She'd taught him all the ways a woman liked to be kissed, how to ready their bodies for pleasure. And how a kiss, if done well, could make a woman cry and cling and shudder.

She'd explained that his enjoyment was an insignificant component. Having been a boy of fifteen at the time, he'd believed her.

Yet it had always left him with a sense of detachment. Whenever he kissed a woman, every taste and press and tease were merely parts of a lesson he'd mastered years ago.

At least . . . until now.

Raven didn't understand the reason, but kissing Jane was different. It felt natural and essential. And he took so much pleasure from this simple, fully-clothed act that he ought to feel guilty. But he didn't.

No, he was too lost in the supple texture of her lips, the

lush taste of her tongue, and the soft purrs of her throat. His fingertips traced the delicate framing of her jaw, the velvety texture of her earlobes, the silken wisps of her hair. He could lose himself for hours in these unending fathomless kisses.

He wanted to know how her brain processed this unhurried exploration. If her skin was covered in tingling gooseflesh like his own. If her heartbeat was unsteady. If she felt the static charge that fused them together, wrapping around them like a coil. If she was experiencing something wondrous and unfamiliar and startling, too. Something that—she would say—required further study.

He smiled at the thought and nipped at her bottom lip.

Jane sagged against him, panting, her breath rushing over his jaw, her hand resting over his pounding heart. "Gentlemen do not unleash their feral appetites on young women in carriages."

"You should be admiring my restraint. This might have happened on the pavement. After all, I am not a gentleman."

"You are by birth. I think you know that now. I'm fairly certain that the earl knows, too. And, whether you like it or not, soon the *ton* will know it. Mrs. Bramly was right about the rumors. In fact, she'll likely be the one to start them," she said with a direness that filled him with amusement. "Oh, laugh all you like. However, if this were happening to me, I'd want someone particularly clever to prepare me for what was bound to happen next with a few lessons to help me blend into society."

He tucked his grin away and affected a pondering countenance. "Hmm . . . Then it is a pity I'm not acquainted with anyone particularly clever."

"Do be serious," she said with a playful swat against his chest. "In a matter of days, the *ton* will descend upon you *en masse*. Would you rather be under their quizzing glass as a curiosity—the plebian orphan boy? Or will you demand that they see the man who unapologetically forged his own life?"

He didn't have to think about his answer. Part of him had resigned himself to this fate the instant he saw the portrait. And he didn't want to be an embarrassment to the earl, either.

"Very well, I'll agree to a few lessons."

She blinked. "You will? Just like that and without any grumbling protest?"

When he nodded, her responding smile beamed so brightly that it seemed to penetrate his skin with warmth.

Unable to help himself, he kissed her again, losing himself in the welcome of her lips until her essence became part of his own. This was all happening because of her. She'd cajoled and pushed him from the start. He'd fought her every step of the way. Yet, somewhere along the way, he'd let down his guard with her, and more than he ever had with anyone else.

It was a startling realization.

He drew back after another lengthy interval and rested his forehead against hers, filling his lungs with her every panting breath. "No protests this time," he said, "but I do have one condition."

"That's hardly fair. You've kissed me senseless and I cannot think of my own name, let alone argue against your condition, whatever it may be."

"Then we are on even ground for once." He touched the tip of her pert nose. "And all I ask is that you don't keep anything from me again. If you ever have doubts, I want to hear them. If you discover anything, even something as inconsequential as those missing ledgers," he said with straightforward firmness, "I want to know about it. If we're working together then we can't have secrets. There's one thing I won't forgive and that's being left in the dark only to be taken unawares later. Do you understand?"

"No secrets," she agreed. Her hands cupped his face, her gaze earnest. "I would never intentionally keep anything from you. Truth and certainty are things we both value greatly."

Satisfied with her answer, he moved to take her lips once more.

But Jane shied away. "I have a condition as well—in the future, you must not introduce me by my given name, or use it in public. I can only imagine what the earl must think."

Raven arched a brow. "Are you accusing me of laying claim to you?"

"Of course not," she said on a breath, her teeth sinking into her bottom lip. "I think you were simply being yourself and forgot the rules."

"And one must never forget the rules," he teased and kissed her again.

Chapter 19

Dear Jane,

  The rumors have begun. Just this morning, my aunts heard tale of a stranger leaving the Earl of W—r's town house on the arm of an indiscernible young woman.

  Please be on your guard. It is only a matter of time before someone will recognize you. Should that happen, I fear any number of plagues will shortly follow.

Your ever-worrying friend,
Elodie Parrish

Dear Ellie,

  Fear not, for this is welcome news. Never before have I been thankful to be so exceedingly plain. I shall use it to my advantage and hold those plagues at bay.

  For now, my battles are against a certain gentleman who is proving to be stubborn (even more than myself). He adamantly refuses to see the value in pur-

chasing calling cards or in hiring a manservant—as if the lack thereof will maintain his anonymity.

> *Your exasperated friend,*
> *Jane Pickerington*

Dearest Jane,

I have heard the most shocking rumor—which is saying quite a good deal considering I never hear anything so far removed in the country. Could it be true that the Earl of W—r's heir has actually been found after all this time?

Have you heard of him? And, more to the point, is he as handsome and as primitive as everyone is saying?

> *Your friend on the fringes,*
> *Prudence Thorogood*

Dearest Prue,

I hope you are sitting down as you read this.

I am acquainted with the man himself. The meeting happened as a result of one of my research expeditions (the details of which are not suitable for a letter). But the answers to your queries are . . . yes.

As for the question of his primitive nature, however, he is actually quite exceptionally levelheaded for a man who suffered the horrors of being an orphan in London. Though he is reticent to share many details regarding his upbringing, what I have learned of him I find admi-

*rable. And while he tends to be somewhat domineering
and overprotective at times, I also find that his loyal
and thoughtful nature far outweighs his flaws.*

*But please do not presume that my observations
are indicative of romantic feelings. No, indeed. These
are merely logical conclusions to the facts presented.
The Earl of W—r would seem to agree. Since their
first introduction, his lordship has requested daily
visits with the estimable gentleman in question.*

*I'll say no more on the matter, but send my fondest
regard to you. I hope you know that you are ever in
my thoughts.*

*Your clearheaded friend,
Jane*

As Jane blew the sand across this letter, she frowned in
speculation.

Was she clearheaded? All her life, and up through the
end of October, she would have answered in the affirmative,
without hesitation.

Now, however, she was beginning to have her doubts.

She blamed Raven, of course. His tendency to commu-
nicate through primitive growls, errant touches and swelter-
ing kisses, had put her mind in a twirling muddle.

Then, just as she was learning to immerse herself in this
form of communication, he stopped without warning. In fact,
he hadn't kissed her since that day in the carriage. It was a
terrible shock to the nervous system, like a plunge in a frozen
lake. Was it any wonder that her thoughts were murky?

Each time he'd come to the conservatory in the past week,
he'd acted the gentleman, even though he still spoke like a
scoundrel.

True to his word, he adhered to the bargain they'd made.

While she presented her lessons, he willingly offered insight into the more scandalous aspects of a man's desires.

One day, he'd arrived right after she'd finished repotting a fig tree. Grinning rakishly at the way she brushed at the residual specks on her bodice, he said, "You're giving me all sorts of filthy thoughts. Want me to help? I'll be incredibly thorough."

She'd chided him for noticing. "A gentleman should never remark on a blemish on a woman's person."

"Unlike other men, I was born to observe the world around me," he'd offered with a shrug of self-defense. "At an early age, I began to notice the differences in anatomy. We had a cook at the foundling home who ladled out our breakfast gruel every morning. She had these enormous and glorious . . ." He stopped when Jane glared at him but grinned at the way she had her hands on her hips. "Well, they'd had me so transfixed that I didn't even realize that the lad next to me had eaten all my porridge. I've never gotten over my appreciation for the fairer sex since, in *every* size and shape."

If the way his gaze had heated as it roved hungrily over her slight form was any indication, Jane shouldn't have had the barest feeling of inadequacy. Besides, there was little she could do about the body nature had given her. She would never have a bosom that would *transfix* a man.

As if sensing her thoughts, Raven had taken a step closer and murmured low in her ear, "I have a particular fondness for little samplings that I could devour in one bite."

❧❧❧

ON ANOTHER day, she'd asked him, "Is physical attraction the primary force that compels a man to seek out a woman?"

"It doesn't hurt," he said absently, smirking while perusing the manual of *Gentleman's Etiquette*.

Thinking about a letter she'd received from Prue and how the gentleman, which her friend referred to as Lord F—, had pursued her to the point of compromising her in the gardens at Sutherfield Terrace, Jane had required more from his response. "What if the gentleman knows he cannot have her?"

To that, Raven had looked up sharply. He closed the book with a snap and dropped it onto her desk, seeming cross. "Sometimes a man desires what he cannot have, and not even he can explain the reason."

He'd left shortly thereafter and stayed away for the two days that followed.

❦❦❦

WHEN HE'D returned, he had regained his usual rakish humor, flirting with her shamelessly as she'd tried to teach him table manners and the intricacies of flatware.

"Show me again how the napkin is supposed to lay across my lap," he'd said blandly. But there had been enough heat in his smoky gaze that suggested he had an ulterior motive.

Still irritated by his unexplained absence, and wondering if the siren call of cyprians had kept him away, she'd tossed the wadded linen at him. "Perhaps you would be better served if you had interests other than sexual congress."

Capturing her wrist, he'd kissed her fingertips and waggled his brows. "You would not say such a thing if you knew how all-consuming pleasure can be."

She'd jerked free, wanting to stomp her foot and be angry at him. And yet, she had to think about the book. Understanding the driving force of a scoundrel's nature would be valuable information.

"Very well, then," she'd said, taking up her ledger. "If you would, describe the sensation wrought by coupling."

Raven had looked at her thoughtfully for some time and softly tucked a tendril behind her ear.

"Pleasure isn't always a matter of physiology, professor. Sometimes," he'd added rather cryptically, "a man can walk away from a rousing conversation, feeling more sated than if he'd spent himself between a pair of comely thighs."

She, of course, had blushed but averted her face to write down every word verbatim.

⊰∘⊱∘⊰∘⊱

THE REMAINDER of the week had progressed similarly. For every lesson she'd given, he'd provided a new insight for the primer.

Jane should be pleased, lack of kisses notwithstanding.

However, the more pages she filled in the ledger, the more she knew that this time with Raven would come to an end. The thought made her listless and anxious at the same time. It made no logical sense. After all, she'd known this from the beginning.

Still, she sighed as she folded and sealed the letter for Prue, leaving it on a salver in the hall.

She came back to the conservatory just as Raven strode through the door. Her chronic arrhythmia erupted again in a flurry of heart palpitations that drew all the blood from her brain, leaving her with that peculiar giddy, spinning sensation.

She pinched the bridge of her nose and wondered if a simple remedy might be to start wearing a corset and being fitted for spectacles.

Raven tossed his hat and gloves to the top of her desk with familiarity. But a frown furrowed the flesh above the bridge of his nose as he stared at her quizzically. "Something amiss, little professor?"

He took a step toward her and reached for her hand. Her fingertips tingled, craving his warm touch.

In the last instant, she shied away and pretended an urgent

need to replace the stopper on her inkwell. "Nothing of the sort, I assure you."

His gaze wandered over her in a slow, speculative perusal, pausing at the pulse at her throat and the crests of her cheeks. Then his mouth quirked as if he were privy to her inner thoughts and believed them all to be scandalous. That one hot look had the peculiar effect of expelling all the air from her lungs, sending her stomach into fits of flutters.

It was decided then. She would begin wearing a corset on the morrow.

He took a step toward her, then two, until only an inch separated them. The crisp scent of the outdoors clung to his clothes. She drew in a breath, catching the pleasing spice of fresh shaving soap, the aroma of leather boot polish and his own tantalizingly earthy essence.

"What's my lesson today, hmm? Physiology, I hope. Or, better yet, female anatomy. Just lay yourself out on the trestle table for in-depth scholarly research," he said, his voice as deep and rich as blackberry jam on rum-soaked cake.

"Paying calls," she whispered hoarsely as if she'd spent the past hour breathing in noxious fumes from an experiment.

She cleared her throat and tried again. "It is a gentleman's obligation to return calls that are paid to him. Morning calls to a person of the female sex, however, should always be of a short duration, otherwise it suggests certain intimacies. Therefore, it is essential to keep your hat and gloves with you."

He chuckled and distractedly skimmed the backs of his knuckles along the exposed inner curve of her forearm, eliciting tingles of gooseflesh. "Does society believe it's impossible for a man and woman to swiv"—he stopped at her narrow-eyed glance—"to share *intimacies* while a man carries his hat?"

"Certainly. If his hands are otherwise occupied then he is ready to leave at a moment's notice and cannot engage in any activity to sully his hostess's reputation."

Raven turned back toward the desk and proceeded to don his gloves and then his hat. "Come closer, Jane. I'm going to demonstrate the first four things that popped into my mind—no, make that seven—in order to better inform you of what a man is capable of while still keeping his hat and gloves."

"Seven?" she asked without the slightest blush. She was genuinely curious now. "I should need to take notes."

Picking up her ledger and the stub of a pencil, she numbered the page and waited for him to begin.

He grinned and quickly surveyed the conservatory. "This isn't the ideal room to have you up against a wall, since these are all glass. Nonetheless, that wouldn't disturb my hat. Neither would taking you against the door."

She considered this for a moment, her mind blank. Then her sketch artist flashed a pair of scandalous drawings and the surface of her skin heated by at least eight degrees. "I don't mean to question your authority on the subject. However, wouldn't those two be the same . . . um . . . position?"

"Not if, for the second one, I'm behind you and you're facing the door, hands braced, feet apart," he whispered, his breath drifting across her cheek as he tapped the tip of his index finger to the paper. "You're not writing."

She blinked, several times. Her throat went dry. And her body seemed to have developed a series of new pulse points that quickened deep inside and caused her inner organs to tilt and clench. "Oh, yes. And the third?"

"This desk would do nicely. Or on this stool with you on my lap and your hands on my shoulders," he said and shifted closer. His boot slid in between her slippers, compressing the layers of her petticoat and skirts until they were molded against her thighs.

Her fingers slipped down the length of the pencil, her nails butting up against the page. "Goodness, I think I put too many pieces of wood in that stove. If you're too warm, we could open the door to the garden."

He traced the flushed swell of her cheek and the outer rim of her ear, blowing softly at the curls trailing down from her temple. "Then either of us on our knees, or both of us for that matter. Hat still in place, of course."

The scandalous portrait flashed in her mind. *Newton's apple!* She was beginning to forget how letters were formed. And yet, she heard herself say, "That's only six."

He readily picked up the gauntlet and settled his hands on her hips, pulling her flush. His teeth flashed with wicked delight at her gasp. "Or I could just lift you in my arms right here until your hips and mine align, and your limbs are wrapped around me . . ."

His warm breath swirled around the whorls of her ear, slipping inside her body on a warm tingling current that reminded her how wondrous it felt to be in his arms.

However, with it, came the reminder that this wasn't going to last—this arrangement or whatever it was between them. She was providing him lessons to fit into society and he was merely assisting her with her book. And she had her reputation to consider.

Absently, she realized she'd dropped the ledger. Her hands were fitted to the curves of his shoulders instead, her breasts taut and aching beneath her bodice. "I'm not . . . thinking properly at the moment."

"Then you must be thinking *improperly*." He nuzzled the underside of her jaw. "You need to share those naughty thoughts with your professor, Jane."

A strangled laugh escaped her, the throaty sound wanton and foreign to her own ears. "I am the professor, remember? And our lesson isn't over."

"Mmm . . . I was hoping you'd say that," he murmured against her skin, skillfully teaching her about the quivering electric currents running through her body.

But from not too far away, she heard her name being called by one of her siblings in a plaintive, "Ja—*ane.*"

They both turned to look at the open doorway, their breaths quick and harried.

"Damn," he cursed and turned away to face the trestle table, his palms splayed on the surface. "I forgot where we were. It's no wonder with all these lessons. They've made it impossible to sleep. And I've eaten that entire bloody jar of damson jam."

"I wish I had more to give you, but that was the last we had in the larder," she answered automatically. But when he looked over his shoulder and his heated gaze dipped to her mouth, she realized he was saying something else.

He just told her that he thought about her when they were apart. He wasn't sleeping. He'd consumed an entire jar of jam. Apparently, he wasn't clearheaded either. And it was because of her.

Her! Jane Pickerington, the plain, forgettable bluestocking.

Her heart fluttered fast and wobbly like the wings of a nectar-drunk hummingbird, crashing into her lungs and leaving her breathless.

Drat! Why hadn't she kissed him when she'd had the chance?

But she knew why.

Because, for her, this was starting to feel like more than just kissing. And more than research, too. Much more.

Chapter 20

After he'd nearly debauched Jane seven different ways in her conservatory, Raven decided to take a few days off from lessons.

They'd both agreed it was for the best.

Lately, it had become nearly impossible to control his desire to bed her. Though, it might have helped if he'd been able to slake his lust elsewhere. And he'd tried, too.

During the previous two days he'd spent apart from her, he'd gone back to Moll's to see if she'd grant him admittance again. She did. After hearing the rumors about his birth, she'd decided to let bygones be bygones. And before he knew it, he was in the parlor with Hester and Venetia on his lap, ready to give him the warmest of welcomes.

Strangely, their cloying perfumes had soured his stomach. Their skillful caresses had made his skin prickle unpleasantly, their hands not nearly as soft as a kitten's underbelly. He'd tried to ignore it, to immerse himself in the wicked delights they'd promised him with heated whispers as they'd nibbled his ears. But time and again, his gaze had strayed to that shadowed alcove in the corner of the room.

Like it or not, all he wanted was Jane.

So he'd paid the girls handsomely for their conversation and left, knowing that he wouldn't return.

He thought about Jane at all hours. He couldn't eat without thinking of the sweet taste of her mouth. He couldn't sleep while her scent still lingered in his bedchamber. Hell, he couldn't even don his clothes without remembering the way her body had felt against his.

In short, he'd become obsessed, lust-addled, and irritable.

For the past few days he'd been ready to bite the head off of anyone who even looked at him sideways, let alone those who muttered under their breath that he was a charlatan and a pretender.

The fact that he still felt like a fraud only made it worse.

All the lessons were starting to make him feel the same as when he'd dressed the part of a gent in order to be allowed into Moll Dawson's. Because of that, he'd stopped his visits to Warrister, as well.

He needed a respite to gather his thoughts about where all this was going. Even though he liked spending time with the old man and hearing tales about young Edgar Northcott and his penchant for mischief, Raven had no desire to become part of the aristocracy. He'd spent too many years abhorring it.

He'd told Warrister countless times that all he wanted was to connect the puzzle pieces of his life, and to find out where he came from. But the earl kept pushing for more.

He wanted to introduce him to society. What a joke!

If the past week of taunts and jeers had taught him anything, it was that society didn't want him. Gents who'd never bothered him before were now issuing insults, begging to draw him into a fight.

Even tonight, as he passed by the faro tables, he heard, "Look, there, at that pretender. He is the very mongrel I spoke of earlier."

"The one trying to rise above his station?"

"Indeed. Though it is clear by his brutish posture and bestial gait that he is more animal than man, and certainly no member of the nobility."

The pair of haughty gents had raised their voices to ensure they were heard. But Raven didn't give them the satisfaction of responding.

Gritting his teeth, he walked on with his head high.

But he hated that Sterling's had become a constant episode of confrontation. Even the ushers and croupiers were treating him differently, some with obvious disdain and others with tongue-tied awe.

If there was anyone who understood these daily provocations it was Reed Sterling. Unfortunately, he'd been at his country estate for the past week and hadn't yet heard the news. Or so Raven thought before he walked into his office the afternoon of his return.

"There's something I need to tell you," Raven began the instant he crossed the threshold. In the back of his mind, however, he imagined how Jane would chide him for such a greeting.

She'd spent an afternoon's lesson on the intricacies of polite *tête-à-têtes*. But she'd been wearing a plum-colored frock that had distracted him with thoughts of jam and kissing, and his contributions to their conversation had been more on the wicked side of things.

Bollocks. He was thinking about her again. He really had to stop doing that.

With a shake of his head, he offered a politely grumbled, "I hope your journey was without incident."

Seated at his desk with the account ledgers splayed in front of him, Reed Sterling looked at him with a bemused grin. "It was, thank you. And, now that you've dispensed with your uncharacteristic niceties, why don't you just tell me what you came in here to say."

"Very well, then," he said, shifting from one foot to the other. "I've recently uncovered a few details about my origins. And it seems that there's a possibility that I might have been born to"—he paused to draw in a deep breath and prepare for the inevitable mockery—"aristocrats."

Reed didn't laugh or even snicker. He merely nodded and looked shrewdly across the desk. "I'd heard a rumor. Apparently, you're all the talk at my wife's matrimonial agency. There were so many young debutantes asking about you that she had to start a file."

Raven cursed and cringed. It was even worse than he imagined. "Please burn it, I beg of you. I've no intention of entering society. And, to be honest, none of this is indisputable."

Briefly, he ran through the paltry list of things that may or may not prove his identity. No matter how it had felt to see the portrait, he knew that this could still just be a series of coincidences.

After all, there were still some rather important questions that needed answers. If Edgar and Arabelle Northcott were his parents, then why hadn't he died in the fire, too? And, for that matter, who had abandoned him on the foundling home's doorstep?

"It seems enough for the Earl of Warrister to believe it. So, why don't you?"

"It should be obvious," Raven quantified, straightening his shoulders. "Surely you haven't forgotten that you were the one who found me beaten, shot and left for dead three years ago. My life has been one scrape after another. It took forever to finally become the man I am. That isn't something I'm willing to give up just to pretend to be someone else."

Before coming here, his life had been controlled by other people—the beadle, Mr. Mayhew; Devil Devons; then Devons's widow. But that all changed three years ago. He'd been free to make his own decisions. He'd found a place where he fit, where, until recently, he'd felt valued.

Did he truly want to give all that up just to enter into another life where he was controlled by obligation and the same high society who already despised him?

"You can't close the lid on Pandora's box," Sterling said, matter-of-fact. "And you can't keep your life the way you had it before. No man can. Refusing to acknowledge change is like shadowboxing. There's nothing to be gained from it."

Raven knew that. But everything was changing too fast and he couldn't gain a foothold.

For the past week, he'd been beleaguered by incessant knocking at his door, and each day there were heaps of calling cards stuffed in through the crack above the threshold. How did people live like this with no peace and no privacy?

"You seem to keep a foot in both worlds easily enough," he said with a jerk of his chin and accusation in his tone.

Sterling chuckled and crossed his arms over his chest. "Perhaps you've mistaken contentment for ease. I will completely admit to the former. I've never been happier since I married Ainsley, but her world isn't always easy to navigate— the dinners, the parties, the calling hours."

"The calling hours," Raven muttered with a disparaging shake of his head. It seemed that every hour he tried to sleep was a calling hour.

"Aye. And there are different rules for peers, too. Especially the women. One false move and ruination not only befalls her but her entire family." He paused as if carefully sifting through his next words. "From our previous conversation, I hazard to guess that Miss Pickerington is still assisting you?"

Raven stiffened, having a sense of where this was leading. "I've no intention of ruining her."

"Does that mean you have . . . other intentions in mind?" If Sterling's brow hadn't flicked with amusement, they might have had words. "An encounter or two with a debutante and suddenly you're thinking of matrimony? Please, I beg of you, don't. Ainsley would see this as an excuse to paste bulletins for her agency all over my building again, believing that everyone here needed to find a match."

The tension Raven felt abruptly lessened, remembering when Sterling was at war with his neighbor, before she became his wife. "Rest assured, Sterling's facade is safe. I'll never marry in the first place, and least of all a hoity-toity debutante."

Yet, as he said the words, a voice in the back of his mind told him that Jane had never acted like a snobbish, high-society deb.

She was different from the rest. She never turned up her nose at him. She didn't put on airs. In fact, there wasn't anything fake or deceptive about her. She was driven by logic and a need to understand the world around her. And there was something altogether appealing about the way she murmured to herself and how her eyes glinted when she had one of her epiphanies.

"Then again, who knows?" Sterling said with a mysterious air, pulling him out of his thoughts. "You may change your mind in the future if that grin means anything. I'll say this, however: the rewards of marrying the right woman far surpass the trials along the way."

Only then did Raven realize that the corner of his mouth was curled upward. Because he was thinking about Jane. Bloody hell!

Abruptly, he frowned. When would this obsession end?

Sterling unfolded from his chair and walked around his desk to clasp Raven on the shoulder with something like brotherly affection. "Why don't you take a few days away from here and get things settled."

Raven surprised himself by agreeing with a nod. Perhaps

all he needed was a couple of days to himself. That should set matters to rights.

"Just know this," Sterling added. "No matter what you choose to do, now or in the future, you have my unwavering support. Always."

A sudden wealth of appreciation tightened Raven's chest. He cleared his throat to hide it. "I'm glad of that. I might need your infamous right hook if Duncan Pickerington asks me one more time if he should call me 'my lord.'"

✠✠✠✠

"Well, what does the Earl of Warrister call him when he visits?" Ellie asked as they sat on the jonquil settee in the upper gallery of the Earl of Dovermere's ballroom.

Jane looked down to smooth her skirts—a regrettable shade of yellow that perfectly blended into her surroundings. She must look like a disembodied head. Which likely explained the odd looks she'd received from gentlemen. Though, at first, she'd imagined she was about to be asked to dance. How foolish of her.

Then again, she wasn't in the mood to dance.

It had been six entire days since she'd seen Raven. In that time, she could have sworn that the earth's rotation had slowed and the days grew longer. She'd even checked the mechanics of all the clocks in the house to be sure they were functioning properly. Regrettably, they were.

"I'm not certain. I've only met with the earl that one day, and I haven't seen Raven to inquire with him. Not since the middle of last week."

Jane thought she'd kept the disconsolation from her tone . . . until Ellie reached over to squeeze her hand.

"I'm sure he's quite busy, settling in to a new life."

"Of course," Jane agreed distractedly, watching the dancers twirl beneath the chandeliers to a three-quarter beat waltz. "And I have been quite busy as well. Not only have I been writing notes for my portion of the book, but I've been preparing the children for their examinations, which they will take before December is upon us and the older boys are home."

"Will they return before the Marquess of Aversleigh's ball in a fortnight, do you think?"

"I'm not certain, though I hope they will. I always love to see Theodore, Graham and Henry's faces flood with color when you remark on how much they've grown, especially while they are within earshot of the young ladies they try to impress," Jane said with a small laugh. She expected Ellie to laugh as well, but instead she looked stricken. "What is it?"

"I just recalled that Aversleigh's ball will include a number of tradesmen and officers. Apparently, they are relations of his lordship's future son-in-law." Ellie's shoulders slumped on a sigh. "I cannot imagine your parents permitting any of you to attend such a party."

Sadly, it was true. Lord and Lady Hollybrook did not condone mingling with commoners.

"The rest of society is gradually altering their views, and yet my parents still want their children to marry up in the peerage and in wealth, or not at all. At least, that's what they should like of their eldest daughter. I'm to set an example, after all." *As my uncle has so recently reminded me*, she thought grudgingly. "Though if my parents could even name each of their children in order, I'd eat my slippers."

"Then why is it so important to them? After all, they married for love, did they not? At least, that's what everyone suspects, due to their number of offspring."

Jane wasn't convinced that procreation and love were one in the same, and was still hoping to find existential proof of the latter. She kept the thought to herself, however.

Flicking her fingers against a stray feather that had drifted to her glove from a passing matron's turban, she answered Ellie's first question. "I'm sure their decision has something to do with my uncle's scandal. Family pride, you know. Even though he was sent off to debtor's prison years ago, they are forever willing to entertain, to fawn, and to do whatever they have to in order to keep the *ton* from remembering it."

"Mmm," Ellie mused, cascading through the blank ivory tiles of the dance card tied at her wrist. "But with tradesmen and officers invited, Aversleigh's ball will surely be a rousing event. And I know that George plans to attend. He has already agreed to at least two dances with me."

"Quite promising," Jane remarked absently, her thoughts straying.

She was thinking about the fact that her friend had been in love with George, the Marquess of Nethersole, all her life. But did Ellie have proof of this all-consuming certainty?

Likely not, Jane decided after a moment. Her friend also made wishes on falling stars, but cared very little about the properties of meteorites. A romantic-minded person wasn't the best resource to provide substantiated evidence, she was sure.

Even now, Ellie was gazing at the chandeliers as if they were stars about to fall.

"I hope that George has sown his oats at last. I want him to see me as more than just his neighbor." She released a slow breath as if she'd finished an incantation. Then, her cheeks pinkened slightly as she glanced at Jane and issued a helpless shrug. "If he isn't, however, at least there will be officers aplenty to distract me. If you were to attend, we would have our pick of partners, I should think."

Again, Jane's thoughts were distracted. Even if she were able to attend, the only person she would want to dance with would not be there.

But then, she sat up straighter as an idea occurred to her. "Officers and tradesmen . . . In such company, any small slip of manners would be completely ignored. Therefore, one would think that such a setting would be the perfect foray into society, particularly for someone who might be a bit . . . savage from time to time."

Not only that, but if Raven attended such a party, perhaps that would show him how well the two worlds could mingle and find acceptance with each other. The more she thought about it, the more she was determined to make it happen.

"You don't mean that he could make his first public appearance at Aversleigh's ball as"—Ellie paused to draw in a dramatic breath—"Merrick Northcott?"

A few heads turned in their direction, eyes glinting with undisguised, rapacious curiosity.

Jane quickly affected a laugh as if her friend had made the most outlandish jest. She gritted her teeth in a semblance of a smile and murmured, "Of course not. Whyever would you think such a thing?"

But the damage had been done.

A roiling sea of busybody whispers rose and fell in waves as it descended from the gallery, down the stairs, past the refreshment table, crashing over the dancers. In seconds, everyone was talking about it. *Newton's apple!*

"Oops," Ellie said.

Jane expelled a patient breath. Any careful plotting she might have done was now out of her hands. There was only one thing left to do. "Come on then. Let's go downstairs. I'm going to need to send two letters of warning post haste."

Chapter 21

Raven's quest for peace and solitude fell apart the instant he answered a knock at the kitchen door two days later. The beanpole valet on the other side declared that his services were a gift from the Earl of Warrister.

A gift Raven was apparently unable to return.

He didn't know why he bothered to let the man in. And no matter how much Raven ranted, Mr. Sanders simply wouldn't stop poking through his wardrobe and trying to *improve* his appearance.

"I'm fine just as I am," he barked as Sanders tried to strangle him with an ink-marked tailor's tape.

"Of course, sir. However, his lordship believes that you should have a fresh suit of clothes before he introduces you to the Marquess of Aversleigh, along with proper attire for the ball. Now, if I could just finish the measurements . . ."

"The Marquess of—" Raven cursed.

At once, he knew who to blame for this persistent pestering. Just this morning, he'd found a letter on the foyer floor. He never would have given it a second look if the paper hadn't been stained with a familiar shade of beet-powder pink.

Curiosity had compelled him to open it.

My dearest Raven,

You are very likely to growl as you read further.
By circumstances quite beyond my control, there

is now a rumor running rampant that you will attend the Marquess of A—h's ball in order to present your-self to society.

Yes, I know you did not intend to make such a debut. However, I must lay the blame partially at your feet. If you had answered the door when I sent a servant with several urgent missives (or, better yet, stopped being so stubborn and employed a butler), this might have all been put to rest. Yet, because of your inaccessibility during these past twenty-four hours, this rumor has spent too long on the lips of the ton. *They are rabidly foaming at the mouths for a chance to look at you.*

As for myself, I'm sure I cannot even recall your face as it has been so long since I've seen it.

Your once, but now forgotten,
Professor

After his second read, Raven had found it amusing. He could imagine Jane scolding him with her hands on her hips, tapping the toe of her slippers on the floor.

But now, with Sanders here sniffing through his shaving kit, Raven didn't find it amusing in the least.

He hadn't meant to respond to her at all. It was best to avoid temptation, after all. Under the circumstances, how-ever, he was too furious to think about bedding her.

So, he went to his desk for a scrap of paper. His mouth curled in a cold smile as he stabbed the surface of the ink with his pen. She wasn't the only one who could send a missive.

❧❧❧

LESS THAN an hour later, Raven heard his front door open and then a rapid patter of footsteps on the stairs.

Jane appeared, breathless and wide-eyed. To the valet, she said, "Oh, thank goodness you're still alive."

In turn, Mr. Sanders stared back at her perplexedly. "I am indeed, miss."

Raven crossed his arms over his chest and glared at her. "So, you've come to beg my forgiveness, have you?"

"Not in the least," she said with an exasperated sigh as she jerked the ends of her moss-green ribbons before setting the straw bonnet down onto the bedside table. "I came because of your missive. If you didn't want me here, then you shouldn't have written the words, and I quote: *Dear Jane, I am about to commit murder. Be warned, I'm laying the corpse on your doorstep.*"

Raven speared the meddlesome valet with a deadly look.

"Pay no attention to him," she said to Sanders, who turned three shades paler as he took a step back. "He's all growl and thunder."

"He tried to shave me, Jane. Came at me with a razor."

She grimaced and shook her head as she patted the valet on the shoulder. "Well, perhaps, it would be best to wait downstairs for a moment. I'll talk with him."

Sanders left without argument. But when the door at the end of the hall opened, Raven heard the sound of thumps from the main floor and then a high, piercing war cry. And it sounded uncannily like one of her brothers.

Raven stared out the open door to the hall and then back at her, dubious. "Did you bring the children?"

"Well, it is Sunday," she said as if that explained everything. "Many of the servants have a portion of the day off from their duties, including the governess and the nurse. We usually fend for ourselves."

"And your parents?"

"Having tea with Lord and Lady Sutcliffe."

No sooner had the valet's steps descended than Raven

heard someone tromping back up, along with a crescendo of wailing as it drew closer. Then eleven-year-old Charles appeared, his short-cropped hair sticking up in brown tufts, his eyes wide in an unmistakable expression of being at his wits' end. Raven imagined he looked the same.

"Jane, you've got to take Anne. She just won't stop crying. I've tried everything, but I think she hates men."

"Nonsense," Jane said and summarily plucked the plump, mop-headed, bawling Anne out of Charles's arms and handed her off to Raven.

Stunned, he didn't know what to do with the soggy-faced creature.

Reflexively, he drew her against his chest so he wouldn't drop her, one hand tucked beneath her nappy-pinned bottom, and the other over the center of her back. The baby quieted after a series of stuttered, snuffling hiccups. She stared up at him with glistening blue eyes surrounded by wet, thorn-shaped lashes as she flexed her little hands on his shirtsleeves.

"Gah," she said. Accompanying the sound, a rainbow-prismed bubble of drool formed from her rosebud mouth.

Then Jane added to her brother, "You see, it's all in the manner in which she is held. She needs to feel secure and safe. You tend to hold her as if she has the plague."

"I just don't want her to wet on me again."

"Believe me, I felt the same way about you." Jane grinned and ruffled his hair. "Go on, now. Keep watch over the rest. Make sure Peter keeps all his clothes, and inform me if the twins start to plot against the valet. I'll keep Anne up here for a minute."

Charles was off like a shot and Raven . . .

Well, he was left holding the baby.

Jane turned a pair of doe eyes on him, her head tilted to the side, her lips curving softly.

"No," he said and quickly put little, sweet-smelling Anne

back in her sister's arms. "You're not allowed to look at me that way with those midnight eyes, which are likely calculating a three-part plan of domesticity. And aye, I see you shaking your head in denial, but you are biting your lip. That always means you're not saying all your thoughts aloud."

She frowned, adjusting her sister on her hip. "An entire library of charts and graphs wouldn't form enough of a plan to domesticate you. You'll always be untamed."

"Never forget that," he said sharply as he pivoted on his heel and stormed back into his bedchamber. "In case you're not aware of it, I'm angry with you. All this madness is due to whatever you said to my"—he growled, frustrated that he still felt like a pretender—"to Warrister. And it was you who told him, wasn't it?"

"I may have sent him a missive, as a courtesy." She sniffed, indignant. "At least *he* responded. At least *he* didn't forget my very existence, like you have done this past week."

Raven detected a twinge of hurt in her tone and that irritated him even more. "No! You don't get to come here with your accusations and soft smiles as if you're the aggrieved party. Because of you, I'm forced to deal with a valet barging into my house, determined to fit me for a suit of clothes in order to attend a ball that I never agreed to go to in the first place."

"I tried to prepare you, but you didn't answer your door. If anything, this entire ordeal should convince you to hire—"

His growl cut her off.

He jerked open his bedside table drawer and picked up a pink letter, unfolding it with a single irritated shake. "You should have discussed this with me before you mentioned anything to Warrister."

"For what purpose? You would have refused the invitation, regardless," she whispered as her sister yawned sleepily in her arms.

"Correct," he vehemently whispered in return, tension roped between his shoulders.

Raven hissed out a breath through his teeth. Then, looking down at the letter, he folded it with care and tucked it back in the drawer before locking it for safekeeping.

When he faced Jane again, he saw her gaze drift absently from him to the tasseled key. Her lips moved briefly in a silent murmur as if she were making a mental note of something.

But he refused to ask her what it was about. Instead he crossed his arms as another edgy growl vibrated in his throat.

When she spoke aloud, her tone was contrite, tender. "I will write to Ableforth this very day to make amends."

"Fine."

She rocked the baby back and forth, stroking her hand along the layers of tiny scalloped ruffles. Gradually, the heavy cherub head settled into the curve of her neck on a soft sigh, a fan of lashes falling against the plump crests of her cheeks. "I suppose I lost my head for a moment."

Raven watched as she pressed her lips to those butterscotch curls and was struck with a strange tug at the center of his chest—a pull that forced an image to form in his mind, of Jane with her own child. But instead of brown hair and blue eyes, he saw a tumble of inky black curls and gray eyes.

A disconcerting jolt rifled through him.

He rolled his shoulders and cracked his neck to free himself of the thought and sensation. "That doesn't sound like you, losing your head."

"No, indeed," she said wryly. "It struck me quite by surprise. You see, I didn't even believe I would have the opportunity to attend Aversleigh's ball. But when I mentioned that to Ableforth, he decreed that he would ensure my parents' acceptance of the invitation. Less than an hour transpired before a messenger from the earl himself arrived at the door. With all pomp and circumstance, he stated his lordship's desire to renew acquaintances with many members of society and hoping to do so at the marquess's ball. Flattered and quite proud of themselves, my parents accepted the invitation on the spot." A laughing breath escaped her as she rolled her eyes. "I then told Ellie and she was thrilled. She was sure that we would find plenty of dancing partners among all the officers and tradesmen invited."

"What *officers*? What *tradesmen*?"

"The ones who will be in attendance, of course. The marquess's daughter is marrying a wealthy American tradesman and this is her betrothal ball." She lifted her shoulders in a half shrug, but there was a mysterious glint in her eyes. "Besides, that is the purpose of the Season—for unmarried men and women to become more familiar with each other. And as Ellie began to proclaim how we were bound to wear out our slippers . . . Well, I'd had one of my epiphanies."

"And just what was your epiphany?" He growled again, folding his arms across his chest.

Her soft smile returned as she rested her cheek on the baby's head and looked up at him. "That I only wanted to dance with you."

He felt that tug again. But this time, it was harder. It ripped through him as if he'd been speared by a harpoon and hauled from the depths of the ocean to break the surface.

He drew in a gulp of air, lungs tight. *Bloody hell. What is this?*

"Very well," he said, disgruntled and pressing a fist to the center of his chest. "Send that blasted Sanders back upstairs."

Chapter 22

Raven didn't need any more lessons. But Jane was determined to teach him to dance like a proper gentleman, and had doggedly cajoled him until he'd given in.

Since he was still brooding over her mention of *tradesmen* and *officers*, what else could he have done?

Even so, before she'd left with *the horde*—as she called them—he'd made it clear that he was attending this ball as himself. There would be no formal introduction to society as Merrick Northcott. Not yet. Perhaps not ever.

The truth was, he'd rather just continue on like this, one foot in each world. If only everyone else could see how much simpler that would be. Then he'd have everything he wanted.

The following afternoon, Raven arrived at the conservatory for his first dancing lesson.

He found Jane building some sort of contraption. It was a box with interconnecting notched wooden cogwheels, fixed to a turn-crank handle that rotated—what looked to be—a large tin grater inside.

So absorbed in her work, she didn't notice that he'd arrived. Not even when he handed her the mallet that had fallen on the floor, out of her reach.

She was disheveled and driven, her hair falling loose from a twisted topknot, a smudge of dirt on her cheek, and the remains of a forgotten wedge of toast balanced on the edge of the trestle table.

He drew closer and lifted his hand, unable to resist tucking a few of those silken brown-and-gold strands behind her ear. "What are you building, little professor?"

She muttered something barely discernible about a *snowflake maker* under her breath as she turned the crank, peered into the box, then frowned at the unmoving grater.

"Want me to have a go?" he asked. "I'm fairly good with my hands."

He didn't mean it as a flirtation, but it managed to pull her out of her fog with a blush on her cheeks. She blinked at him several times, her pupils contracting then dilating warmly.

"You're here," she said, the whisper of her sweet breath flavoring the air between them.

Damn, he wanted to kiss her. It had been ages since he'd tasted her mouth. But it was that very desire that gave him reason to hold back. He was only a temporary fixture in her life. She belonged in society and he . . . didn't know where he fit yet.

So, Raven settled for wiping the smudge off her cheek, then nodded to her contraption. "A 'snowflake maker'?"

She smiled and slipped a handkerchief from her sleeve to swipe at her cheek. "Indeed. This is for our toboggan race on Christmas morning. You cannot always depend on Mother Nature to bring the snow precisely when you wish for it, so I thought I'd make some myself. The children and I love Christmas, even if most of the *ton*—including my parents—look at it as a silliness enjoyed by rustics. But the children and I put together a grand celebration. It's our little tradition. We enjoy making puddings and sugar-dusted biscuits and we hang garlands and ribbons from the staircase."

She smiled and her gaze went distant as if she were picturing all the years of merriment. And Raven had a burning need to know what that felt like. To be surrounded by family. To have traditions to look forward to, year after year.

Feeling like a mawkish fool, he turned his attention to the mechanism. After a brief examination, he saw why it was failing and reached inside to secure the coupling.

"And what about you? Do you have any favorite Christmastide—" She broke off abruptly and her hand fell on his sleeve. "I apologize. That was thoughtless of me."

He shook his head, absolving her. The last thing he wanted was to diminish her joy with the reminder of his past. So, he made light of it for her sake.

"Let's see . . ." he mused. "One year, I got a peppermint stick and a lengthy hug from the cook. Lost the sweetie, but the memory of that big-bosomed embrace will linger in my heart forever."

Looking over his shoulder, he winked at Jane and she swatted him on the shoulder.

"*Scoundrel,*" she chided, almost tenderly. Then she reached for his hand. "Come along then. It's time for your lesson."

Raven let her tow him from the conservatory before he mentioned, "I already know how to dance."

She cast him a doubting look. "I don't know what type of dancing you've been doing with your ladies of the evening—and I'm sure I shouldn't want to know—but today's lesson is learning the proper steps and the proper form. Every position you present to your partner will also be viewed and judged by the entire *ton.*"

Unconcerned, he focused his attention on the long expanse of columns, arched niches, and murals in the main hall. At the far end, Charles, Phillipa, and the twins were carrying chairs and tufted hassocks out of a nearby room and placing them on the Axminster runner.

"What's going on over there?" he asked her.

"Merely a history lesson. The children are reenacting the battle of Trafalgar." Then she briefly paused in her trek toward the staircase and called out, "But remember, children, there will be no eggs, apples, or any foodstuffs for that matter, used in your cannon fire. I don't want a repeat of the Battle of Flodden. The carnage and the resulting odors of that were nearly enough to cause Mr. Miggins to quit us all on the spot, and he'd already lived through several actual wars."

A quickly chorused "Yes, Jane" answered.

Suspicious, Raven eyed the four of them huddled close and whispering.

"You know," he mused, "if I had an entire houseful of potential projectiles at my disposal and was only given orders against using food . . . Well, I'd instantly start thinking of all the other things I could use that would do the most damage—rocks, clay pots, actual cannon balls if I could lay my hands on them."

"Newton's apple! We have several of those in the garret. Father collected them at one time. Mother had them gilded," she said absently and stopped on the bottom tread. Then, in a surprisingly resounding voice from her small form, she issued a warning. "Your artillery can have no greater mass or weight than a pair of Peter's woolen stockings rolled together. Is that clear?"

Groans of disappointment preceded another, far less enthusiastic, chorus of "Yes, Jane."

She slid Raven a glance and curled her hand over his arm as they continued up the stairs. "Thank you. You're terribly clever about anticipating mischief."

"That's how I first found you, after all," he teased and couldn't resist adding, "*and* your glove." He even tsked her. "Naughty, Jane."

She tensed at his side and drew in a breath, doubtless to

claim that it was all innocent, once again. But the appearance of Miggins at the top of the stairs quieted her excuse and left Raven with the upper hand.

Miggins bowed. "A pleasant day, Mr. Raven?"

Looking down at the pink color staining Jane's cheeks, he grinned. "Getting more pleasant by the minute, Miggins. And you?"

"I have nothing of which to complain, sir. Miss Jane," he added, turning his attention to the blushing mistress of the house. "Would you care for a tray sent to the ballroom before we begin?"

"No, that won't be—"

"I'm positively famished, Miggins. I could eat a horse."

"I'm afraid the last of the horse was served at dinner," the butler said, completely deadpan. Not even a quiver of jowls. It was all the more hilarious when Jane—who was trying so hard to be offended and self-righteous—suddenly erupted in laughter too hearty to be stifled behind her hand.

Raven grinned at the ever-sedate butler. "I'll take whatever Jane usually fancies."

"Very good, sir."

Jane gradually quieted on a hiccup as the butler left through a camouflaged door, tucked into the staircase landing.

She dabbed the wetness from the corner of her eyes. "I always knew there was mirth hiding in those jowls. Leave it to you to bring it out of him."

"I take no credit. It was obvious from the day I met him that he's content to be here with all of you."

"And we love him dearly," Jane said and Raven felt something like a pang of envy in the pit of his stomach. He sobered at the thought. "Which is one of the reasons why I've asked if he shouldn't mind assisting us for your lesson. He and I will demonstrate while you observe. I believe you'll have the steps sorted rather quickly."

A sudden wash of tension flooded every fiber of his being, itching beneath his skin. That one simple, thoughtless, statement cast him as an outsider. Someone who didn't belong.

He knew this, of course. But the reminder that he was only here to be molded from a poor, pitiable orphan and into a gentleman had caught him off guard.

"Aye. I'm an excellent mimic. I can pretend better than any stage actor," he said tightly, jaw clenched. "As I said, I already know how to dance. I've had years of experience with country dances and reels. Or did you imagine I was living under a rock before we met?"

"Well, no. But . . ." She frowned, lifting her curious gaze. "That isn't what I meant at all. In fact—and forgive me for saying this—but you're a terrible mimic."

He stiffened, the roped muscles beneath her hand rigid. "You're mistaken."

She shook her head. "You may have fooled others, but it's true, I'm afraid. You don't do a single thing like anyone else, especially when you put on aristocratic airs in an effort to blend in. You do everything your own way. As I said when we first met, you even move differently than other men."

As they made their way down an ivory-and-gold wall-papered corridor toward a set of white-glazed doors that stood ajar at the end, she continued. "My statement was in regard to your skills of observation. You are quite adept at understanding the way of things at a single glance. Not only with people, but with my contraption just a few moments ago. I don't think there's anyone like you. And I wouldn't insult you by expecting you to be like someone else."

Raven was left speechless.

She hadn't been casting him as an outsider at all. In her own logical way, she was paying him a compliment.

Every ounce of tension drained out of him at once, as if a hole had opened up in the floor beneath his feet and simply gobbled it all away. And yet, he wasn't feeling empty. Something else had taken its place. Something powerful that made him want to pull Jane into his arms and kiss her.

As they neared the threshold of the ballroom that hosted a bank of mullioned windows on the far side, he planned to fulfill that desire in just a few short steps.

Regrettably, he discovered that they weren't alone.

Seated at a piano bathed in the afternoon light, was a young man with a Caesar hairstyle of short disorderly nut-brown curls and aristocratic features. He bore a striking similarity to all of the other Pickerington males Raven had met thus far, but seemed to be a few years older than Charles.

"Hullo there," the young man said with a casual salute of his hand before he stood and sketched a bow. "You must be the one I've heard the others chattering about—the infamous suitor who dared to return. You're the only one, you know. All the others have abandoned their pursuit shortly after they'd survived tea with us."

"I'm not exactly a suitor," Raven corrected, refusing to give the wrong impression that he was a permanent fixture. Even so, when he felt Jane uncurl her fingers from his sleeve, he was compelled to place his hand over the top of hers, keeping her in place. "I'm more of a . . . foundling, you might say."

"Eh, we're all foundlings here. Jane simply found *us* in the nursery and has been watching over us ever since." He took a step forward and slid a palm across his coat front before extending it. "I'm Henry, by the by. Welcome to our clan."

"Raven," he said and was forced to release Jane in order to shake hands.

She slipped free, taking her warmth with her. "Henry is home from school after concluding his examinations early. He'd decided to assist"—she cleared her throat pointedly—"some of the other boys in his house with their work. The schoolmaster thought it best to *permit* him to return home early for winter holiday before he finds himself in any more mischief that might warrant permanent expulsion."

"And as punishment for cheating," Henry said to Raven with a grin, "I've been relegated to the task of playing an assortment of instruments for your dancing pleasure. So, what shall it be—a stuffy minuet? A fast-footed quadrille? A lively Scotch reel? A dreadfully boring country dance?" He paused to roll his eyes. Then, he perked up and chafed his hands together as he continued. "Or . . . a salacious waltz? I just happen to have a melody I've composed, poised and waiting on the piano."

Raven didn't know why it surprised him that Jane had a composer in the family. And she'd once said they were all quite plain. Well, he couldn't find anything remotely ordinary about any of them, least of all her.

"The only one I'd care to learn is the waltz," Raven answered, knowing that was a proper excuse to have her in his arms.

"Huzzah!"

"Absolutely not, Henry," Jane chided. "I won't reward your misbehavior at school by presenting you with an audience to admire your latest work. You're not allowed to enjoy yourself one bit."

"Aw, you're just tetchy because you're forbidden to dance the waltz."

"Forbidden?" Raven's brows rose with mock alarm. "Why, Jane, just how terrible are you? And should I bandage my feet before or after the lesson?"

"Your feet have nothing to fear. I'm only forbidden because I have yet to earn a voucher that permits me to waltz at Almack's." She lifted her shoulders in an inconsequential shrug. "Mother was going to make a request last Season, but she forgot."

"And she forgot again this Season, as well," Henry muttered, disgruntled. "Much like Father forgot to send a carriage for me at school, so I had to hire a coach for the drive home."

Jane stepped forward to cup his shoulder. "Remember what I always say?"

"Yes, yes. I should consider these instances as lessons in resourcefulness."

She pressed a kiss to his cheek, then wiped it off with a pass of her thumb before he could.

Facing Raven, she cocked her head to the side, her lips murmuring silently. Then, aloud, she said, "We would require two more for a proper quadrille. Therefore, the waltz seems our best option."

"Somehow, I shall carry on." He nodded solemnly, pretending disappointment and forgetting all his reasons for wanting to keep his distance from Jane.

✧◦✧◦✧

THE INSTANT the music began and Raven swept Jane into his arms, all her thoughts of lessons fluttered off in a dozen heartbeats.

His steps were sure and quick, as if he'd been dancing all his life. The possessive angle of his shoulders kept his posture from being precise, but she didn't mind. It felt too wondrous to be in his arms. His hold was firm but still gentle, and close but not stifling.

She could hardly believe this was his first waltz, and that all he'd done was watch Mr. Miggins a few moments ago. However, for reasons beyond her understanding, it made her giddy to be his first.

Perhaps it was all due to the fact that she'd missed him terribly, and for the first time in a week she felt alive.

A laugh bubbled past her lips as he swept her into a turn and her gaze held his. "Now, I know what I've been missing. It will be difficult to return to watching the dancers from a distance."

"What if you were to waltz without permission?"

"Scandal," she said with a lift of her brows, still smiling. "Of course, I've never been asked, so I'm not entirely certain. As my brother so eagerly mentioned, I hardly have suitors lining up at the door. Should any manage to look past my unremarkable appearance and idiosyncrasies, they would soon find that my dowry was a less-than-tempting two thousand pounds."

"Those gents are all idiots," he said simply and left it at that.

She felt him draw her closer, the shift of his palm gliding over warm silk, his fingertips brushing the tiny cloth buttons down the back of her dress. They turned together, effortlessly gliding over the polished floor. She breathed in the scent of him, enthralled by a tender aching sensation beneath her breast that begged her to press against him.

The three-quarter beat melody sped by in a rush. More than anything, she wanted to slow down and savor this feeling of contentment thrumming inside her. Their time was coming to an end. Not only today, but the lessons and his need for her assistance would soon be concluded.

Then, she knew he would go on his own path and likely never think of her again.

When the last note of the piano faded, she averted her face to hide her thoughts. He was always too good at reading them.

"You are quite the exceptional dancer, Raven," she said a little breathlessly, focusing on the lesson at hand. "Your form and steps are somewhat more predatory and possessive than what the *ton* would consider graceful. Additionally, you could not hold your partner so improperly close without causing a stir."

"And yet," he said, bending to her ear, "I didn't hear a word of reprimand or correction from my instructor in the midst of it."

Somehow her hand had drifted to his chest where the heavy thud of his heart nudged the center of her palm. It had a three-quarter beat, too, much like her own at the moment . . . *bum-BUM-bum . . . bum-BUM-bum . . .*

What a fascinatingly intimate thing to notice.

Not only that, but the insteps of his boots slid along the outer curve of her slippers, corralling her into an embrace. There, in the middle of the ballroom.

"I was distracted by my study of the . . . um . . . mechanics of it all," she said and reluctantly took a step back, her protesting body slow to retreat.

Scanning the room, she saw that Mr. Miggins had gone— likely to return the tray to the kitchen—and Henry was at the piano, scribbling notes onto his sheet music.

"Let's waltz again. I'll do much better this time," he said, a deep edge to his voice as he moved closer and seized her hand, twining their fingers together with delightful friction. He slid his other hand to her waist, skimming to the small of her back.

She cast a glance to her brother before she whispered, "If you did any better, my dress would go up in flames."

He grinned rakishly. "I'm willing to take that chance. I imagine you'd look fetching without it."

"Such a scoundrel."

"Take care, Jane," he chided softly. "That phrase is beginning to sound like a term of endearment. If I didn't know better, I'd think you liked scoundrels."

"Before you say another word," Henry called from the

bench, still not lifting his head from the pencil nub and paper, "I must warn you that the acoustics in this room are exceptional. So if you plan to have your way with my sister, please wait until *after* I've gone."

Face flaming bright, her eyes narrowed into slits at Raven. Then she scoffed and turned to her brother, hands on hips. "You shouldn't be eavesdropping, Henry. In the very least, you might think about defending my honor."

"You're managing well enough on your own. And I daresay you'd know more ways to kill a man in a duel than I do. Which, by the by," he said distractedly, "would make an excellent opera. Yes. I can hear it now. A bluestocking murder of a scoundrel on a cold November morning. Why, it practically writes itself! The opening score would begin with a shot, a clash of cymbals, and a high keening E sharp . . ."

"I think we've lost our chaperone," Raven said and his gaze lowered to her lips. "Seems to me that we should adjourn to the conservatory for . . . research."

"I cannot." She hated that those words fell from her lips. "I promised the children we'd start our Christmas puddings this afternoon. It takes weeks before they're ready to be steamed. And I know," she dropped her voice to the barest whisper, "that time would escape us if we engaged in more . . . research."

He growled in response, his grip possessive as he brought her hand to his lips. "You're right. I'm in a mood to be quite thorough."

His warm gaze never left hers as he kissed each knuckle, and every vulnerable niche in between. Her knees went weak.

Before she could stop herself, she asked, "Will you come back tomorrow?"

From the piano, Henry cleared his throat and Jane made a hasty amendment.

"For another lesson, of course," she said in a rush. "You

still need to improve your polite parlor conversation and—
Oh! I just had another epiphany. You could come to dinner
and meet my parents."

"Your *parents*?" he parroted with a horrified grimace.

"Opus two," Henry remarked with a snicker, "the bluestocking spins her matrimonial web on a new victim."

Jane sent a glare to her brother.

Before Raven acquired the wrong impression, she slipped
her arm into his and ushered him out of the ballroom and
away from Henry's interfering ears.

"I have no ulterior motive," she said once they advanced
to the corridor. "I simply believe there is no better way for
you to gain experience on practicing superficial conversation
than with the two leading experts in society. To be honest, I
don't know why I hadn't thought of it before."

"I work in a gaming hell, Jane. What am I possibly going
to converse about—the odds of winning at faro?"

"Oh, believe me, they'll do all the talking," she said. "It
will be excellent practice for you."

Raven's mouth twisted with patent skepticism. "I don't
know. It just seems a bit *too* proper."

"If it makes you feel any better, they likely won't even
realize you're there. I often have dinner with them and they
are startled to look down the table to see me."

Unfortunately, it was all too true. She was so plain and
forgettable that even her parents couldn't seem to remember
her. But after all these years, it didn't bother her. Not much.
In fact, hardly at all.

A pair of astute gray eyes studied her for a long moment
and his head fell back on a taut sigh. Then he grumbled under
his breath, "What the hell. It's just dinner, eh?"

Chapter 23

Jane knew this evening was bound to be a disaster. Dinner with her parents? What *had* she been thinking?

Oh, but she knew. She'd been under the spell of the waltz. She hadn't been thinking at all about how humiliating it would be for him to witness how utterly unimportant she was to her parents. And he would soon realize how she wasn't at all what a debutante ought to be.

At that point, he would see her as an oddity like the other gentlemen had, and whatever connection they'd shared would soon be severed.

She was a bundle of nerves. Waiting outside the door to the drawing room, she fanned her hands at her sides in an effort not to wrinkle her gown with the perspiration that dampened her palms.

Inside, her parents were trying to recall which one of them had invited a guest to dinner.

Jane had already told them three times that *she* had issued the invitation, but they paid no attention. They never did.

But none of that mattered now, because Raven was here. Early, in fact.

In his usual commanding prowl, he traversed the length of the hall in a floor-eating stride. A tailored dark blue coat drew her attention to the breadth of his shoulders and his trim torso in a cashmere waistcoat. He looked exceedingly handsome in his snowy cravat with his hair tamed back from his forehead.

A pair of frostbitten eyes stood out in sharp relief beneath the dark slash of his brows. The only thing that hinted at his reluctance to be here was the muscle ticking along the hard, chiseled ridge of his mandible as he clenched his teeth.

But then his gray gaze warmed as he drew closer, and witnessing it eased some of her agitation. He took in every inch of her form in a single, thorough sweep, from her lips to her pointlessly low-cut bodice and all the way down the rose-colored silk gown to the ruffled hem.

By the time his eyes met hers again, they were smoldering in blatant hunger, as if he'd come to dinner and believed that she was the intended buffet. No one had ever looked at her the way he did.

A pleasant fluttering stirred in her stomach and lungs, twirling in giddy circles. She laid a hand over her midriff, feeling peculiarly breathless. "Thank you for coming. Truth be told, I don't know what possess—"

"Is that our guest?" Lord Hollybrook asked, coming up behind her.

She turned and took a step into the drawing room as Raven followed. "Yes, Father. I'd like to introduce—"

"No. No. Don't tell me," her father said, falling into his practiced guise of blandisher by grinning and wagging his finger. Then he tapped that same digit against the side of his pursed lips as he scrutinized the cut of Raven's clothes. "I know! You're the King of Waistcoats. That cut is positively smashing. You must tell me who your tailor is. I'm giving mine the sack this instant." Then he genially held out his hand and offered, "Beauregard Pickerington, Viscount Hollybrook, and you are—Oh, wait just a moment, for I have spotted the most divine creature across the room.

Love, come hither and greet our guest with your beatific smile. Sir, I am delighted to introduce my own Clementina, Viscountess Hollybrook."

"An honor, my lord, my lady. I am Raven."

"Yes, I'm sure we've met before. Raven . . . Raven . . . Ravenscroft. Of course! Excellent family, excellent." Beneath a carefully coiffed dishevelment of short, sandy-silver hair, Father squinted, displaying two small fans of faint wrinkles beside each blue eye. "And which one are you?"

"Dearest, how rude," Mother said. With a graceful fingertip touch to her own coiffure, smoothing one errant pale strand back into the arrangement, she sashayed across the Axminster carpet in a dramatic mazarine blue gown.

"Yes, yes. Quite right," Father said. "None of that matters when our trenchers await in the dining room and our empty goblets are eager for libation."

Her mother issued a tittering laugh as she placed her hand on Father's proffered arm. "Lord Hollybrook paints quite a barbaric portrait of my place settings. *Trenchers*, indeed. The silver has been in my family for three generations. Or would it be four, now, dear?"

"Hmm," he mused, escorting his wife from the room without a backward glance. "Let's see. It was either your great-grandmama's mother, or your great-grandmama's great-grandmama. Then again . . ."

Left alone in the parlor with Raven, Jane shrugged. "And there you have Lord and Lady Hollybrook. I trust the introduction was as painless as promised."

Raven looked away from the vacant doorway to her, his brow knitted in perplexity. "I ought to correct their assumption. I don't want to mislead your parents into thinking I'm someone else."

"I'm afraid it won't matter. Dinner will commence in a similar fashion. By the end of the evening, you'll have acquired at least three different names and titles and an entire history they will have pieced together from snippets of random rumors heard at parties. Why, even I have been called Janice and Jeanette—along with other forms, therein—for an entire service before one of them recalls that I was named after my father's mother," she said in a nervous ramble, hoping to hide her embarrassment.

But Raven wasn't fooled. She could tell in the way his eyes held hers as he took her hand. Then he brought her fingers to his lips and pressed a warm lingering kiss that helped to soothe her.

"Regardless of how the night progresses, I'm glad I came," he said, settling her hand on his sleeve. "And you look lovely in that shade of pink. It makes your skin shimmer in the candlelight."

Her breath caught at the unexpected compliment. "Goodness. If that is your foray into practicing polite social conversation, then you don't require any lesson."

"I wasn't being polite. Although, I was stopping myself from adding that you look like a sugar-glazed confection."

"I suppose that isn't too scandalous."

He bent his head to whisper. "A confection that needs to be unwrapped with my teeth and savored slowly on my tongue."

His warm breath brushed the sensitive lobe of her ear, and the deep timbre sent her pulse rollicking beneath her skin like popping corn over a fire. It simmered in a place deep inside, where her inner anatomy tilted and thrummed.

If she could find her voice, she might have called him a scoundrel. Then again, she imagined he already knew that he was.

Jane entered the dining room in a glow.

Unfortunately, the pleasure wasn't to last because dinner proceeded as she'd expected.

Her parents were dragonfly conversationalists, skimming the surface of topics without ever lingering long. They were so used to altering their viewpoints to embrace popular opinion that they usually ended with an entirely different argument than when they began.

"Well, Ravenscroft," Father said, "I suppose you'll be attending the Marquess of Aversleigh's ball. All the best people are, you know."

Raven nodded and cleared his throat. When he glanced to Jane, she knew he was going to explain who he was.

But before he could, Mother interrupted. "It's for Aversleigh's oldest daughter. Her betrothal ball is sure to be the event of the year."

"No, Clementina, indeed." Beauregard shook his head, a frown knitting his tawny brows. "Remember, she's marrying a commoner."

Mother gasped. Her opinions typically served as an enhancement to his, like a sprinkle of salt over a bland meal. "I'd only remembered that the future son-in-law had a great fortune."

Father scoffed a single word, a look of utter disgust pinching his nose. "Trade."

"I simply don't know what the world is coming to," Mother answered, apparently forgetting that her own family's wealth had begun with fur trading. "Well, one thing is for certain—no daughter of ours will ever marry below her class. I'd sooner send her off to America to live with your sister."

Jane looked at the far end of the table and wondered if the woman seated there realized she was in the room, or remembered having given birth to her. Though, after eleven children, perhaps it all became too confusing. Even so, she had rarely felt so invisible.

"Then again," Father mused, "what if he were well-endowed in the bank account? After all, if it's good enough for Aversleigh . . ."

"I've always liked Americans," Mother said, reaching for her goblet. "Their accents and coarse phrasings are so . . . amusing."

Father raised his glass in salute. Setting it down again, he said, "How long will it be until Jane has her debut?"

"Our daughter has been out for two years, dear," her mother said. Then she blinked blankly. "Or is it three?"

"Three?" Father stopped cutting into his lamb and addressed his wife. "I'd have thought she'd be married by now. You only had one Season, if I recall."

Mother dabbed her napkin to the corner of her mouth then issued a distressed sigh as if preparing to impart the worst news imaginable. "Well, she still reads a great deal."

With a row of peas balanced on his knife, Raven frowned toward Lady Hollybrook's end of the table. "Many men admire a well-read woman, especially one who has a—"

"You're quite right, Raversleigh," Father interjected, busily cutting away again, knife and fork screeching over the fire-glazed porcelain. "We should support them in their endeavors. Yet, you must concede that there is a limit. This reading habit, for example, all began with an innocent collection of books from Roxburghe's library, eons ago. I never thought it would bring about a bluestocking in the family. Gratefully, it was only a temporary malady. Turned her attention to plants and flower cuttings, if I recall. Perfectly acceptable, that."

"Oh, but what a jolly time you had bidding for those books," Mother added with a smile, the topic of bluestocking plagues snuffed like a candle flame. "You were so triumphant and crowed about it for months. The Duke of Tuttlesby absolutely loathed you for outbidding him."

"And speaking of Tuttlesby, I heard a rumor that his

nephew—Woodbine, I believe—is on the market again. Had some sort of scrape-up with his prior betrothal or something of the sort. Regardless, we've been invited to dine with the duke later this week. Perhaps"—Father used his fork tines to gesture in Jane's general direction—"our daughter might entice him. We could have a duchess in our family one day, if we played our cards right."

Jane stared down at her plate, begging the stewed turnips in a white cream sauce to bring an end to dinner. But turnips were hateful vegetables. They never did what one asked.

Dinner plodded onward, dragging her along with it by the hair.

Father's next topic was his decision to hire a sportsman. He planned to use the conservatory for exercises to improve his own constitution. Then he grumbled, complaining that he'd found *a great deal of nonsense and clutter* that would need to be cleared out of the room first.

Jane only hoped that his usual forgetfulness would erase that idea before she lost her sanctuary.

Raven tried to speak on the behalf of all learned women several times, only to have the topic *and* his name change each instance. He looked so frustrated and perturbed each time that she wanted to reach out across the table and smooth her fingertips over his ruffled brow.

The obligatory after-dinner conversation moved to the music room. It involved a brief spell where Jane was prodded into *delighting* everyone on the harp.

Mother had insisted that she learn to play at a young age. Jane, having always been a relatively small person, loathed that bully of an instrument. It was nearly two times her size and forever left her shoulder sore and her fingertips feeling freshly plucked.

She studied the pink surface now as she walked alone with Raven toward the main hall.

One of her parents should have been with her to act as chaperone, but Mother had begged off the duties of hostess with a headache, and Father had followed her to their wing of the house, professing knowledge of a cure-all tonic.

They both had left in absentminded fashion, conversing with each other and forgetting to bid their daughter good-night or their guest farewell. And, doubtless, they never imagined their plain daughter would need a chaperone.

After all, who would ever be tempted by her?

"Ravenscroft to Raversleigh, and then to Rosburton might make sense, I s'pose," Raven said, walking at a leisurely pace beside her. "The one I can't understand is Thackeray."

"Well, at the time, I believe Father was speaking of quitting Holly House before Christmastide to stay in his hunting box. Then Mother interjected that she always loved that house because it rests on a hill overlooking quaint *thatched* cottages." She slid him a wry glance. "Naturally, you became Lord Thackeray."

"Ah," he mused. Then a tight exhale left him as they walked on. "There were several times when I tried to—"

"I know. You never had a chance but the sentiment was felt, all the same," she said, smiling fondly up at him as her tender-skinned fingertips stroked the cuff of his fine woolen sleeve. "It isn't purposeful, what they do. It is simply . . . the way my parents are."

"That doesn't make it right."

"It's the same in many society families. The nannies and the governesses raise the children and those children, in turn, become veritable strangers to their parents and little more than figures in a family portrait. Asking them to change would be like expecting a fern to grow oranges."

He laid his hand over hers, stroking the fine skin that covered tissue and metacarpals. A warmth spread through her nerve endings and along her limbs, seeming to converge in the center of every heartbeat.

"I understand why you carry your reticule now," he said quietly. "And your need to have every item on hand to take care of yourself, and others, in any given situation."

Looking at her, his expression altered to something so intimate, so knowing, that it felt as if he were seeing her in the bath.

A wash of embarrassment made her want to cross her arms over herself.

Because if he could know her this well, then he could also see her inadequacies and deficiencies—the ones that had always made her forgettable and invisible.

Slipping her arm free, she stepped under one of the arches lining the hall to adjust a crooked picture frame. "Well, I was an inquisitive child. I peppered my parents with so many questions that my uncle took pity on them and taught me to read early on. A new world opened for me when I learned that books could give me the answers." She realized she was babbling and waved a hand in a nervous gesture to the dimly lit doorway at the end of the hall. "And it all started there, in the library."

From the corner of her eye, she saw him move a few steps in that direction. Felt his intense curiosity. Then he looked back over his shoulder. "Show me."

The gleam of genuine interest in his gaze eclipsed her embarrassment. Not even Ellie or Winn or Prue ever wanted to see the library. She'd dragged them there, of course, on several occasions, but they'd never *asked* to go.

She couldn't resist the impulse to take his hand, and she smiled as his fingers automatically enfolded hers.

Only a single sconce was left burning on the wall by the door. The embers in the fireplace had all but extinguished, leaving a faint apricot glow to the room that didn't reach the vaulted ceiling or the *trompe l'oeil* upper gallery.

Nearby, Raven was already drawing volumes from the shelves and skimming through the pages. But it was his look of awed amazement, like a man viewing the phosphorescent glow of algae beneath the water's surface, that made her smile. She always felt that way, too.

Coming up beside him, she peered over his shoulder at the book he was studying with interest. The subject was botany. The page, plums.

A rush of warmth pulsed from her heart to the surface of her skin and she leaned back against the shelves to gaze up at him, cementing this feeling of joy in her memory.

He closed the book, returning it before giving her his full attention. Propping his shoulder against one of the horizontal ledges, he brushed his fingers along the exposed length of her arm, exciting nerve endings from elbow to wrist.

"It was nearly impossible to act the gentleman tonight. There were so many times I wanted to reach across the table and take your hand," he said, lightly threading his fingers with hers. "So many things I wanted to say to your parents."

It would have been easy to relax into his touch, but his statement sounded too much like pity for her ears. So she straightened, slipping her hand from his as she walked to the center of the room to organize the cluttered map table.

"It wouldn't have mattered," she said, affecting an air of nonchalance. "Besides, I accepted their indifference long ago."

But Raven didn't let her get too far. He stopped in front of her and crooked a finger beneath her chin to capture her gaze. "If this dinner hadn't been part of a lesson and I hadn't vowed to be on my best behavior for your sake, then I would've slammed my fist down on the table, unleashed the growl that was chained in my chest all evening, and appeared every bit the brute."

Jane instantly knew she'd been mistaken. It wasn't pity she saw in his face but something else. Something forceful and earnest and tender.

"I wanted to rail at them, Jane." Drawing her closer, he bent his forehead to hers as his rough-padded fingertips drifted to her nape, working in massaging circles that eased her unnecessary worries. "I wanted to tell them that they were idiots for not seeing that they have an exceptional daughter. The cleverest, prettiest bluestocking I've ever known."

Stunned, her mouth went dry, lips falling slack. He slid the length of his nose against hers and she closed her eyes to savor his affectionate nuzzling, the port wine taste of his warm breath on her tongue.

Her heart didn't flutter beneath her breast. No, instead it lay down like a purring cat, rolling over and exposing its underbelly. "That doesn't sound at all like you. There wasn't a single scandalous comment in your entire declaration."

There was a rakish grin in his low voice when he said, "I also would have told them that you have lips sweeter than damson jam, and that I sleep with your scent on my bedlinens every night. But I don't think they would have understood."

His lips grazed her cheek. Her temple. Her brow. And all the while, the artist standing on the portico of her brain was sketching Raven in bed, naked, and thinking of her.

"I must have poured out too much lavender water that night."

He murmured a low, knowing growl as the tip of his nose whispered across her eyelashes, his fingertips teasing the wispy tendrils at her nape. "Perhaps there's a primitive side to your nature and you wanted to leave your scent behind, hmm? You'd be scandalized by the dreams I've had ever since."

Her palms glided up the sleeves of his coat to curve around his thick shoulders and neck as she rose up on her toes. The spiced scent of bay rum clung to his clothes, blending incomparably well with his own fragrance. She inhaled deeply, fighting the urge to bury her nose in his shirtfront.

"Tell me what scoundrels dream about," she said, her inner scribe at the ready. "Scandalize me."

Chapter 24

One of them moved first. Jane wasn't certain which. All she knew was that their mouths captured each other, colliding in symbiotic need.

A sudden, startling glut of pleasure quickened her blood. It pooled deep in her midriff where their bodies met, separated by fabric and gathering heat. But this malady inside her demanded more. She needed pressure to assuage it.

Scarcely had the thought entered her mind when one of Raven's hands roved along the curve of her spine, splaying possessively and pulling her flush against the hard plane of his torso. They were now so close that she could feel the buttons of his waistcoat and the tiny silken bow of her chemise ribbon between her breasts. She nearly sighed in relief. This was so much better. Almost enough, in fact. But not quite.

She still wanted more.

Hungrily, she opened her mouth beneath the insistent pressure of his, their tongues tangling in a delicious port-and-pudding-tinged impact. She loved the textures of his kiss. The firmness of his lips. The damp silk inside. And the sharp edge of his teeth, paradoxically gentle as he nibbled into her flesh while the flat of his hand coasted over the generous slope of her bottom.

Then he cinched her tighter, lifting her feet effortlessly off the carpet. A gasp escaped her as she groped for purchase, gripping his shoulders. This position aligned their bodies in a perfect placement—navel to navel, chest to chest—and it caused the last remaining breath to shudder out of her in a rush.

He grinned at her, nipping her chin. "Surely, you're not scandalized already. I've barely begun. And there's so much of your little body I've yet to touch. To taste."

He was trying to make her blush, she knew. Well, he'd succeeded. Even so, she saw the challenge in the arch of his brow, testing her determination and willingness.

She threaded her fingers through the short silken strands of his hair and played the mimic, nuzzling against his nose, pressing soft kisses to his cheek and brow. Then she nibbled into the corner of his mouth. "Perhaps I'll be the one who tastes you first."

He growled, his lips fusing to hers in a searing kiss and, next, she found herself perched on the edge of the map table.

Perhaps she may have been too bold just now? But when his teeth rasped deliciously over her earlobe, and the hot drift of his breath on her skin awakened a siege of new receptors, she could not compel herself to recant. Instead, her neck arched in supplication under the skillful mastery of his tongue as he laved the pulse at her throat.

This wasn't about research for the book, and her brain wasn't the only part involved. Her heart, body and mind were completely enmeshed.

No one ever saw her the way Raven did. Not even Ellie, Winn or Prue understood the pain at the core of her lifelong need to bury herself in books and facts. To them, she was intelligent and capable—the friend always prepared with a plan. To the *ton*, she was merely a culmination of oddities and idiosyncrasies. To Raven, she was still all those things. But she was more, too. She was a woman, someone desirable despite her peculiarities. Perhaps even because of them.

He proved it now in the way he kissed her and held her

face so tenderly. And also in the way he tilted her head back as his mouth hungrily ravaged hers, like a man half-starved and hunched over a bowl of ripe fruit. But she felt the slightest tremor in the hands that cradled her cranium as if he were suppressing a stronger desire than he revealed.

Jane wanted him to gorge himself on her. And the very notion made her feel juicy beneath her skin, compelling her to mold her body to his.

"You don't have to hold back. Not with me," she said against his lips.

His hand tightened at her nape, a low sound vibrating deep in his throat and tingling her lips as he fed it to her. Without any argument, he slid her closer to the edge of the table, nudging her knees apart until their hips were flush.

She felt the hardness of him roll with sinuous command against her as he greedily swallowed her gasp. Having studied sketches of the male anatomy a number of times—not to mention her statue encounter—she knew what this part of him was, and knew that the process of copulation required a man's penis to gain an erection. It had all seemed so clinical in the texts. Mere lines on a page. Being an active member in the process, however, was quite a different matter altogether. Her body responded in heated, liquid pulses. She clung to him.

Wanting more, she suckled the tip of his tongue deeper into her mouth. He drew in a surprised breath, then exhaled a gruff grunt, his hips hitching against hers. A corresponding identical reaction happened in her, hips tilting, welcoming.

Friction at its finest.

Shifting her closer still, he eased her back onto the table amidst the crinkle of forgotten maps and a crunch of taffeta. Intuitively, her knees lifted higher, locking him in the throbbing cradle of her thighs. She needed to keep him here. Forever.

"What are you thinking? I have to know all the thoughts turning in this lovely skull," he said in a rasp against her lips, his fingertips gently tracing the outline of her face, skimming the shell of her ear, the line of her jaw.

His tenderness only made her want to hold him tighter.

She slipped beneath his coat and embraced him, bearing him down upon her aching breasts and quivering midriff. "I'm thinking about friction, and the combustion properties of silk and wool when rubbed together. I'm thinking about hard, geometric angles and how I never fully appreciated them until now. And I'm thinking about the canning temperature of jam."

He smiled against her lips. "And why jam, exactly?"

"Because I'm certain that my insides have turned liquid, like a pot of plums and sugar bubbling over." Her hips arched, tilting automatically in that same instant so there was no mistaking her meaning.

His eyes were the color of smoke and steam, burning down into hers. Then he took her mouth again.

Jane stopped thinking. She gave herself over to the feel of his hand rising along the curve of her waist, splaying over the cage of her ribs, and settling with firm possession over the swell of her breast.

She knew she was small. Certainly not endowed like any of the prostitutes she'd seen that night at the brothel. But the vibration of Raven's gruff growl of satisfaction put any insecurities to bed. The hard bud of her nipple crested against his heated palm. Skillful flicks of his thumb drew it tighter still as his mouth scorched a damp path down her throat with tender bites along her clavicle. A glorious agony!

Teasing the edge of her gown at her shoulder, he gripped the silk and the ruffled edge of her chemise and petticoat, tugging them down together. Still not one to wear a corset, she soon found the moon-white globe exposed to the flicker of pale apricot light. And to Raven's ardent attention.

His breath came out in a hot rush against her vulnerable skin. "Ah, Jane. Just look at you, all cream and berries and . . ."

His observations ended on a brush of lips. She gasped in wordless pleasure as his mouth closed over her, his tongue laving the crest with slow, wet licks. Holding him to her breast, her fingers tangled in his hair. She never knew anything could feel so electric and wondrous, sensations collecting on a current, coiling tightly inside her body.

Just when she thought the pleasure couldn't get any more intense, he suckled her flesh. *Volta's battery!* Her back bowed off the table. Rapture bolted through her like lightning and settled in demanding throbs between her thighs.

Seeking pressure against the ache, she twined her legs around his hips. But he didn't comply. Instead, he shifted to one side, and a frustrated huff left her when she hadn't the strength to pull him back.

"Shh . . ." he said against her lips, kissing her tenderly. "So impatient. Some experiments take time, you know. We have to gather information. Test the response of our subject."

His hand eased down her midriff, covering her navel with his palm, his fingertips resting just above the thin layer of taffeta and cambric, and the shallow rise of her mons.

Anticipating the direction of his next touch, her body quivered with the barest amount of trepidation, her breath held captive in her lungs. But he altered course, skimming over to the curve of her waist. He gripped her hip in a tender massage as his lips nibbled softly into hers. And he reassured her endlessly until her own impatience caused her to list toward him.

She needed more. Ever astute, Raven already seemed aware of this. His dexterous hand followed the slope of her bent leg down to her hem . . . and beneath.

Jane started thinking again. She wondered if her woolen stockings were too chaste, too unworldly a garment compared to what he'd encountered before. Or if he thought her too small as he covered her kneecap and spanned the circumference of her thigh.

"You're perfect," he whispered as if she'd worried those thoughts aloud. "So soft. I never knew anything could be so soft, Jane. I want to take a bite of you. See if you'll melt on my tongue like freshly fallen snow. And I want to kiss you here . . . all along this silken path . . ." The tips of his fingers brushed her bare inner thighs, almost tickling, almost soothing her trembling limbs. His lips glided back and forth over hers, matching the gentle up-and-down sweeps beneath her skirts. "I'll stop whenever you ask. But please don't ask. At least, not yet."

His rough plea sent a surprising thrill through her and, giving him her full trust, she nodded in acquiescence. He reassured her with every kiss, and with every touch as his hand descended.

She felt the first brush of her damp curls with an acuity of a butterfly's antennae. He continued with scholarly care, cataloguing every panting breath of his subject, collecting her responses to his tender exploration. Then he cupped her fully.

A breath staggered out of her and her knees reflexively clamped shut in shy embarrassment, even as her hips arched in invitation. The combination of movements effectively pressed him harder against her. And strangely, his breathing was now strained with erudite patience.

The way his hand molded to her, caused her pulse to

bump against the curve of his palm. He pressed back and she bit into her bottom lip on the most excruciatingly lovely ache.

"Your hand feels quite different than my own," she said in a hurry of hoarse nervousness. Staring up at his face, she saw his eyes close as he went still. At once, she worried she'd spoiled everything. "I didn't ask you to stop."

"I know. I'm merely taking a moment to savor the vision of my naughty little professor hiking her nightdress above her hips and playing underneath the coverlet."

"Playing," she scoffed but with a smile, wondering if he noticed that he'd said *"my* little professor."

"Exploratory research, then?"

This time she rewarded him with a kiss, cupping his cheek. "Better."

He inhaled deeply, satisfied in some way. Mouths locked in an embrace of their own, he shifted, rising up and angling his body possessively. And with one leg drawn over hers, his finger winnowed her curls with tender deftness, cultivating her pleasure until she forgot all about being nervous or scandalized.

All she wanted was him. She told him this secret in the way her lips and fingers touched his face and throat, his nape and shoulders. She wanted him to feel the affection spilling from her heart in heavy gushes and flooding every vein. So she eased her knees apart and heard his murmur of approval.

His studies resumed. He investigated the sensitive folds with expert care and long-fingered gliding strokes, teasing ripe flesh until the tips of his fingers were saturated with dew. Then he slowly delved inside the swollen seam on a hiss as if scalded by her heat.

Undeterred, he navigated an erotic path up to the tender

throbbing pearl, chasing the pulsing sensation in furtive circles. Her gasp echoed in the library. The aged leather-bound tomes were surely scandalized, blushing in red and burgundy hues. But she didn't care.

Her hips tilted eagerly. She wanted to skim through the lesson to reach the final exam. He eased that one clever finger away from the bud and she whimpered in protest before she understood he was following the narrow runnel down to the vulnerable opening.

Her senses heightened in helpless anticipation.

Then the blunt tip nudged inside and he cursed under his breath, the husky sound like a pained prayer. "You're even softer here. Soft . . . and wet . . . and snug."

He punctuated every word with another nudge, knuckles edging inside one by one, stroking the inner walls. Her body closed around the gradual invasion and he shuddered, his palm pressing against the inexorable pulse.

She was lost in the exquisite torture of it all and arched her neck to drag in a breath. In that same instant, his mouth descended to her exposed breast, overwhelming her nervous system with heady sensation.

He feasted on her pale flesh. The tight swirling flicks of his tongue matched the firm rotation of his palm against the throbbing bud, his finger driving deep into the narrow channel. A new restlessness settled inside her, drawing tight.

Her own explorations had never been this in-depth. Her fumblings had left her damp-skinned and frustrated. But this was so much more—a chemical reaction with perfectly measured components. Coupled with the application of this luxuriant friction, she felt on the verge of detonation.

Tingles scattered out from her core in cascading ripples, keeping her from being embarrassed over the slick sounds of her desire. She wanted this—whatever it was—too much. Her hips bucked involuntarily, riding counter to his rhythm.

And Raven captured her lips on a groan as if the cataclysm were happening to him as well.

His finger thrust faster into the slick constriction, his palm rubbing in circles, urging her on and on until she could hear the crackle of her own blood rushing in her ears.

Every part of her exploded at once.

She shattered like a firework in the night sky, hanging suspended in the heavens beneath Raven's skillful, unending caress as he dragged out every last flicker. Then he coaxed her into a slow, easy descent to the earth again.

She went boneless onto the map table, an awed sigh floating up from her lungs in a vapor that surely sparkled. Eyes closed, she said on a sigh, "Gunpowder must be so happy when it ignites."

He chuckled against her throat, then dipped his head to press a kiss to her bare breast, spurring another voluptuous kick from her body. Just a small firework, but it made her smile nonetheless.

"Is that what it will feel like for you? Will you describe it while it's happening?"

Slowly, he withdrew his hand, her body closing on emptiness. Then deftly he situated her clothes before gathering her in his arms. His mouth pressed to her temple. "I'm not going to strip you of your maidenhead in the library, Jane."

She frowned, slipping her hands inside his coat and feeling the tandem, thundering beats of their hearts. "Whyever not? It seems like a perfect place to me, and I can feel your readiness for copulation against my thigh."

To be sure he knew her determination well enough, she wriggled against him.

He let out a low groan then stilled her, holding her tighter. "The door isn't even closed, let alone locked. Aren't public displays of this nature frowned upon in polite society?"

"At this hour of night, a closed door would only indicate

to a passerby that those within are engaging in activities that require concealment. Logically, an open door is our best chaperone."

Thankfully, she also knew that Mr. Miggins had retired for the night, so she'd never worried. Then again, after the kissing began, she hadn't been thinking about anything or anyone other than Raven.

If someone had caught them . . . the consequences would have been dire.

While Jane had never worried that her escapades would cause her ruin—primarily because her parents were decidedly indifferent to her activities—being found *in flagrante delicto* on the map table would have been a different matter altogether.

Even with her virginity still intact, she would have been sent from London. Away from her friends. Away from her family. And, most definitely, away from Raven.

The realization sent a cold chill through her.

She burrowed closer. "In hindsight, I suppose it was reckless. But we'll plan the next time better," she said against his waistcoat. "I'll steal away from Ellie's one evening and—"

"There isn't going to be a next time," he said. "Now don't stiffen up on me and think it's because you're lacking in worldliness. It isn't that at all. In fact, it's the opposite. I want you, which you clearly know. All I can think about is how good it would feel to lift your skirts and fill your sweet body with my flesh, right here on this table."

The chill evaporated under a blushing wave that trembled through her at the tableau he formed in her mind. She looked up at him, still not understanding.

He kissed her forehead, then both of her cheeks, and against her lips he said, "I don't want you to regret me."

"I wouldn't."

"Jane, I'm not going to claim my birthright. There are still too many unanswered questions for me. It could be years before I find the answers, and maybe not even then."

"I don't care about any of that."

"Your parents care. And you may think you don't care, but in the future when you find some proper chap you might want to marry, you'll remember this night and wish you hadn't given yourself to me first." He smiled tenderly and brushed the fine tendrils away from her cheek. "All I can give you are fireworks. Eventually, you'll want something more. Believe me, I've traveled this road and I know where it ends."

She shook her head to argue, but a yawn slipped out. She was suddenly overwhelmed with exhaustion.

Sleepily, she twined her arms around him once more. "Don't leave yet. I want to disprove your hypothesis."

"Let me play the part of the gentleman while I still can, hmm?"

He kissed her tenderly once more, then left without another word.

Jane lay back on the map table and closed her eyes. She wondered why Raven, who was usually so astute, didn't realize that he'd already given her more than fireworks. So much more than she ever expected to find from a study of scoundrels.

Chapter 25

The following afternoon, Raven stood at the window in the Earl of Warrister's paneled study and watched the Marquess of Aversleigh drive off in his carriage.

"Well done, my boy," Warrister said from behind him. "Reginald was quite impressed. Your lack of loquacity only amplified your aura of mystery, I'm sure."

Raven's mouth curled into a wry smirk, not missing the earl's heavy-laden sarcasm.

"I didn't know what to say," he admitted, turning toward the bemusedly grinning old man at his desk. "You just introduced me as your grandson and the marquess shook my hand genially, without any hesitation or doubt from either of you. But you must have doubts."

Warrister shook his head. "I knew the instant I clapped eyes on you that you were—you *are*—my grandson."

The earl had made this very statement on their previous visits, as well. But the question of certainty still rattled around in Raven's skull.

"People tend to see what they want to." He hesitated, weighing his next words carefully. "Considering all the hope you must have had over the years, and then to receive a letter from your housekeeper, no one could fault you for wanting to find a long-lost grandson."

Warrister picked up a walnut from a dish and absently

cracked it open, leaving the shards to litter the desk. "I'm neither senile, nor a romantic fool."

"That may be true"—Raven broke off when the earl's wizened eyes speared him—"I mean, of course, you're not," he amended and gained a grunt of forgiveness. "But there's still a few pieces of the puzzle missing. It doesn't make sense that someone would have saved me but never bothered to come to you for a reward, like all the others had."

He didn't want to hurt the man when all this came to nothing. And he knew it would come to nothing. He sensed it. There were too many questions left unanswered. Too many ways he could be taken off guard if he allowed himself to believe.

Only children had blind faith. Like all the times he'd had the notion of running away from the workhouse to gain freedom, just to be caught unawares when he least expected. Then dragged back and punished. The brutal memories still caused a shudder to roll through him—the darkness of the cupboard, the *scritch-scratch* of rat claws skittering closer, and the sharp, tiny edges of their teeth.

Without thinking, he stepped closer to the fire in the study to ward off a cold chill. Staring into the flames, he recalled a multitude of harsh life lessons when he'd foolishly allowed hope to eclipse the need for certainty. He'd never make that mistake again.

"Believe it or not, I've considered the same questions," Warrister said, drawing Raven's attention. Then, tapping a finger to his temple, he added, "Not senile, you see. *And* I have a man making inquiries at that foundling home. He had a brief discussion with the beadle, a certain Mr. Mayhew. But my man said that Mayhew seemed to be a very nervous fellow. Especially when asked how his bank accounts increased substantially during the years of the French Terror.

Regrettably, Mayhew eluded my man before we could get to the bottom of the mystery."

Frowning, Raven asked, "But what does Mayhew have to do with any of it?"

"Only time will tell. He could be the key to everything, or it could come to nothing." The earl shrugged, unconcerned. "Regardless, you're still my grandson."

Raven expelled an impatient breath.

Warrister chuckled and slapped the meat from the nutshell into his palm then popped it into his mouth, chewing it with a twinkle-eyed grin. "You're just as stubborn as your father.

"I remember the day Edgar came into this very room to tell me he'd decided to marry a French girl he met by happenstance," Warrister continued, a reminiscent smile on his lips. "His mother and I had chosen a debutante from a good family, but he wouldn't have her. Edgar and I had our share of words that day, but he'd never wavered. Just stood there with his fists and jaw clenched." He arched a brow and made an offhand gesture to Raven's own posture. "But it turned out that he was right all along. Arabelle proved to be a kind, caring and loyal woman. She looked at my son as if the heavens and earth had converged to form one perfect person. Much like the way Miss Pickerington looks at you, I imagine."

Raven forced himself to keep a neutral expression. But in the center of his chest, he felt that painful, burning harpooning again. "I'm sure I wouldn't know."

Warrister chuckled again. Easing back against the leather upholstery of his winged-back chair, he steepled his fingers. "Are you going to marry the gel? If you are, you'll need the title to satisfy her father. And she has plenty of brothers and sisters for whom to set an example."

"You've been spying, it seems."

"I have my sources."

"Well, you can't use her to badger me into being introduced as Merrick Northcott at Aversleigh's ball," Raven said, straightening his shoulders. "I'll go there as myself and as your grandson, if you like, but I don't want the title. And I don't need it either because I'm not planning to marry. At all."

For the first time all afternoon, Warrister's smile fell. "It will be your duty to carry on the Northcott line with legitimate heirs. Miss Pickerington comes from a robust family line. However, if you don't want her, I'll find someone else for you."

"I don't want *any* wife," Raven said with an irritated swipe of his hand in the air as he began to pace the floor. "I've been intimately acquainted with a number of them and, let's just say, I wouldn't be willing to share. I keep what's mine."

The years he'd been the plaything of Mrs. Devons and her friends had left a sour taste on the back of his tongue when it came to the notion of marriage. In addition, there were countless society wives who'd whispered propositions in his ear at Sterling's while their husbands played hazard in the next room.

"I see," Warrister said, thoughtfully staring into the fire. "Then I suggest you end your acquaintance with your . . . *Jane*, as you called her. She's likely to have misunderstood your intentions. And too long in any gentleman's company, without explanation, will not bode well for her reputation."

After last night in the library, Raven knew the earl was right.

He couldn't risk seeing Jane again. If she'd meant nothing to him, he never would have stopped. He'd have taken her, there on the map table. But the very fact that he had stopped told him that his initial feelings of merely liking her had turned into a genuine affection.

If he gave himself over to it, he'd become vulnerable.

There'd be no telling when the rug'd be pulled out from under his feet. That's what would happen. That's what always happened.

So, from now on, it was better if he just kept his distance.

"It's already done and over," he said with a tight shrug and went back to the window to stare blindly at the traffic in the square.

Behind him, Warrister cracked another nut. "I'm sure Aversleigh will be delighted to hear that. He has a son your age, Lord Manning, a widower without an heir. He doesn't keep much society, though. Bookish sort of fellow. From what I gather, however, Miss Pickerington had made quite an impression on him this past spring. Apparently, she said something or other that inspired an idea to improve the condensing engine he'd been building for some time."

Raven twisted around, biting back a low growl in his throat. "And why are you telling me this?"

"No reason," Warrister said flippantly. "Other than knowing that the two of them will be attending the same dinner at the Duke of Tuttlesby's tomorrow evening. If you like, I could garner you an invitation. Tuttlesby is an old friend."

Incredulous, Raven almost wanted to laugh. "I don't need an invitation. As I said, there's nothing between Jane—*Miss Pickerington*," he corrected, "and myself."

The old codger merely smiled in response.

❧❧❧

Dearest Jane,

Your last letter saved me from another visit with the widow and her spinster daughter down the lane. As I write this response, I am blissfully alone in the parlor where I can pretend this is a mere visit with my aunt and uncle instead of a life sentence.

As you may have surmised by my lack of mentioning the topic of Lord F— in these past four letters, I have been at sixes and sevens since his unexpected presence in the village. His pursuit has been nothing more than a plague upon my conscience.

Thankfully, I need not worry about him any longer. After our last meeting, he went away without a word, and his lack of correspondence indicates that I shall never hear from him again. I am relieved, of course. Indisputably relieved.

Your friend,
Prudence Thorogood

Standing in the pale November light, Ellie lowered the letter and crumpled it to her bosom. She stepped away from the garret window in slow, mournful steps. "My heart is breaking for her. To have this terrible man pursue her at such lengths goes beyond the pale! Well, that settles it—I shall speak with my aunts about a long visit with Prue when winter ends. And I shall write to her more than thrice per week."

"I shall do the same." Jane nodded and continued perusing the assortment of trunks in search of the one containing the ball gown from her presentation at court two years ago.

However, in the back of her mind, her thoughts were similar to Prue's.

Raven hadn't returned. She thought that, after the evening they'd shared, he would have awakened yesterday morning wanting to see her with the same yearning that she felt.

For the purpose of the primer, she tried to describe the sensation. But there were no words. It was more of a feeling. She likened it to being one of the clematis vines that covered trees in the corner of the conservatory. They grew quickly, tendrils reaching out blindly to seek purchase on the branch of a neighbor tree, connecting them both in an autumn flowering arch.

Logically, she knew she wasn't a vine on a tree. Even so, she felt herself reaching out blindly, waiting for Raven to take her hand.

But deep inside, she feared that he would stay away again. He seemed to only want to get so close before he put distance between them.

"How is the scoundrel portion of our book faring? Did you receive those chapters that Winnie promised?" Ellie asked, trying on a feathered bonnet from atop a dressmaker's dummy. Tying the green ribbons around her neck, she stepped over to the oval standing mirror to pose like a sketch from *La Belle Assemblée*.

"I did, and they will be quite useful. However, I am not of the belief that Lord Holt belongs in the scoundrel portion of the book," Jane said, avoiding mention of her own study of a true scoundrel and the worries that were plaguing her. "And what about your hunt for a certain gentleman neighbor?"

Ellie issued a disconsolate sigh in response and began searching through another trunk. "George recently returned from the country and he has been in a fractious mood ever since. I don't know what to make of it."

It seemed that all three of them—Jane, Ellie and Prue—were having similar experiences with the men in their lives.

Behind her, Ellie clapped and said, "Jane! I've found your gown!"

Turning, her breath caught as her gaze skimmed over yards and yards—well, perhaps not too many yards considering she was so short—of pale silvery-blue taffeta, spilling down to a Vandyked hem. "I'd forgotten how lovely it was."

"You're so silly," Ellie commented with a grin on her lips. "Don't you realize that this is the precise color of your scoundrel's eyes?"

Jane blushed, only now realizing why she'd been determined to wear this gown to the ball. Because it reminded her of Raven.

But was he *her* scoundrel?

When she first began her research for the primer, she never would have wondered such a thing. Her study of scoundrels had begun with perfectly sound reasoning.

Now, she worried that she was perilously close to losing her head.

Therefore, she decided at once that it was time to resume her dedicated focus on the primer.

"That will do nicely," she said, adopting a neutral tone. "What do you think I should wear to the Duke of Tuttlesby's dinner tonight?"

Ellie scoffed. "I thought you said you were going to claim a headache and stay home. After all, how could either of us be in the room with that horrid Mr. Woodbine after the way he treated our Winnie when they were betrothed? Well, not unless we were planning to poison him."

Jane considered the possibility for a moment or two.

Then she shook her head. "No. Winnie is content. And surely, we must be beyond the timeframe when poisoning would have been appropriate."

"Hmm . . . true." Ellie sighed, forlorn. "I hope I do not look back on a life of misspent opportunities. Then again, who's to say I don't have a terrible carriage accident on my way home? It could be that all I'll have to show for my efforts to marry George is a gravestone in the family plot not too far from his own."

"Fear not. I would plant flowers that would bloom all year for you, and design a mechanical watering device that would be powered by the wind so they would never wither."

"Thank you ever so." Ellie laughed and found another gown. "You'd look smashing in the cerise gown this evening. It is the color of love. Perhaps it will inspire one of the gentlemen there to woo you."

"I shan't hold my breath. I recall wearing that last spring with little success, other than an invigorating chat about condensing engines with Lord Manning. And then, afterwards, I never saw him again for the rest of the Season."

"Well, with any luck, it will inspire the right man to do more than just talk."

"The right man," Jane murmured, holding the gown at arm's length as if eyeing it critically. In the back of her mind, however, she was still thinking about Raven.

"Would you like to hear something amusing?" Ellie asked, digging toward the bottom of the trunk to find the matching slippers. "Ever since I was here for tea with you and your scoundrel, I started to wonder if you were falling in love with him . . ."

Jane went still, but her head started to spin like a whirligig. She felt giddy and somewhat nauseous as if she were going to laugh and vomit at the same time.

". . . he is handsome, after all," her friend continued, oblivious, her voice echoing inside the trunk. "And scads of rakish appeal. I even admit that my own heart fluttered. But, of course, no one could ever take George's place."

The truth came to Jane in that same mysterious way that brought pages of text to the forefront of her mind. Suddenly she knew an answer without ever having asked herself the question.

And she, who had begun her research in part to find evidence of love, had somehow stumbled upon it without having taken a single note.

"Oh, Ellie," she said, mystified. "I do believe I am."

Chapter 26

It was the most frustrating evening of Raven's life. He never should have come to the Duke of Tuttlesby's dinner party in the first place.

Yesterday, he'd left Warrister's town house feeling completely sure of himself. Only to return early this morning to beg for a bloody introduction to Tuttlesby and gain an invitation to His Grace's dinner. The earl hadn't even bothered to hide his merriment.

So, before Raven had left, he'd said, "This changes nothing."

To that, the old codger had grinned. "Of course not."

Arriving at Tuttlesby's soiree, he'd met a pompous windbag named Woodbine, an assortment of *accomplished* debutantes—or so their parents said—and a certain Lord Manning.

But no Jane.

He felt duped. Manipulated. He thought Warrister had planned the whole thing.

After dinner, they all gathered in the parlor. Raven's irritation only mounted as Lord Manning took him into his confidence to wax poetic about the brilliant Miss Pickerington. By all accounts, she was his muse for the engine improvements he'd created. And, while Manning droned on and on, Raven had the unsettling picture in his mind of Jane and Manning standing in the conservatory, surrounded by their dozen children.

"I'd hoped to see her this evening," Manning said, cleaning the golden-rimmed spectacles against the knee of his trousers. "But I learned, shortly before I arrived, that Lord and Lady Hollybrook had sent their apologies, stating their daughter was unwell."

The news sent a shock through Raven, banishing all the hot irritation and turning it cold. He never even thought she could be ill.

He stood and, without begging anyone's pardon, left to fetch Sterling's horse from the stables. Then he rode to Westbourne Green in the light of the full moon, under a cold midnight sky.

He never expected to see a light within the Holly House conservatory, the frosty window glass aglow from within.

He rubbed his hand in a circle on the pane and peered inside to find Jane at her desk, her pen fervently scribbling over a sheet of paper.

Tapping on the glass, he saw her head turn instantly. And as she walked to the door, he was perplexed to see her dressed in a deep red gown, her hair gradually coming undone from a coiffure. She appeared as though she'd gone out this evening.

"I thought you were unwell," he said the instant she opened the door.

She looked at him queerly, tilting her head to the side. "That is an odd way of greeting me. What would give you cause to believe I'm ill?"

"Apparently, everyone at the Duke of Tuttlesby's dinner party."

"Oh, that." With an absent shrug, she latched the door behind him, then proceeded to walk back to her desk. "I had a pressing matter on my mind so I claimed a headache. But wait." She stopped on the path and turned back to him, eyes wide. "Were *you* there?"

"Is it so hard to believe that I was invited? And besides, wasn't that the purpose of your lessons?"

"Well, yes. I mean, no. I—" she stammered perplexedly. "I only wanted you to find a level of comfort in society."

Crowded by vines and branches, he took her by the shoulders to turn her around, gesturing with a wave of his hand for her to proceed toward the clearing.

"Were you aware that I'd planned to attend before you went, or was this mere happenstance?" she asked once they reached her desk.

Issuing a noncommittal grunt, he walked by her to the stove, sloshing the kettle to ensure there was enough water for a cup of tea. Then he lifted the curfew and stuffed a few fresh pieces of kindling inside.

When he faced her again, her lips slowly began to curl up at the corner. "You did know, didn't you? That's the reason you went to that stuffy old duke's party."

Feeling like seven kinds of fool, he sidestepped the question and jerked his chin toward her desk. "So, what's your *pressing matter*?"

"Oh, simply a chart of progression. It is always difficult to accurately number every part of the process after a result has been unexpectedly obtained."

He didn't know what she was talking about but it was better than him having to explain the reasons he'd gone to the duke's dinner. "Let me help, then. Talk through the stages and we'll number them together."

"Hmm. Yes, you would offer the best assistance in this particular matter. Sometimes you know my thoughts better than I do." Distracted from her interrogation, she studied the page in earnest. "Now, I do not believe it began in the brothel; however, I cannot discount the initial spark of interest. This, as you know, led me to study your person in such depth as to scrutinize your brown thread."

He felt his brow pucker in bemusement and he chuckled, still ignorant of her topic. "Yes, I recall the moment."

"Then later in your bedchamber," she continued, "there were those instances when you were attempting to shock me. I admit, I had been shocked. But, more importantly, I had felt another spark. At the time, I'd passed it off as mere curiosity. Until I saw your books. Then I felt something else that I could not define. It was only later that I gave it a label of admiration."

"Admiration," he parroted, feeling the warmth from the stove blanket him.

"I've always admired you for creating a life out of nothing and pushing through every obstacle in your path. You're quite an exceptional man."

He stared down at her profile and knew that it wasn't the fire making him warm.

The tip of her finger absently drifted over her notes. "Seeing all your positive qualities, here on the page—not to mention how those sparks of interest turned into something far more earth-shattering on the map table—I cannot fathom how the conclusion evaded my consciousness for so long."

"And what conclusion is that, exactly?"

From over the top of the paper, she blinked at him as if bewildered by the question. "Why, that I love you of course. I've been trying to figure out when I first fell. It's a vital component for my research."

She came up to him and shared the page, her puckered brow and pursed lips so earnest that she didn't seem to realize that he'd gone still. Or that he'd stopped breathing.

Her declaration had taken him completely by surprise. The words rushed in his ears in a sudden sweet flood, threatening the walls he'd constructed to protect himself over the years. It was terrifying. It was wondrous. And it was maddening, because he didn't know what to do.

"Now, if you could take a look at this chart. Have I missed any of the crucial moments when it might have—"

Raven turned her in his arms.

He heard the paper crumple between them and her soft gasp of surprise as he lowered his mouth to hers. He had to tether himself to something grounded, something real, something logical. And Jane was all those things.

Smart as she was, she knew exactly what he needed. She pulled him into the welcome of her slender arms as they twined around his neck.

At once he was engulfed in her powdery scent, her body rising to meet his. Yet, somehow, he could still feel her words as if they were branded in his ears and scribed on his lips and tongue. Every tender press and soft sigh caused another deluge of this terrifying, wondrous thing to ram relentlessly against his fortress.

His heart pounded back with equal force. It felt like he was surrounded by a rising flood beyond his control. So Raven clung to her tighter, lifting her off the stone tiles. If he was going to drown, then he was keeping her with him.

He'd never had anyone love him. Never had anyone of his own before. And Jane *was* his.

According to her rules, he'd claimed her the day he'd introduced her to his grandfather by using her given name. And who was he to argue with propriety?

"You're mine now," he growled, needing her to understand.

Against his lips, he tasted her smile. "If I am yours, Raven, then you are mine."

Chapter 27

Jane was lost in Raven's ardent embrace. There was something desperate and fierce in the way he held her, his hands fisting in her clothes. And he'd never kissed her this way before, taking possession of her lips in searing passes and deep, fathomless pulls as if he were branding her.

How could she focus on her chart when her entire being was fully immersed in the love she'd only just discovered today?

So she gave herself over to it, slanting her mouth beneath his. The chart could wait until later. Much, much later.

His skin felt smooth against her lips and chin, smelling clean and freshly shaven. And his tongue tasted sweet like brandy as he held her tighter against him.

He growled in appreciation as his hands roamed down her body, claiming every inch he touched, splaying into the dip in her spine, molding over the curve of her waist, and the plump flesh of her bottom, delighting all her senses. After experiencing the map table, her body responded with eager pulses that descended quickly to the cradle of her thighs.

"Where are you taking me?" she asked, feeling the shift of their bodies with his sure-footed steps along the path.

"To your napping spot."

His voice was so low and deep that it sent a flutter directly to her midriff. Breathless, she asked, "Planning to tuck me in, or are we napping together?"

"Whatever you like. But first, I'm hoping to . . . expand your research."

He lifted her higher, just enough for her to feel the hard outline of his flesh. There was no mistaking his meaning.

A thrill trampled through her, along with a hint of trepidation. "And are you going to be thorough?"

"Quite," he said resolutely and nipped lightly on her chin. A silver glint of wickedness sparked in his gray-smoke irises.

But any qualms she may have had were abandoned the instant he commenced a scorching path down her neck. She surrendered her throat to his openmouthed kisses, loving the way he laved the tender pulse that throbbed helplessly and wantonly for him.

"How shall we begin? And will I need to take notes?" she asked when they reached the secluded chaise longue.

He lowered her feet to the tiles in one sinuous slide of her body over his, awakening thousands of tingling receptors. Lifting his hands to her hair, he deftly withdrew the pins holding her coiffure in place, loosening the silken strands to fall softly against her nape and shoulders.

"I'm going to start off by sampling every inch of your delightful little body," he said tilting her chin up for a kiss. But then he stopped and frowned in speculation. "Why are you biting your lip? What is it that you're holding back?"

She released her lower lip and shook her head. "Well, for you to have access to *every* inch, I could not be wearing any clothes. And that thought reminded me of the first time I was naked in the conservatory. It involved a study of an ant colony that went awry, and an unsuspecting gardener who has never been able to look me in the eye again."

Raven laughed, tilting back his head and holding her close. "There is no one else in the whole world like you, Jane Pickerington."

With a smile lingering on his lips, he cupped her face and

kissed her so tenderly it was as if he was telling her something else altogether. Something true and earnest. It drifted inside her with every caress, floating down into the deepest part of her heart in a secret whisper.

He didn't draw back to speak the words aloud. That wasn't his way. But she felt the promise in them all the same.

He continued this rare kiss, his fingertips skimming lightly over her buttons as the coolness of the air contrasted with the heat of his touch. Her dress soon became a puddle on the floor, followed an instant later by a ripple of her petticoat and then her chemise.

She was positively shameless. Naked aside from her stockings and slippers, she felt no shyness, only fascination with the ardent hunger in his gaze. And it was because he was looking at her. *Her!*

"*Jane*," he murmured on a hot breath that rushed over the crest of her shoulder and fell lightly against one pale pink nipple. It pebbled against the airy sensation. He cursed in appreciation and this breath took the same path, too, drawing her flesh tighter still, her small breasts feeling heavy and ripe. "You are a living fantasy. I don't even know where to begin because I want all of you at once."

"Hold that thought, glutton," she teased, lifting her hand to his cravat. "After all, if you're planning to be thorough, then so am I."

Though, having little experience with undressing a male over the age of four, she fumbled a bit with untying the length of raw silk. His coat was slightly damp, and only then did she hear the soft pattering on the glass.

"You rode in the rain," she said inanely, blinking up at him with worry. "You must be dreadfully cold."

Though he didn't appear cold at all with the slashes of burnished color over the crests of his cheeks and bridge of his nose. And his gaze smoldered down at her when he said,

"Then you'd best make haste to get these wet togs off."

She did her best. But the tailored superfine wool clung to his broad shoulders and the sleeves turned inside out along the way. She unfastened the buttons of his waistcoat and leaned forward to nudge the garment down his arms. Then she gasped as her nipples grazed his shirt, the linen abrading the sensitive rosebud flesh into taut peaks.

He grinned against her lips at her discovery. His hands splayed over her back to draw her flush against him, teaching her the delicious lesson of contrasting textures of fabric against bare skin.

"Oh, I quite like that," she breathed, rubbing her shivering flesh against the warmth rising through his clothes.

On a low growl, he swiftly stripped out of his shirtsleeves, letting them fall unheeded to the floor. She nearly chided him for skipping through one part of her research, but then he gathered her back into his arms and . . . *oh, sweet anatomy!*

He was so firm where she was soft. So enticingly coarse where she was smooth. The dark furring of crisp, springy hairs across his chest abraded her nipples to pleasure-stung peaks that sent a quickening to her womb.

"You should have told me about this. Had I known, I might have stripped you from your clothes while you were still pink," she rasped huskily, inhaling the delicious spice of his neck as he tilted her head back to take her mouth again.

He smirked as his fingertips skimmed over her shoulder blades, along her spine and over the ample globes of her buttocks, arousing her in gently gripping passes. "My naughty little professor."

She felt the hardness of him pressed thickly against her middle, and she slid her hands down his torso on a slow exploration to the waist of his trousers. But she paused along the way to appreciate the firm breadth of his chest, sliding her fingers through the fascinating curls. His brown nipples hardened to taut discs beneath the attention of her lips. And the muscles along his abdomen quivered slightly as she splayed both hands over him and slid around to his narrow, tight waist.

Unable to help herself, she pressed her nose against the fine trail of hair dusting his stomach, above and below his navel. She breathed in the intoxicating scent of male skin and heat and musk. And since she was already there, she peppered his flesh with kisses.

His hands caressed her shoulders and arms and ribs, and stole underneath to cup her breasts. She straightened then, arching into his palms, breathless and greedy. Fascinated, she watched as his thumbs gently circled her nipples, every rotation exciting the pulse between her thighs as if connected by the same mechanism.

"I'm positively shameless. In all the novels I've read about women suffering scandalous male advances, they always faint to save their virtue."

His lips rasped against the shell of her ear, nuzzling gently into her loose curls. "If you want to save your virtue, you'd better tell me quick."

"I wouldn't dream of asking you to stop. Not when I'm thrumming from head to toe and waiting to become a firework again." She knew she sounded wanton but she didn't care, not even when he chuckled. "I'm simply wondering why they never write novels where the heroine is brave and admits that she is curious, too."

He nipped at her earlobe as her hands drifted to his fastenings. "I knew from the moment we met that your curiosity would be my undoing."

She blushed at the compliment. Then, without even looking, the buttons slipped free. She was amazed at her own deftness. And as she turned her head to press her lips to his, she let the fall front . . . fall.

The heavy heat of him reared out through the opening and lay thickly against her belly. He snaked an arm around her slender waist and pulled her firmly against him, biting out her name on a groan of unabashed pleasure.

She pushed away, but only far enough to steal between their bodies, to find and explore the silken flesh. His phallus was fascinating and hot. She ran the tip of her inquisitive fingers along the granite-hard column, sensing the rush of scorching blood inside the engorged tissue. Her small ivory hand investigated his dusky length, the thick veined shaft and mushroomed head. Then her thumb rolled over the glistening bead resting at the top. She heard his breath shudder, felt it flow through her in throbbing, liquid beats.

"You're wet, too," she whispered, but soon found herself lifted off her feet.

He enfolded her against him as he laid her back on the chaise longue, his hands coasting over her body, touching, teasing, stirring. However, when she moved to reciprocate, he issued a short grunt, took both her wrists in one hand and lifted her arms above her head.

"Did I do something incorrectly?" she asked.

Poised over her, he shook his head in a brush against her lips. "No, Jane. In fact, you've been an exemplary pupil. You've earned the high marks for today and now it's time for your reward."

"Then I want to touch you more."

"If you do, then our lesson will end far, far too soon," he said with a rueful smirk. Then gazed down on her with something akin to wonderment, his free hand tracing the wispy arc of her brow, the slope of her nose and the outline of her lips. "You're always surprising me, you know. I think that's just one of the reasons."

"One of the reasons for what?"

He answered her in a kiss—a kiss that was apparently

meant to obliterate her ability to think because that's precisely what it did.

She didn't bother to struggle against the hand that kept hers locked above her head. She simply gave herself over to the pleasure of his touch as he navigated every slope, curve, and contour of her body until she was writhing beneath him, urging his palm to cup her sex. And then he did. His hand was a welcome shield against her, his fingertips teasing softly through her damp curls.

She wanted that sweet explosion. Wanted to feel the plunge of his finger stroke the slippery, sensitive lining of her walls.

"Please," she begged against his lips as his finger caressed and teased her into a frenzy.

"All in good time." Then he withdrew, and nudged her thighs apart, settling the heavy weight of his erection between them. She tried to slip out of his grip, to guide him back to where she wanted him, but he chided her with a nip on her chin. "But first, clasp your hands together and keep them up here for me, hmm?"

She pursed her lips in speculation. "Will I like this lesson as much as the other one?"

"Even more," he promised, rewarding her acquiescence with a wet kiss . . . on her breast, and flashed a wicked grin when she gasped.

He gave ample attention to both her breasts, teasing them to sensitive peaks before blowing a cool stream of his breath over the budded, damp flesh. She quivered, the sensations throbbing low between her thighs. If he continued like this, she might have her explosion without even having the aid of his hand.

She whimpered in protest when he stopped that, too.

But then she forgot all about her pique when he began trailing hot kisses down her body and she felt the glide of his tongue circumnavigate the rim of her navel.

Lifting her head, she watched him with fervent curiosity as he descended further. But the lower he went, the harder it was for her to catch her breath. Her stomach issued a nervous shudder and he laid a soothing hand over her as he blew gently into the triangular thatch of sable curls.

"What precisely do you intend to—*ohhh*."

He nuzzled brazenly into her sex. Breathing in deeply, his eyes closed on a low, prolonged growl that vibrated to her core.

She gasped from the yearning he created. She was so taut and eager and lust-addled that she thought nothing of his broad shoulders prodding her legs further apart. She simply obeyed. Her eyelids felt heavy as she watched his dark head poised at her sex.

Holding her gaze, he opened his mouth over her. Then his tongue slid along the seam of her flesh in one . . . slow . . . lick.

"Mine," he murmured savagely against the tender crevice, laying claim to that part of her as well.

The warmth of his mouth settled over her again in a deep, indecent and thorough kiss. She blushed even as her body arched against the swirling of his tongue and the slow, tender suction. She trembled, her hips tilting of their own accord. He slid his hands underneath her. Lifting her off the chaise, he feasted, his tongue sliding in long wet strokes, mouth suckling in tight controlled swirls.

She gripped the curved molding above her head. Her back arched, hips hitching against the undulations of his tongue. A quickening rush danced through every nerve ending, ready to erupt.

Strangled sounds escaped from her throat in soft moans and pleas. Jane never knew anything could feel like this. The scientist in her couldn't be bothered to think about research at the moment. Her inner scribe was fanning herself with blank pages. But the artist on her portico had a series of very scandalous paintings underway.

"Raven," she rasped, hoping to convey how much she needed him . . . to stay right there . . . always. He seemed to want her complete surrender and he had it. She was his.

Then he slowly slid a finger inside her and she spasmed at once in a choked explosion, every limb tightening. Her skin tingled in a cool rush on the surface, a cascade of molten heat below. Her womb clenched and quivered. Her inner muscles gripped him greedily, trying to drag him deeper.

The next thing she knew, her thrumming body was gathered into his arms as he pressed wild, urgent kisses over her brow and nose and cheeks. She felt his body tremble with the intensity of his desire. The vibrations brought her to the awareness of his unassuaged erection. It felt even more imposing now as it prodded thickly against the tender, swollen niche.

But he did not thrust inside her. Not yet. He drew in a breath, exhaling it slowly against her temple. Then he eased his mouth over hers and lingered for endless minutes.

Tasting a salty essence that wasn't there before, she blushed. This was *her*. Even after all the intimacies they'd shared, she was shocked by this discovery while, at the same time, it caused a new ripple of arousal to quicken her womb.

She sighed, wrapping her arms around his neck. "If I didn't love you before, I would most definitely love you now."

Electrified silver filaments gleamed in his eyes as he gazed down at her beneath the drowsy hood of his dark lashes. And he kissed her again as his hot, hard flesh nudged her. But the snug entrance did not yield immediately. It teased them both in promising throbs and residual pulses, leaving her panting. Even so, she liked the feel of him there against her sex, the weight of his body over hers. The comfort of his surrounding embrace.

He soothed her in slow passes, his hands skimming down every curve and into every hollow. He urged her knees up against his hips, first one, then the other. Open for him, she felt the broad head of his erection pass between her labia, and it excited her to feel that he was bathed in her own warm fluids.

He inched inside. His breath hitched and he cursed, murmuring against her lips about how soft she was. How much he wanted her. Needed her. Only her. And her heart rejoiced. But her body barely yielded before it closed around the thick flesh, pushing against the invasion.

He withdrew and took the bolster pillow, positioning it beneath her hips. Then he settled over her and kissed her again, teasing her mouth as he edged inside her body in a series of slow, shallow thrusts.

The friction, grip, and slide of their flesh coming together renewed the incendiary throbbing of her sex. Instantly, she wanted more. Wanted all of him.

Tightening her legs around his hips, she wiggled, attempting to impale herself.

A strangled sound left Raven. "Patience. Remember, this is new for both of us. I don't want to hurt you, and I don't want this to end quite yet."

"But can't you . . . be patient . . . later?" she panted and gained a growl from him, his hips jerking reflexively.

He pushed deeper into her shrinking body, his kisses more urgent, his tongue stealing past the seam of her lips. She could feel the trembling of his limbs as he strove to remain gentle, coaxing her body into full acceptance. And she did want him, so much that tears were gathering in her eyes.

"Relax, my little professor. Yes, darling. A bit more. You feel so . . . *Ah.*" He stopped on a curse and clenched his teeth as if the sharp burn and sting he caused was shared by both of them. Wedged firmly inside her, he spoke in panting breaths against her temple. "Almost there."

Jane's eyes flew open on a start. *"Almost?"*

He didn't answer her. Perhaps he couldn't, if the glazed intensity of his gaze told her anything.

So this time, *she* soothed *him* with her fingertips brushing the perspiring locks away from his brow. Her lips explored his throat as he withdrew and took a moment to breathe. But he returned to his quest, eager and ardent, his kisses desperate as if he were suffering an unbearable malady.

Then he plunged deep—impossibly deep—and held. Jane bit down on her cry, unable to bear him feeling that he'd hurt her after taking such pains to avoid it. But his flesh scalded hers like a branding iron.

Raven took her mouth in a kiss so primal that, at first, she didn't know what it meant. This one was not in his lexicon. He'd never kissed her like this before either. But then as his body began to move in those unhindered liquid thrusts, she understood.

In this moment, he'd *truly* claimed her. She was irrevocably his.

And as the thought entered her mind, the ache gave way to the throbbing friction building with every grip, every slide. Yielding fully, she took him inside the clutch of her body, welcoming his invading flesh, loving him all the more.

"Yes, I'm yours. Only yours," she said against his lips between soul-claiming kisses.

Breathing hard, he ripped his mouth away from hers on a possessive growl. Their gazes locked, bodies joined in a perfect rhythmic frenzy. She clung to him, nails biting into his shoulders, hips rising to meet his. And he filled her, over and over again.

To her amazement, that bundle of nerves started to sizzle

and flare to life once again. Waves of tingling sparks gathered tightly in her core until she thought she would die in his arms.

And quickly, she cried out, splintering apart, her body riding the spasm as a shower of tingling sparks cascaded through her.

Then Raven made a choked, guttural sound. His hips hitched inside her before he wrenched free, spilling in molten rivulets against her inner thigh.

✿✿✿

HUNCHED OVER Jane's warm body, Raven expelled a low oath in the sweetly fragrant curve of her neck. He kissed her there, lingering and panting as his heart rammed against his chest in thick gushes.

It had never been like that before. He couldn't even call what they'd done *swiving* or *tupping* or any of the other crass words in his vocabulary. It had no name that he'd ever used before. This was something altogether different.

All he knew was that the instant she'd given him her unconditional love, he'd felt a surge of joy so profound that he couldn't contain it. He'd had to show her, in the only way he could, that she had utterly claimed him, heart and soul.

He'd never been lost so completely. Never been so attuned to every quiver and tremor and breath, so much so, that he hadn't known where he ended and where she began. They were just . . . one.

Bloody hell.

Jane lifted her head to press her lips against his shoulder, her fingertips skimming his back in a silken caress. "Is that a good *bloody hell*, or a bad one?"

He didn't realize he'd spoken aloud. Though, it wouldn't surprise him if he hadn't and Jane had simply developed a method for reading his thoughts. She was far too brilliant and beautiful and soft . . . and yes, she did taste sweet everywhere.

"Good. Definitely good," he rasped, near to collapsing from utter bliss.

Then he felt the residual slickness against her thigh and cringed.

"But a bit of bad, as well. Jane," he said, rising up to look into her eyes and brush the tendrils from her temple, "I nearly spilled inside you because I didn't want to leave. No, that isn't cause to grin up at me. That's a dangerous desire and one I've never had to deal with before. Ever. As you might imagine, I wouldn't risk putting another orphan in the world."

She tried to school her features and purse her lips thoughtfully, but she wasn't fooling anyone. He could see the delight in her eyes as she finger-combed the hair back from his brow.

"I'm sure I should be alarmed, and perhaps offended, if not by your words then by your serious glower," she said, smoothing the delicate pad of her thumb over the furrows. "At the moment, however, the anxious portion of my brain is asleep and all I can feel is complete contentment. Well, and a bit of pride. After all, you are the experienced one. Therefore, it would seem that I'm something of a prodigy."

Even though he was trying to be serious, she drew a low grunt of amusement from him and he couldn't resist taking her lips once more.

She distracted his thoughts with the sinuous slide of her leg against his. All at once, his body felt too heavy to support, urging him to ease against her. Her lips weren't moving in that soundless murmur, and yet she was still casting spells over him.

"But when that other part awakens," he said, needing to get out the words that were crowding his mouth before she hypnotized him, "I don't want you to regret or to fret that I would leave you to face any unforeseen consequences alone. I would take care of you."

It was almost terrifying how quickly the image of having her as his wife, and of their child growing in her body took hold of him. Like a picture waiting on the next page of a book. It seemed so simple, even though it wasn't. It couldn't be.

Jane rolled her eyes and rose up to nip his chin with her teeth. "Such a romantic proposal. You're speaking as though you acted alone in this. I was a full participant, if you'll recall."

"I most certainly recall. In fact, I will be recalling your participation for years to come." *For all the years of my life,* he thought.

"Scoundrel," she said with warm affection. "Well, I hope it will ease your mind to know that I don't expect to marry you. This is all quite new to me. I haven't even had time to consider how we would fit into each other's lives."

Neither had he. So, he should feel relieved. He was completely sated and lying naked with a soft, willing woman who wanted only to research the intricacies of lovemaking.

Then why did his chest feel tight, as if a book had closed and he never had the chance to turn the page?

Chapter 28

Within a matter of seconds, Jane had figured out how they would fit into each other's lives.

Perfectly, she thought.

Of course, she was pragmatic enough to realize that without a bond of marriage between them or even an understanding, theirs was only a moment-by-moment affair. However, she was in love enough to hope for a lifetime with him.

Her inner scribe dutifully listed all the obstacles in their path in one column and the ideal solutions in the other. All the while, the artist on her portico was painting fireworks and hearts in vivid reds and pinks.

No matter what path he chose—whether he claimed his birthright or not—he belonged with her. At least, for now.

After gently cleaning the residual fluids from her body with the handkerchief from his discarded coat, he gathered her back into his arms. Then he draped the shawl over her and held her close, skin to skin. These glorious sensations were certainly worth exploring at length.

They caressed each other in a leisurely manner as if they had all day. But it was nearly time for the servants to wake, and soon Mr. Miggins would be making his usual rounds through the house.

As if he sensed this too, Raven held her tighter. "Do you know how impossible it will be to leave you?"

His forehead pressed to hers and his hand rested on her

cheek. She turned to kiss his wrist, wanting to tell him that it would be equally as impossible to let him go. Yet, as her mouth parted to speak the words, her lips came in contact with a trio of tiny upraised scars that were usually hidden by his shirt cuffs.

He immediately tried to pull back, but she stayed him with a light touch. Or rather, he *allowed* her to stay him. He went completely still while enduring her close examination.

Unlike the smooth mark on his arm, these were silver-skinned and asymmetrical. They did not resemble burns or even cuts. Here, the flesh appeared torn and jagged, and it turned her stomach to imagine what might have caused them.

"Relics from my old life in the workhouse," he said remotely.

She kissed him there again and lingered over each of the three until she felt him relax. "Is this what you didn't want to talk about that day we met your friend, Mr. Rollins? That cupboard he mentioned?"

"Aye. It isn't a pretty story."

"But it's still part of you and I'd like to know it. That is . . . whenever you want to tell me."

His heavy breath rushed across her cheek. "I don't ever talk about it. But I don't mind telling you, if that's what you want."

She waited quietly, expectantly.

Then he nodded. "Bill-Jack and me both had our time in that cupboard. In fact, every time we'd tried to run away, we'd end up getting caught by Mr. Devons or one of the older boys who worked for him. Usually, he'd keep us in there for an hour or two. After all, he needed us to be able to work. The old devil was a greedy prig and mean as hellfire. He liked to toss in a bone after he shackled one of us, signaling the rats to come through a hole in the wall. And in the dark, I'd listen to them gnawing it. Feel their feet crawling on me as I tried to kick them off."

Feeling him shudder from the memory, she held him tighter, smoothing her hands over his shoulders and nape, pressing her lips to his throat.

"The last time," he swallowed, "lasted two days. The old devil had gotten himself killed and the workhouse closed for a spell. But the thing was, the bastard forgot to throw a bone into the cupboard that time. I was fifteen, but scrawny and thin-skinned so the shackles cut through as I struggled to escape. I don't know if it was the scent of blood that lured them out. All I know is that I turned into their next meal. They started at the wrist, but there are other scars on my legs. And I don't know how long it took of my kicking and fighting before I'd killed them all."

Jane was trying to absorb this without bursting into tears and sobbing against him. Squeezing her eyes shut, she held him tighter and kissed the place above his heart, her own breaking. In response, he stroked her back and pressed his lips to her temple.

"And it was Mr. Rollins who'd found you?"

"No, it was Devons's widow," he said. "She took me into her home, tended my wounds for weeks and fed me as much as I could eat until my cheeks were fat and my belly soft. Then, she told me I'd never have to go back to the work-house again and that I could live with her."

"You must have been so grateful." Jane expelled a sigh, her own relief blanketing the sadness over what he'd endured.

"Aye, and I wanted to please her. So, when she told me that I'd be sleeping in her bedchamber from that point on, I never thought twice about it."

Jane frowned. "Well, that's peculiar. Was her house quite small and you had no other room in which to sleep?"

"If I recall, her house had five bedchambers, well turned-out."

"And yet she . . ." Jane looked at his arched brow and at the hint of mirth lingering in his eyes as he watched her puzzle this together. "Do you actually mean to tell me that she seduced you?"

"I wouldn't've called it that at the time. Young men at that age are gluttons for pleasure. I readily accepted my new role."

She was appalled. To her, Mrs. Devons wasn't any better than her husband had been. The only difference was a more comfortable cupboard and the rat was female.

"Did you love her?"

He thought for a moment. "No. But for a time I was intensely enthralled by her, not to mention indebted. I was elevated to—what I thought was—a fancy middle-class world, where there was always food enough to eat, clean clothes, and an abundance of . . . enjoyable activities."

At the sound of his chuckle, she began to ease apart from him. But he pulled her back, securing her in a possessive grip.

"There was nothing between Mrs. Devons and I."

"Mrs. Devons and me," she muttered crossly.

And he had the nerve to grin. "There was nothing between us beyond the physical, so stop your frowning, my little jealous professor." He kissed her furrowed brow. "By the time I'd reached my eighteenth year and my body had grown from nourishment and vigorous exercise"—he paused to wink—"my features had lost their boyish softness. Her interest waned. By my twentieth year, my only use to her was in servicing her friends whose husbands were otherwise occupied with mistresses."

Jane thought she was appalled before. But this? "She *sold* you to her friends?"

"I didn't see it that way. I was given a choice. I could either make my own way, or stay in a life I'd grown accus-

tomed to. Or should I say, *to which I'd grown accustomed*?"
he teased, nuzzling her nose as his fingertips stroked lightly
through her hair.

She didn't feel like correcting his grammar this time.

"I *chose* to stay," he emphasized.

"Oh? And have the women at Moll Dawson's chosen to
stay as well?"

He stiffened marginally, his jaw tight. "As a matter of
fact, yes. The two women you saw me with that night chose
to work at Moll's in order to save the money to open a dressmaker shop. Venetia is a widow who lost her home and all
her belongings when her husband died and his relatives
swooped in to devour the carcass. And Hester has a son
being raised by a parish vicar and his wife, and she's working to make a home for him. They both tried to earn enough
money as respectable seamstresses, but they were starving
and living in a rathole. So they *chose* to work for Moll. For
many it is a choice of survival."

"I understand that," she said crossly. "There are few op-
tions for women outside of society and within it as well.
It isn't uncommon to be sold into marriage for the sake of
wealth, but that doesn't make it right. And I absolutely abhor
the idea of you being used for someone else's pleasure, or
used at all."

She wrapped her arms tightly around him, trying not to
think of all the other women who'd been the recipient of his
kisses and caresses. All the women who knew what it was
like to feel his body move within them.

Those gray eyes searched hers for an interminable, probing moment. Then, gradually, a soft smile curved his lips
before he brushed them across hers. "Such a fearsome little
warrior. Who knew you possessed such a primitive side to
your nature?"

Her eyes narrowed and she wiggled beneath him, attempting to slide away. "If a man had done the same to me, or I to him, wouldn't you feel a little . . . primitive?"

"I would hunt him down and gut him," he said on a series of tender kisses as he pulled her closer.

"Do you still see Mrs. Devons?"

He shook his head. "Our acquaintance, such as it was, came to an abrupt end, around three years ago when we bid our farewells. She left on the ferry for a continental tour. And before I left the wharf, I was attacked by two men and left for dead."

Shifting her attention and concern to the more deadly crime against him, she touched the puckered scar between his ribs. She'd discovered this during these explorations, and looked at him inquiringly. "A projectile from a firearm?"

He nodded. "Pistol."

Lifting herself up on her elbow, she pressed her lips there and lingered. "Did they try to rob you?"

His hand cruised lightly down her back and along her arms as if he couldn't get enough of touching her. "No. The odd thing was, their only intent was to kill me. They'd said as much, wanting to make sure the deed was done."

She turned to look down at him, feeling her brow crease with worry. "But why you?"

"Couldn't say." One shoulder lifted in a shrug as if it were just a matter of happenstance. As he continued, he skillfully threaded his fingers through her hair, massaging her scalp and the back of her nape. "That was the day Reed Sterling found me. Without hesitation, he brought me back to his gaming hell, fetched a physician and gave me a place to live. It was the first time I had honest employment, with a salary enough to buy a ramshackle row house of my own, along with enough left over to visit a brothel . . ."

She gasped and swatted him. "Is that truly all that matters to you?"

"You didn't let me finish." He laughed softly and shifted suddenly to capture her hands and playfully anchor them to either side of her head as he moved over her. "I was going to add that it also gave me the chance to meet a curious little bluestocking who turned my comfortable world on its head. I'll never be the same again."

She rolled her eyes.

"I mean it, Jane," he said, his gaze unguarded now as he softly smoothed the curls away from her forehead, tracing her hairline in a simple, untutored caress. "In my whole life, I've never felt this content before. I never even imagined that someone like you existed in the world. You're so smart and caring and pretty. Your lips move in this amazing way when you're thinking. And sometimes you're absentminded and far too curious for your own good. But there isn't a single thing I'd ever change. My only wish is that I'd found you sooner."

That was the moment when Jane understood that it was possible to love someone and to keep falling in love with them over and over again. Her heart turned in a joyful revolution beneath her breast.

The thick evidence of his renewed arousal was unmistakable and her body responded to this with a sweet clench.

She sighed, smiling when he kissed her again, softly, endlessly, threading their hands together. And a long while later, after he had her whimpering and unable to bear the emptiness inside her, he slowly eased into the damp, tender constriction once more.

Chapter 29

It was after dawn and Jane hurriedly tucked the combs in her hair as Raven fastened up the back of her gown. "Now I understand why my friend Winnie and her husband Asher have lingered so long on their honeymoon. It would have been so lovely to stay just as we were all day, perhaps even for weeks."

He chuckled and kissed the back of her neck. "I'm not a machine. Though, I'd do my utmost to perform to your alarmingly high standards."

"I didn't mean . . ." She trailed off and blushed, looking at him over her shoulder. "Actually, I might have meant precisely that."

Yet, even as she said the words, every subtle shift and movement afforded her the intimate knowledge that the inner workings of her body had altered. She was sore in places she'd only ever noticed in anatomical sketches. And a good, long soak in a hot bathing tub would certainly ease those aches. But there wasn't time.

Their loveplay had lasted longer than she'd realized. They'd lingered over kisses and tender caresses that had joined more than merely their anatomy, but their very breaths and souls. Gazing into his eyes as her body had welcomed each deep, slow thrust, she'd felt as if every question her heart had asked throughout her life had finally been answered.

She knew she would never be the same. Never share such a deep understanding with someone as she did with him.

"I don't want you to leave," she said, sagging back against him, reluctant to acknowledge the distant clap of servants' footsteps in the hall as the house awakened.

His arms stole around her waist on a possessive growl. "Tell your parents that you're visiting your friend, then come to me. Wear the veil so no one knows and we'll spend all day in bed. All week. *Hell*, all month."

"I'm giving the children their examinations this morning. My other brothers will be arriving the day after tomorrow for holiday and—*Oh!*" She gasped and turned in his arms, her hands skimming over his broad chest and shoulders to the silken black locks at his nape with familiarity. "Tomorrow is the first of December . . . your birthday."

He blinked. A bemused grin tipped up the corner of his mouth like one side of a weighing scale. "*My birthday*. I don't think I've ever said those words aloud before. Orphans, as you might imagine, only think those types of things. Let those thoughts out and you open yourself up to all types of unfriendly hazings."

"Then you've never celebrated, at all?" she asked, hiding the twinge of pain in her heart when he shook his head ruefully. "Well, that is going to change. The children and I are going to bake you a cake and have you over for tea."

"Oh, goody, more lessons on how to lay a napkin on my lap," he chuckled, but his gaze was soft as egret feathers as he held her and bent to press his lips to hers.

But before they kissed, a large crash sounded in the hall, shaking the floor at their feet.

Raven chuckled. "Toboggan races again?"

She turned toward the door as a chill skated down her spine. Something was wrong. "That wasn't the twins. One of them would be cheering. And Phillipa would have dashed in here by now if it was Charles."

And as she took a step, she recognized the discordant pained moan that echoed down the corridor. "Raven, I think Henry is hurt."

✥✥✥✥

ONCE THEY reached the hall, Raven saw Henry in a tangle of broken toboggan parts and a portion of the railing that had been severed in the middle of the staircase. The young composer was lying on his side, grimacing in pain and clutching his arm.

"Where can I find your family physician?" Raven asked before they reached him. Jane answered him in a strained whisper and he dashed away from Holly House to fetch their neighbor a quarter mile down the lane.

He returned with Doctor Lockwood within minutes, after having demanded an immediate audience with the master of the house. Apparently, used to such interruptions, Lockwood was not offended by Raven's brusque mannerisms and came without delay.

When he returned to deliver the doctor, Jane had already fashioned a splint around Henry's arm. On the outside, she appeared perfectly calm, reassuring not only her injured brother but each of her siblings that all things broken could be mended. She even asked if one of them could name the bones in the arm.

But in her eyes, Raven saw her fears and doubts, wondering if her brother would heal properly and be able to fulfill his dreams as a pianist and composer. And he saw her interminable love for her family. There wasn't anything she wouldn't do for them.

The thought gave him pause.

He ached with the need to pull her into his arms, to hold and reassure her. But to do so would irreparably damage her reputation. He saw that now, clearer than ever. So, he clung to the shadows, ensuring that no servant looked his way and her parents didn't see him as they rushed past.

His place wasn't at her side. She needed someone who had a name. Someone who came from a solid, respectable family. But he still existed in the shadows of uncertainty, on the fringes between her world and his. And she seemed to know that, too.

I don't expect to marry you . . . I haven't even had time to consider how we would fit into each other's lives.

Those words had been a relief then. Now, they scratched at his conscience, itching inside his head like a whirring cyclone of dried leaves and pine needles.

Before he left, even in the midst of all the chaos, she still found him. Across the vast hall, her gaze sought his for comfort. He held it for as long as he could, then nodded with a promise to return later.

He hated leaving her. And he felt no peace in his thoughts as he rode against a bracing morning wind, plagued by one single question—How did he fit into her life?

⠀⠀⠀⠀⠀⠀⠀⠀⠀⠀⠀✧✧✧✧

WHEN RAVEN returned to Holly House after midnight, he still didn't have the answer to the question that had plagued him all day. The only thing he knew for certain was that he wanted to see Jane, and to ask her how Henry was faring.

The door to the conservatory was unlocked, the only light within came from the pale orange glow of the embers beneath the iron stove's curfew and the gray moonlight shining down through the domed ceiling. But Jane wasn't there.

He found a letter on the cushion of the chaise longue,

with his name scrawled in her familiar hand. And, for just an instant, a jolt of fear trampled through him.

As he reached for the folded page, his mind started to spin in circles with the countless nightmares that could be written within. Of all the different ways the rug could be pulled out from under his feet.

Last night was a mistake . . . We live in two different worlds. I see that now . . . I don't really love you after all . . .

Raven inhaled a fortifying breath before he opened it.

Then he exhaled with a smile.

Inside, there were no words, but an interior sketch of the house—every room, because she was meticulous in the best possible way—and a tiny *x* inside a corner chamber on the second floor.

A few minutes later, he knew that he wouldn't have needed the sketch at all. The powdery fragrance of lavender drew him to her door and inside, where he turned the key in the lock.

He found Jane asleep in a pale yellow chair by the hearth.

She looked so small and vulnerable with her legs curled up on the cushion beneath the tucked hem of her nightdress. The soft fan of her lashes drifted shadows against her cheek. A spill of glossy curls rested on the arm of the chair. A book lay unattended on her lap, and a sputtered chamberstick sat on a rosewood drum table beside her.

She'd waited up for him as long as she could, it seemed. The thought brought another smile to his lips and a swelling warmth inside his chest.

He crossed the room to kneel in front of her and slipped the book from beneath her hand, setting it aside. She stirred, her fingers flexing over his, and her lips tilted upward even before she opened her eyes.

"You're here," she whispered.

He leaned in to kiss those tender-padded fingertips and kitten-soft palms. "How did you fare today, and how is your brother?"

Her free hand combed through his hair in gentle soothing strokes that eased away all the irritations that built during these long hours apart. He found himself resting his head on her lap and pulling her close.

"Henry will be fine in a month or two," she said. "Doctor Lockwood is confident that the break will mend without any lingering effects, as long as he avoids all toboggans in the near future. Which shouldn't be difficult now that it's in one hundred and seventy-four pieces."

Leave it to Jane to know the exact number. "You counted them?"

"The children did. It helped to keep their minds off their worries. Most of them were concerned for Henry. The twins, however, were lamenting over the fact that, with only one toboggan left, there would be no race down the hill toward the canal on Christmas Day and no way to win. They were quite sore at their brother and told him outright that he should know better." She yawned and bent to kiss his head, lingering to rest her cheek there. "He is fourteen, after all. And he'd never been given to flights of reckless-ness before."

Raven could feel the turn of her thoughts. "Did you ask what compelled him?"

"After the good doctor and our parents left the room, Henry told me that he is in love," she said with a soft smile. "Apparently, his *muse* lives in the village near the board-ing school. She is the loveliest creature in the entire world, of course. But the heart-thief is also poor, has no family connections, and he knows that our parents would never ap-prove the match. So, in his own dramatic way, he decided that getting tossed out of school and engaging in other wild behaviors would show Mother and Father that he wasn't worth their high expectations. He wants them to wash their hands of him so that he can have a life of his own choosing."

She sighed, the smile fading from her eyes as she averted her gaze to worry a loose thread from his sleeve.

He took her fingertips and kissed them again. "And what did you tell him?"

"I assured him that he can depend upon the rest of his family to support him in whatever life he chooses, and that I would always be here for him."

A faint shiver rolled through her body and into him. It reminded Raven of what she stood to lose if they'd been caught this morning. She would have been sent away, like her friend.

He hadn't been thinking of the risks she'd taken. He'd only been lost in his need for her. And so he'd claimed her as his own . . .

But was she truly his?

"We'll need to be more careful from now on," she said, her thought mirroring his. "On the nights you come here into my bedchamber, you'll have to leave by dawn. And I will go to your house as often as I am able."

His conscience pricked at him. This wasn't what he wanted for her. She deserved more than these clandestine encounters and the deception of her family. She deserved the world handed to her on a tray that she could dissect at will in order to discover its contents.

"Oh, and here. This is for you." She twisted to slip a folded page from beneath the chamberstick and handed it to him.

Still bothered by his thoughts, he sat back on his haunches and stared blindly at it. But when he blinked and realized what it was, his heart started racing in panicked beats.

It was another of her sketches. This one was of a tree filled with slanted charcoal slashes, and on most of the branches hung names and dates written in ink.

A Northcott family tree. And his name was there, too.

He stared at it, speechless. All his life he'd wanted a family. All his life he'd wanted to know his name. So then why, for the past weeks, had he done nothing but doubt all the evidence shown to him?

But Raven knew why. *Fear.*

Fear of a hand clamping down on his shoulder and capturing him as he tried to run for freedom. Fear of the cupboard doors closing him in the dark, the click of the latch, and the quiet that came before the rats scurried in through the hole in the wall. Fear of losing his place if he didn't whore out his own body. Fear of dying on the wharf with nothing to show for his life.

Fear had taken too much from him. It was time to be done with it.

No more, he thought, and he stared at the page. Emotion stung the back of his eyes, clogging his throat, and he didn't know what to do with it.

"Happy birthday," she whispered. "Of course, it is only the past seven generations. I'm afraid that I shall need to complete more resear—"

He cut her off with a searing kiss. Fitting his mouth to hers, he let the deluge of his overflowing heart fill her. She had made all this possible. And, in the process, she'd pushed her way into his life and embedded herself into his very soul. He wouldn't even be surprised if part of it was indelibly stained pink.

Gathering her in his arms, he stood and carried her warm body to her small canopied bed. He lay down, facing her so that their heads rested upon the pillow. And for the next few hours, he simply held her and kissed her until they both fell asleep.

Raven awoke before dawn with Jane's drowsing head cradled in the crook of his shoulder and her hand over his heart. All of the questions and confusion that had overwhelmed him these past weeks had vanished from his mind in a soft cloud of lavender.

Everything was clear.

He knew the life he wanted, and it was with Jane. But he also knew that her parents would never let her marry a mere orphan with no cemented family ties.

The only way he could keep her, would be to claim his birthright. Completely.

Chapter 30

December

Later that morning, Raven discovered that negotiating with the Earl of Warrister was like dealing *vingt-et-un* to a seasoned Captain Sharp.

They sat across from each other in the library as they'd done on the first day, each one carefully sizing up the other.

There was a triumphant gleam in the old codger's gaze. "That's all settled, then. I'll give a formal announcement at Aversleigh's ball next week."

That would be perfect, he thought, already imagining Jane's reaction as he was introduced as Merrick Northcott. He would keep it a surprise until then. And after the ball, he would ask her to marry him and they would begin a new life together.

He wasn't afraid of the unknown any longer. There was nothing waiting to pull the rug out from under him. Jane would never be this certain of his true identity otherwise. He trusted her unequivocally and knew that she would never lead him astray if she had the smallest doubt.

So, he was taking the plunge.

"But no sooner than that," Raven said, keeping his elbows perched on the armrests. He knew that if he gave in too easily, Warrister would only ask for more.

"Then you'll live here starting that night."

They'd had this particular discussion several times in the past weeks, but Raven was always firm. "No. I'm keeping my own house. I'm a grown man, after all."

The earl shook his head. "No. There's just too much for you to learn. Or were you under the impression that gentlemen of the peerage fritter about all day, ringing for their servants and riding through the park? Spend their nights gaming and whoring?"

Well, actually . . . Raven thought wryly but he earned a dark, exasperated look.

"Just as I thought," Warrister said. "You'll have investments and estates to manage, tenants to look after, farms to oversee, along with a hundred other things. I'll need time to teach you."

Estates and lands? That sounded like an inheritance that he didn't really earn. "I don't want to be handed anything. That isn't why I've come here."

"You're a Northcott and my heir. Whether you like it or not, these responsibilities will fall to you," he said, his features set and immovable. "Had I found you as an infant, you would have been raised in my house. I'd have had a lifetime to prepare you, but that time is coming swiftly to an end."

Raven didn't want to think about losing the man he'd only just discovered. But even he knew death was an inevitable part of life. And, during whatever time they had left, he realized with a pang of yearning, he wanted to make the earl proud.

He drew in a deep breath and let it out slowly. "I wouldn't know the first thing about estate management."

"You have a sharp mind from the work you've done for Mr. Sterling. And from what Sanders tells me about your house, you've got a good head for property and for knowing what repairs would need to be done. I used to manage it all on my own," he said, looking down at his gnarled hands only to shake his head. "But I've had to rely on my stewards for too many years."

Raven offered another short, conciliatory nod. "I'll need

to give proper notice to Reed Sterling. He is not only my employer but like a brother to me. I won't abandon him."

"Understandable," Warrister said, then sat forward with a glint in his eye, as if he felt he'd gained the upper hand. "And you can keep your house as long as you hire servants."

He paused, considering. "I will concede only to hiring a cook for the time being."

"I want you here in the mornings to break your fast and we'll discuss your duties while my mind is still sharp."

"My lord, I highly doubt there is a time of day when your wits are not edged with the precision of a cutpurse's blade," Raven said, surprised his palms weren't sweating by now.

"Grandfather," he said with resolute tenacity. "You'll call me grandfather from this point forward. Is that clear?"

The old codger was always pushing for a bit more. But a grin tugged at Raven's lips nonetheless. "Very well . . . Grandfather."

Even after such an intense debate, Raven felt lighter somehow when he left the room. As if a great stone had been pried from his chest.

He had a grandfather now, and he had Jane. They were all the family he needed. All he ever wanted.

Knowing he would see her again this afternoon for tea, his thoughts were distracted as he walked down the stairs to the foyer. He nearly collided with a man stepping in from the rain.

The figure in the doorway paused, back turned to shake the droplets from the brim of his beaver top hat. "Take my coat, will you? And fetch me a whisky while you're at it."

Raven remembered the voice and instantly bristled, the hair on the back of his neck standing on end. Staring at the sharp profile, the hawklike nose and silver streaked sandy hair, he recalled the man from a confrontation at Sterling's.

Straightening his shoulders, Raven growled, "Take off your own bloody coat."

The man whipped around, blue eyes flashing daggers. They widened in twin recognition. "You! What are you doing in my uncle's home?"

"Paying a call on *my* grandfather."

It felt good to say it aloud to another person.

It felt even better to see the shock on this prig's face.

Raven said nothing more and simply walked past him, through the open doorway. Yet, it didn't escape his notice that the man was likely Lord Herrington, his father's cousin—the same man who'd been campaigning for years to be named Warrister's heir.

This was Raven's first lesson that, while a man might wish to have a family, he could not always choose them.

෴෴෴

JANE PUT away all the jars, vials and gallipots from the trestle table in the conservatory, then dressed it in linens and her mother's finest china and silver. She baked a special cake for Raven's birthday tea, and Mrs. Dunkley set it on a porcelain pedestal in the center of the table, enrobed in pink icing and sugared flowers.

For the occasion, Jane wore a dress of rose-and-white stripes with flounced sleeves. She wanted to surprise a laugh from him with this color scheme, reminding him of the night they'd met.

Busy fussing with an intricately folded napkin, she heard the door to the garden open and then close. Her heart started turning in an endless revolution. She bit down on her lip to keep from grinning too broadly. He was here.

She turned and her breath caught at the sight of Raven entering the light-filled chamber. He wore a fine suit, the charcoal-colored broadcloth tailored perfectly to his form, and his jaw was freshly shaven above a starched white cravat.

Stopping before her, he bowed, then presented her with a bouquet of bright pink flowers.

"For you, Miss Pickerington." His gray eyes gleamed with mirth as he glanced to the table. "It seems we are of like mind as usual."

She smiled and took the flowers, her hands trembling slightly. She didn't know why she was nervous all of a sudden. Perhaps it was because no one had ever brought her flowers before.

"They're lovely." She drew in their sweet aroma, gathering them close. Then, without warning, he picked her up by the waist and twirled her around in circles. Her head fell back on a giddy laugh as she clung to his shoulders. "You're crushing the flowers."

"A lesson to you to put them down sooner. You should have known I'd need to have you in my arms straightaway," he said, nipping lightly along her exposed throat. "And you are positively delectable in pink. Then again, you're quite tasty out of it, as I recall."

Her body clenched with tender yearning at the reminder. "Hush now. You mustn't say things like that because Henry is joining us for tea. No doubt Charles, Phillipa, and the twins would already be here, but they are still writing their final examination essays."

"Then you leave me no choice but to put you over my shoulder and carry you back to my cave so that I can have my way with you."

As if to prove it, he held her tighter. His grin brimmed with wicked intent as he began to prowl toward the door.

"You wouldn't dare!"

"With you, I think I would dare to do just about anything," he said with a mysterious glint in his eyes. Yet, with patent reluctance that made her heart flutter even more, he lowered her to the stone tiles.

They both heard her brother's disconsolate shuffle in the hall. But, ever the scoundrel, Raven stole a quick kiss the instant before Henry appeared. Therefore, her cheeks were in high color when he ambled in.

He looked between them before rolling his eyes. "I don't have to be here for tea, you know. I can go somewhere else and be alone in the silence."

Recovering herself, she dashed over to her desk to put her disheveled bouquet in one of the jars she'd stashed earlier.

She clucked her tongue. "If melancholia were contagious, I should shoo you from the room post haste. But even Doctor Lockwood said that you should move around a bit during the day. He believes that bed rest is important to aid recovery, but so is good circulation. Thirty minutes out of bed and in the sunlight will do you a world of good, I'm sure."

"She's a hard taskmaster, this one," Raven said, commiserating with Henry. "But perhaps this will help to ease some of the ailment you suffer."

Reaching into his coat, he withdrew a folded packet of papers. He held them out to her brother, who reached reflexively with the arm encased in a sling and winced before remembering to use his other hand.

Henry issued a taut sigh as he took hold of them. "And what's this, then?"

"Open it and discover the answer for yourself," Jane huffed.

Her brother slumped down in a chair and spread the pages wide. He stared at them for a moment, then smiled and laughed out loud. "Compositions for the left hand. You're a right solid fellow."

Raven shrugged and came around the table to hold Jane's

chair. "I just happened by a little shop this morning and thought these would keep you occupied during your recovery."

As she sat down, she smiled up at him, her heart twirling again. Her arteries were surely loomed in a tight swirl like ribbons on a maypole by now.

He gestured to the center of the table with a nod. "And what's this?"

"It's a fortune-telling cake," she said as he took the place beside her. "There are small trinkets tucked inside, so be careful that you don't bite down too hard."

"Just don't get a button in your slice—that's not a proper fortune," Henry said.

"I dunno." Raven glanced to Jane. "I wouldn't mind a button, as long as it had brown thread. What other fortunes are in there?"

Henry listed them with absent finger-taps on the table as if he were already practicing the music. "There's always a sovereign. Mother used to get a little cherub in hers, but by the time Theodora was born and the nursery expanded to two rooms, everyone agreed that we should lose that one. And cook always puts a ring in Jane's cake, but she's never gotten it in her slice. Then last year, one of us—and I'm not naming names—put a spinster's thimble inside. Unfortunately, she didn't get that slice either. But her friend did."

"And it wasn't very kind of you," Jane chided and turned the cake, repositioning it to better her chances. "Thankfully, Ellie is rather fond of thimbles and didn't take umbrage."

Raven laid his hand over hers and slipped the cake knife free. "So then which slice do you normally get?"

"Nothing," Henry chortled. "Her slice is always empty."

"Ah," Raven said thoughtfully. "The slice of possibility, where your future is what you make of it."

Jane smiled and lifted her brows smugly at her brother. "Precisely. It doesn't matter what the slice holds. In reality, we all forge our own paths."

However, as she watched Raven cut into the cake, she still hoped to finally get that ring.

Chapter 31

⌒

After Raven and Henry left the conservatory, Jane went up to the garret in search of the matching slippers for the gown she planned to wear at Aversleigh's ball.

She'd found them quickly but spotted a few stains that needed tending. Thinking about the solution she would use, she wasn't paying much attention to where she walked and accidentally tripped over a small black-lacquered casket.

She landed, sprawled out on the floor. But she simply laughed at herself, far too content to be bothered by the bracing sting in her palms and smarting knees on the hardwood planks. She did, however, cast a glare to the culprit.

And felt a jolt of surprise.

It was a box from among her uncle's things. She must have forgotten to have it brought downstairs on that first day Raven had come. Of course, it likely didn't contain anything of import. But ever curious, she opened the lid.

It was full of letters. Examining them in the bright shaft of light through the dormer window, she saw that they were written in French and addressed to *Jean Louis*, as in John Louis Pickerington, her uncle.

She frowned in perplexity. More letters written in French to her uncle? It seemed too coincidental not to be related to the letter from Raven's mother.

However, this was not Arabelle Northcott's handwriting. In fact, the script was small, with letters crowded together in utilitarian fashion. This writer, she surmised, was not given to wasting good paper. And the signature on the bottom was not Raven's mother's either. It was signed only with a single name—*Helene*.

The paper was a fine quality, similar if not identical to that of the letter from Raven's mother to Uncle Pickerington.

Scouring through the depths of the box, there seemed to be more than a dozen letters, all in the same hand.

Jane skimmed the French text quickly and realized it was a love letter. Helene, it seemed, was passionately in love with Uncle Pickerington.

Letter after scandalous letter was written with an open eroticism that made her blush. But there was a vulnerability here in these pages, as well. When Helene described her bitter escape from a cruel husband—whom she called *le Sinistre*—and her fears that if she bore him a son then her husband would never let her go, it was impossible for Jane not to hope for the author's happiness.

Perhaps her uncle felt the same. Why else would he have kept the letters?

Hmm . . . why indeed.

Something began to niggle at the back of her mind. But she lost her train of thought as she read further. When Helene mentioned pining for him while he was busy teaching English to her mistress, a chill went down Jane's spine.

Her uncle *had* worked for the Northcotts after all. Proof of it was right here in her hand, written on paper from the Northcott household.

But the question was, why had he lied about it?

He'd been having an affair with a woman who'd likely been the Northcotts' maid. Was he ashamed? Perhaps. After all, the woman was also carrying *le Sinistre's* child in her womb.

The child.

"Wait," Jane said into the stale air as the pieces started to fit together.

Her eyes drifted to the corner of the page. She must have looked at the dates before, surely. Yet now, seeing the month and the year scrawled in black ink made her pulse thicken with dread.

Fingers numb, she fanned out every yellowed letter, putting them in chronological order.

All the dates were from the year 1799, except for the last letter. It was dated January of 1800, little more than a week before the fire.

And in the letter were the damning words: "It has happened. I have borne the monster a son."

A son.

This meant that there was another male infant in the house at the time of the fire.

Dismayed, Jane realized that these weren't just random letters left forgotten. They cast doubt on Raven's legitimacy.

Was that the reason he'd been left on the foundling home's doorstep and no one had bothered to claim a reward for his rescue?

She didn't know the answer. But she wished with all her might that she could turn back time and stop herself from opening this box.

THE MORE Raven thought about it, the more eager he was for his new life to begin.

Of course, not even he was surprised to realize that his first order of business was to do something special for Jane. She'd done so much for him, after all. And knowing how much she loved her family, he knew exactly what to do.

After his birthday celebration, he'd spent the better part of the day making inquiries about her uncle's debts, and then arranging to pay them off in secret. Soon, she would have all her family together again.

His second order of business was to hire a cook. And he knew just where to find one.

Late that night, he walked the pavement toward Moll Dawson's, hoping he'd find Bess in her usual spot. But as his polished shoes landed on the stone, every step had a queerly tardy echo.

As if someone were following him.

Raven whistled a tune into the cold December air, his breath misting in a cloud beneath the lamplight. He paused, pretending to pat his pockets for a cheroot, and surreptitiously glanced over his shoulder. Just beyond the shadow of the previous lamppost, a figure paused, too. And it wasn't likely that he was alone.

Walking on, Raven kept watch on the narrow inlet of an alley up ahead where the lamplight didn't reach. One of two things would happen up there. Either he'd encounter his shadow's bedfellow, waiting in the dark for the two of them to come at him at once . . . or Raven would lie in wait and teach this bloke a lesson he'd not soon forget.

Approaching the alley, he heard the shuffle and scrape of a heavy step. He rolled his shoulders in readiness for whatever emerged from the dark and whatever came up behind him.

"Well, if it ain't me long lost chum from our foundling days and old Devil's work'ouse," a piercing voice drawled, squeaking at the ends in familiarity.

Raven stopped as the large-bellied shape emerged, the fleshy cheeks giving the grown man with a scruffy beard a boyish appearance. "Gerald Tick?"

The two of them had been part of the same group of boys that Mr. Mayhew had sold to Mr. Devons for his workhouse.

"The one and only," he said with a sneering brown-toothed grin as he spat on the ground. "Look at you in your posh clothes. Rumor 'as it that you ain't no orphan anymore. Well done, you."

Wary about this reunion, he stayed where he was. But behind him he heard the approach of those *echoed* footfalls on the pavement. This time, when he looked over his shoulder, the figure was standing in the lamplight. And another grin greeted Raven.

"Surely, you remember me, little flightless bird. Devil paid me right 'andsome to track you down whenever you'd run off."

Raven remembered the taunts and the jeers of *"little bird, little bird, likes to eat rat tails for worms"* every time he was locked in that cupboard. "Bertie Woodcock."

The man laid a three-fingered hand over his heart. "You do remember. I'm touched, I am."

"And to what do I owe this unexpected pleasure, gentlemen?"

"Gentlemen," Tick screeched in a laugh.

Woodcock took a step forward. From his sleeve, he pulled out a cudgel and smacked it sharply against his palm. "I dunno whot it is about you, but Mayhew and the old Devil weren't the only ones who hated you. Believe it or not, there's a bloke who don't just want to teach you a lesson. Wants you dead and buried, 'e does. Says 'e's willin' to pay to make sure it's done right this time."

Chapter 32

Later that night, Jane paced the floor of the conservatory. Her thoughts were always clearer in this space. She'd brought down the black-lacquered casket with her, along with all those terrible letters that cast doubt on Raven's legitimacy.

In her mind, she ran through the facts in quick succession. The proof working in his favor was the mark on his arm, the January he arrived at the foundling home—the same month as the fire—and his resemblance to the portrait of the Northcotts. All relatively solid arguments, she thought with a nod.

Then she stopped abruptly on the stone tiles as the opposition chimed in.

None of it was wholly indisputable. Logic dictated that every fact could be twisted and seen as coincidence by those who wanted to deny his claim. And they would . . . if this information surfaced. *If* . . .

Could she keep it a secret? Should she?

He could be the maid's son, her mind whispered. She growled in frustration and shook her head, hating the turn of her own thoughts.

The truth was, someone had saved a child from the fire and left him on the doorstep of the foundling home. Could it have been a mother who wanted to save her son from a *sinister* husband and father? If so, then where was Helene now?

So many unanswered questions. Jane's head was starting to throb.

She had to tell Raven.

But she knew what this would do to him. If she told him about these letters, she'd break his heart. And yet, if she didn't, she'd be breaking her promise. He hated secrets.

Before she knew what to do, she heard a tap on the glass.

She quickly stashed away all the letters and closed the casket, stuffing it under her desk for good measure. Then she rushed to the door.

But it wasn't Raven standing in the cold December drizzle.

"Duncan!" she said, stunned and out of breath. "What are you doing here so late? And why have you come to the conservatory door?"

Her cousin shifted from one foot to the other and dragged off his hat, worrying the brim in clumsy folds. "Because he told me not to come . . . but, if I was going to ignore him and come anyway, that I should come to the conservatory. So here I am."

"Whyever would Raven tell you not to come?"

"Doesn't want you to worry. Said he'd be just fine. It's only a little blood, that's all."

Jane went cold all over. "Duncan, you have to take me to him."

Her cousin nodded and sighed with relief. "That's just what I told him you'd say."

Grabbing her reticule and the shawl from the chaise longue, she blew out the lamp and followed her cousin into the bitter night.

❧❧❧

WHEN SHE arrived at Raven's house, Duncan took her in through the back. In the kitchen, she encountered a rheumy-eyed old woman with hunched shoulders and a cackling laugh, who chided Duncan for not listening to the *randy gent*.

Knowing that Raven was opposed to people in his house, Jane was obligated to ask, "And who are you?"

"Me name's Bess," she said with a proud sniff. "And I'm 'is cook, I am. Got a kettle on the boil and everythin'."

Not wanting to waste time arguing the fact that Raven would have told her if he'd hired a cook, Jane walked out of the kitchen toward the upstairs. She paused only long enough to call over her shoulder, "Bring the kettle when it's ready."

When she found Raven in his bedchamber, her heart dropped to the floor.

He was sitting in his chair with his feet propped up on the hearth and a wide, bloody strip of silk tied around his shoulder—a cravat. Dangling from his uninjured arm, he loosely held a bottle of whisky by two fingers.

"Bollocks," he cursed after a look over his bare shoulder. "I told Pickerington not to tell you."

"And you knew he would, regardless, which essentially says you wanted me here." She bustled over and leaned down to press a kiss to his lips. Lingering, she felt the sting of tears at the corners of her eyes. "Tell me what happened, so I know who to murder."

"You wouldn't do that. I know you too well, Jane. You'd likely teach them a more effective way to wield a knife and inform them of its metallurgical properties." He chuckled, but hissed as she peeled back the makeshift bandage.

The ghastly sight stole her breath. A trio of slices were gouged deep into the flesh, the wounds glistening bright red.

She swallowed down her gasp. "They did well enough on their own, I'd say."

"Fear not, professor. They left all the anatomical parts you like best."

"This isn't a time for jesting," she scolded, her throat dry. Tears were stinging her eyes now and she turned away quickly.

At the bedside table, she lit the *rat de cave* and every taper she could find in the drawer, then set them along the edge of the mantel. "Someone has severely cut into your arm. I'm going to have to stitch you up. It's fortunate that I always carry a needle and thread. And I met your new cook, apparently. She'll be bringing up the kettle with boiling water shortly."

"That'd be Bess," he said, tipping back the bottle for another swig. "She saved my life tonight."

"Then I love her already."

He eyed her warmly. "You throw that word around quite a lot these days."

"Only when I mean it."

No sooner had the words left her lips than she found herself ensnared by the waist, toppled onto his lap, and pulled to his lips for a demanding kiss that stole every sip of air from her lungs.

"None o' that now," came that gravelly cackle from the doorway as Bess strolled in. "He fought a good fight and gave them back plenty of their own, he did. But he's weak as a wee lamb now. I had to finish off those two buggers with me basket o' posies. Only most people don't know that I keep rocks in there. Big 'uns, too. That makes it too heavy so no one will filch it, see?"

"Bess, I don't know how to thank you," Jane said.

"Aw. T'weren't nothin'. He saved my life more times than not by giving me enough coin for a place to sleep and a hot meal. And now, he's given me a post. I'm a respectable cook again, I am, with a cozy room belowstairs. It's all I ever wanted." Then she glanced at his cut shoulder and cringed, gulping audibly. "But I'm a bit squeamish when it comes to bloody hunks of meat, so I'd best be headin' on back down the stairs. Need to check on that big lad, make sure he's cleanin' out the cupboards instead of the larder. Though, he deserves to eat his fill from tottering out of the mews like he did, just at the right time. Why, he even sent his light-o-love away, so that he could help the randy gent into a carriage."

As Bess left the room, Jane fished out the supplies she needed from her reticule. Unfortunately, some of her vinaigrette concoction had spilled and the spirit of hartshorn left a powdery substance on her needle and thread. Therefore, she decided to drop those in the basin and pour boiling water over them. Not knowing how long it had been since he laundered his linens, she tore strips from her clean petticoat to serve as bandages.

"It'd be easier to do that if you removed your dress first," he added helpfully, taking another swig.

She took the bottle out of his hand. "I need to use some of this for before and after. Now brace yourself."

And while she had the courage, she bent down and quickly doused his wound.

He howled a curse up to the ceiling, nearly shooting out of the chair. "Damn it all, Jane. Give a man some warning."

"I did," she rasped, her nerves getting the better of her.

"Perhaps a little more than a second, next time."

She nodded and took a swig herself, choking on the burn. Then she handed it back to him, while she readied the needle and thread. "It's a shame Ellie isn't here. She would stitch a lovely design on your flesh. And it's a shame, too, that I didn't get a thimble in your cake."

"Jane," he said quietly, holding out his hand. "Come here."

She did and he pulled her onto his lap again, nuzzling her nose, breathing in deeply.

"Just so you know, I only want your needlework on my body," he teased, soothing her trembles with gentle sweeps along her nape and spine. "And I want you to stay right here, close to me, hmm?"

She nodded. Even though she wasn't entirely steady, being near him made her feel better than before.

Expelling a deep breath, she surveyed his wounds. She chose the largest cut first. Knowing that he needed her strength and not her tears, she summoned the objectivity of her inner scientist to help her through the task.

Then she applied the needle to his flesh.

Raven took another swig. Leaning back against the chair, he closed his eyes. The muscle ticking along his jaw was the only indication that he felt pain.

"It's a gruesome and deep cut. Were they trying to sever your arm?" she said, her own attempt at humor falling flat.

"They were after the mark," he said, every syllable uttered in a carefully controlled monotone as if any inflection would cause him further pain. "I knew these blokes. Ne'er-do-wells from my past life. Said that the person who hired them wanted to make sure I was good and dead this time and needed proof."

"'This time'? That suggests someone had tried before."

"Aye. That's been puzzling me, too." He squinted his eyes closed and hissed in a quick breath as she reached the deepest part of the cut and had to tug a little for the skin flaps to meet.

He continued after a minute, his voice edged with strain. "The first person who ever talked about the mark, outside of the foundling home, was Mr. Devons. When he shackled me inside that cupboard that last time, he told me that he was finally going to get something worthwhile out of me. Said he'd mentioned his workhouse boys once or twice in a pub and that someone perked up at the tale of the lad with the raven on his arm. I didn't think anything of it at the time. My thoughts were on the hole at the back of the cupboard.

All I know, is that he left to meet this person and it was the last I ever saw of the Devil."

"Do you think the person who queried him about your mark was responsible for his death?"

He shrugged reflexively, then stiffened, biting down a groan before he took a healthy gulp from the bottle. "Dunno. I'm sure he had enemies."

Jane kissed him on the shoulder after she finished the first set of stitches, tying off the thread. Only two more sets to go.

"Then there was the attack on the wharf," he mused. "I found it peculiar then and even more so now that they never tried to rob me. And I'd had a few pounds tucked in my pocket from"—he stopped and appraised Jane carefully, glancing down to the needle—"well, it doesn't matter who."

Jane instantly knew it was that horrible Mrs. Devons who'd paid him. But she managed to keep her stitches light and easy for his sake.

"There were two that got me—one from behind and the other dead on. My arms were caged before I got much use out of them. The first bloke pulled down my coat as the other ripped my shirtsleeves. Seeing the mark, the second bloke said, 'This is him.' I didn't know what he meant, but I didn't want to find out either. When I saw that pistol, I knew my life depended on getting away, but I still caught the ball in my ribs."

This news didn't sit well with her. She finished the second set of stitches, feeling more anxious than before.

To her, these accounts cemented his legitimacy. But they also left her shaken. "So, in other words, there is someone who knows who you really are. And this person is willing to kill you in order to keep anyone else from finding out. Who could know about the mark and is threatened by it?"

"There's only one person I can think of who'd stand to gain from my death."

They shared a look.

"Lord Herrington," she said. "But that would mean he'd have known about you all along. That would mean he knew that the legitimate heir had survived the fire."

Thinking back to the letters, this made sense. If Herrington knew about Raven, then he likely saw him as the only obstacle to the earldom.

"I'd thought about that, too. But, by all accounts, there wasn't another survivor of the fire. So then who pulled me out? If it was Herrington, wouldn't he have just let me burn with the others?"

She shivered and burrowed nearer to Raven's heat.

Knowing that he'd been so close to death, and so often, it was too much to think about. And yet, it was all she could think about.

"I d-don't want to t-talk about this anymore," she stammered, fear and agony clogging her throat.

She was glad she'd finished the last set of stitches, because her eyes began to flood, her vision obscured. She blinked and the hot deluge streamed down her face in wet runnels. Blindly, she swiped at the strips of linen and began wrapping his arm, knotting the ends.

"Shh . . ." he said, holding her face tenderly, kissing the tears from her cheeks, her eyelashes, her lips. "It was really you who saved me tonight, you know."

"Me?"

"Mmmhmm." His lips grazed hers in intensely slow sweeps. "But I knew I couldn't die yet. Not when everything was just starting to go right. Not when I just found you."

His intention was likely to keep her from crying again, but tears flowed from beneath her closed lashes regardless.

"But there was a moment—" His voice broke, the sound of it hoarse and lost in a way she'd never heard before. He locked eyes with her, the gray filled with rife panic as he fisted his hand in the back of her dress. "There was a moment when I was afraid I'd never see you again. Ever. And I thought of my body being locked in a coffin, lowered into the cold ground and never feeling your warmth. I couldn't bear it, Jane."

He kissed her again, frantic and desperate, pulling her closer, as if she could never be close enough. Shifting beneath her, he rearranged her legs to straddle him. The position forced her knees higher, tucked under his arms, until she was curled flush against him, heartbeat to heartbeat. And seated on his hard, insistent heat.

His aroused state shocked her. But what surprised her even more was the way her body instantly responded in urgent, fluid pulses, hips rocking forward. It felt so primitive—this sudden overwhelming need for intimacy. The need to prove that he was alive and safe and hers.

She fused her mouth to his, craving to be closer still. Raven's thoughts seemed to match her own. He reached between their bodies and jerked at the fastening of his trousers. He kissed her hard. Lifted her. Then impaled her deeply in one slick thrust.

A primal, feral sound roared from his throat as her gasping body gripped his flesh.

They moved together in a wild, panicked rhythm, both seeking assurance. One driving harder and harder. The other willingly impaled over and over again . . . until they both cried out, clutching and breathless, locked tightly in a torrent of thick liquid shudders.

For long moments after, they simply breathed together, lungs rising and falling in perfect harmony, their heads bowed toward each other as if in prayer.

Chapter 33

Three evenings later, the Marquess of Aversleigh's ballroom brimmed with music and gaiety and the glimmering light of a dozen chandeliers.

Officers, tradesmen, and haute society all mingled beneath the golden glow as a crush of lively dancers reeled and twirled on the floor. There was so much laughing and clapping and foot-stomping that even Jane's smiling parents were caught up in the merriment.

She stood with Ellie near the archway between the ballroom and the winter garden—an octagonal room with a glass dome overhead and a reflecting pool below. Together, they furtively tossed biscuit crumbs from a small tin Jane carried in her reticule to the shimmering Amur carp.

"Do you think he decided not to come?" Ellie asked, her voice raised to be heard over the din.

Aside from Duncan and Bess, Ellie was the only other person who knew about Raven's injuries from earlier in the week. But no one knew that it might have anything to do with the mark on his arm. Or his claim to the earldom.

Jane closed the lid and dropped the tin into the reticule discreetly tied at her waist, and smoothed her gloved hands over the long placket beneath the gathers of her full pale taffeta skirts. Then she looked over her shoulder to the door for the thousandth time and sighed.

"He sent a missive earlier that he might be late," she said

distractedly. "But he did not give a reason. He only told me that he has a surprise for me and not to worry. Which, of course, makes me worry all the more."

Ellie squeezed her hand. "You're sounding a bit too much like me, Jane. Is this what happens when you fall in love?"

She laughed, but gave no answer as a movement by the door caught her attention.

One of the liveried footmen approached the butler, who spoke to the Marquess and Marchioness of Aversleigh before the footman bowed and departed.

The marquess lifted his hand to the orchestra and they abruptly fell silent.

"Rather mysterious, is it not?" Ellie whispered.

But Jane felt tingles skitter warmly over the surface of her skin. She smiled. "Raven is here."

In the next instant, a dark-headed figure appeared in the doorway. His frostbitten gaze skimmed the partygoers at a glance before settling on her.

She felt the contact keenly in the sudden flip of her stomach and fluttering beneath her breast. But what sent a gasp through the entire ballroom was the older man beside him, leaning on his arm and holding a cane.

"The Earl of Warrister," the butler announced, his voice ringing out to the far expanse of the terrace windows and up to the vaulted ceiling. "And Mr. Merrick Northcott."

A collective gasp sucked all the air out of the room. Jane felt her heart rise to her throat as Raven's gaze locked on hers again.

"A surprise, indeed," Ellie said. "I thought he had no intention of claiming his birthright."

"He didn't, as far as I knew."

"Well, perhaps his decision has something to do with you. Because, if I'm not mistaken, those are your parents he's talking to."

Jane was in utter shock. With everything that had occurred in the past week, her brain couldn't seem to process
any more. So she merely stared at him like a gape-mouthed
carp.

Whatever he said to her parents, he received a nod. He
bowed in return, kissed her mother's hand, then stepped
down from the dais that overlooked the ballroom and crossed
the floor, parting the expectant dancers.

Jane was captivated by the sight of him in the tailored
satin-trimmed black broadcloth and high, snowy cravat that
accentuated the chiseled cut of his jaw and chin. He prowled
toward her, every step purposeful, every eye watching his
progress.

Then, the music began again.

He stopped in front of her and inclined his head. "Miss
Pickerington. Miss Parrish. How fetching you both look tonight."

"Pretty words," Ellie said, surreptitiously dabbing her
eyes with a lace handkerchief. "Though, they might be more
convincing if you'd actually looked in my direction."

His mouth curled in a smirk. "I saw you in your gold-
colored finery, Miss Parrish. So did the officer coming this
way to ask you to dance."

She let out a small gasp as she looked over his shoulder
and saw that he was right. But Jane already knew that he
was aware of every person, always on his guard. To her, he
merely held out his hand in expectation. And her fingertips
pulsed with longing.

"A gentleman asks," she whispered.

He leaned closer, a low deep breath of amusement brushing her cheek. "I think you're the one who needs lessons—
lessons on remembering that I'm not a gentleman. However,
on this particular occasion, I asked your parents for permission."

Reaching out, he snatched her hand and then stole around to the center of her back. Before she could recover from shock, he pulled her into his frame for a closed waltz, his steps quick and light and leaving her breathless.

A minute or more passed before she could say, "You likely should have honored your host by dancing with his daughter first."

"Would you have liked to see me dancing with the marquess's daughter?"

"No," she said without hesitation and he grinned. But there was something that needed to be mentioned. "Should I call you Merrick now, or do you prefer Mr. Northcott?"

He pulled her a fraction closer than propriety permitted and gazed down at her warmly. "To you, I will always remain Raven. Northcott to all others."

She smiled, glad for him, but it wavered under a blanket of apprehension. Not because she doubted his legitimacy. No, after his attack, she was convinced that he was indeed legitimate. Her only uneasiness came from the fact that whoever was responsible for attacking him was still out there. "Do you think it is entirely safe to make a public appearance?"

"Aye." His wounded arm twitched in a small shrug and he winced slightly, but without a single misstep. "I'm likely in less danger the more people know about me. I have a grandfather now, a name, and a family. And it's all because of you. My only regret is not believing you sooner."

"Raven, there's something I need to tell you," she said as that sense of disquiet prodded her conscience.

She'd made a promise, after all. And besides, she believed telling him about the letters would come to nothing.

"And there's something I need to tell you, as well. Don't look now, but I think that's Baron Ruthersby."

Jane startled and saw that horrid man from the brothel speaking with the marquess. "What if he remembers us?"

"Don't worry. You were beneath the hood and wore a mask, and he was likely too drunk to recall much of the night, regardless. Just be sure he doesn't hear you speak. That should be simple enough since you'll be on my arm the whole night," he said with a rakish wink. "Now, what is it you have to tell me, hmm?"

"Later," she said, not wanting anything to spoil the evening.

Besides, there were too many eyes watching with speculation, too many whispers behind their fans. Too many people who would doubt him if there was the slightest speculation.

At the thought, a shiver of foreboding skated over her scalp and down her nape.

In the same instant, the music ended abruptly on a discordant screech of violin strings and everyone looked over to the orchestra.

Jane gasped. Standing there was none other than Lord Herrington.

She curled her hand protectively over Raven's. "You should leave before he does something worse."

"I'm not going anywhere. Whatever he has to say, let him say it."

∽∾∽∾∽

THE BALL at the marquess's town house was a lavish affair, far surpassing anything Raven had ever experienced. But there was no accounting for Aversleigh's taste in guests.

Why did Herrington have to be invited, tonight of all nights? And he looked three sheets gone, at least, wobbling on his feet. Then, hefting a goblet high, he tapped the crystal with the gold ring on his right hand in high, piercing *clinks*.

"I have a toast," he began, words slurring together as he pointed his glass to Raven. The gesture caused the crowd to turn at once, shifting as if to make a path for whatever insults were about to be propelled his way. "To you, who-ever you are, for duping my uncle and all these guests. But you'll never fool me. You're no son of my cousin. You're no Northcott."

"Stop this, nephew," Warrister growled, struggling to rise from the settee where he'd been sitting and talking with the marchioness. "You're only going to make a fool of your-self."

"Oh, but I have proof that casts more than a shadow of doubt on this pretender's legitimacy."

"Let him speak," Raven said, affecting a tone of bore-dom. "He can't say anything I haven't already heard."

But beside him, he felt Jane grow still and heard the subtle intake of her breath. And it might have been his imagination or the shifting of candlelight, but her complex-ion appeared somewhat paler.

He curled his hand comfortingly over the one she had resting on his sleeve, trying to warm the gloved fingers that had gone unnaturally cold.

"Challenge accepted." Herrington sketched a bow, slosh-ing his drink. Then he moved away from the orchestra and went down the steps to the ballroom floor, speaking to the crowd along the way. "What my uncle doesn't know is that there was a maid who worked for my cousin, and she gave birth to a child that January, just days before the fire. So, you see, there were two infants in the house that night." The crowd gasped and Herrington ate it up with a gloating grin. "Yes, indeed, two infants."

Surprised by this news, Raven sought Jane's gaze. But her stark attention was fixed on Herrington and her hand slipped out from beneath his.

A cold chill slithered into Raven's stomach, turning it to stone. Could she have known about the other child?

No. It wasn't possible. He trusted Jane and knew that she would never keep anything from him.

Herrington held up two fingers and waved them around as he started to amble toward Raven. "Some of you might ask why that could be important. Well, *that* is the most important part of all. And it has something to do with Miss Pickerington's uncle."

He paused to empty his glass before he continued. "It just so happens that Mr. John Pickerington worked as a tutor in my cousin's house, teaching his French wife to speak English. During that time, a maid arrived in a delicate condition, having left her husband. She'd begged for a post and a home for herself and her unborn child. Yet, all the while, she was hoping to trap some man into taking her away, wanting him to claim her husband's child as his own. She attempted this with me as well. Of course, I—as a gentleman—put her in her place," he said smugly with his hand splayed over his chest. "Mr. Pickerington, however, was fully ensnared. He gave her money. Bought her baubles. Promised her the world. He would have done anything for her. Anything. Even, I dare say, try to pass off her son as the lost heir."

Raven absorbed this information, and felt the *click* of damning puzzle pieces sliding together. It made sense, albeit in a strange, twisted way. But it accounted for the missing information.

"Nephew," Warrister warned again, but his voice had gone weaker, hoarse.

Herrington ignored him, stopping behind Jane. He peered around to look at her as if playing a game of hide and seek. "Ah, Miss Pickerington, you don't appear surprised by this tale. Perhaps it is some great family secret."

She looked up at Raven, eyes wide and the clear mark of guilt written in her unblinking stare. "Raven, I was going to tell . . ."

He looked away, sickened. Duped. And agonizingly tired of being used by nearly everyone he had ever known.

He'd thought she was different from the others. After all, what could she have to gain by any of this?

But he knew it had to be something. It always was.

For her, it likely started out with her study of scoundrels. A book. He'd been her research project. Then she found the mark and decided to make a gentleman out of him. Coincidentally, the bluestocking required a gentleman to marry, in order to have the life *she* wanted. Never mind the fact that she'd destroyed the life *he'd* wanted.

And he'd played perfectly into her hand. He'd forgotten all his rules.

"And what about you, Mr. Raven—whatever your name actually is? What secrets do you have?"

"I'm hiding nothing," Raven said harshly.

Out of the corner of his eye, he saw tears roll down Jane's cheeks. Disgusted by the sight, he jerked a handkerchief from his pocket and pushed it into her grasp. Then he looked to his grandfather.

Color was rising from Warrister's neckcloth as he glared at Lord Herrington. Raven tried to go to him but Herrington blocked his path, arm extended to press that goblet-clenching fist to his chest.

Rage simmered in Raven's blood. Instead of unleashing it, he drew in a breath, refusing to make a further spectacle that would injure the heart of a kind old man.

So he signaled the footman to help the earl back to the settee.

Herrington tsked. "Such concern. How sweet, indeed. You play your part well. But what do you think my uncle will do once he realizes he was manipulated from the start?"

"There was never any deception on my part."

"Of course, you would say that," Herrington continued,

clucking his tongue. "You and the Pickerington family are thick as thieves. Here you are courting Miss Pickerington so that one day she'll become a countess. All the while you're paying off her uncle's debts so that he can be free of prison. It certainly seems that such a tremendous display of *gratitude* wouldn't be necessary if you were, indeed, legitimate." He scoffed, his voice rising to a bellow. "The truth is, you're a complete fraud, trying to pass yourself off as the heir and take advantage of a senile old man."

"That is enough." Raven pushed aside the bracing hand and stepped toe to toe with Herrington, seething. "You've made your points perfectly clear, and have made it equally impossible to believe anything other than your truth. But leave the earl out of this."

Before Raven left, he looked to Warrister one last time. "For what it is worth, I never wanted the title. I only wanted a name. A family."

❧❦❧❦❧

ALL EYES in the room watched Raven leave, including Jane's. Then every eye descended on her.

She looked to her parents, who were—of course—already bowing to popular opinion. Ellie had tears in her eyes, but she was all the way across the ballroom. And Herrington was smiling.

He held the goblet out to her. "Your prize cup, madam."

Furious and heartsick, she slapped it away, glad that it fell from his hand and shattered on the floor. "Isn't it enough that you've tried to kill him several times? Did you have to murder his spirit as well?"

She didn't wait for an answer, just dashed out of the ballroom and after Raven.

He was already across the lamplit street, eating up the

pavement toward Covent Garden with prowling, long-legged strides. There was no way she could catch him on foot.

She hailed a hackney and, once she was beside him, she called out, "Please get in. Let me explain."

To her surprise, he didn't hesitate. Leaping inside before the carriage had stopped, he sat across from her, his cold stare boring into hers, in the light of the carriage lanterns.

"I made a mistake in not telling you."

"A mistake?" He arched a brow. "No, Jane. A mistake happens by accident. You *chose* not to tell me something monumental. You broke your word. You promised that you would tell me everything. You, who always needs to be prepared for every situation, left me in the dark. I can never forgive you. Not for this."

The words were spoken with such glacial certainty, that Jane felt as if she'd fallen through the ice of a frozen lake and was left floundering. "I only just discovered the letters in the attic. I didn't even know until the night you were attacked, and by then it didn't matter. Nothing else mattered."

She hoped the recollection of their night together would bring him back. The tender confessions. The desperate joining of their bodies. The love they both felt. Even though he'd never said the words, she'd felt it spilling out of him and into her.

"All you had to do was tell me. That simple," he said through clenched teeth and then looked out the hackney window as if dismissing her from his presence.

"Simple?" She swallowed down another jolt of panic. "If I had shared the contents of those letters, I know precisely what you would have done. You would have turned your back on your birthright. On your family. And you would have done it without thinking twice. You've spent your life keeping everyone at a distance. You even put conditions on

your time with me, keeping a barrier between us, disappearing whenever I got too close."

His gaze swerved back to her, a smile twisting his mouth as he drawled, "Oh, that's not true, Jane. In fact, I'd say you and me have been quite close. Quite close, indeed."

"It was different with us, from the very beginning," she said quietly.

"You'd like to think so."

"You're doing it now. You're trying to hurt me to keep me far away. You've lived most of your life without letting anyone in. You keep yourself locked up like your bedside table," she said, trying to get him to see reason.

"You keep talking about my flaws and failings. Well, what about yours, hmm?" He growled. "You know how your parents don't give a damn about you? Well, have you ever once thought that it might be your own fault? That you and your little quirks are nothing more than a constant headache? Who wants to deal with all the chaos that follows you?"

She flinched at the attack, feeling it penetrate the vulnerable surface of her heart.

But she swallowed down the pain. Trying hard to believe that he didn't mean it, she shifted to the edge of the bench and laid her hand on his knee. She needed to convince him that she hadn't abandoned him.

"I understand your reasons for saying these cruel things," she said. "You've been hurt so badly throughout your life that you expect it now, from everyone. But I'm telling you that I made a mistake. Please don't let this consume you and ruin us. Raven, we belong together, no matter who you are."

Desperation made her reach out for his hand. She had to pry his folded arms apart, so that she could lay his palm against her cheek.

"Stop it, Jane. Just stop it." He pulled free, shrugging her off, voice rising as he continued. "You're more cruel and cunning than any of them because you made me want this. You made me believe I had a family. Then you just stood there while it was being ripped away."

She shook her head, frantic, tears clogging her throat. "I didn't know what to say. I knew shortly after Herrington began that you wouldn't believe me."

"Pity, that." He tsked. "So, tell me, Jane. Were you just amusing yourself for a bit of research, hmm? Will this be part of your book—a scoundrel's lessons?"

"No. Please listen—"

"At least I got something out of it, too," he sneered, deaf to her pleas. "Though, in hindsight, I think the manner of payment for your services is rather steep. You may want to go a bit easier on the next bloke who falls for your lies. But I'll say one thing in your favor"—he reached across and set his hand on the carriage door—"you make it easy for everyone to walk away and never look back."

Opening the door, he leapt down to the street without a backward glance.

Jane wanted to call out to him. But when she opened her mouth, only a deep wrenching sob came out, the agony so overwhelming that no sound accompanied it.

She doubled over, her mouth frozen open as if in a silent scream that no one would ever hear. And for the first time in a long while, she felt completely alone and utterly invisible.

Chapter 34

~~~~~~

The first thing Jane did upon arriving home was to collapse into Mr. Miggins's arms. The stoic butler did not seem at all surprised, but simply put his arms around her and let her have a good cry. When she'd managed to collect herself enough, he gave her a handkerchief and told her that he'd have the kitchens send up a nice tray to her rooms.

The tea did nothing to console her. It was simply a liquid with leaves, heated to a certain temperature, and she couldn't even bring herself to care about the properties of steam. All she did was lie beneath the coverlet and cling to any part that still carried Raven's scent.

It was impossible to believe how quickly it had ended.

In fact, she couldn't believe it. Her mind refused to accept it.

There was no logic in their separation, not when her skin still recalled the sensations of his touch as if expecting him to stride in and brush the hair from her face and hold her close. Not when her lips still pulsed with the tender memories of their last night together and might forever be bruised from his sweetly frantic kiss. And not when her heart still belonged to him.

The artist on her portico had painted an entire series of imagined scenarios of their future together. Her inner scribe kept a catalogue of his language. It contained the meaning of every growl and grunt, along with every type of caress and kiss.

She was not a person given to nightmares, but she imagined this was what one felt like—the inability to escape, the racing panic to get away from the most painful moment of her life.

How did one move on from such devastation?

The answer did not come. And likely never would.

Jane didn't expect to see her parents that night. Nevertheless, they slowly strolled through the doorway and looked around her room, as if touring a museum or a shop, seeming to pay no attention to the young woman sobbing into her coverlet.

"Have you c-come to tell me s-something?" she asked when she was able, her voice breaking in hiccupped sobs.

"It is all out now, dearest," Mother said. "Everyone is talking about how he was nothing more than a fraud, like the others before him."

"He's not a fraud. He just doesn't know what to believe. There were two children in that house, true, but that doesn't mean he isn't Merrick Northcott."

"That's neither here nor there. With everything that has come out, Mr. Northcott—or whoever he is—has lost favor with the *ton*."

"And no daughter of mine is going to be ruined with all of society watching."

Jane went cold and still. "What do you mean?"

"I think it was in the way that Lord Herrington indicated that you were conspiring to marry that man," Mother said with a nod as if agreeing with herself. "It was all very scandalous. And so many people noticed the way you had rushed off after him. It might have been forgiven when he was the heir, but now . . ."

"Then we heard a strange accounting from a certain Baron Ruthersby. As soon as you left, he came to me and declared that he'd met you in a brothel of all things. Even though it couldn't be true, the damage has been done, nonetheless. The Marquess of Aversleigh overheard him," Father added with a stern frown. "Therefore, I've no choice but to send you to America. Fear not, though, I'm sure everyone will eventually forget about this entire episode, much like they forgot my brother's misdeeds. Or at least they had done . . . until tonight. Now who's to say how long it will be before their memories are erased once more?"

Mother issued a sigh. "I'm only glad no one discovered that John had been at the Northcott estate on the night of that terrible fire. I shall never forget seeing him covered in all that soot and ash, stumbling in here and sobbing at your feet. Quite alarming, indeed."

Jane startled. "My uncle was there the night of the fire?"

"Yes, yes, muttering on and on about a murderous Frenchman and a woman named Hortense or Heloise or—"

"Helene?"

Mother flitted a graceful hand in the air. "None of it matters now, I'm sure. All water under the bridge. And, perhaps, in time it will be the same for your scandal, dearest. You will write to us, won't you?"

Jane blinked numbly, trying to process this new information. But it was impossible to focus, given that her life was falling apart around her.

Yes, she'd known about the risks and, had she been caught, this would have been the likely outcome. But it was all hypothetical then. It hadn't happened. It hadn't yet exploded in her face.

Now it was all too real. "What about the children? I can't leave them. It's almost Christmas."

Her parents looked to each other in confusion. Then her

father spoke. "I don't see what that matters. It's obvious that you'll have to be gone before the January freeze. I'll make all the arrangements and, in the meantime, have your maid begin to pack your things."

"Good night, dear," Mother said and walked beside Father out the door.

Jane was losing everything—her home, her family, and her future. And it was all happening in the course of one night.

It was just like Prue. Her friend had suffered this same fate, and was now living letter to letter.

Perhaps it was that realization that jolted Jane out of bed.

When this had happened to Prue, all her friends had rallied together to do everything they could. So, first, Jane sent a letter to Ellie, begging for her counsel.

Second, she sent a messenger with the black lacquered casket full of letters to Raven's house, in the fervent hope that, if she provided him with all the facts, he would see that she'd been telling the truth. That he could still trust her. Then, perhaps, they could heal the wounds between them. Perhaps . . .

And third, she needed to learn why her uncle was at the Northcott house the night of the fire, and what he knew about it. Unfortunately, she didn't know how she could get past the prison gates to find the answers.

Then a thought occurred to her. If she couldn't get into the prison, she just might know someone who could. Someone whose title could open any door.

The following morning, Ellie arrived.

But shortly thereafter, so did the black casket.

The letters were still inside, along with a gallipot of salve, an empty jar that once contained damson jam, and a black glove. There was no note addressed to her. No words telling her to stop and desist. Only silence, as if he'd already managed to forget her.

In that moment, she learned that unbearable, heart-twisting agony wasn't the worst pain imaginable. There was another ache that hurt even worse—the cold desolation left behind of a love wrenched from the very center of her soul.

❧⊷❧⊷❧

MUCH TO Bess's dislike and lamentation, Raven demolished room after room of his house.

He started with the main floor, taking a sledgehammer to the walls from dawn to dusk without much break in between. Then from dusk to dawn, when all was quiet, he'd spread fresh plaster on the bare lath.

He moved from room to room, stopping occasionally to grab a new bottle of whisky and take a piss. Sometimes he'd find himself lost in a slow blink with his shoulder propped up against the wall. But then he'd rouse himself and get back to work.

The first day, Bess left out a tray and told him whenever he had a visitor. But after being barked at for her efforts, she stayed belowstairs from that point on. She turned everyone away, too, just like he asked. Not that there was anyone who stopped by after the first day.

Warrister sent several missives, but they were all in a pile on the table by the door.

And Raven had to stay away from his bedchamber because Jane was everywhere within it, her scent on his bedclothes, her memory in his chair, and her letters still tucked in his drawer.

But after a week of tearing his house apart, Raven needed something else to distract him.

When he walked into Sterling's office and asked to return to his post, Reed's brow furrowed in confusion. "You want to continue working for me? What, have you just given up after the debacle at Aversleigh's ball?"

Raven shrugged. "I just need to know where my next step will land. I need some certainty."

"Isn't Miss Pickerington your certainty? I had the impression the last time we talked that she was a big part of your decision to claim your birthright."

"I'm sure you heard what happened. Because she duped me, I lost everything. I can't forgive that."

Sterling scrubbed a hand over his face. "Can't you?"

Raven just looked at him, stony-eyed.

"How did she do it, then?"

"She uncovered vital information that could have stopped this entire nightmare, but she kept it from me. She'd made a choice to deceive me."

"Did you ever think she might have had a good reason?"

Raven was already exhausted by this conversation. "There is no good reason for that. In my experience, there are only bad reasons."

"Very well. I have something to tell you," Sterling said. "I've been keeping something from you and from everyone here. And it's something I've known for quite a while, in fact."

Raven waited for it, crossing his arms, jaw tight.

"I've decided that Sterling's isn't going to be a gaming hell any longer, but a proper gentleman's club. And the reason is because I'm going to be a father," he added with a smug nod. "Is that a good enough reason to keep a secret?"

Raven relaxed. Somehow, his mouth remembered how to curve into a smile and his hand reached out to slap Reed good-naturedly on the shoulder. "Well, look at you, all puffed up and proud. Congratulations, old man."

"I'm glad you forgave me for that," Sterling said with a wink.

"Come on, now. It isn't the same at all."

Raven expelled a breath. He'd had enough. And he was

tired of thinking about Jane constantly, so he certainly didn't want to keep talking about her.

"Perhaps Miss Pickerington just wanted you to have what she thought you deserved. Perhaps she feared you would give up if something stood in your way."

He growled and threw up his hands, stalking to the door. "And perhaps I'm tired of always having to fight to survive. I just want my old life back. I just want to wake up in the morning and know who I am, who I've always been. Come to work. Go home to my house. That's all. So, can I have my position or not?"

"Of course," he said. Then, before Raven could leave, Sterling halted him with one final comment. "Word of advice from someone who understands a bit about fighting. Don't do it unless it matters to you. But when it does, you've got to fight like hell for it."

⁂

BILL-JACK ROLLINS never had an earl in the gatehouse before and he didn't know quite what to do with one.

So, he doffed his hat and scuffed the dust from the toes of his boots. "Good day to ye, Lord Warrister. 'ow can I be o' service?"

The old earl straightened his shoulders and gave the courtyard a flinty-eyed stare. "Take me to Mr. John Pickerington's chamber, if you please."

Chapter 35

I‍t was nearly Christmas and there were no garlands on the stairs or above the doorways. There were no beribboned kissing boughs, and no family puddings in the larder, waiting to be steamed.

Jane could barely summon the desire to walk into the conservatory. However, whenever she did, she went to the chaise longue for a good cry.

"I've had enough of this, Jane," Ellie said sternly, wagging her finger. Her reprimand was lessened, however, by the blatant concern in her stricken features. "Let's have a walk in the cold air. I've heard it's very good for the constitution."

"I would likely freeze to death on purpose, and I don't want that weighing on your conscience."

"Then we'll walk down the hall to the library."

Jane closed her eyes, futilely trying to keep the memory at bay. "Not the library."

"Then what about your desk? Surely, you can manage ten steps."

"I don't see the point of it."

"The point is," Ellie huffed, "that there is paper and ink and a plan that needs to be formed. You're not simply going to allow your parents to ship you off to America, are you? At the very least, you could think up a grand escape like you did for Winnie earlier this year. All turned out well for her. And it will for you. Why, even my aunts are determined to keep you if your parents attempt to go through with it."

"Thank you, Ellie, but it doesn't matter any longer."

"Of course, it matters. What about our book?"

"I'm afraid that you will be left in charge of its completion. My name will have to be omitted, of course, or else it will never be published otherwise. And I wouldn't be able to live with you and your aunts without risking your reputation. I won't do that to you."

"Oh, Jane why did you risk your own?" Ellie asked, worrying the seams of her cuffs with a flick of her manicured thumbnail. "You told me that you knew from the outset that he might never claim his birthright. So falling in love with him was a foolish choice. You'd never have been able to marry him and live here with your siblings like you'd always planned. Your parents would never have allowed it."

"I know. I even tried to convince myself that I wasn't aware of the full risk of ruination." Jane shook her head, feeling silly for trying to fool herself. "But I would have married him regardless, or even stayed by his side without marriage. I was willing to risk everything. And I did. I love my siblings, but they will eventually grow up and move away and start families. But I want a family, too, and children of my . . . own." Her voice broke on the painful reminder. "And I wanted that with him, even if it meant never being allowed back into this house."

Ellie stared, agape, and slowly sank down onto the foot of the chaise longue. "You truly love him that much?"

"I do. But it is a one-sided love." Apparently, it always was.

"The worst kind of love." Her friend nodded in commiseration. "But how can you be certain of his regard, or lack thereof, if the two of you haven't spoken since the night of the ball?"

In Ellie's eyes Jane saw a glint of promise. At least, one of them still had hope.

"I sent him another missive this week, absolving him from any obligation toward me," Jane said with numb desolation, recalling the miserable moment her courses had come, leaving her with no possible tie to Raven. "He never responded. And in his lack of response, he has made his desires indisputably clear."

"I hate him," her friend decided, her fist on her lap. "I know you don't, but I must. He has wounded you too severely. The Jane Pickerington I knew would have marched up to his door and given him a piece of her mind . . ."

Ellie's words trailed off and her gaze went distant and unfocused as she stared toward the frosted window glass.

The old Jane would have been able to surmise what she was thinking. But this Jane was only half of herself, having already given Raven a piece of her mind along with every bit of her heart.

◈◈◈◈◈

"ONE OF your lovelies finally came to see you," Bess announced from the door. "Been wonderin' when this would 'appen."

Raven's reflection went still in the washstand mirror, the razor poised in his hand. His heart stopped, too, and every thought went directly to Jane. Was she here?

Slowly, he lowered the razor and wiped the shaving soap from his jaw.

"Well? Am I to send 'er away?"

"No," he heard himself say, his voice distant to his own ears. "I'll be down in a trice."

As Bess flounced out of the room, he realized that in the past he would have just said to bring this particular caller upstairs. But he couldn't now. He had to keep his guard up. There was no way he'd allow himself to be manipulated again.

He dressed more carefully than he usually did for a day at Sterling's. But he didn't want Jane to know that he'd spent every moment of the past fortnight doing little more than thinking about her.

He kept his focus on straightening his cuffs as he ambled down the stairs, refusing to look at the figure waiting in the foyer until he reached the nadir. And there he stopped abruptly.

It wasn't Jane.

A wave of tension rolled through him, clawing up his back, chafing his skin. On an exhale he said, "Miss Parrish. To what do I owe this unexpected visit?"

She held up a stack of the post that had piled on the table, withdrawing one as if she were planning to discard it like a card in a deck. "You haven't even bothered to read it. I knew I was right to hate you, using my friend the way you did."

"I think you have that the other way around. Your friend was the one who toyed with my life as if it was of little consequence to her."

She scoffed. "Then, I imagine, you consider being sent to America, away from her family and friends, of *little consequence*."

Raven took a step forward, and another, his heart thudding in his chest and their last night together playing poignantly through his mind. "Why is she being sent away?"

"Because of you, of course," she hissed, narrowing a pair of amber-colored viper eyes. "Though, if you'd bothered to read her letter, I'm sure you would have known already."

He snatched it out of her grasp and ripped it open, skimming the short missive for any word of a child. His child . . . their child . . . A family, with Jane.

And in that second of searching, he felt such hope that he knew he'd been fooling himself all this time.

Jane was right. And so was Sterling, for that matter. Raven had pushed her away because he was afraid of losing her. He knew that when doubt was cast on his legitimacy, he'd never be allowed to marry her. And the thought of never having her was even worse than losing any stupid title.

His hands gripped the page, his gaze settling on the text. *You are under no obligation to me now or in the future.*

Lowering the paper on a breath, he turned to the stairs and scrubbed a hand over his face. He understood too clearly. No child . . . No Jane . . . Nothing.

His life was what it had always been. What he'd made of it. He had employment, coin in his pocket, and a roof over his head. It was all a man could want.

So then why wasn't it enough for him any longer?

"What about the book?" he asked, knowing how much it meant to her.

Miss Parrish huffed and said, "It's up to me to finish, now. Jane must keep her name from being associated with it because of all the talk of her ruination."

He whirled around. *"What?"*

"Do not pretend that you care. You had to have heard of the things Baron Ruthersby said, and yet you did nothing. If I had the power, I'd wish the plague on you."

Raven hadn't heard. He'd been blocking out every comment and every whisper in an effort to return to his old life. But there was nothing to return to. Nothing left for him without Jane.

He'd been an idiot not to have seen it before.

"Miss Parrish, I have a favor to ask of you."

And then, he was going to have a little chat with Ruthersby.

Chapter 36

Jane awoke to the sound of Theodora giggling in the corridor, and light flooding in from below her bedchamber door. Checking the clock on the mantel, she saw that it was not quite seven o'clock in the morning. Exhausted but curious, she slipped out of bed and shrugged into her wrapper to investigate.

Opening the door, she saw the wall sconces were lit all along the corridor, adorned with evergreen and sprigs of holly. Strange. She hadn't noticed these decorations last night.

Stepping further into the hall, she saw her cherub-faced little sister being lovingly mauled by a little ball of white-and-brown fluff. "The puppy is kissing me, Jane."

"I see that. But where did you find . . ." Her question trailed off as she saw another ball of fluff gambol down the corridor.

This time, Peter followed—*sans* clothing, of course—and pointing. "Bird."

"You're not supposed to be upstairs yet," a whispered voice said.

"Ellie? Whatever are you doing here at this time of morning?"

Her friend froze in midstride before she could reach Peter and the puppy. "Um . . . Jane, why are you not still asleep?"

"I believe I posed my question first."

Ellie looked over her shoulder fretfully and then back to her. "Would it be too much to ask for you to pretend that you're sleepwalking and simply turn back around?"

"It's no use, Miss Parrish." The words were said in an all-too-familiar deep growl, as Raven slowly ascended the stairs like a figure out of a dream. "I knew it would be futile to attempt to surprise someone as clever as Jane."

He stopped abruptly when he saw her, his gaze holding hers.

Neither of them was breathing. But she could feel her pulse hammering at her throat, and see his doing the same above a silver cravat. His frost-colored eyes heated as he took her in from head to toe, drawing out a twinge of longing from her heart.

She steeled herself against it and tied her frilly wrapper shut. "Why are you here?"

"To wish you a happy Christmas," he said softly.

"Christmas isn't for five more days." She knew this because she was leaving for America in four.

He shook his head and began to walk toward her, the air seeming to crackle between them. The closer he came, the more her skin tingled and yearned.

So she took a step back and held up her hand to stay him, all the while feeling the sting of tears prick the corners of her eyes.

He stopped, his brow knitting together. Then he scrubbed a hand over his face. It was only when he drew it away that she noticed the weary exhaustion beneath his eyes.

"Jane," he whispered, the single syllable spoken with raw agony. "Don't send me away. Not yet. Come downstairs with me, first, and see what all the children have done."

He held out his hand. She was helpless to resist.

A static jolt stole beneath her skin when their fingers

clasped, curling into each other with achingly tender familiarity. Her breaths came out, stilted and shallow. She moved
beside him, trying not to absorb too much too fast.

Perhaps Ellie was right and she *was* sleepwalking. These
days had been nothing more than a cold fog surrounding
her. Surely this couldn't be real.

She turned to her friend as she passed her at the top of
the stairs and whispered, "Pinch me, quick."

Ellie smiled and obliged her. And on her other side, Jane
felt Raven relax marginally.

The stairway was woven with evergreen garland and
dark red ribbons. The main hall glowed with bright golden
light as Theodore and Graham, home from school, were assisting Henry with lighting beeswax tapers by the dozens.
Phillipa and Charles were hanging paper snowflakes. But
most surprising of all was Mr. Miggins trying to wrangle a
tumble of puppies into a shawl-lined basket.

"What is all this?" she asked in wonderment, turning
around in a circle.

A hesitant smile curled the corners of Raven's mouth.
"As I said, we're celebrating Christmas today. And the cook
is mixing the batter right now for a fortune-telling cake for
your birthday."

"My birthday is in June," she said, perplexed.

"I know. Ellie told me," he confessed, shifting from one
foot to the other as if nervous. "I wanted you to celebrate
these special days with your siblings, so that you'll have a
memory to take with you."

"Oh," she said, dejected. He must have heard the news
from Ellie about her parents sending her away. Those blasted
tears threatened again. "I don't know why you would bother.
You and I have bid our farewells."

"I'm making a muck of this," he said, chagrined. Then
he pointed an accusatory finger at her. "You were supposed

to be asleep for another hour, then it would all be clear. Charles," he called out across the hall. "Did you take that pouch to the cook, yet."

Her brother smacked his palm to his forehead, then he trotted over and gave the small leather sack to Raven. "Blast! I knew I was forgetting something. Apologies. Got caught up in watching the twins make snow outside with your new contraption. Too bad it's all melting. But it makes a great snowball . . . while it lasts."

Jane looked toward the windows to the side garden just as Sebastian and Tristram strolled in through the door, pushing a familiar wooden box, while wet globs of snow dripped from their heads.

She looked to Raven. "You put wheels on my snowflake maker? That was quite clever of you."

He shrugged. "It was your design. But this," he said, placing the pouch in her open hands, "was going to make everything clear. At least, as soon as you had your cake. You see, there was going to be one of these in every slice."

He untied the drawstring.

A swirling ribbon of hope filled Jane. Then she looked down and . . . frowned.

"You were going to put *buttons* in every slice?"

"What—" He glanced down, his mouth set in a grim line, just as the twins started snickering. He growled. "Sebastian. Tristram. I can just as easily take away that new toboggan."

In a blur of movement that could rival Phillipa on her best day, they both dashed forward and began to unload pocketful after pocketful of golden ring trinkets into Jane's waiting hands.

Her breath caught and slowly she looked up at Raven.

"You were right, Jane. I pushed you away because I was afraid. I knew I'd lose you when it turned out that I wasn't anyone anymore."

"I don't care about your title. I never have."

He smiled and brushed her damp cheek with his finger-tips. "I know. But your parents wouldn't have let me marry you. If we went against their wishes, then you wouldn't see your siblings and that would break your heart. So, I thought that I'd just say some terrible, unforgivable things and keep you at a safe distance from me, and close to them, then every-one would be content."

"And that turned out swimmingly," she said wryly as her heart fluttered painfully beneath her breast in anticipation.

"I've been going mad these past fourteen days. I deserved to be in hell after what I said. And I didn't mean a word of it," he said earnestly. "You're not forgettable, Jane. I've spent every moment apart wishing you were. I've nearly torn down my house with a sledgehammer. I need you, every brilliant part of you."

Trying not to let her heart overpower her thoughts again, and blocking out the sound of Ellie's sighs, she said, "But I've brought you chaos since the moment we met. That, I'm afraid, is indisputable."

"Only the best kind of chaos, the kind I can't live with-out. And there's something else I realized, too. My life is one massive locked cupboard without you. So, you've got to marry me."

She sniffed and tears spilled down her smiling cheeks in a great flood. "Is that truly how you're going to propose? I think it was more of a command than anything else."

"How about this, then?" He lowered to one knee. "I love you, Jane Pickerington. It happened when you had your first epiphany. I didn't want to ask what it was. Because if you'd have told me, right then and there, that you thought we should get married and have a big, chaotic family . . . well, then . . . I just might have carried you off that day."

She was trembling now, shaking so much that some of the rings began to tumble from her hands, pinging and jingling to the floor. So, she sat down onto his knee, put her arms around his neck and let the buttons and rings fall in a clatter as she kissed him.

Then she whispered, "If that's true, then I had an epiphany just now, too."

Chapter 37

For the first time in his life, Raven was truly happy. He was filled with hope for the future. And, if he were honest, it was slightly terrifying.

He was so used to being a miserable, jaded cynic that he didn't know what to do with this feeling. So, he reached for Jane's hand and, when she squeezed his in return, he instantly relaxed.

She laughed brightly, looking away from the first flakes of downy snow falling outside the carriage window and back to him. "I cannot believe we're dashing off to Gretna Green, while my parents are still asleep. I think Ellie is actually looking forward to telling them the news. She even borrowed my vinaigrette."

Raven lifted her fingers to his lips and held her gaze. "I promise that you'll get to see your siblings often, even if we have to steal inside the house."

On the other hand, he didn't think there would be any need to sneak around. He'd had a lengthy *chat* with Ruthersby and the baron had agreed to recant his claims about seeing Jane at Moll Dawson's.

"I'm not worried any longer," she said with scholarly certainty. "I have this strange sense of peace about it all, which requires no planning or overthinking whatsoever. Regardless of what happens tomorrow or the days that follow, I know that I'm precisely where I belong."

He couldn't resist stealing a kiss and lingering over her plum-sweet lips. He'd been such a fool to spend those days apart. And a fool not to trust her. He should have listened to her and *fought like hell*—as Sterling said—against his own demons.

A love like theirs was too precious to lock away. He'd never lose sight of that again.

Ending the kiss, he put his arm around her and snuggled her closer as she rested her head against the crook of his shoulder on a contented sigh.

"Do you mind if we make one stop along the way?" he asked, thinking about wasted time and all the unopened letters waiting on the table in his foyer.

She feigned a gasp of shock. "Was that actually a politely worded question?"

"Forget I asked," he teased and called up to the driver to take them to St. James's.

Less than a quarter hour later, they were standing at a black door, opened by a rather cross housekeeper who tapped her foot on the floor. "So ye've returned, 'ave ye? Took your time about it."

"It's a pleasure to see you, as well, Mrs. Bramly. Is my"— he stopped and cleared his throat—"is the earl at home this morning?"

"In the library. You know where it is." She jerked her head toward the stairs, then tromped off in a snit.

As Jane walked up beside him, she whispered, "At least she doesn't think you're a ghost any longer."

"No, she only wishes I was."

The familiar sweet fragrance of old books greeted Raven as he stepped into the library through the partially opened doorway. Warrister was in his usual chair. But he wasn't alone.

Herrington was there, too, hands braced on the mantel

and his arms and shoulders tense as though he were in the midst of an argument.

At the sound of the door creaking, he turned his head, then sneered.

Warrister looked over at the same time and his countenance brightened with affection, tinged with a frown of scolding. "Here you are, at last. I've sent an invitation to your house every day for a fortnight."

"My humblest apologies," Raven said instantly, pleased to be here and even gladder that Jane was on his arm. "In fact, today is a day for apologies. As I confessed to Miss Pickerington earlier, I have recently realized that I tend to shut out the people I want most in my life when I fear I'm about to lose them. I'm afraid I did that with you, as well. But I am here to admit that I would like, very much, to remain in your life. No matter who I really am to you."

"Of course, my boy. There's never been a question of that."

Herrington scoffed.

"Hush, nephew. Make peace with the fact that he is your family."

"How can you say that, after everything I've told you?"

"Because there are many things I know, which you do not. However, *I* did not choose a public forum to air mine. That should serve as another lesson for you." Warrister turned his attention to Jane. "Miss Pickerington, my deepest gratitude for the heartfelt correspondences, along with the parcel. With your assistance and research, I believe I've finally gained a complete understanding about the events that transpired so many years ago."

"I was more than glad to be of assistance," she said with a modest shrug. "I don't like unanswered questions either."

Raven looked at Jane with a measure of surprise. Apparently, even when they were apart, she'd been campaigning for him, believing in him. And all the while, he'd been a confounded idiot.

She blinked up at him and nodded as if reading his thoughts, and it took every ounce of his control not to kiss that smirk off her lips. He'd wait till they were in the carriage.

"Those letters were invaluable," Warrister said.

"What letters?" Herrington asked crossly.

"The ones in the casket, there on the mantel. They were from the maid, Helene Bastille. I believe you were acquainted with her, nephew," the earl said carefully and Herrington stiffened, his gaze riveted on the black box. "Read through them if you like. I daresay, without the letters, I never would have thought to look at the maid, and then to her husband for the answers. But, as it turned out, that was the key." Then, as if he'd just commented on the weather and nothing at all earth shattering, he turned to Jane with a smile. "My dear, would you be so kind as to hand me those papers, waiting on the table by the window?"

"Of course," she said and received a pat on the hand when she returned, along with an invitation to sit beside the earl.

Raven pulled up the chair for her, his brow puckered in confusion. He heard himself ask, "What key?"

"The key that finally unlocked the whole truth," the earl said with an ambiguous air that demanded the forbearance of his audience. "In those pages, Helene Bastille refers to her husband as *le Sinistre*. The name could easily be disregarded as merely a moniker that an abused wife might have given her estranged husband. However, it means a great deal when one discovers that there was an infamous French spy by that same name." He paused, lifting his brows thoughtfully. "Not only that, but *le Sinistre*'s method of covering up his tracks was through arson."

Arson? A shock jolted through Raven, the hair at his nape

standing on end. He looked from Warrister to Jane, and to the casket beneath Herrington's hand on the mantel. He'd never bothered to look at the letters. Not even when he saw that Jane had translated each and every one. At the time, just seeing her handwriting had nearly broken him, so he'd sent them back.

"Does that mean this . . . *le Sinistre* . . . is responsible for setting the fire that day?"

Warrister nodded solemnly. "I believe so. From what I have uncovered, he had several contacts in England—traitors willing to sell British secrets and others who engaged in smuggling for him. Regrettably, one of those traitors had fallen in love with his estranged wife and planned to flee with her child. I can only imagine that this was the reason *le Sinistre* brought his wrath down upon my son's household."

Herrington whipped around, fury marked in his high color. "If you think for a moment that I had anything to do with this, then you're sorely mistaken!"

"Calm down, nephew. I'm making no such accusation."

"Then what are you doing? Why are we even talking about Helene in the first place? Unless you're about to tell me what I already know, that this imposter"—he flung an arm toward Raven—"is really her child."

Raven straightened, head high and ready for confrontation. If he was the maid's child, then that's who he was. There was no changing it.

"No need for a battle," the earl said, exhaling his impatience. "Let's put that aside for the moment. I should like to read the final letter that my son wrote to me. It should clear up many of the doubts plaguing both of you," he said looking from one to the other.

"'Dear Father,'" he began, the rasp in his voice redolent with emotion. "'I shall arrive straight to the topic of your last letter and tell you that yes, your grandson is perfectly hale. He grows stronger by the day and seldom cries, which is likely because Arabelle keeps him with her always. I am teeming with jealousy—or I would be if I could love either of them less.

"'But there is news to report of another birth in this house. You may recall that maid I mentioned, the one who sought sanctuary with us from her husband. She has brought a son into the world just today. A boy with dark hair and dark eyes and a healthy set of lungs.

"'Merrick acts very much the elder infant and studies this other child with equanimity. He is ever-stoic, and I have never seen a more inquisitive child in my life. He studies us with that pale watchful gaze like a king, waiting for us to entertain him. And I am embarrassed by the amount of foolishness I've put forth simply to earn a smile.

"'Today, it finally happened—the smile—and I did nothing to inspire it. My only activity at the time was sitting near the bassinet in our rooms and reading aloud. I heard a gurgle and a coo that stopped my oration. I turned to attend to him, but he simply stared back, expectant. So I read again and—*behold*—there it was. A smile. I am happy to report that Arabelle was positively teeming with jealousy.

"'I look forward to seeing you in the springtime, Father, and be assured I will read your every letter to your grandson. Your son, Edgar.'"

Raven felt as if his heart was in his throat and he swallowed thickly. Looking to Jane, he saw that her own heart was swimming in her eyes.

But, of course, Herrington had something to say about it.

He cast a sweeping gesture to Raven. "That letter gives no proof at all. Everyone knows that the color of a child's eyes often alters after birth."

Raven fought the urge to growl.

"Yes, I thought you'd say as much." Warrister drew in another deep breath before he continued. "What I have here is a complete confession from Mr. Pickerington which should finally end this speculation."

He shuffled the pages on his lap. "Pickerington mentions working for my son and his affair with the maid, Helene. He further admits that he'd been intending to run away with her, *and* to having double-crossed her husband—the man to whom he'd been selling secrets while working for many notable military families—*le Sinistre*."

Raven watched as Jane read the page and her face paled. He went to her side and took her hand.

Tears spilled down her cheeks. "My own uncle. If not for him then you would have had . . ."

"Shh . . ." He knelt down and wiped the tears from her cheeks. "None of this is your fault."

"Quite true. No one in this room is to blame," Warrister said, looking warningly at his nephew. Then, skimming through the pages once more, he paused briefly, closing his eyes. After a moment, he cleared his throat and continued. "According to Mr. Pickerington's account, he was set to abscond with Helene the night of the fire. Regrettably, he arrived too late to save anyone—" He broke off, his voice gravelly. "Anyone other than the child in my son's outstretched hands, as his body was being consumed by flames."

The breath fell out of Raven's lungs. Beside him, Jane stifled a sob in the cup of her hands.

Warrister looked into his eyes, holding his gaze as he reached out and put a warm hand on his shoulder. Then he nodded and Raven knew.

There was no ounce of doubt any longer. There never would be again.

Then the earl turned back to his nephew. "In these pages,

he even mentions seeing you that night and how he'd hoped you wouldn't hear the baby crying from underneath the bench. How he'd hoped it was dark enough that you didn't see the soot on his clothes."

Herrington cringed as he pressed his fingertips to the center of his forehead. "I did see him that night."

Warrister nodded, unsurprised. "I suspect you didn't tell me that you saw him because that would lead back to the maid. The maid had ensnared you, as well, despite what you said at the ball." Then softly, he added, "She was likely playing her part with both of you."

"I was supposed to go to her that night but I waited. And then I waited . . . and all because I didn't want her to think she had power over me." Herrington cursed, a low mournful sound. "Uncle, you don't know how often I've regretted making her wait and what could have happened if I'd been there sooner." He gripped the earl's hand. He held it for a moment, then let it drop and looked to Raven. "But that still doesn't mean that this man is my cousin's child."

Warrister drew in a deep breath, then turned to Raven. "Show him the mark, my boy."

Numbly, he stood and shrugged out of his coat. His thoughts lingered on the horrifying image of his father emerging from that house on the hill, determined and skin still burning as he carried his child to safety.

Overwhelmed by a torrent of emotion, Raven didn't bother to remove his shirtsleeves. He just took hold of the linen and ripped.

The sound echoed in the room. It was followed by Herrington's choked sob as he staggered back from the sight of the scarred shoulder.

"The ring," he whispered. "That's from the signet ring I found on my cousin's body. He was sprawled on the ground, arms outstretched. And his hands were"—he broke off, slowly lifting his own hands in imitation, his gaze haunted— "as if he were holding a chalice or something precious."

Warrister stood and walked across the room, looking away from the fire and toward the new snow falling outside the window. He withdrew a handkerchief from his pocket.

Raven sat down in his grandfather's chair beside Jane. He felt her brush the pads of her fingers against the wetness on his cheeks.

After their collective shuddering breaths fell silent, Warrister said, "Nephew, you'll make it known that Merrick Northcott survived. That Viscount Northcott lives."

"I will," he said. Then looked to Jane. "I apologize for what you've endured since the night of the ball, Miss Pickerington. I wish you had slapped *me* instead of the glass from my hand. I deserved it, and much more."

Raven looked at Jane, curious. He didn't know about this. *Damn*, he wished he'd seen it. In fact, he wished he'd punched Herrington, and much more. Unfortunately, they were family. *Bloody hell*.

Jane nodded to Herrington in forgiveness. She was far too generous, in Raven's opinion.

"And I realize now that you didn't try to murder Raven, after all," she said. "It's here in my uncle's confession."

She showed Raven the letter.

He saw that the scrawl was much altered from the one he'd read in those ledgers. The hard slant was barely discernible, and the words were like the ramblings of a madman.

Apparently, Mr. Mayhew had been blackmailing Pickerington for years.

The beadle at the foundling home had been watching from an upper floor window the night Pickerington had left an infant on the doorstep. Then, once word had spread about the fire and the earl's belief that his grandson survived, Mayhew approached Pickerington.

The tutor had been terrified about anyone associating him with the fire and having his treasonous activities discovered. Mayhew used this to his advantage, as well as all the other information he had in his possession. He knew all of Pickerington's secrets because he, too, had been working for *le Sinistre*.

But while Mayhew had carefully covered his own tracks, Pickerington had not. So Mayhew used everything he could against Pickerington, including the one thing that mattered most—family.

Pickerington knew that if his treasonous secret came out, it would have signed his own death warrant. But worse, in his opinion, a public trial and hanging would forever blacken the family name.

The threat had been enough for him to pay Mayhew any amount, even enough to beggar himself.

But as the years dragged on in debtor's prison, Pickerington had decided that it would serve him better to get rid of the only real link between him and his crimes.

And the only way to do that was to have Raven killed.

"Now, I understand why all the money my father has been sending has barely kept my uncle in coal. If he wasn't paying Mr. Mayhew, then he was hiring murderers to—" Jane's voice broke as she turned away from the page, her forehead pressed to his chest. "He isn't the man I remember at all, and I cannot apologize enough for all he has done to you."

Raven dropped the letter on the floor, dismissing it, and took her face in his hands. "No. It is not your place to apologize. And, besides, there is nothing either of us can do about our relations," he said with a wry glance to Herrington.

The man chuckled in response and cursed under his

breath. "Further proof that you are your father's son. Edgar was ever-quick with the quip and I received the lash of it more times than not." He sighed, resigned. "I suppose I deserve to be plagued by you."

Warrister turned away from the window, a pleased smile on his lips. "At last. And to celebrate the reunion of our family, I'll host a dinner this evening and—"

"Beg pardon, Grandfather," Raven interrupted and shrugged back into his coat. "Jane and I have a previous engagement in Gretna Green. We're on our way there now."

Warrister started to bluster. "No grandson of mine is getting married over a blacksmith's iron. No, you'll have the wedding here in London. The banns will be read—"

"I've spent a lifetime apart from her and I refuse to wait a minute longer."

Warrister's mouth set in a stubborn line. "I'll secure a special license with the archbishop post haste. You'll be married tomorrow and then we'll have a wedding breakfast."

Raven took Jane's hand and curled it over his sleeve. "On this topic, I'm afraid, I cannot be moved. Jane needs a new chapter for her book—*How to Marry a Scoundrel*."

The Mating Habits of Scoundrels
continues with Ellie's story . . .

THE WRONG MARQUESS

Coming 2021

*G*ive in to your Impulses!

These unforgettable stories only take a second to buy and give you hours of reading pleasure!

Go to *www.AvonImpulse.com* and see what we have to offer.

Available wherever e-books are sold.

AVONIMPULSE